THE

Accidental

BESTSELLER

THE
Accidental
BESTSELLER

WENDY WAX

BERKLEY BOOKS, NEW YORK

THE BERKLEY PUBLISHING GROUP
Published by the Penguin Group
Penguin Group (USA) Inc.
375 Hudson Street, New York, New York 10014, USA
Penguin Group (Canada), 90 Eglinton Avenue East, Suite 700, Toronto, Ontario M4P 2Y3, Canada
(a division of Pearson Penguin Canada Inc.)
Penguin Books Ltd., 80 Strand, London WC2R 0RL, England
Penguin Group Ireland, 25 St. Stephen's Green, Dublin 2, Ireland (a division of Penguin Books Ltd.)
Penguin Group (Australia), 250 Camberwell Road, Camberwell, Victoria 3124, Australia
(a division of Pearson Australia Group Pty. Ltd.)
Penguin Books India Pvt. Ltd., 11 Community Centre, Panchsheel Park, New Delhi—110 017, India
Penguin Group (NZ), 67 Apollo Drive, Rosedale, North Shore 0632, New Zealand
(a division of Pearson New Zealand Ltd.)
Penguin Books (South Africa) (Pty.) Ltd., 24 Sturdee Avenue, Rosebank, Johannesburg 2196,
South Africa

Penguin Books Ltd., Registered Offices: 80 Strand, London WC2R 0RL, England

This book is an original publication of The Berkley Publishing Group.

This is a work of fiction. Names, characters, places, and incidents either are the product of the author's imagination or are used fictitiously, and any resemblance to actual persons, living or dead, business establishments, events, or locales is entirely coincidental. The publisher does not have any control over and does not assume any responsibility for author or third-party websites or their content.

PRINTING HISTORY
Berkley trade paperback / June 2009

Library of Congress Cataloging-in-Publication Data

Wax, Wendy.
  The accidental bestseller / Wendy Wax.
    p. cm.
  ISBN 978-0-425-22767-1
  1. Women authors—Fiction. I. Title.
  PS3623.A893A65 2009
  813'.6—dc22
                          2008054352

PRINTED IN THE UNITED STATES OF AMERICA

10 9 8 7 6 5 4 3 2 1

This book is dedicated to every writer—aspiring and otherwise—who has a story to tell, a love of the written word, and a burning desire to see the fruit of their labor on a bookstore shelf. In a prime position. Cover out. With full publisher support behind it.

Acknowledgments

Although writing is generally an individual sport, few novels emerge from a vacuum. A number of people helped me bring *The Accidental Bestseller* into being, and I'd like to thank them here.

Thank you to Sandra Chastain, Berta Platas, and Karen White—who is my Faye, Mallory, and Tanya all rolled into one—for using their considerable brainpower to help me turn the kernel of an idea into an actual story. And to Missy Tippens for her insights into the role of a minister's wife as well as the realities of writing inspirational romance; she is *not* Faye, but was generous enough to lay out the parameters in which Faye might exist.

Thanks, too, to the Chicago contingent, Rachel Jacobsohn, Sue Ofner, and Karen Lothan, who helped me figure out where Faye might live as well as the logistical details of her life. And to Susan Jacobsohn, trainer extraordinaire, who knows absolutely everyone and has the phone numbers to prove it.

Thanks to my brother, Barry Wax, who took me to the inspiration for the Downhome Diner in our hometown of St. Pete, and who has become a voracious reader in his own right.

Finally a great big thank-you to my agent, Stephanie Rostan, for all that she did to see this story into print. And for sharing her editorial experiences and inside knowledge of the publishing industry—even though I now know all kinds of things that I kinda wish I didn't.

1

*The profession of book writing makes
horse racing seem like a solid,
stable business.*
—JOHN STEINBECK

Kendall Aims's writing career was about to go down for the count on that Friday night in July as she hurried down Sixth Avenue toward the New York Hilton.

It had taken many blows over the last year and a half—the first when her editor left Scarsdale Publishing to have a baby, leaving Kendall orphaned and unloved; another when her new editor, a plain, humorless woman named Jane Jensen, informed her that her sales numbers were slipping. And still another when they showed her the cover for the book she'd just turned in, a cover so bland and uninteresting that even Kendall didn't want to open it. And on which her name had shrunk to a size that required a magnifying glass to read it.

She landed on the ropes when the print run for this new book was announced. Kendall's first thought was that someone had forgotten to type in the rest of the zeros. Because even she, who had given up on math long ago, could see at a glance that even if they sold every one of these books, which now seemed unlikely, she'd never earn out the advance she'd been paid.

Looking back, it seemed as if one day she was perched prettily on the publishing ladder, poised to make all the bestseller lists, and the next the rungs had given way beneath her feet, leaving her dangling above a bubbling pit of insecurity and self-doubt. Not to mention obscurity.

Tonight her publisher, like all the other publishers participating in this year's national conference of the Wordsmiths Incorporated, or WINC as it was affectionately abbreviated, had hosted an obligatorily expensive dinner for its stable of authors. There Kendall had smiled and eaten and pretended that she was happy to write for them while they pretended that even after eight years spent proving otherwise, they still intended to make her a household name.

Now one filet mignon, two glasses of wine, and a crème brûlée later, Kendall hurried through the hotel lobby barely noticing the knots of chattering women scattered through it. The waistband of her panty hose pinched painfully, and her toes, more used to Nikes than Blahniks, throbbed unmercifully. She felt, and she suspected looked, like what she was—a suburban Atlanta housewife whose children had left the nest and whose husband barely noticed her. At forty-five not even expensive highlights and a boatload of Lycra could disguise the fact that her body had given up its struggle against gravity.

She reached the lounge and was already scanning the crowd for familiar faces when two women stepped up beside her. One was tall and blocky, the other short and round. A cloud of nervousness surrounded them.

"Let's just walk through and pretend we're looking for someone." The tall one was clearly in charge, her broad shoulders set in determination.

"Do we have to? We don't know anyone and we aren't anyone, either," the other one whispered. "What if we do see an agent or an editor? What are we supposed to do then?"

Kendall flushed with memory. She might have been either one of these women ten years ago. Shy, insecure, and dreaming of publication, she'd been stuck on the fringes of her first national conference desperate to sell the book she'd somehow managed to write, but unable to imagine how it could possibly happen.

"We're just going to make a quick pass," the taller one promised. "At least we'll be seen. And be sure to keep an eye out for any opportunities. Half the point of being here is to network."

"But . . ."

"Come on. Just follow me. The worst thing that's going to happen is nothing."

Kendall smiled, drawn out of her own misery for the first time since she'd arrived in New York early that afternoon. She and Mallory and Tanya and Faye had met at their first Wordsmiths Incorporated conference in Orlando; all four of them wannabes who'd stood, knees knocking, waiting for their turns to pitch ideas during editor and agent appointments. Fifteen minutes to try to sell yourself and your talent to a twentysomething girl who held all the power and couldn't understand why you, who might be as old as her mother, or possibly her grandmother, were unable to keep your voice from cracking as you delivered your carefully memorized pitch.

They'd bonded then and there, four women of disparate ages and even more disparate backgrounds, drawn together by their fear and longing.

How many times during that first conference had Mallory dragged her through the cocktail lounge insisting they had to work the room and get their names out there? How often had the four of them sought each other out in that sea of two thousand strangers, carving out their own ground, pooling their strengths and resources, vowing that all four of them would beat the odds and see their books in print?

Miraculously, they'd done it, continued to do it. Against all those frightening odds.

Kendall's own chin went up a notch. Her career might be faltering, but she did, in fact, have one. She was multipublished by a major New York publisher and so were her friends. They'd all done respectably, though Mallory was the only one of them who'd hit the all-important *New York Times* list regularly.

Somewhere inside this bar the three of them waited for

her, back from their own publisher dinners and parties, a warm cozy oasis in the middle of the Sahara of publishing.

Her children might not need her anymore; her husband, well, she wasn't ready to think about what, if anything, he wanted from her anymore. But she had her friends and she was somebody in this world. A smallish somebody perhaps. Not as big as Mallory. Or as prolific as Tanya. Or in as hot a space as Faye. But she had value here; her name was known. She wasn't finished yet.

She couldn't be finished.

Because if she wasn't an author, she was nothing. And nothing was the one thing Kendall Aims was not prepared to be.

. . .

"There you are!" Mallory St. James moved quickly and surely toward Kendall, a tall, elegant figure in sleeveless black silk. Velvety brown hair brushed slim shoulders and diamonds glittered at her ears and throat. The two women next to Kendall gasped in recognition, but Mallory's smile stayed firmly in place.

"We thought maybe you'd pounded Plain Jane to a pulp over dessert and been carted off to jail." Mallory pronounced their nickname for Kendall's new editor with relish and managed to avoid making eye contact with the obviously eavesdropping women. "Tanya and Faye are holding down our table. The wine is on its way." She slipped her arm through Kendall's then acknowledged their gaping audience. "Ladies," she said with both warmth and enough distance in her tone to prevent a request for autographs. "My friend here has to be rushed to our table. She's clearly in desperate need of a drink."

Kendall marveled at Mallory's social dexterity; she'd become a master at making the readers who bought her books and kept her on the lists feel good without encouraging them to become too familiar.

The taller one's hand flew to her chest and a delighted smile washed over her angular face. "You see," she said to her companion as Mallory led Kendall into the bar. "I told you we needed to come in here. Mallory St. James actually spoke to us!" Her voice vibrated with excitement. "I bet that was her friend Kendall Aims."

The bar was knee-deep in men and women of all shapes and sizes. Rings of chairs surrounded too-tiny tables. It looked and sounded as if all two thousand conference attendees had tried to cram themselves into the lounge at the same time.

"Good grief, you've just made their entire conference," Kendall said, as they worked their way through the crowd. "They can't wait to get out of here to tell somebody they talked to you. They didn't even notice me until you arrived. I used to have a career of my own. Now I'm Mallory St. James's friend."

Mallory shrugged her bare shoulders, unperturbed. Kendall hated the whine that had crept into her voice. Normally the four of them laughed over the idea of anyone being in awe of any of them. They'd started together and held each other's hands through the giddy heights and rock-bottom lows that were an inevitable part of publishing. Envy and resentment had never been factors in their relationship, and Kendall was horrified to be feeling both now.

"I know that was not a note of self-pity I just heard in your voice." Mallory nodded to a knot of women who'd fallen silent to observe their progress.

"A note." Kendall snorted. "That was a fugue. A full-fledged symphony. My entire career is in the toilet. I just keep praying that nobody flushes."

"Interesting metaphor." Mallory continued to nod and smile, but never checked their pace enough to invite interruption. "But there's not going to be any flushing. All you have to do is walk off with the Zelda Award tomorrow night and Scarsdale will be looking at you in a whole new light."

A woman at the bar pointed them out to her friends. Two more tables stopped talking as they passed.

"Do you think we should have just had a bottle of wine in the suite?" Kendall could feel the weight of the eyes on them, assessing, wondering, trying in a glance to glean Mallory's secret for making all those bestseller lists. Curious how close she was to Kendall, whose career was nowhere near as big.

"No, no hiding." Mallory's lips barely moved behind her smile. "Besides the WINC board wants us published folk to be visible. You and I are bona fide evidence that a writer's dreams can come true."

"Maybe we should warn them that sometimes those dreams turn into nightmares," Kendall said. "I don't remember them covering that in any of the conference workshops." She smiled evilly. "Let's propose a workshop for next year—'Caught in the netherworld. Stranded in the mind-sucking midlist.'" She referred to the dreaded spot in the middle of the publisher's list of offerings in a given month. The top slots, the books the publisher was most excited about, got the biggest orders and the most publisher support, perpetuating those authors' positions at the top of the publisher's and ultimately the bestseller lists. The rest of their authors were thrown out there, much like shit flung at a wall, while the publisher waited to see who "stuck," or so it seemed to Kendall.

Kendall had originally clung to the wall and even begun to inch up it; now she seemed to be sliding back down at an alarming pace.

"Great idea," Mallory said. "Except no one wants to hear the truth. Just like no pregnant woman actually wants to listen to those delivery horror stories. Everyone wants to believe that once they sell their book the struggle is over, when it's really just beginning."

Kendall looked at Mallory, whose rise had been nothing short of meteoric, and an ugly pocket of envy filled her heart. How had she sailed through so unscathed when Kendall felt so badly bruised and beaten?

Kendall pushed the bitterness away as Mallory slowed. She looked up as Tanya and Faye, still dressed from their publisher parties, waved their hellos.

"Hey, over here!" The youngest of their foursome, Tanya Mason was thirty-five with blond hair that could only be described as "big" and an oval face dominated by a pointy chin and cornflower blue eyes. Her accent was pure country and so was her attitude. She wrote stories about single mothers like herself for Masque Publishing, with the occasional NASCAR hero thrown in.

"You are way behind, Miss Kendall," Tanya crowed as Kendall and Mallory reached the table and dropped into their seats. "I had to slap Faye's hands away to save you a glass of this fine red zinfandel. Of course, I could barely move my arms to get at her after the white-water rafting trip through the Hudson River Gorge that Darby dragged us on today."

Kendall felt the room and the curious eyes recede as she accepted a glass of the red zin. "I think Masque should be paying you a bigger advance to compensate for the inevitable hospital bills," Kendall replied. Tanya's editor, Darby Hanover, was both highly competitive and a notorious jock with a passion for hair-raising adventure. Her favorite authors often found themselves a part of those adventures, even those like Tanya whose spirits were willing, but whose muscle tone was weak.

"Hazardous duty pay," Tanya said, "that's it for sure. And to think I came in a whole day early to lose the use of both of my arms."

Faye rolled bespectacled eyes at Tanya, though the eyeglasses couldn't hide the twinkle that resided there. She was sixty, referred to herself as "full figured," had cropped salt-and-pepper hair, and was the wife of the charismatic televangelist, Pastor Steve, though you'd never hear it from her.

A former film and broadcast producer, Faye wrote novels for the increasingly popular inspirational market. She was also their group's head cheerleader and chief organizer, planning their biyearly brainstorming retreats and keeping them all in touch with each other.

Where, Kendall wondered, would she be without the three of them? Still standing on the outside with her nose pressed against the glass looking in, no doubt. None of them, not even Mallory, would be where they were without the others.

"OK," Mallory said, raising her glass. "I propose a toast to Kendall Aims, soon-to-be winner of the Zelda."

"Here, here." They clinked glasses and drank, the wine sliding easily down their throats as the warmth of friendship wrapped its comforting cloak around them.

"We better drink to that again. Because if I don't win, I won't be held responsible for my actions." Kendall held her glass out for a refill.

They drank in silent accord and ordered a second bottle. At that moment every one of them believed better things lay ahead, that wanting could make it so, and that the bonds of their friendship had already been sufficiently tested.

2

*A person who publishes a book willfully appears
before the populace with his pants down.... If it is
a good book nothing can hurt him. If it is
a bad book nothing can help him.*
—EDNA ST. VINCENT MILLAY

Kendall came awake slowly, her subconscious aware of her unfamiliar surroundings before the rest of her. Her head pounded slightly and her mouth felt thick and wooly. Her jaw ached from laughing and talking.

After too many bottles of wine, they'd come back to the suite and sat up talking until almost 3:00 A.M.—hours that had been remarkably good for the soul but not so good for the eyes and skin.

Last night Kendall had felt optimistic, if not the master of her destiny at least a participant in her future. But that was when the awards ceremony was still a comfortable day away, when the one thing that might rapidly revitalize her career seemed attainable. They'd hashed out her odds last night, pronouncing them highly favorable, dissing her competition, and imagining the look on Plain Jane's face when Kendall was called up to the podium to accept her Zelda. Which would, in an omen of good things to come, they'd decided, be presented to her by Mallory.

But now the comfortable cushion of time had been ripped away and the fear had begun to steal in. Not winning was unthinkable, but the ceremony was tonight, the winner's name already written and stuffed inside the envelope; no amount of positive thinking or deal making with God at this point would change the outcome.

She lay still beneath the covers with her eyes tightly shut, wishing she could block out what was to come as easily as her eyelids blocked out the morning light.

Sound sifted through the heavy drapery—car horns and construction, irate voices, the hum of a big city waking up and going about its business. At home she'd be hearing the neighbor's sprinkler system, birds conversing over the feeders in the backyard, the hum of a lawn mower.

She was going to have to leave this dark, safe, unexposed place. She was going to have to spend the day getting ready for an awards ceremony that could expose her in ways she could not let herself think about. Her heart beat too fast and fear churned in her stomach.

The sound of hushed voices in the living room of the suite reached her, and Kendall knew she couldn't hold off the day much longer.

Forcing herself into an upright position, she opened her eyes. Perched on the side of the bed, she probed carefully inside herself for the courage she needed, but found only a pronounced sense of dread. Still she managed to draw on her robe and stand, then padded into the living room, where she found Faye curled up on the couch with her feet tucked up beneath her fuzzy pink robe.

Tanya stood at the coffeemaker, already dressed, her back to the room. The garish flower arrangement Scarsdale had sent Kendall perched on the bar beside her along with the untouched bottle of champagne. Kendall had decided she'd open it tonight—but only if she won. She'd drink it to toast the bargaining chip that would finally force Scarsdale to invest in her.

The sound of fingers striking a keyboard came from behind Mallory's closed bedroom door. "She's already working?" Kendall asked.

"She said she had to do her twenty pages before we left for

brunch." Faye shrugged, clearly not feeling the flash of guilt at not working that immediately smote Kendall—not that Kendall had all that many twenty-page days even when she was writing.

Faye's face was devoid of makeup, her black-rimmed glasses stark against the white of her skin. She untucked her legs to reveal fuzzy slippers that matched her robe. "Some of us are obsessive compulsive about our work. Some of us are not. Some of us aspire only to breakfast and a day at the Red Door Spa." She smiled warmly. "And a Zelda for a friend."

Kendall dropped down on the sofa next to Faye and laid her head on Faye's fuzzy pink shoulder.

"How are you feeling?" Faye's tone was soothingly motherly.

"Queasy."

"I told you you shoulda taken those two aspirin last night *before* you went to bed," Tanya said, as she brought a steaming mug of coffee to Kendall. From a distance she could have passed for a teenager in her denim miniskirt and layered tees, her hair pulled back off her face with a wide headband. "It's always better to head off a hangover at the pass. Otherwise you spend the whole next day trying to get rid of it."

Kendall took a tentative sip of coffee, welcoming the liquid burn on her tongue and the jolt of awareness it shot through her. "I was surviving hangovers when you were chasing boys on the elementary school playground," she said, though she didn't think her queasiness had anything to do with the amount of alcohol she'd consumed. "I'm fine." Or she would be once she got through this day. She really should call Melissa and see how her trig exam had gone yesterday. And she probably should check in with Cal—she had a vague recollection of trying to reach him too late last night but there'd been no answer.

"I'm glad to hear it," Tanya said. "I slept like a baby. The note in my room says those sheets are Egyptian cotton with a six-hundred thread count. When I hit the list, I'm going to buy two sets of sheets just like that. Though they might look kinda out of place in Mama's double-wide." She sighed. "Do you think there's really a job where all you do is count the number of threads in a sheet? It sounds a whole lot easier than the Laundromat and the diner."

Gretchen Wilson's "Redneck Woman" rang out in the suite. Tanya reached for her purse and rooted around for her cell phone. "Oh, Lordy. I hate this thing." She lifted the phone to her ear. "My number one fantasy is no longer stealing Brad from Angelina; it's being completely unreachable."

"Somebody better be bleedin' or on the way to the hospital," she said into the phone. "I'm at conference. You remember I told you that's the same as workin'."

Tanya sank into the wing chair across from the couch and crossed her long legs. Her feet were encased in strappy sandals with a heel that made Kendall's feet ache in sympathy. Her wide mobile mouth turned downward.

"No, Loretta, I told you, you could *not* go to the mall this weekend. You are supposed to be helping Granny with Crystal."

Tanya drew a deep breath. Her calf swung up and down in agitation. "Don't call your little sister that, Loretta. How many times have I told you . . . Ret! Retta? No! Don't put your grandma . . ."

Tanya closed her eyes. Her leg stopped in midswing. "Hello, Mama. Yes, everything's fine *here*." The emphasis on the last word was apparent. "No, Mama. I have *not* had a chance to call Kyle to see if he can pick up the girls for the day. You know how unreliable he is. And you said you'd be fine. I'll be back tomorrow night."

Tanya sat silent for a moment, her body still. Kendall was careful not to make eye contact.

"Yes, I know how your migraines get. You go on and lie down for a while. Crystal is nine years old. She can make her own breakfast. All she has to do is pour the Cocoa Puffs into the bowl and add some milk. It's not rocket science, Mama. They're big girls now. No one expects you to do everything for them."

Tanya stood and walked away from them toward the window, her shoulders hunched in, her voice intentionally low.

"I know, Mama." The back of Tanya's head went up and down. "I know. And you know I appreciate it. I'll be back tomorrow in time to make dinner."

Tanya flipped the phone closed. When she turned to face them, her eyes shimmered with unshed tears. Frustration filled her voice. "Everything is too much for my mama. Everything has always been too much for her." She swiped at her eyes with the back of one hand. "I swear, if I have to get a third job I will. And I am selling that proposal for a bigger book this year, you see if I don't." Her long-fingered hands smoothed the sides of her miniskirt. "And then the girls and me are going to move into our own place. One with an actual foundation. And a yard. And our own freakin' bedrooms."

Faye straightened on the couch next to her and Kendall could tell she was dying to go offer comfort to Tanya, but Tanya smiled a wobbly smile and shook her head. "You two go get dressed now, OK? I'm going to go pull Miss *New York Times* away from the laptop that she had surgically attached to her fingers. I need food and then I need our day of pampering so bad I can taste it. Do you think we'll get to ride in Mallory's limo again?" She was already heading for Mallory's door. "I want to be sure to get a picture of me emerging gracefully from it for the girls."

• • •

Somehow, she'd never be sure exactly how, Kendall made it through the day. Mallory and Faye and Tanya led her from one activity to the next, distracting her with a steady stream of chatter and laughter, pretending they didn't notice her ever-increasing anxiety and decreasing levels of participation.

It took everything she had to make it from brunch at Tavern on the Green to four hours of primping and prodding at the Red Door where they all had manis and pedis followed by massages, facials, and hair appointments. From there Kendall and Mallory had raced back to the hotel for the awards ceremony run-through, where Kendall had been forced to confront her competition—a formidable group of much bigger name authors who had all already won at least one Zelda.

Now she sat in the reserved section of the grand ballroom, wedged between Faye and Tanya, her palms and underarms sweaty, her lips completely dry; an apparent trick of body chemistry in which her armpits and hands somehow sucked all the moisture from the other parts of her body.

Her hair in its updo felt stiff and unnatural, the black evening gown too low cut. Her arms, which she knew were too heavy to be bared this way, were covered in goose bumps in the over-air-conditioned space. The body shaper—she wasn't sure when they'd stopped calling them girdles, but she wasn't fooled—was too short and bit uncomfortably into her crotch.

There were quiet whispers and rustlings in the back of the ballroom while the video history of the founding of Wordsmiths Incorporated played out on a supersized video screen. But around her, in the section reserved for finalists and their "dates," tension hummed like a high-voltage wire. A Zelda could do anything from attracting a bigger agent or better offer at another house to reaffirming your value with the ones you already had.

Though many authors quibbled with the judging being done by potentially jealous or competitive peers, no one would argue the prestige of winning. Or pretend that they wouldn't give their first-born child to carry a Zelda home with them on the plane.

Kendall licked her dry lips and silently thanked God they didn't have cameras on the waiting finalists like they did at the Oscars. Who but an actor could pretend to be comfortable waiting to find out his fate? Or happiness when someone else won?

Were all the other finalists as nervous as she was? She stole a glance around her, but Kendall didn't know any of them well enough to tell whether they were as engrossed in the ceremony as they looked. Or silently screaming the words "Freak out!" from the Chic song "Le Freak" in their heads like she was.

Kendall gnawed her lip again and contemplated the ramifications of pulling out her purse to reapply lipstick. If she did actually end up on the stage, magnified on the pounds-adding, pore-revealing screen, she didn't want her lips to look like the cratered surface of the moon. On the other hand, any move to primp now could be construed as an indication that she believed she was going up on that stage to receive a Zelda soon. Which would appear foolishly overconfident and totally pathetic in the event that she didn't.

Worse, it might tempt fate to decree she not win in the same way that washing your car could bring on rain.

Kendall drew another deep breath and tried to stem the tide of her thoughts. Which even now in her panicked state she recognized as completely pointless and stupid.

The winner was already determined, she reminded herself for the hundredth time. Nothing she did—or thought—now was going to change the name on the card that Mallory was going to read.

As one, Faye and Tanya each took one of her hands in theirs.

Looking up, Kendall saw Mallory's name flash across the screen. Music swelled and a deep, prerecorded voice began to recap Mallory's astounding ascent from debut author to permanent resident on the *New York Times* list.

Pictures and video flashed on the screen: Mallory looking beautifully coiffed and elegantly dressed on a television talk show set; Mallory signing books for a line of avid fans that snaked out the front door of a Barnes & Noble; Mallory with the publisher of Partridge and Portman himself; Mallory at her computer in her tastefully appointed home office, conspicuously overdressed for writing, presumably pounding out yet another bestseller.

Kendall forgot about her lips and everything else. Faye and Tanya squeezed her hands so tightly that her fingers went numb even as her heart began to pound much too quickly.

Then the video screen filled with the real-life Mallory St. James.

There was Mallory, striding out onto the stage with her deep brown hair swept into a sophisticated French twist; Mallory, whose bare shoulders in the strapless dress were white and lovely and whose sinewy arms were perfectly toned.

And who Kendall knew did not need to wear a crotch-splitting body shaper beneath the full length white Grecian gown.

Kendall braced herself as Mallory cleared her throat and flashed her megawatt smile into the camera lens. She offered a silent prayer as Mallory began to read the names of the finalists for Best Mainstream Women's Fiction, beginning with her own.

3

*Almost anyone can be an author; the business
is to collect money and fame from
this state of being.*
—A. A. MILNE

Kendall held her breath as her air-brushed face filled the mammoth screen, making her immensely grateful that she'd spent the money on a makeup artist and photographer to ensure that her head shot made her look like an assured professional writer, and not her everyday self.

The cover of her book, *Dare to Dream*, appeared beside her screen photo, its stylized bold black-and-gold stepback cover and her name in twenty-four-inch point across the top, the best cover art she'd ever been given, a gift from the publishing gods, which apparently, based on her latest cover, was never to be repeated.

The four other finalists received the same exposure and then a hush of expectancy filled the room—a potent form of silence that was as pulse accelerating as a drum roll.

Kendall wanted to hide her eyes behind her hands as Mallory lifted the envelope, but managed to keep them in her lap.

Her mind raced from thought to thought at speeds so dizzying she could barely keep up with them. Maybe she should have written a speech after all so that she struck the right tone between deserving and appreciative and didn't forget to thank anyone in the event she actually won. It was always so embarrassing to hear a writer ramble disjointedly—it made you wonder how focused his work could possibly be. Kendall often spent hours polishing a paragraph or a phrase in a manuscript, but it was hard to sound eloquent extemporaneously, especially in front of a live audience.

Kendall sighed. Writing a thank-you speech had felt even more jinx inducing than applying lipstick during the ceremony. She simply hadn't been willing to take the risk. It mattered too much.

Mallory's hands encasing the envelope shook slightly; her manicured fingernails fumbled with the seal.

Please God, Kendall thought, as she clasped her own hands together, don't let me trip on the way up there if I win. And don't let me humiliate myself too badly if I don't.

So much for allowing only positive thoughts and energy.

Mallory managed to get the card out of the envelope and Kendall stopped trying to feign nonchalance and began to pray in earnest. She realized as she did so that she hadn't addressed God in any way since her father's fatal illness five years ago. And if God hadn't responded to that life-and-death situation, what were the chances that He was going to bother with a matter as small as Kendall Aims's career?

"Just this one award, God," Kendall prayed silently. "I know you have all kinds of things to deal with, but please just let me win. I won't ever ask again, I promise. Just this one thing tonight. To save all I've worked for."

Mallory pulled the oversized card free of its envelope and lowered her gaze to read it. Her eyes skimmed the card and then she glanced quickly down at Kendall, but Kendall couldn't decipher the message in her eyes.

The praying, begging, and negotiating going on in her mind coalesced into a single desperate "Pleeeeeaaassssseeeee!" that echoed in her head and filled her very soul.

Mallory leaned into the microphone and her lips began to move. "And the winner of the Zelda for best mainstream women's fiction is . . ."

Mallory looked directly at her and Kendall's body began to rise from the chair of its own volition. She was halfway out of her seat when the winner's name left Mallory's lips and reverberated through the ballroom, but Kendall could barely hear it for the ringing in her head.

Finally the name broke through the barriers of sound and resistance and registered in Kendall's brain as Faye and Tanya yanked her back down into her chair.

The name was a name she knew well. It rolled easily off the tongue and had a very definite ring to it. Unfortunately, the name was not hers.

. . .

Hillary Bradford Hines walked up the steps to the stage and moved to the podium where she embraced Mallory, took the statuette in her hands, and stepped toward the microphone to give her acceptance speech.

Kendall didn't hear a word she said. Nor did she hear the wrap-up of the ceremony, the announcements about the reception to follow, or a reminder about airport shuttle reservations for the following morning.

She'd lost. Lost the award, lost face, lost her last hope. She was, in the most literal sense, a loner. Unlike the mythical story character, she was not going to be entering that innermost cave. And she would definitely not be returning with the elixir.

The ballroom began to empty and Mallory began to make her way toward them.

Kendall and her two human bookends had not yet exchanged a word. Kendall was simply too numb to move or speak, and she suspected Faye and Tanya were experiencing similar technical difficulties.

Kendall watched Mallory's progress as if watching through a fog. People stopped her, called out to her as if they knew her, and Mallory dealt with each and every one of them with that peculiar mix of warmth and distance.

Finally Mallory reached them. "I'm so sorry!" She moved a group of chairs out of the way and swooped down to hug

Kendall. "I wanted to warn you as soon as I saw that damned card, but I didn't know how. I'd convinced myself your name would be on it—it should have been," she added hastily, "and I almost said it anyway. Wouldn't that have been interesting?"

Kendall still couldn't speak. And apparently neither could Faye or Tanya. All three of them just sat silent and staring.

"OK." Mallory stepped back and folded her arms across her chest. "Which one of you is 'see no evil'?"

Tanya broke the silence. "I wish you woulda announced Kendall instead. Hillary Bradford Hines is already so big she could hit the *New York Times* now with a grocery list. This win won't make a speck of difference for her." She put a protective arm around Kendall. "I think we should demand a recount."

"Yes, because that worked so well for the Democrats in Florida," Faye weighed in. "This is not the end of the world; it's just a temporary setback. Kendall doesn't need a Zelda to have a career. It might have helped, but plenty of people have done just fine without one."

Kendall knew she should reply but she just couldn't seem to manage it. Stray words and images formed in her brain but she couldn't form them into thoughts, let alone complete sentences.

Loserloserloser continued to echo in her mental abyss. For the life of her, she couldn't come up with a word to replace it.

"Kendall?" Mallory whispered her name. "Are you all right?"

Kendall opened her mouth but nothing came out.

Faye cupped Kendall's chin. "Kendall?" She spoke very clearly and slowly. "Everything's OK, Kendall."

Kendall was horrified when her vision blurred, beyond horrified when the first tear fell and she had to fight off the urge to bury her face in Faye's pillowy shoulder and wail like a child.

She just couldn't figure out what to do next. She'd spent the last two months convincing herself that winning a Zelda would turn things around. Now she was supposed to convince herself it didn't really matter?

The four of them remained huddled there, locked together in Kendall's misery.

The cleanup crew began to break down the ballroom.

"Listen," Mallory said. "I have to leave for the reception. I need to have a quick word with Zoe and Jonathan," she said, mentioning her editor and publisher.

Kendall's editor and publisher were probably out there, too, as was her agent. But they were the last people in the world she wanted to see right now. Kendall shook her head, sending the tears dribbling down her face onto the bodice of her gown.

"I can't."

"Of course you can," Faye said. "And you will."

Kendall sniffed and swiped at the tears. Her whole stupid face was awash with them.

"You are not going to slink off like some loser," Mallory said.

Kendall's head snapped up on hearing the word that was still filling her brain spoken aloud.

"So you didn't win," Mallory continued. "Neither did Karen or Laura or Susan or Dora. In fact, the number of people who didn't win tonight is a lot longer than the list of those who did. The Zelda would have been a good way to try to get your editor and your house more firmly behind you. Maybe Sylvia could have negotiated a few more bucks out of them on your next contract. Or taken you elsewhere a little more easily. But like Faye said, it's not the end of the world. We'll just have to give your next move some real thought. I'm sure if we all put our heads together we can come up with a plan of attack. Let's just get through the night and we'll start the discussion over breakfast."

Kendall sniffed and dashed away the last of her tears and resisted the urge to remind Mallory that this was all very easy for her to say. She didn't need a Zelda or anything else to boost a sagging career. Her career was in even better shape than her body.

Kendall's chin shot up. She was not going to take this out on Mallory. Or allow herself to appear as pathetic as she felt.

"Right." She stood and her henchwomen stood with her. "Just let me go fix my face. I'll meet you at the reception."

"I'll go with you. I need to powder my nose." Kendall saw the look Tanya shot the others as they separated, but she was too lethargic to protest.

In the ladies' room, Kendall sat in the stall for a very long time, holding her dress up off the floor while she searched the veins of pink marble for the strength to get through the rest of the night.

A loud knock on the stall door roused her from her contemplation of the floor.

"Are you coming out anytime soon, Kendall?" Tanya's voice reached her from the other side of the door. "There's a good-sized line of desperate women waiting out here, and if we don't hurry all the hors d'oeuvres will be gone."

"Be right with you." Reluctantly Kendall left the stall, smiled an apology to the waiting line of women, washed her hands, and repaired her makeup all without forming a single coherent thought. She then followed Tanya obediently out of the bathroom and toward the roar of voices. Her brain seemed to be moving at half its normal speed, but she was too glad of the protective numbness to wish it away.

They passed clumps of writers as they crossed the expansive upstairs lobby. The women wore everything from short black cocktail dresses to long formal gowns aglitter with sequins, their shapes ranging from hourglass to building sized. The men had dressed up too, after a fashion, and everyone juggled plates of finger foods and cocktail glasses. All of their mouths were moving either to talk or chew. Or in some unfortunate cases, both.

"Oh, shit," Tanya whispered under her breath as she checked her pace. "Plain Jane at six o'clock."

Kendall glanced up and sure enough there was her editor,

Jane Jensen, wearing shapeless black, her short dark hair held off her pale face with child-sized barrettes.

A split second after Tanya's warning, Jane Jensen glanced up and made accidental eye contact with Kendall.

"'Oh, shit' is right," Kendall agreed, knowing her editor would now feel compelled to acknowledge her. Which would compel Kendall to respond.

Kendall resisted the urge to flee as the younger woman approached; it took even more effort to keep a pleasant smile on her face.

"Sorry you lost," Jane said, her tone neither regretful nor surprised. "I thought *Dream* might have had a shot." Her plain face was as devoid of expression as her voice. "It was probably the best thing you've done."

The backhanded compliment carried the weight of a slap. In all their dealings with each other, Kendall couldn't remember the woman ever displaying an ounce of real enthusiasm for Kendall or her books.

Beside her, Tanya's jaw jutted out in a combative way; Kendall could feel her friend practically pawing the ground like a bull ready to charge.

Kendall placed a hand on Tanya's arm. She was too weary even to let someone else start something on her behalf, and Tanya didn't need to piss off an editor at a major publishing house at this stage in her career.

"Thanks, Jane." Kendall tightened her grasp on Tanya's arm and tugged gently. "That means a lot coming from you." She purposely kept her tone as expressionless as her editor had. "If you'll excuse us, we're going to get something to eat now," Kendall said, as they made their exit, though not even the normally therapeutic qualities of junk food were likely to cure what ailed her.

They hadn't covered much ground when Kendall heard her name called. "Hey, kiddo," Daisy Maryles, the executive editor of *Publishers Weekly,* said as she strode up to her. "Tough luck. I really thought you had it this time." Daisy's friend and sidekick, Bette-Lee Fox of *Library Journal* was with her and held her arms out to Kendall for a bracing hug. Carol Fitzgerald, founder of Book Report Network, completed their triumvirate.

Kendall had met and bonded with the threesome early in her career and always enjoyed the way they riffed off each other. Drawn to their warmth and collective quick wit, she made a point of seeing whichever of them was available whenever she was in New York. They were smart and funny and, in an industry where people rarely meant exactly what they said, they could always be counted on to speak their minds.

"Scarsdale should be ashamed, burying that book the way they did. The only thing they gave it was a cover," Carol said, as she stepped up to hug Kendall.

Bette-Lee nodded her agreement. "I loved *Dare to Dream*. It was your best yet." Funny how her comment mirrored Plain Jane's but managed to be so positive.

"Thanks, ladies." Kendall's smile was wobblier than she would have liked. "You remember Tanya, don't you? She writes for Masque and is working on a new single title idea that's absolutely killer."

They talked for a few minutes and Kendall felt herself regaining some of her equilibrium. She saw Mallory at the center of a group of women not too far away and spotted Faye coming out of the reception ballroom. All she could think of was burying herself in the midst of them and letting them comfort her until it was time to fly home.

She and Tanya said their good-byes to Daisy and crew and began to move toward the buffet tables, but they didn't get far. "Oh, no," Kendall said, coming to a stop.

"What? What is it?" Tanya asked. "If it's that Plain Ole Jane again, I'm going to give her a piece of my mind this time. That woman doesn't know good writing from a hole in the ground."

"Not Jane," Kendall said. "Worse. Over there next to that potted palm."

She waited while Tanya focused on the sight that had stopped Kendall in her tracks. Her agent, Sylvia Hardcastle, was engaged in deep conversation with Plain Jane's boss, Scarsdale's associate publisher, Brenda Tinsley, and even from a distance Kendall could tell it wasn't going well. They stood watching while Sylvia shook her head hard then stepped in to crowd the other woman, her body language clearly combative.

"Oh, God, they must be talking about me," Kendall said with a moan.

"Whoo-eee, Sylvia's looking mighty hot under the collar," Tanya observed. "Look how she's squared off. Any minute now she's gonna go for her six-shooter. Who else does she have at Scarsdale?"

"Nobody," Kendall said. "Nobody but me."

As they watched, the associate publisher pursed her lips and turned her back on Sylvia. The panic she'd been fighting off all night wedged itself in the pit of Kendall's stomach.

"I'll be right back." Kendall left Tanya and moved toward her agent, trying as she walked to come up with scenarios that she could live with for the scene she'd just witnessed. There weren't any.

"What just happened?" Kendall asked in greeting.

Sylvia shook her head slowly.

"What?" Kendall's panic intensified, though she would not have thought that possible. She had never seen Sylvia Hardcastle at a loss for words. Never. "What did she say?"

"You want a blow by blow or you want me to cut to the chase?" Sylvia was originally from Brooklyn and when agitated her Manhattan veneer began to peel away.

"The chase."

"They don't want to go back to contract. They're dropping you. Oh, except that they want the book you owe them before you disappear."

Now it was Kendall's turn to be speechless. She'd come to hate it at Scarsdale, couldn't bear working with Plain Jane, resented everything they had promised and then failed to do for her.

But she had always assumed she'd leave them for a juicier contract at an even bigger publisher. It had never occurred to her that they'd dispose of her first.

Kendall's mind filled with disjointed images of what lay ahead: the gossip and speculation, the expressions of sympathy from writers who would be thanking their lucky stars that it was her and not them who'd been cut loose.

Being homeless and adrift with no publishing house behind her, she would no longer be operating from a position of strength. What were the chances another publisher would be excited about her when Scarsdale had decided she wasn't worth keeping?

Kendall looked Sylvia in the eye. "They actually expect me to write another book for them under these circumstances?"

"Yep."

"Can't I just give them back the advance and call it a day?" Not that she still had the advance they'd paid her for the last book of her current contract. In fact, almost every penny of it had gone toward Jeffrey's and Melissa's college tuitions.

And even if she'd still had it, Cal would never support her giving it back. He already thought her grossly underpaid for the amount of time it took her to write a book. He'd just tell her to write the book, hand it in, and move on. But of course he was an accountant not a creative type—to him a novel was a product, something you produced and sold like a stick of deodorant. He had no understanding of the gut-wrenching required to write a four-hundred-page manuscript.

"Brenda just made it abundantly clear that they intend to hold you to your contract," Sylvia said.

"But they'll just bury it. They've done almost nothing when I was supposedly of value to them. What will they do now that they're getting rid of me?"

"I told her you'd want out. She told me we'd have to call their in-house litigator to pursue that conversation. I don't think you want to get caught up in that."

"But I can't write a book for them under these circumstances. They can't be serious. There's just no way."

Sylvia sighed. "Sometimes this business really and truly sucks. And this is one of those times."

Another of Sylvia's clients approached. Her unforced smile proclaimed her a newbie who had no idea what lay ahead.

"Call me Monday after you get back to Atlanta," Sylvia said as the younger author drew closer. "And we'll talk this through."

"Right." Atlanta was a world away, her everyday life shrunk to insignificance by the disaster that had befallen her. She looked up to see Mallory, Tanya, and Faye moving toward her, her own personal Mod Squad. But after this last blow, Kendall could barely stand, let alone share the complete implosion of her career.

"None of us have had dessert yet. Let's go get something chocolate." Mallory was doing the talking but all three of them were eyeing her as if she were a piece of glass that might shatter at any moment. They had no idea how right they were. And she couldn't tell them.

"Can't do it." She'd gag if she got within smelling distance of chocolate. And she absolutely could not discuss this latest disastrous development without completely freaking out. Even the slightest hint of sympathy would push her completely over the edge.

"Listen, I'm really beat right now," she said. No lie there. "I know you guys want to help, but I need some time to myself. I just can't talk about anything right now."

"Let's all go back to the suite then. We don't have to talk if you don't want to. We'll just—" Faye began.

"No!" Kendall looked away, willing the hysteria out of her voice. If they knew how bad off she was, they'd never leave her alone. "I have to get some sleep. I'm way beyond exhaustion, you know?" She heard the quiver in her voice, but was helpless to eliminate it. "And I really need some time to myself."

The three of them conferred silently. Mallory acquiesced for the group. "All right, but we're going to have a powwow in the morning. You're not in this alone, Kendall. None of us is."

"Right." She hugged them all good night, but even as she did, she knew Mallory was wrong. They might want to be there for each other, they might even smooth the path a bit on each other's behalf whenever they could, but when it came to putting the words on the page and living with what they'd written, they were all alone.

At the moment, she was the one whose career was facing extinction; she was the one who was supposed to write a book, which was tantamount to giving birth, and then put that baby in the hands of people who would either ignore or abuse it.

"I'll see you all in the morning," Kendall said, and she headed back to the room. Once there, she closed her bedroom door and sat on the side of her bed for a very long time, mesmerized by a small comma-shaped stain on the wall. Unable to think or plan, Kendall just breathed—a steady in and out that she hoped would calm her. But that never happened.

When she heard a key in the door, she reacted without thinking, sliding under the covers still dressed, like a child about to run away from home.

Home.

It came to her then, in the dark as she listened to the others getting ready for bed. She couldn't wait for her Sunday afternoon flight out. She'd never make it through Mallory's promised powwow or brunch or the limo ride to the airport afterward. She wanted to go home right this minute. She didn't know how she was going to make it happen, but she needed to be home in her own house and her own bed as soon as humanly possible. If not sooner.

Moving on instinct she hurriedly changed her clothes,

packed her suitcase, and phoned the airline. Then she was scribbling a note and propping it on the cocktail table and tiptoeing out of the room, without a single thought in her head except getting back to Atlanta as quickly as possible.

4

Every novel is an attempt to capture time, to weave something solid out of air. The author knows it is an impossible task—that is why he keeps on trying.
—DAVID BEATY

The 6:00 A.M. flight out of LaGuardia deposited Kendall at the Atlanta airport at 8:29 on Sunday morning. Exhausted, she deplaned and made her way to baggage claim then took the shuttle to the remote parking lot where she'd left her car. She felt as if she'd been gone an eternity rather than a mere forty-eight hours.

Traffic on Interstate 285 was light and she made the trip to the northeastern suburbs in record time, pulling into the driveway of her house on the dot of 10:00.

The twins were in Athens at their last week of the summer session. Cal's car wasn't in the garage and there was no sign of him in the house. After bumping her suitcase up the front stairs to the master bedroom, she wheeled it through the bedroom into the master bath and propped it open to get out her nightgown and toiletries.

She was creaming off her makeup—applied so hopefully yesterday afternoon in New York—when she looked into the bathroom mirror. Unable to face her ravaged reflection, she stared beyond it to the mirror image of the bedroom behind her.

Kendall's fingertips on her face stopped in midmotion.

Carefully she cupped her hands beneath the stream of water and rinsed off the remaining cold cream then patted her face dry with a hand towel. Only then did she turn around to consider their king-sized bed, which she noted with a peculiar mixture of resignation and horror, appeared patently unslept in—the comforter, shams, and pillows aligned exactly as she'd left them on Friday morning—a feat Cal would never have attempted to duplicate.

The garage door rumbled open downstairs, announcing Cal's arrival at the same time the possible ramifications began demanding access to her heretofore numbed brain.

An interior door slammed and Cal's footsteps sounded on the back stairs. They were not the eager steps of a lover, but the long, dragged-out footfalls of a husband who had not been expecting his wife home quite yet. And who might even now be trying out explanations for why he hadn't answered the house phone all weekend.

Kendall stood there in her rumpled nightgown and makeup-less face as Calvin walked into the master suite freshly showered and shaved. His gym bag dangled from one hand.

"You're home early." He stepped up and bent his tall, spare frame to give her a kiss on the cheek along with a whiff of minty mouthwash and woodsy cologne. "How'd the conference go?"

Kendall's antennae quivered. Sunday morning usually found Cal still in bed or stubble faced and surly behind the Sunday newspaper. But here he was all bright eyed and bushy tailed. Her gaze stole to the crisply made bed. His gaze followed hers and then came back to her face.

"Did you win?" Cal's tone was calm, matter of fact. It contained no admission of guilt and no real interest in what she'd suffered over the weekend.

Kendall looked directly into his eyes, not wanting to see the truth there. Her brain began to poke at all the evidence, but some self-preserving censor commanded it to back off, for which Kendall was thankful. If there was such a thing as a good time to find out your husband was cheating on you,

Kendall was pretty sure nine out of ten women would agree that this definitely was not it.

Like a pigeon bent on Capistrano, she'd managed to sneak out on her friends, get to the airport, onto a different flight, and then drive home almost entirely on instinct. And those instincts told her she absolutely could not handle the end of her personal life right now. Not on top of the demise of her career.

Those self-preservation instincts turned out to be pretty heavy duty. One minute Kendall was staring into Calvin's face, the next the air was whooshing out of her lungs and her brain was going wonderfully mushy.

Then her knees buckled beneath her and everything went dark.

. . .

Mallory St. James had breakfast with Faye and Tanya before dropping them at JFK for their flights home to Chicago and Tampa. They spent the meal and the limo ride trying to reach Kendall, whose note had said only that she'd decided to go home early and would be in touch when she got herself "back together."

"I can't even let myself think about what time of morning she must have left," Faye said, picking half-heartedly at her eggs Benedict.

"Sylvia must have hit her with something pretty big for her to bail like she did," Tanya agreed, pushing her plate away.

"Well, I don't like how she ran out on us." The bright yellow yolks on her fried eggs stared accusingly at Mallory. "I only let her off the hook last night because I figured we'd all be able to help better this morning." Mallory looked at the others and knew they were feeling as guilty and out of sorts as she was. "We've always shared the bad times along with the good."

Tanya shot her a piercing look. "When did we ever help you? I'm not aware of you having a bad time." She flipped her hair over one shoulder. "Except maybe that cover where they used that shade of blue you didn't like?"

Mallory put down her fork and attempted to still the rush of anger. These women who knew her best knew her so little, but then that had been her choice, not theirs. "I'm so sorry I haven't had more problems." That you know about, she added silently. "If it's any consolation, I feel like shit about it. Sometimes I'm afraid to mention anything good that happens because I don't want to make you feel bad."

There was a heavy silence. Mallory felt like a hen that had surprised the whole henhouse by laying a ten-pound egg. They prided themselves on being honest with each other, but they were women. Sometimes they put protecting feelings above the truth. Or looking self-sufficient above asking for help. And, of course, the version of her past that Mallory had shared with them had been carefully edited. If she ever admitted the real reason she wrote so compulsively, would they understand?

"Well that's not right, Mallory." As always Faye was the peacemaker. "We're glad for your success, aren't we, Tanya?" A salt-and-pepper eyebrow sketched upward above the dark frame of Faye's glasses. Her gray eyes were warm.

"Of course we are." Tanya took a sip of orange juice. "I'm just all worked up about Kendall. I feel like we failed her last night. And I hate to think about her all alone in Atlanta right now dealing with everything on her own."

"She has Cal," Mallory said, not sure why she said that when she knew better than anyone that being married didn't guarantee you a safety net.

They all sighed. They'd been friends too long for any of them to hold out any real hope of Cal as a comfort.

"And Melissa and Jeffrey are only an hour away at UGA in Athens," Mallory said as they divvied up the bill for the food they'd barely touched. "Kendall's a big girl. She'll be fine. Let's just promise that whoever reaches her first will let the others know."

Now Mallory stood in the foyer of her newly renovated Greenwich Village brownstone, trying to shrug off the nagging sense of worry that had ridden home with her. They all cared about Kendall and wanted to help her, but a woman had to build her own safe harbors and escape hatches in this life.

"Mal? Is that you?" Her husband, Chris, called out.

"Yes." She sat her suitcase down on the marble floor and propped her laptop up against it.

"I'm in the kitchen."

Mallory pushed through the far door of the circular entryway and stepped into the sun-dappled kitchen, by far her favorite room in the house. Two banks of windows framed the lush walled-in garden and allowed one to sit at any spot at the kitchen table and still have a view of it.

Chris, who had overseen the seemingly endless renovation and managed to make it possible for her to work throughout it, stood at the stovetop set into the octagonal island. The hair at his temples had begun to gray perfectly and his chiseled jaw and carved cheekbones made him look more like a male model in a Williams-Sonoma ad than an actual living, breathing, cooking spouse.

Chris waved his spatula at her. "Thought I'd make osso bucco for an early dinner. Or are you full from eating in restaurants all weekend?"

Mallory pinched a handful of grapes from a bunch in a cut-glass bowl on the counter and popped one in her mouth, feeling his positive energy lift and buoy her. "Sounds good," she said.

"Do you want to go to a movie while it's simmering? Or maybe adjourn upstairs for a nooner?" He moved up behind her and nuzzled the nape of her neck, smelling of man and meat, a fairly potent combination. Mallory knew from experience that he could put her in the mood in five minutes flat if she let him.

Her gaze strayed to the clock on the microwave and she struggled against the temptation. What could be better than an afternoon in bed with Chris? Certainly not the pages she had to write. For a long moment Mallory considered shrugging off the clock and throwing herself into her husband's arms. But making love wouldn't keep her in charge of her destiny; she already knew that writing could.

Turning, she gave him an apologetic peck on the cheek and ducked under his arms. "It's way past noon, and I haven't done my twenty pages yet."

"It's Sunday afternoon and you've been gone all weekend. Don't you think you could start thirty minutes later?" Disappointment thickened his voice. "Better yet, why not take the rest of the day off?"

But Mallory never ever took the day off. No matter what.

She kept her voice purposely light. "Can't," she said. "You know I have to do my pages first. I always do my pages first." What a dreary fact of life that was.

A look of irritation passed across his face. *He* was irritated? Mallory folded her arms across her chest. At the moment even arguing seemed more attractive to her than sitting down to work. "When did that become a problem for you?"

"It's not a problem," Chris said, stepping away from her and back to the simmering pan. He fixed his gaze on the cookbook propped on the counter. "I'm thinking about six o'clock for dinner. Will you be able to take a break then?"

But now Mallory found herself unwilling to let him sidestep the issue he'd raised. "You didn't think my having to write first was a problem when it was paying for this money pit we live in." The words were out before she could stop them. "Or making it possible for you to leave the architecture firm and go out on your own."

She was going too far, she knew it, but it was such a relief to let loose after a weekend of thinking about each word before it was uttered. In her study she'd have to think about each word before she wrote it.

"I said, no problem, Mal. There's no need to turn this into a big thing."

As always, Chris refused to engage. There were no knockdown drag-outs in the Houghton/St. James household. The man had been determinedly even-keeled practically every minute of their twelve-year marriage. Usually she treasured his calm. Sometimes she wanted to kill him for it.

"Fine," she snapped. "Then there's no problem." She walked briskly to the foyer to retrieve her laptop and then walked back into the kitchen. "I'm glad to hear it!" She was practically shouting now. Perversely, the calmer he got, the more agitated she became.

Angry, she stomped past him and into her study where she slammed the door to prove it.

But once she was behind the closed door of her office, it took an immense act of will to cross to her desk and sit down. Because the real truth was if there was anything she didn't feel like doing right now it wasn't making love to Chris.

It was writing.

She glanced around to make sure she hadn't made the admission aloud.

In fact, she almost never felt like writing anymore. Which was something she'd studiously avoided mentioning to Kendall, Faye, and Tanya, as well as her expensive Park Avenue therapist, and her annoyingly wonderful husband.

It used to be that she could simply sit down, boot up her computer, and the words and images would flow effortlessly from some deep well inside of her. But it seemed the well had dried up. Nothing flowed from her anymore, not even drivel. Now each word was painstakingly mined and placed. Great spans of time were spent attempting to create characters that differed in even a small way from the characters she'd written before. And then she had to find the words to describe them.

She caught herself staring out the window searching the gnarled oak in the garden for inspiration. Stray noises reached her from the kitchen, and she regretted the angry words she'd hurled at Chris. Maybe she should go out and make up with him, coax him into bed for a change.

That would be far more pleasurable than trying to eke out today's twenty pages. What better way to procrastinate than in bed?

No. Mallory booted up her computer and took out her notes. She was a professional writer and she had work to do. If she was going to make her deadlines, she was going to have to write her twenty pages today, tomorrow, and every day after that. If she allowed herself to think about the number of words she needed to produce, the sheer weight of them would crush her.

She couldn't let that happen. Because writing had been her ticket back to the world of financial security and she could never allow herself to forget it.

Mallory lifted her fingers above the keyboard and prayed she would find some kernel of something buried deep inside then chided herself for the thought.

If no kernel presented itself, she would have to invent one. She didn't have the time to wait for inspiration, divine or otherwise. If she waited until she really felt like writing, it would never happen. And then all of the lovely things that filled their lovely home and their lovely life would cease to exist. No sane human being would let that happen more than once in a lifetime.

Mallory shifted purposefully in her seat. She couldn't afford to be afraid. Nor could she afford to run out of words. So thinking, Mallory St. James tuned out her hurt husband in the other room, her hurt friend down in Atlanta, and the smell of the simmering osso bucco. Then the woman who had once been known as Marissa Templeton placed her fingers lightly on the keyboard and began to type.

5

*Books choose their authors; the act of creation is
not entirely a rational and conscious one.*
—SALMAN RUSHDIE

Unfortunately fainting was only a temporary escape. You couldn't rely on it on a regular basis, though it occurred to Kendall, when she came to on Sunday evening on the bed where Cal had placed her, that the women of Scarlett O'Hara's day probably hadn't fainted so often because their corsets were laced too tightly, as was rumored, but because there were so many unpleasant things they didn't want to deal with.

Kendall could relate. Between her failing career and her suspicions about Cal, the list of things she simply could not face was growing by the minute.

When the kids were still at home, when the foundation of her career could still bear weight, she might have tried to discuss things with Cal or suggest seeing a marriage counselor to help them save what they'd had for the last twenty-three years.

But with everything collapsing around her at the same time, Kendall was afraid to talk to Cal. She had a very bad feeling that if she did, the first words out of Cal's mouth would be, "I'm leaving!"

Earlier when he'd lifted her from the floor, she'd roused long enough to refuse to let him call a doctor or take her to the nearby walk-in clinic. Claiming exhaustion, she'd curled on her side and feigned sleep until she finally nodded off for real. Now she lay awake beside her snoring husband, staring at the wall trying to figure out her next move. When nothing came to her, she eased carefully off the bed, tiptoed into Melissa's bedroom at the opposite end of the hall, locked the door, and slid between her daughter's sheets, where she fell asleep sometime before dawn.

A sharp knock on the door awoke her about 8:00 A.M. Monday morning. "Kendall? Are you in there? Are you all right?"

Only half awake, Kendall tried to process her next move. For lack of a better alternative, she remained quiet while Cal rattled the doorknob. "Are you all right, Kendall?"

No response.

"We really need to talk."

If there was anything in the world Kendall did know, it was that she didn't want to do that.

"I've got to work on the Bryer report tonight," he said finally when she didn't say anything. "But I'm not leaving until you tell me you're OK."

"I'm OK," she called from bed, wanting him to leave.

"I'll try to be home by ten," he called back. "There are some things I want to tell you."

Most likely the very things she didn't want to hear. Kendall lay in bed listening to Cal clomp down the stairs and tromp through the kitchen to the garage. She thought he might have been whistling. Then the garage door went up, actually making Melissa's bed vibrate. Kendall felt it go down, too, but she stayed in bed awhile longer listening, just in case he had just pretended to leave in an effort to flush her out.

Exhausted, she wandered downstairs and poked in the refrigerator for something to eat but found only half an out-of-date container of blueberry yogurt and a shriveled peach, which she disposed of. Whatever Cal had been doing all weekend had not included a trip to the grocery store. Or eating at home.

Settling for coffee, Kendall carried the steaming mug into her office and set it next to her computer monitor. Still looking for comfort, she checked her e-mail and found one each from Tanya, Faye, and Mallory giving her hell for sneaking out on them. Each message ended with the instruction, "Call me."

When the phone rang, she practically leaped for it, thinking it was one of them, but it was Sylvia, which she would have known if she'd taken the time to look at the caller ID. At the sound of her agent's voice, Kendall envisioned a new family crest, something fancy in Latin for Avoidance at All Cost. *Avoidus, avatas, avant?*

"Hello?"

"Boy, you sound like shit," Sylvia said.

"Thank you," Kendall replied. Catching a glimpse of herself in the computer monitor, she added, "I look like it, too."

Taking a deep, hopefully bracing breath, she waited for Sylvia to get to the point of her call. Since it was Sylvia, this took about two seconds.

"I talked to Jane at Scarsdale this morning. If you want to give them back that thirty thousand dollars in order to terminate your contract, I can make it happen. But I don't advise it. Brenda Tinsley is notoriously vindictive. I think you'd be better off giving them the book and then moving on."

Kendall, of course, didn't have the money anyway and given the state of her marriage, she couldn't quite picture Cal dashing off a check out of their savings. For all she knew he was already squirreling away everything he could; yet another thing she should be paying attention to.

"Kendall?" Sylvia's voice broke the silence. "I know this is really hard, but you're a pro, you can do it. While you're writing I'll start putting out feelers at other houses. How far along are you?"

Kendall closed her eyes and breathed deeply. She hadn't written a single page, not one. She'd originally been very excited about the idea—a book about four writers at various stages of their careers loosely based on her, Mallory, Tanya, and Faye. But with all the bad news and lack of interest from Plain Jane, Kendall had been unable to hold on to that enthusiasm. Then the kids had gone off to college and left the house so empty she couldn't seem to think. Then Cal had started disappearing physically and emotionally and she'd gotten caught up in the possibility of winning the Zelda.

"Kendall? You can meet your December first deadline, right?"

Kendall instructed her brain to do the math. It was August 1; that would give her exactly four months, which was one hundred pages a month. If she worked six days a week, she'd have to write five to six pages a day. She normally wrote a book a year and took up to seven months for the actual writing of it, but she knew plenty of people who wrote much faster. With the kids gone and her time her own, she should be able to manage it, assuming she didn't let the story meander or take any wrong turns.

Except, of course, for the fact that she could barely think, let alone write. And if her marriage actually ended . . . No, she could not let herself go there. "Sure," Kendall said, trying to sound perky, willing to settle for upbeat. "Shouldn't be a problem."

For anyone but her at this time in her life.

"Good," Sylvia said, and then added in an uncharacteristically gentle tone, "You're very talented, Kendall. Don't let them throw you. Just get this book done and then we'll find you a more appreciative home."

Kendall lay on the couch the rest of the afternoon in a half-awake, half-dozing state, flipping from channel to channel until she settled on Turner Classic Movies. *Houseboat* with Sophia Loren and Cary Grant was the afternoon feature.

The phone rang periodically, but she didn't answer even when she saw Faye, Tanya, and Mallory's numbers on the caller ID. Her misery didn't seem to be interested in company.

With no food in the fridge and the idea of actually dressing and leaving the house unimaginable, she began to forage from the pantry. A bag of chips, two granola bars, and a handful of ancient vanilla wafers got her through the day. At 9:30 that night, she dragged herself back up to Melissa's bedroom, locked the door, and climbed into bed, where sleep eluded her until long after Calvin had come home and rapped on the door. "Kendall?" he'd called.

She squinched her eyes shut and pretended it was all just a bad dream.

"Damn it. This is unbelievable. You can't think we're going to be alone together and not talk to each other?"

As if this would be the first time this had ever happened.

"At least give me a sign that you're alive," he said.

She knocked three times on the wall behind her head then shouted, "I'm alive! But I have nothing to say to you!"

Kendall listened to him stomp off then spent the rest of the night staring up at the ceiling trying to understand how her life had unraveled so rapidly. At dawn she fell into a fitful sleep and was once again awakened in the morning by Cal's voice on the other side of the door. "Kendall, this is ridiculous. I've got to leave for the office. Open the door so we can talk."

She remained silent. After all these years of begging him to communicate more, it figured he'd want to do it now when there was nothing he was likely to say that she'd actually want to hear.

"I'm not leaving until you at least answer so that I know you're alive," he shouted.

Kendall debated whether to respond or not.

"Seriously, Kendall. If you don't answer right now, I'm calling nine-one-one and then I'm going to break down the door."

For a moment Kendall actually considered remaining silent just to see if he'd follow through on his threat. But since her goal was avoiding a discussion with Calvin, she reasoned that his coming into the room via battering ram or otherwise would make that close to impossible.

"I'm alive," she shouted back. "And I'm not stupid." She let him think about that for a couple of seconds. "Now go away and leave me alone!"

Agitated and exhausted, she waited for him to leave for work, then pulled on her robe and dragged downstairs. There she skimmed through her e-mails while munching on a breakfast of Ritz crackers and chocolate bits. She didn't go back into her office or near her computer that day nor did she see any reason to shower or dress. Whenever her thoughts strayed to the manuscript she should be writing or the husband she should be talking to, she'd scavenge something from the pantry and carry it back to the couch for consumption.

She cried and ate stale marshmallows while watching Doris Day and Rock Hudson trade insults in the romantic comedy *Pillow Talk*. By late afternoon when she began flipping between talk shows, her body had worn a comfortable hollow in the family room couch and Oprah was on her way to becoming Kendall's new best friend.

Despite her attempts to numb it, her brain raced madly, changing gears so rapidly that she couldn't hold on to a thought long enough to examine it. She did nothing all day, but felt as if she'd climbed Everest and then been trapped on its peak surrounded by air that was too thin to breathe.

Desperate for sleep and without any plan other than avoiding Cal, she went upstairs at 6:30 P.M., locked herself in Melissa's room, and took two sleeping pills, telling herself that if she could just get a full night's sleep she'd be able to think again.

In Melissa's bed she breathed in her daughter's still-girlish scent, closed her eyes, and finally fell into a dark cocoon of sleep. For a time she floated in the nothingness, her head bound to the pillow, her fears tunneled far off in the distance. And then there was a soothing, disembodied nothingness that stretched out into infinity.

She woke at noon, slow and dim-witted, and when she ventured out of her sanctuary, the house was silent around her. On the kitchen counter she found a note from Calvin. "I'll be home early. Don't bother locking the door. We're going to talk."

Four or five times that day she reached for the phone to call Faye or Tanya or Mallory, but she couldn't make herself dial. She sat at her computer trying to work herself up to writing, but after a full hour the only words on the screen were "Chapter One." After a second hour she'd added, "Page One."

When she clicked over to e-mail and saw messages waiting from Faye, Tanya, and Mallory, she cried, but didn't read or return them.

She was still sitting at her desk staring despondently at the blinking cursor when a phone call came in from Scarsdale Publishing. Too numb to weigh the pros and cons, she answered.

"Hello?" The quiver in Kendall's voice betrayed her and she followed it up with a sniffle that she hoped would be attributed to a cold or allergies.

"Ms. Aims?" The voice sounded breathy and unsure.

"Yes." Kendall groaned inwardly. It had to be some sort of bookkeeping or technical question. She should never have picked up.

"Ms. Aims, this is, um, Lacy Samuels. I work for Jane Jensen at Scarsdale."

The name was vaguely familiar, but she had no face to go with it. "Yes. Have we met?"

"Well, no. I, um, just graduated from Smith. I'm Jane's new editorial assistant."

Kendall waited impatiently, much too drained to engage in small talk with Plain Jane's slave labor.

"So, um, I'm calling because Jane has asked me to take over your next book for her."

At first the sleeping pill grogginess protected her from the truth. "I'm sorry," Kendall said. "What did you say?"

"I've, uh, been given the honor of editing your next book. I just wanted to, um, introduce myself and let you know how much I'm looking forward to working with you."

Kendall's brain was starting to kick in now and she really wished it wasn't. "Did you say you are going to be my editor? That *you* are going to edit *my* book?"

"Um, yes, yes, I did. Jane apparently, um, feels that I can bring something to your work."

The silence stretched out and the girl kept trying to fill it. "And, of course, there's, um, so much I can learn from you."

Kendall tried to gather her wits about her. It was, of course, a clear indication that Plain Jane didn't plan to waste a moment of her time or an iota of Scarsdale's resources on Kendall's last book for them.

"How old are you . . ." Kendall looked down at the name she'd scribbled on a nearby envelope, not remotely concerned whether the question was PC. ". . . Lacy?"

"Well, um," the assistant said quietly, "I'll be twenty-two next week."

Kendall couldn't bring herself to speak. She'd thought things couldn't get any worse than they already were, but she'd been wrong.

"But I was at the top of my class," Lacy Samuels assured her. "And everyone says I'm very mature for my age."

. . .

Kendall hung up the phone and sat, unmoving, for what felt like an eternity. She didn't go to the pantry to forage for food nor did she get up to wander the empty house or burrow back into her spot on the sofa. All of those actions were beyond her.

She was still staring out her office window when Calvin drove his BMW up the driveway and pulled it into the garage. It was 3:00 P.M., she hadn't showered or washed her hair for two days, and she was still wearing her bathrobe. She waited, suspended in time while he entered the house and walked into her office then sat on the loveseat to her left.

After all her ducking and weaving, she still wasn't prepared for the blow he dealt her. Scarsdale's repeated jabs had weakened her; Calvin's uppercut sent her crashing to the mat.

"Kendall?" Her husband's tone bore not a trace of the quarter of a century they'd been together.

Kendall kept her gaze on the cherry tree outside her window and wished she were the squirrel currently perched in the fork of outstretched limbs. If Calvin noticed her unkempt appearance, he made no mention of it. There was little more than a moment's hesitation before he spoke.

"Things haven't been so good between us for a long time," he said.

Oh, God, she thought, it's really happening. She drew in a breath and kept her eyes on the squirrel who was gnawing on something he held in his front paws.

"When the kids were at home, it made sense to try to keep up appearances for them."

So that was all he'd been doing, keeping up appearances.

"But now that they're gone, well, life's too short to spend it pretending."

She had a wild thought that Calvin had been watching Turner Classic Movies, too. Because everything he said sounded like it had been lifted from an old movie—and a bad one at that. Her husband of twenty-three years was dumping her and the best he could do was string a bunch of clichés together?

When she finally turned to face him, she fared no better in the dialogue department than he had. "You're seeing someone, aren't you?"

The words hung in the air between them, a trite accusation that came nowhere near addressing the gulf that stretched so wide between them.

"Yes," he said, without a hint of apology. "But I don't see any reason to get into that."

Something hot and heavy surged inside of her at the unfairness of it all. Her publisher didn't want her anymore and neither did her husband. They both just expected her to do whatever the hell they wanted and then quietly get lost.

The squirrel dropped whatever it had been clutching and used all four paws to spring onto another branch and trip lightly down the trunk of the tree to the ground. Kendall watched it scamper off.

What did it say about your life that you envied a four-legged rodent with a bushy tail?

"No," she said. "Of course you don't. You've never seen any

reason to consider anyone else's feelings or point of view. You just make decisions and we're all supposed to go along with them."

His jaw clenched at her response, but that was his only reaction. She had the feeling he'd rehearsed this whole scene, hackneyed dialogue and all. Probably while she'd been holed up in Melissa's room. Or maybe for a long time before that.

"I want a divorce," he continued. "I have an attorney and I think you should find one, too."

Part of her wanted to shout, "Fine! Who needs you?" and stomp off to find someone who would represent her; someone who would take him to the cleaners and make him rue the day he'd done this to her and the kids. The other part of her wanted to curl up in a tight little ball and pretend this conversation had never happened. *Avoidus, avatas, avant.* She should have stayed in Melissa's room longer; there was one thing she'd been right about—she absolutely could not handle this right now.

Panic began to kick in; her fight-or-flight instincts stirred. Her fists clenched in her lap as thoughts bombarded her. And then, oh, thank you, God, that soothing numbness took hold, filling and surrounding her. She didn't black out this time, but everything slowed and went slightly out of focus. Neither of them moved and yet Kendall could feel the distance between them widen.

One singular thought swam through the undercurrents of her brain and broke through to the surface: She didn't have to do anything about this right now. Not one thing.

She looked into Calvin's eyes and read the urgency there, his burning desire to be done with her so that he could continue to do as he liked.

But Calvin Aims's wants and needs no longer had anything to do with her. For the first time since she'd met him twenty-five years ago, she didn't owe him any special consideration. She didn't owe him anything.

She felt his growing impatience, but it no longer carried any weight. If she wanted to, she could simply go back and lie down on the couch in the family room and watch Oprah and eat her way through the pantry. Just because Cal wanted an answer didn't mean she had to give him one. In fact, the very fact that he wanted one was all the more reason not to give it.

"I'll think about it," she finally said quietly, grateful for the merciful numbness. "Maybe you should take some things with you when you go."

Cal's face telegraphed his surprise. Clearly during his rehearsals he hadn't wasted any time imagining how she might react. But then imagination had never been her husband's strong suit.

Slowly she got up from her chair then turned and walked away from him. In the family room, she fit her body into its groove in the couch and pulled the old afghan around her then aimed the remote at the television. Oprah's theme song came on, drowning out the sounds of Calvin going through dresser drawers up in the master closet as well as his clomping down the stairs and the slam of the garage door as he left.

Then she flicked to *The Kristen Calder Show,* which was also broadcast from Chicago and whose host had been hailed as the next Oprah. Her guests were a woman who'd gone to jail for maiming her abusive husband and another who'd driven the sports car her husband had given to his girlfriend into the deep end of their swimming pool—a crime for which a jury of her peers had refused to convict her.

"Right on, sisters," Kendall thought, as she lay wrapped in her cocoon on the couch. But in her current numbness she couldn't imagine ever marshalling the energy to punish Calvin for his crimes. She wasn't even sure she could make it to the pantry.

At the moment, as far as Kendall could see, she had absolutely no reason to move at all.

6

If my doctor told me I had six minutes to live,
I wouldn't brood. I'd type a little faster.
—ISAAC ASIMOV

Tanya Mason sat at the flaked Formica dinette in the mostly silent trailer. From the back bedroom her mother's snores sounded in a dead-to-the-world rhythm that originated in a liquor bottle.

From the second bedroom came the occasional snuffle or sigh from her daughters accompanied by the squeak of the metal springs on the old iron bed that took up most of the room. Later, when she finished this chapter, Tanya would squeeze in between them to grab the three to four hours of sleep that would see her through her breakfast shift at the Downhome Diner on Thirty-fourth Street South and the afternoon at the Liberty Laundromat, just around the corner.

Her only light came from the beam of the desk lamp she'd placed on the dinette and a small slice of moonlight that poked between the panels of the once beige curtains, now dingy from years of her mother's cigarette smoke, that hung at what her mother called the "picture window." Even though the only picture provided was of the septic tank that served the 1960s-era mobile home park.

Normally, no matter how tired she was after working two jobs, feeding the kids, and helping them with their homework and then getting them to bed, Tanya was eager to get to her writing, which she saw not only as her ticket out of the life she now lived, but a welcome daily mental escape from reality.

Her books were peopled with women like herself who found themselves alone and facing adversity but who, unlike her, still managed to find themselves *and* true love and got to live happily ever after.

Each night as she worked out her characters and their stories, she lived her heroines' triumphs and fell in love with the heroes she created for them; honorable men who not only pursued them but once committed stayed put—unlike the not-so-honorable Kyle P. Mason, who had married her and fathered Loretta and Crystal only to crumple at the first signs of real life, admitting as he fled his responsibilities that his first love was NASCAR and the fast cars he sometimes got to work on.

Tonight the words and images just wouldn't come. And when she closed her eyes to try to picture her characters and put herself in the scene, she saw Kendall's stricken face instead.

A hacking cough sounded at the back of the trailer and then there was the shuffle of feet as Trudy Payne came out to the living area. Shriveled and wizened well beyond her fifty-one years, Trudy had been only sixteen when she gave birth to Tanya. If she knew who Tanya's father was, she had steadfastly refused to name him.

Tanya had seen pictures of her mother before she'd gotten "caught" with Tanya, but there were none that came after. That would have required a camera and some sort of interest in documenting the train wreck Trudy's life had become.

Tanya guessed she should be grateful that Trudy hadn't aborted or abandoned her. She knew firsthand how hard it was to support and raise a child by yourself. But while Tanya relied on hard work and her dreams to sustain her, Trudy had turned to alcohol and cigarettes and the stream of men who provided them; a stream that had shrunk to a trickle now that Trudy had gotten old.

"You seen my smokes?" Trudy's voice had always had the

sound of a stick being dragged across gravel, but now it was punctuated by a perpetual whine.

Tanya studied her mother in the half light. Her blue eyes were wilted and her skin had turned leathery. Her blond hair came out of a bottle now and didn't resemble anything created by nature. Even in the more forgiving light, it was impossible to believe that this woman was only a year older than Mallory; she might have been a hundred.

"Did you hear me? I asked if you'd seen my smokes." Trudy's whine had turned ornery.

"No," Tanya replied. "And by the sound of that cough you'd be better off if you never did find them."

"Always think you know best," Trudy muttered, "but you ended up no better off 'n me."

Her mother settled for a shot of whiskey, which she poured with a shaking hand and a defiant glare. "I went three whole days without a single drink while you was gone, so don't give me that look of yours."

"Oh, Mama," Tanya said. "When did alcohol ever solve one little thing in your life?"

Trudy took a swallow of the amber liquid. "Just tryin' to take the edge off." Trudy's whine laced through her lament. "I've kept my part; I don't drink a drop when I'm takin' care of the girls. But I don't see no big advantage in facin' the world so stark sober as you."

Tanya didn't argue further; it wasn't as if they hadn't covered this ground a thousand times before. Trudy's promise not to drink around the girls had been the only thing that had made moving in with her possible. Trudy had never shown that kind of restraint when Tanya was a child; the idea had never occurred to her.

"You never did say much about that conference you went to," her mother said now. "What do you think those fancy friends of yours want with you?"

"We're all writers, Mama," Tanya said, as calmly as she could. "And we started at the same time. We all help each other."

"Lotta good that's done you." Trudy downed the remaining whiskey and brushed the back of her hand across her mouth. Mercifully she didn't belch.

"We wouldn't even still be in this trailer if it wasn't for my books," Tanya said. "And just 'cuz you don't think much of what I do and who I am, doesn't mean nobody else does."

Her mother snorted but didn't ramp up for a fight, for which Tanya was grateful. She put up with a lot and bit her tongue as often as possible, but she would not let Trudy ruin her daughters' opinions of themselves or Tanya's faith in her friends. Faye and Mallory and Kendall had saved her as surely as if they'd reached in and pulled her physically out of a garbage Dumpster. If it weren't for them, she'd have no one's opinion of herself except her mother's. And she sure as hell would never have written a book, let alone fifteen of them.

Her thoughts circled back to Kendall and how upset she'd been after the awards ceremony. It was odd how she'd lit out for home without even telling them. And now she wasn't responding to their calls or e-mails.

A shiver of unease snaked up her spine and Tanya promised herself she'd send another e-mail before she quit writing tonight and place another call to her from the Laundromat tomorrow.

"Don't you stay up too late now," her mother said as she shoved her glass onto the counter. "You know I can't get up with them girls in the morning. Especially after a night like this when I don't do anything but toss and turn the whole damned time."

Tanya knew better than to mention the heavy snores she'd heard coming from Trudy earlier. Or the fact that this probably wouldn't be her last shot of whiskey before morning. Her mother liked to dish out the criticism, but she surely couldn't take it.

Trudy retreated into her room, hacking as she went, but Tanya was no longer seeing the bitter woman who had given birth to her. She was seeing her current heroine, Doreen Grant, who was wiping the cute little bistro table at the beachside café where she worked. She kept straightening her uniform and fussing with her hair because her brother was supposed to be bringing one of his oldest friends in for lunch—a NAS-CAR driver Doreen had had a crush on since childhood.

Eyes closed, Tanya could hear the rush of the waves over the sand and see the seagulls wheeling overhead. The hero would be wearing cutoffs and have his T-shirt hanging over one broad shoulder so that he could be bare chested. He and Doreen's brother would tease her about the old days, but that spark would be there between him and Doreen. He might fight it for a while, but that boy had met his match.

Tanya gave a happy little sigh as the scene unfolded in front of her. Then she placed her fingers on the laptop keyboard and began to type.

. . .

Later that morning in the northern Chicago suburb of Highland Park, Faye Truett stretched and yawned then opened one eye experimentally. It was 6:00 A.M., not yet time to roll out of bed but too late to turn over and go all the way back to sleep.

Beside her, her husband Steve, or Pastor Steve as he was now known in almost every corner of the civilized world, slept on, his breathing even and peaceful in the morning quiet.

Faye turned her head so that she could see his profile, which she had always considered Kennedyesque. In fact the older Steve got, the more Faye thought he looked exactly like Jack Kennedy might have had he been allowed to reach the age of sixty-four. She, however, was no Jackie. Nor did she want to be.

Steve sighed in his sleep and rolled closer, draping an arm across Faye's waist, or what was left of it. Sometime in her midfifties everything had begun to widen and soften no matter how many hours Faye spent on a treadmill or at the gym. Sitting at a computer all day most days hadn't helped. Steve, with whom she had been sleeping for the past thirty-nine years, didn't seem to notice. Or perhaps he was just too smart to comment.

She settled her head against her husband's shoulder and

marveled at the twists and turns of their life together. Even Faye, who now wrote fiction for a living, thought her real life had turned out much differently than anything she might have made up.

She and Steve had met in a comparative lit class at Northwestern University in the late sixties, fallen in love, and married the June that Faye graduated.

They started out normally enough; Steve went into sales at a large Chicago ad agency, and Faye, who dreamed of one day writing a novel, became a producer for a film production company. Like most of their friends, they juggled careers and the rearing of their children. They had three in five years: Steve Jr., Kai, and Sara—all of them now married and producing grandchildren, though only Sara still lived in town.

On his fortieth birthday, Steve, who had been a lapsed Catholic since Faye had met him, decided to take a class at Seabury-Western Theological Seminary on the Northwestern campus. In hindsight, Faye should have paid more attention to this. But at the time it seemed a commendable use of Steve's spare time. He'd downplayed the whole thing, billing it as an intellectual and spiritual exercise—not a second calling or the beginning of a second career.

In fact Faye missed every single warning sign right up until the day, on her own fortieth birthday, when Steve announced his plans to leave his lucrative advertising job to start the Clearview Church of God and Television Ministry.

Despite the fact that all three of their children were in college.

It was, Faye thought now, a miracle that she—and their marriage—had survived the shock.

Steve's hand skimmed down the swell of her hip and back up to her waist in a soothing yet sensual movement even as Faye's thoughts continued to center on the past.

Overnight they'd gone from "comfortable" to strapped as they'd eaten through their savings to support three college tuitions in addition to Steve's new aspirations.

During those turbulent years she'd put her own writing

dreams on hold to ghostwrite the two God for Dummies books and *Rich God, Poor God,* which had put Pastor Steve on the ministerial map. Then she'd used her broadcast background and contacts to help launch his television ministry. She'd done what she had to do to keep her family afloat and Steve's dream alive. And found an additional source of income she'd never mentioned to him and of which he remained blissfully ignorant.

Steve had never looked back, but Faye had. He'd wanted her on the air and by his side, a package deal like the Bakkers once were or the Osteens out in Texas were now. But while Faye loved Steve and her children and believed strongly in God, a public ministry and a husband who globe-trotted in the name of Jesus was not what she'd signed on for.

Still she did her best. And when the kids were out of college and his ministry became both successful and highly profitable, boasting a facility with a 2,300-seat Worship Experience Center, full-service Starbucks café, childrens' facilities, and film and recording studios, Steve told her it was her turn. That was when she'd attended her first Wordsmiths Incorporated conference where she met Kendall, Mallory, and Tanya. From that day onward she'd considered herself a professional writer even though it took her two more years to sell her first novel—at least the first work of fiction written under her own name.

Steve's questing hand moved beneath her nightgown, drawing it up to cup her breast. "I missed you," he murmured against her skin, and against all odds, she felt the same shimmer of anticipation that she'd felt as a coed. Whatever they'd gone through, however their paths had diverged, they'd always been able to find their way back to each other. And they'd always been good in bed.

"You haven't said much about the conference. How'd it go?" he asked.

"It was all right," Faye said, not really wanting to talk about it.

"Just all right?"

"Yes." Any other time this week Faye would have been grateful to discuss the subject, but right now she wanted to turn off her brain and enjoy the feel of Steve's hands on her body. "Kendall didn't win and she got some other bad news she was too upset to share with us."

"That's too bad." Next to his looks, Steve's voice was his biggest asset. It was warm and soothing, the perfect register for communicating conviction and concern. Faye sometimes had to listen closely to separate the true feeling from the professional sympathy.

Once he'd realized Faye wasn't going to join his religious bandwagon, Steve had supported Faye's writing—in fact, being his wife had certainly boosted her inspirational romance career, but he'd never really understood her attachment to Kendall, Mallory, and Tanya. "She's the one in Atlanta, isn't she?"

"Yes." Faye didn't want to ruin the moment with irritation over his lack of interest in the details of her life. Between his speaking engagements and television production schedule and her book deadlines, their time alone had become increasingly rare. There'd been a time when they talked about everything; now it seemed like they had to pencil each other in and work down an agenda to cover the most important topics.

Subtly Steve lifted his arm to check the wristwatch he was never without and Faye noticed that his fingernails were newly manicured and his palms felt smoother than hers.

"Do you have any other books due out?" Steve asked, running one smooth palm across her hip. "The ladies of the congregation love your inspirationals; I thought we might look at cross promoting on the website. Maybe I should have someone call your publisher to see if we can work out some kind of agreement." He rested his palm on the no longer gentle swell of her abdomen, his fingers splayed. But now Faye was thinking about the book she was working on and whether it was a good idea for anyone from Clearview to contact Psalm Song.

Faye's amorous mood began to evaporate just as Steve's seemed to be kicking in. In real estate it might be location,

location, location. In lovemaking it seemed keeping one's mouth shut might be the key.

"I don't think I have time for this right now." Faye began to pull away. "I really should get up and get to work."

There was a long silence, and then with obvious reluctance, Steve withdrew his hand and pillowed it with the other beneath his head. "Right," he said, as Faye pushed the sheet aside and stood, smoothing her nightgown back down. "Me, too. I've got to be at the church for a meeting at 9:00 A.M. And I'm doing a radio sermon at noon."

Despite his reasonable tone, Faye could tell that her refusal had irritated him. He had the same wounded air the children used to get when she criticized their dishwashing technique, or lack thereof. Or refused to take them somewhere they'd asked to go.

She padded away from him toward the bathroom aware that her rear view was a whole lot "fuller" than it had once been. For a brief moment she wondered if she should have just gone ahead and given in. After all, he was, as he sometimes liked to put it, one of God's quarterbacks. There were probably scores of religious groupies just dying to give their all for the team.

Faye turned in the bathroom doorway to find him still studying her from bed and a part of her acknowledged that she should probably be grateful that her husband still found her desirable. But Faye didn't like the idea of feeling obligated. And she really disliked the fact that he didn't know who Kendall was and that he seemed to see her writing as something that might please his parishioners or benefit his ministry rather than something marvelous that she alone had created.

Shampooing her hair, she tried to picture where Kendall was and what she was doing at that exact moment, but she kept drawing a great big blank. Faye wrapped her dripping hair in a towel and wiped steam from the mirror so that she could apply her makeup and dry her hair.

She could hear Steve moving around the bedroom, getting

ready. The phone rang and the sound of his murmuring reached her though she couldn't make out the words. It was barely 7:00 A.M. and already she could feel him slipping into full Pastor Steve mode. Drawers opened and closed and she imagined him cradling the phone against one shoulder while he tied his tie and strategized with one of his personal assistants.

But Faye's thoughts were already circling back to Kendall. She'd left numerous messages and while she'd tried to give her friend some space, enough was enough. If she had to, she'd get on a plane and fly down to Atlanta.

But first she'd check in with Mallory and Tanya. Surely someone had heard from Kendall by now.

7

I'm not saying all publishers have to be literary, but some interest in books would help.
—A. N. WILSON

The offices of Scarsdale Publishing occupied all ten floors of a glass and limestone skyscraper on West Thirty-sixth between Fifth and Sixth Avenues midway between the Empire State Building and the New York Public Library.

The massive marble lobby, like the rest of the building, had been built to impress. A burled walnut security desk sat exactly in the center of the space, elegantly blocking access to the bank of elevators behind it. The wall to the left was dotted with elaborately framed portraits of the publishing house's most famous authors. On the right Plexiglas-topped pedestals displayed first editions of those authors' releases dating back to Scarsdale's inception in 1922.

Scarsdale's beginnings as a family-owned company whose fortunes were built on western dime novels and true confession romances were well documented, but the company had been gobbled up early in the cannibalization of New York publishing and had changed hands too many times to count. It was now owned by the media conglomerate American Amalgamated and was operated by people who knew a lot more about the cost of paper and the color of the ink on the bottom line than the art of publishing.

An uneasy truce existed between the editorial and business

sides, but the days of buying a book based solely on literary merit or an editor's gut reaction were long gone.

Lacy Samuels was blissfully unaware of all of this on the Friday morning following her conversation with Kendall Aims. Lanky and somewhat awkward, Lacy had deciphered her first written word at the age of four and had spent the last eighteen years inhaling every one she encountered, from ad copy on cereal boxes to leather-bound editions of the classics.

Having graduated at the top of her class at Smith, she took her English degree very seriously. Despite her worship of the written word, she had recognized early on that she was not a writer herself, but was certain that her destiny was to discover and nurture into print the next Great American Novel.

Toward this end, in between the grunt work and coffee runs, she had begun to work her way through the mounds of unsolicited manuscripts, referred to as the slush pile, that she had originally believed would yield at least one undiscovered gem that might propel her out of the bottom of Scarsdale's editorial heap. Unfortunately, despite six months of concerted effort, she'd barely made a dent in the constantly replenishing piles that littered the editorial offices and had been forced to concede that the quality of the work, even to her inexperienced eye, was appalling.

Which was why she had been so excited when Jane Jensen had assigned her to work with Kendall Aims, who as a multipublished author should provide a much speedier and more enjoyable route to an editorship.

Except, of course, for Kendall's worrisome reaction to her call.

Lacy sat at her desk, worrying her lip, trying to figure out whether or not she should bring this up with her boss. On the one hand, she didn't want to give up the opportunity to prove herself editorially; on the other, she didn't want to be foisted on an author who didn't want to work with her. She was still debating her best course of action when her phone rang and Jane called her into her office.

Jane Jensen's dark hair was held back with a black-and-white polka-dotted headband that looked much too perky for the rest of her. She wore a generic black top and pants that did nothing to disguise or enhance her chunky figure, and she wore neither makeup nor jewelry. Lacy, who was not exactly a fashion diva herself, felt downright trendy beside her. If she didn't care about her job so deeply, she would have been on the line to the people at *What Not to Wear* to nominate her boss for a fashion intervention.

"Good morning," Lacy said, as she entered Jane's corner office and came to a stop across from her desk.

"Maybe," Jane Jensen replied. "The jury's still out on that."

Lacy smiled weakly; she'd discovered the hard way that no response was expected to her boss's sarcasm.

"Call Stephanie Ranson—you'll find her name on the agent list—and tell her I'm looking for something with at least a touch of paranormal to fill in the slot Sandra Adams was slated for." Sandra Adams was a first-time author Jane had bought who'd been unable to revise her manuscript on time. "She owes me for this whole fiasco. Tell her I expect to see something by Monday.

"Then get hold of somebody in the art department and find out what happened to that new cover we were promised."

"I'm not sure anyone is in the art department today," Lacy said, as she scribbled Jane's directions on her pad. During the summer, Fridays were hit or miss as everyone seemed to work fewer hours. "Aren't they taking off—"

"I didn't ask for an attendance report," Jane snapped. "Just find somebody. Call somebody's assistant and tell them I need that cover *now*. I don't care what you have to do, just take care of it."

Lacy nodded and added the note to her growing list.

"Call Picata," Jane said, naming a nearby Italian restaurant that was so heavily frequented by Scarsdale employees that it was referred to as the Scarsdale cafeteria, "and make a lunch reservation for two under my name. Carolyn Sinclair is in town and I'm meeting her there at one." The day Jane had stolen Carolyn Sinclair from another publishing house was the happiest Lacy had ever seen her. To say that Jane was competitive was like saying there were a few Starbucks in New York City. Jane had practically done a happy dance on the top of her desk when Sinclair's agent had pronounced the deal done.

Some day, Lacy thought, she'd have big name authors and her own corner office. And when she did, she intended to treat her assistants a lot more gently than Jane Jensen. The only people Jane treated well were those a lot higher up on the food chain.

"I want you to type that memo for Brenda Tinsley about the sales catalogue." Brenda, the associate publisher at Scarsdale, was a tall, terse woman who was way up there on Lacy's personal intimidate-o-meter. As the second in command to the publisher, Brenda was often referred to as "the hand of God."

"Find Kara in publicity and tell her I want a copy of the stops on Carolyn's book tour to take with me to lunch. Then ask her to make a call to Carolyn's agent. We need to do a little stroking here and I can't do it all by myself."

Lacy made the required notes, wondering how in the world she was supposed to find all these people when the building felt as quiet as a tomb. If she reached anybody any more senior than herself today it would be a miracle.

She suspected that once Jane left for lunch she wouldn't be seen again until Monday. Lacy waffled once again about whether to bring up her conversation with Kendall Aims or leave it for next week. Deep down, she felt the author's reaction was an important piece of information, but her boss's reactions were often difficult to predict. Occasionally she was friendly and approachable, sharing with Lacy the knowledge acquired over her two decades in the business. More often she resorted to sarcasm or shrieked like a fishwife. Lacy had heard more than one staffer mutter about Jane not taking her meds or needing to get her dosage right, but she'd never known if this was idle gossip or a simple statement of fact.

Jane looked up from her desk. "That's all for now," she said, with all the emotion one would use to shoo off a fly. "I'll probably have a few more things for you before I leave for lunch."

Lacy didn't move, still unsure.

"What? What is it?" Jane's dark eyes signaled her impatience. It didn't look like she was about to engage in a teaching moment.

"I, um." Lacy looked for the right words, but couldn't find them. She already regretted not leaving the moment she was dismissed. "I, um, spoke to Kendall Aims yesterday like you told me to."

Jane just continued to stare at her as if she couldn't imagine why they were discussing this. Lacy fervently wished they weren't.

"And, um, she didn't seem too happy to hear from me." She shifted nervously from foot to foot. "I had the impression she was surprised to be working with me. I, uh, think she would have preferred someone more senior."

Jane's mouth tightened with displeasure. "Is that right?" She stood and came around her desk then leaned back against it in a casual pose not at all in keeping with the ramrod tightness of her body. "As far as I'm concerned, Kendall Aims is a mediocre midlist author who needs to be happy with whomever *I* assign her."

Lacy noted the jangle of emotion that always seemed a tad too close to Jane Jensen's surface and knew better than to comment. She stood completely still, much as you might freeze if you stumbled across a snake coiled to strike.

"This is your opportunity to show me what you can do," Jane said. "I suggest you make the most of it."

Lacy licked her dry lips, but it was the only movement she allowed herself.

"If you're smart," Jane continued, "you won't waste a drop of energy worrying about the Kendall Aimses of this world. I guarantee you she's sitting in her white columned McMansion down in Atlanta right now pounding out this manuscript just as easily as you or I could go downstairs and hail a cab."

This sounded somewhat unlikely to Lacy, who had a great deal of respect for anyone who could produce a four-hundred-plus-page manuscript on a regular basis, but again, she knew better than to comment.

"Do you understand?"

Lacy didn't, not really. But she nodded her head as if she did and forced herself to make eye contact with the woman across from her.

When she was certain Jane was finished speaking, Lacy prepared to leave. As she did so, she noticed a row of Kendall Aims's titles on a lower shelf of her boss's bookshelf. This time the internal debate over whether to speak was briefer.

"Maybe I should read some of her work so I can be familiar with her style," Lacy said. "Do you mind?"

"Fine." With almost complete indifference, Jane waved her toward the bookcase. "Take them. She's all yours now." Jane watched as Lacy gathered the paperbacks and balanced them against her chest to carry back to her cubicle. "But I wouldn't get too attached."

. . .

Kendall was definitely at her desk, but she was not, alas, pounding out a novel. Or much of anything else except a rousing game of FreeCell. Then Tetris. Then Minesweeper.

She had intended to bury herself in her writing and had hoped to get chapter one roughed out, but the day was almost gone and other than her page and chapter headings the screen was completely blank.

Except for that damned blinking cursor.

Every once in a while she stopped between games long enough to make a trip to the pantry or check e-mail or click back to Word—where that damned cursor blinked back.

She both wanted and needed to write. If for no other reason than to blot out Cal's defection, she craved the oblivion of words and imagined images, but no matter how many times she curved her fingers over the keyboard, she couldn't find the right words with which to begin.

Graham-cracker crumbs littered her keyboard and gathered in the lap of her robe. Her notes lay strewn across her desk, but she didn't have the will to decipher them. Her face felt sticky from junk food mixed with tears. It desperately needed to be washed—just like the rest of her. She considered taking a shower but was oddly reluctant to go upstairs where she'd have to see how much Calvin had taken with him.

Just past noon a strange car drove up the drive. From her office window, which fronted the street, Kendall watched what turned out to be a bright red Jaguar pull to a stop. The driver-side door opened and she got a flash of a magnetic Realtor's sign, though she couldn't read the name of the firm. A long shapely leg poked out of the car and a tall, willowy blonde emerged.

Feeling slightly ridiculous, but unwilling to be spotted by anyone who looked that put together, Kendall eased carefully out of her desk chair and onto the floor so that she couldn't be seen through the triple window under which her desk was centered.

She crouched there as the tap of high heels on the brick walkway announced the blonde's approach. Kendall held her breath even as she berated herself for being such a wuss. It was her house, her prerogative how she dressed and what she did in it. She didn't have to hide. If she wanted to she could meet the woman's gaze through her office window and simply choose not to answer the door.

Instead she crouched beneath her desk like some modern-day Lucy Ricardo waiting for the woman to go away.

The doorbell rang, the multitoned chime echoing loudly through the empty house. Kendall waited, barely breathing, for the stranger to go away, but after a couple seconds' wait the bell rang again. It rang a third time.

And then, unbelievably, a key turned in the lock and the front door of her home swung open.

"Hello?" The woman stepped all the way into the foyer and looked right through the open French doors into Kendall's office. Her gaze slid down to Kendall, who was still crouched on the floor.

Kendall's mind, which had been moving incredibly slowly up to that point, began to race through possible options.

The phone was on the opposite end of her desk, too far away to reach, and it seemed unlikely the intruder was going to stand idly by while Kendall lunged for it and dialed 911.

Their gazes met—the intruder's a clear and very startled blue, Kendall's undoubtedly wild and unfocused. An empty marshmallow bag, left over from last Thanksgiving's sweet potato casserole, blew off the desk and landed on the carpet beside her.

A strange woman had just walked into her home and found her cowering beneath her desk. After a few agonizing heartbeats and an unadulterated adrenaline rush, the most salient fact sank in: The strange woman had a *key*.

Kendall straightened with all the dignity she could muster and cinched the belt of her robe tighter around her waist. "Who are you?" She looked the woman up and down, trying to understand what was happening. "And what are you doing in my house?"

The woman took a step forward, pocketed the key, and offered her empty hand, which Kendall ignored.

"Cal," the blonde began then stopped. "Mr. Aims told me you were considering putting the house on the market. I'm Laura Wiles. I'm with Harvey Regis Realty." She flashed a brilliant smile. "I'm a ten-million-dollar seller."

Putting the house on the market?

There was a whooshing sound in Kendall's ears that threatened to drown out the rest of the woman's words. Surely she'd misheard. Or misunderstood. She and Calvin had moved into this house as young marrieds and raised Melissa and Jeffrey here.

She swallowed purposefully, like she did on a plane to compensate for changing altitude, in an effort to clear her ears.

"Anyway, Cal, um, Mr. Aims gave me the key so that I could take a look around and start working on the listing. I rang the bell first like I always do. I'm really sorry for barging in on you. I didn't realize anyone was home."

Kendall swallowed again and willed the whooshing sound to recede as she considered the woman in front of her. Laura Wiles was somewhere in her midthirties, a good ten years younger than Kendall. Her hair, which was salon cut and artfully highlighted, hung past her shoulders. She wore a light pink summer-weight suit over a lacy white camisole. Her dainty feet were encased in pointy-toed three-inch heels. Diamond studs sparkled at her ears and her lipstick matched her suit exactly.

More importantly, she was on a first-name basis with Kendall's husband. And Calvin had given her a key.

Kendall dropped her gaze and was confronted with twin chocolate stains on the lapels of her robe. The hands that she smoothed down her sides encountered frayed patches of terrycloth and other unidentifiable sticky spots.

Her tongue moved over her dry lips and she got a taste of cheddar cheese from the stale Cheetos she'd uncovered at some point that morning. What she looked like began to sink in and she could tell by the Realtor's face that her disheveled state had not gone unnoticed.

"I see I've caught you at a bad time. I'm so sorry for intruding. I'll, um, just let myself out and come back another—"

"Give me the key." Kendall held out her hand, palm up.

Laura Wiles, whose name was now branded in Kendall's head for all eternity, took another step back. But her chin went up and her eyes telegraphed a warning. If there'd been any doubt, Kendall now knew this was not some uninvolved Realtor who happened to call Kendall's husband by his first name. This was *her*, the woman Calvin was getting ready to jettison his old life for.

And he thought he could give *her* the listing on the house Kendall hadn't agreed to sell.

Kendall stood stock still with her hand extended while

adrenaline pumped through her bloodstream and her mind raced. Their gazes were locked and Kendall had this bizarre image of them standing there all day in some sort of Mexican standoff until Calvin finally came home and . . . what? Kendall's brain adamantly refused to go there.

"I suggest you give me the key now," Kendall said. "You may have my husband for the moment, but you will never get the listing to my house." The younger woman blanched and Kendall felt a small surge of victory. "I will personally burn this house down over my head before I'll let you list it or live in it. Do you understand?"

Kendall watched as the other woman considered her options. Kendall's hand had begun to tremble from being stuck out there for so long, but Kendall didn't pull it back.

"You're crazy, you know that?" The Realtor reached in her pocket and pulled out the key. "Look at you." She shook her head, the professional mask gone, allowing the disgust to show on her face. "No wonder he doesn't want you anymore." She wrinkled her nose and dropped the key in Kendall's outstretched palm with her French-tipped fingernails.

"Frankly I couldn't care less about the house," Laura Wiles said succinctly. "It would be a hard sell anyway. And I certainly have no interest in living in it."

She settled her Coach bag firmly on her shoulder and stared Kendall in the eye like a gunslinger fingering the ivory handles of her Colt .45. "But I'm going to keep your husband, *Mrs.* Aims. That much you can be sure of."

Kendall watched the blonde leave. She relocked the front door behind her then stood in the foyer for a long time trying to absorb what had just happened.

There really was another woman. Calvin had already moved on and her little tussle with his girlfriend had accomplished absolutely nothing. The small flush of victory she'd felt when demanding the return of her key had all but faded. Life as she knew it was now over.

Kendall walked into her office and stared down at the desk she'd tried to hide under and knew one thing for sure. She couldn't write—or even think—here. She couldn't *be* here. She would not stay in this house one more minute than she had to.

Moving now at a speed she hadn't come close to all week, Kendall practically flew up the stairs where she dumped her conference clothes out of the suitcase that still sat on the bedroom floor, then ran hot water for a shower. While she washed her hair and rubbed soap into her poor food-caked body, she realized there was only one place she could go.

Letting her hair dry on its own, she dressed, threw jeans and T-shirts into the suitcase, and raced back downstairs where she gathered her notes and a yellow pad and stuffed them into the case with her laptop. On her way to the garage, which she hadn't set foot in all week, she raided the pantry one last time for the fuel she would need to get her where she was going.

*Writing is easy. All you do is sit staring at a
blank sheet of paper until drops of blood
form on your forehead.*
—GENE FOWLER

There is an unwritten rule of writing that the number of trips to the refrigerator a writer makes is in inverse proportion to how well a manuscript is going. When the fingers are flying over the keyboard and the brain is fully immersed in the scene being created, food is completely unimportant. But when the fingers slow and the focus blurs, or worse, when the writer sees nothing but the blank screen and the hypnotic blink of the cursor, food beckons. As does, oddly enough, a load of laundry, the flossing of one's teeth, and the complete rearrangement of a kitchen pantry or walk-in closet.

When it comes to bailing out of a scene that is not working, even the most onerous—or fattening—of tasks will do.

Which would explain why Mallory was now on her fifth trip to the refrigerator, her fourth to the bathroom, and in the middle of her sixth game of Minesweeper. It was only 10:00 A.M.

"Shit!" She pulled her hair down from its crooked ponytail, raked it back up with both hands, and refastened the elastic band, thinking how shocked her readers would be to see what she really looked like when she worked. Or tried to.

Then she got up, yet again, to pace her office, stopping to stare out at the gnarled oak, the black wrought-iron fence that bound it, the taffy-pulled clouds strung through the blue sky.

With a groan she dropped back down into her chair and closed her eyes, desperate to see her characters and the airport lounge in which she'd placed them. But all she could see was how little she'd written and, when she let herself, Kendall's stricken face.

Her mind began to race down dead-end paths as the panic closed in. Chris was out and the house was completely quiet, just as she normally liked it. But today the quiet felt both oppressive and judgmental.

How could you justify not producing when absolutely nothing stood in your way?

She breathed deeply, taking in great gulps of air in an effort to get enough oxygen to her brain to fend off the paralyzing images: blank pages that translated into no manuscript to turn in, her agent and editor turning their backs on her, a book signing to which no one came, the repo vans taking away her possessions.

She knew exactly what this felt like, this snatching away of a life, and there was no way in hell she was ever going to experience it again.

Mallory left her desk yet again and wandered into the kitchen. At the counter she poured herself another cup of coffee. Slowly, as slowly as was humanly possible, she stirred in the nonfat creamer, opened a packet of sweetener and mixed it in. Sipping the milky mixture, she moved to the pantry, where she opened the sliding louvered doors and carefully contemplated her choices—all of them way too fattening. She'd consumed the healthier choices hours ago.

If she didn't find inspiration soon, she'd get too big to fit in her desk chair. Maybe she should go outside and take a walk, burn up a few calories. Get a little fresh air to clear her head.

But that smacked of procrastination, or worse, an admission of defeat. She could not even contemplate that the day's twenty pages might not get written; like the dieter who skips just one trip to the gym and then never goes again, it could be the beginning of the end. The slip that led to the fatal slide.

The trips to the refrigerator, the computer games, surfing the Web in the guise of research, the load of laundry she'd started out of desperation—all of those time wasters had put her behind where she wanted to be. But as long as she didn't leave the house, as long as she didn't stray too far from the laptop or desktop on which her manuscript was stored, she could not avoid the need to do the pages. Leaving the house felt much too dangerous; she might not come back.

Mallory turned her back on the pantry. Her life, and its security, depended on the words she put onto the page. All she had to do was write them.

She walked back to her desk and put her butt in the chair, which as every writer knew was more than half the battle. If she stayed here and faced down the page, she would find the words she needed. She was a writer, ergo she would write. She just needed to clear her mind so that her characters could present themselves to her.

A flourish of music and the icon of a feathered quill announced an instant message from Faye.

Mallory knew she should ignore it. Normally she didn't even have her sound up or her computer online while she wrote, but now she seemed to invite distraction at every opportunity. A click of the mouse and the IM screen appeared.

"I'm worried about Kendall," Faye's message read. "Haven't been able to reach her. Have you?"

"No," Mallory typed back. "She's not returning my calls or e-mails. What about Tanya?"

Mallory waited for a response.

"No. Something's wrong."

The words flew between them. They were in agreement that someone needed to do something, but they weren't sure what.

Faye typed. "I've got to finish this chapter, but I think I have Cal's cell phone number somewhere. I'll call him tonight."

"Thanks," Mallory typed, already feeling guilty for not offering and also envying Faye the matter-of-fact "I've got to finish this chapter." That meant she'd actually managed to *start* one. "Keep me posted."

"Will do." Faye signed off and Mallory clicked back to Word. The screen was still blank.

She had had Cal's number at some point, too, she thought, opening her desk drawer and beginning to paw through the jumble of business cards and scribbled contact info that she hadn't yet put into her BlackBerry.

Her fingers moved nimbly through the odd items that filled the drawer: a photo loop, a business card from the firm Chris was with when they met, a masseuse she'd heard about and been meaning to try, a promotional pen with a writer's name on it.

Maybe she could find Cal's contact info and get it to Faye. And maybe she could organize this drawer while she was at it. The act of sorting and throwing out might free up her subconscious so that it could figure out the story she was working on.

As she rifled through and tossed things out, she realized that her desk was even messier than the drawer and she decided to tidy that, too. No wonder she couldn't think straight with all this . . . turmoil around her. She didn't need to panic or be afraid. She'd just give herself the rest of the morning to straighten up her office. First thing after lunch, she'd get right down to work.

· · ·

Kendall was in her car heading north toward the one place that Calvin didn't like and couldn't touch: the home in the North Carolina mountains that her grandparents had left her.

No blond-haired real estate agents would be prancing up her front walk there. In that neck of the woods a person didn't traipse onto another person's land without expecting to meet up with the business end of a shotgun. She regretted how civilized they'd become; granny's shotgun would have come in handy when Laura Wiles had come to call.

Kendall barely checked her speed as she merged onto Highway 85 at Spaghetti Junction and expertly changed lanes to avoid the slowpokes in the right-hand lanes. About an hour and a quarter into her drive she spotted the swell of foothills that heralded the beginning of the Blue Ridge chain. She passed the scenic overlook at Tallulah Gorge, where a member of the tightrope-walking Flying Wallendas had performed headstands as he crossed the gorge on wire, then continued along the two-lane highway toward Clayton, Georgia, where uncomfortable signs of progress reared their heads: a big boxy Walmart stood next to a shiny new Home Depot, their tar-topped parking lots rectangular slashes in the red clay landscape. The red dust of construction hung in the air and settled on the hood of her car.

At the new twenty-four-hour grocery store, she stopped and bought a haphazard mix of junk food and staples along with a case of assorted wines.

She was through the tiny towns of Mountain City and Dillard in a matter of minutes and then began to wind her way upward, the air cooling as she climbed. Kendall lowered the windows to allow the crisp mountain air to caress her cheeks and rifle her hair. Curtains of kudzu shrouded the landscape, looking much too vibrant for a vine bent on suffocation. To the right, the mountainside fell away in a dizzying drop, leaving vistas of air and sky and tree-topped mountains.

She breathed deeply, savoring the mixture of altitude-cooled air and sun-warmed earth as she passed over the seamless border between Georgia and North Carolina. Mountain laurel, rhododendrons, and fat blue hydrangeas spilled over stone walls and split-rail fences. It was hard to ignore the signs of new construction, but she did her best, focusing instead on the spill of water down a distant rock face, the sun-bleached clapboard of antique stores, and the home-hammered shelving and hand-lettered signs of on-your-honor vegetable stands. Around the next bend a lone horse grazed in an expanse of meadow. From somewhere beyond a cow lowed.

The old and the new did not always coexist happily or

seamlessly here, but for Kendall there was still enough of the long-known to make the drive one of homecoming. And when she turned onto the unpaved road that continued to wind upward to her grandparents' homestead, each tree and shrub seemed planted in order to point her way there.

The house itself was old and worn. It sat in the clearing, its last coat of gray paint long since faded. Two brick chimneys, one at each end of the house, poked up from its oft-patched roof. Two basement-level bedrooms and a bath crouched underneath, their large corner windows maximizing both light and view. Porches and decks shot off the one-story structure providing views, if not architectural symmetry, in almost every direction.

Up here there was no garbage pickup, no mail or newspaper delivery, and no local cable service. Kendall had whiled away her summers here, tending the flower and vegetable gardens with her grandmother, taking long rambling hikes with her grandfather, sitting wordless on one of many wood rockers with a book in her lap, her gaze lifting every so often to follow a hawk riding an updraft or to locate a distant peak of the Blue Ridge Mountains.

She was twenty-five when her grandparents died and left her the house along with the money to maintain it. She tried to share the house with her new husband, but Calvin never warmed to its rustic charm or understood the hold it had on her. He preferred the restaurants, shops, and golf farther north in Highlands, and once the kids were old enough, Kendall brought them instead—all three of them spending the two months of summer together with only occasional visits from Cal.

Now she carried in her groceries and her overnight bag and dropped them on the kitchen floor. In a burst of energy, she went from room to room, throwing open windows and removing dustcovers from the furniture. She carried the outdoor furniture from the screened porch out to the back deck and plopped down into a chair so that she could prop her legs up on the deck railing. The trickle of a distant waterfall carried on the wind and there was a tinkling of wind chimes outside the master bedroom.

The stillness both filled and surrounded her, muffling, if not halting, the litany of fears and disappointments that had been running nonstop through her head. She wasn't fooled. The panic wasn't completely gone. It lay coiled inside her, ready to rear its diamond-shaped head and strike at the slightest provocation.

But for the moment she was in the one place she felt safe calling home and once she pulled herself together—please, God, let that happen soon—all she had to do was write a book. And find an attorney. And get a divorce. And explain it to her children. And . . . No, she couldn't think about any of that right now.

Because right now she was going to sit on this deck where her grandmother once shelled peas and her children had swung lazily in the old rope hammock and do absolutely nothing. That was all she had to do. Just sit right here and breathe.

For as long as she felt like it.

Kendall inhaled then exhaled. And then she repeated the exercise, drawing the fresh piney air deep into her lungs. And then, with the steady drone of insects as background, she closed her eyes and tilted her face up to the late afternoon sun and let the breeze sweep over her skin.

• • •

An hour and a half after their conversation, Faye received an e-mail from Mallory with nothing but Calvin Aims's name and cell phone number in it. She printed it out and left it sitting in her printer tray while she finished the chapter she was on and roughed out notes for the next.

She'd offered to help because she was worried about Kendall, but she wasn't looking forward to speaking to her friend's husband. The few times she'd met him, he'd struck her as self-important and self-centered. His support of Kendall's writing career had been totally monetary, and he'd managed to get in plenty of digs about her disappointing earning power

when he'd finally understood how little most midlist writers
earned.

Some markets were more lucrative than others, but the
publishing business was very cyclical; what was hot one year
might be over the next. There were paranormal writers who
couldn't get arrested five years ago, who were riding the crest
today. The same had happened to historicals, comedies, chick
lit, mystery. If it had been popular, it also had not. And a
writer couldn't necessarily change her voice or style, simply to
fit the current market.

She worked steadily through the afternoon and then broke
at about 4:00 P.M. to see what could be organized for dinner.
The freezer bulged with carefully labeled Tupperware and
disposable containers undoubtedly delivered by female parishioners convinced that Pastor Steve might starve to death
without a wife to cook for him for two and a half days. Never
mind that he had a married daughter who lived less than a
mile away. Or opposable thumbs completely capable of removing plastic wrap and operating a microwave.

Faye selected a tuna noodle casserole, a loaf of crusty cheese
bread, and a rectangular container labeled, "Maybelle's marvelous marbled brownies." After all the food she'd consumed
in New York this weekend, she was not about to quibble over
a few extra calories now.

She had no doubt that if she ever disappeared for more
than a day or two, the women of the congregation would be
lined up to provide Steve with much more than casseroles and
home-baked desserts, but she chastised herself for the un-
charitable thought.

Tonight it was just the two of them for dinner—an unusual and welcome occurrence. Tomorrow Faye would babysit
their granddaughter, Rebecca, while their daughter, Sara,
took her yoga class and did her Saturday afternoon stint in the
church resale shop. Sunday was largely spent at church,
though Faye sometimes got up very early to work before she
had to leave for the morning service. Every once in a while
when she was on deadline, she worked the entire Sunday, not

out of disregard for the day of rest, but because she believed in a God who understood the importance of meeting one's deadlines and commitments. And who, she hoped, would also understand the lengths a woman might go to in order to protect and support her family.

Faye set the casserole and brownies out on the counter to defrost and went out into the garden to cut flowers for the center of the table. She was arranging them into a cut-glass vase when the phone rang. Answering, she was delighted to hear her granddaughter on the line. "Hello, Gran Gran," Rebecca singsonged into Faye's ear. "Mom tole me you were back from France."

Faye smiled. "That's con*ference*, Becky. France is a country in Europe."

The five-year-old's voice dissolved into a giggle. "I see Egypt, I see France, I see Gran Gran's under—"

Sara's voice replaced that of her daughter. "Rebecca Simmons, how many times have I told you to think before you speak?"

"But . . ."

"I'm sorry, Mother. I don't know what's gotten into her lately." Sara lowered her voice. "I think it's that Lowry girl she's gotten friendly with. She does not get enough supervision in my mind."

"Oh?" Faye put the upper oven on preheat and unwrapped the casserole. The brownies looked good even in their frozen state.

"I let Rebecca play there last Saturday afternoon while you were in New York. And when I picked her up at five in the afternoon, her mother was lying around in her bathrobe reading one of those trashy romance novels." Her voice went even lower. "The kind with S-E-X in it and a bare-chested man on the cover." It was clear Sara was completely scandalized.

Faye frowned at the disapproval in her daughter's voice. Faye had always thought of motherhood as a softening experience, but becoming a parent had turned Sara from mildly opinionated into downright judgmental, a change in her daughter that Faye wasn't sure how to address.

"I know how to spell, Mama." Becky's voice piped up in the background. "I learned it on *Sesame Street!*" And then, "Why are you whispering about the number six?"

Faye covered her mouth to disguise her laugh. Still she felt compelled to defend her profession and her colleagues. "And I would think you of all people would know that romance novels do not deserve the adjective 'trashy' attached to them," Faye said. "The romance writers I know produce well-written stories for today's women, not trash. Your mother included."

"Oh, mother," Sara chided back, "you don't write books that need clinches to sell them. You write for the inspirational market, that's not the same thing at all. Why I'd have to move away in shame if you ever put your name on a book like she was reading."

Faye thought about her own body of work. And about Tanya juggling her daughters and her jobs while still trying to hold on to her dream of publication. Then she thought about Kendall, who wrote more mainstream women's fiction and whose identity was so caught up in her writing. And Mallory, with her kick-butt heroines and twenty-pages-a-day compulsion and the fame to show for it.

The writers Faye knew wrote very different things, but they wrote because they had things to say and because they were compelled to do so. There was nothing like expressing your feelings on paper, even if you had to disguise them as a fictional character's.

And, as she well knew, sometimes the writing was about the money and what it could do for your family. That was legitimate, too.

"Sara, that's quite enough. You sound like all those ignoramuses who read a romance novel back in the stone age or once read some titillating back-cover copy and think they have the right to judge. When you can sit down and produce a four-hundred-page manuscript that can transport a reader somewhere else for a spell, maybe I'll allow you to criticize."

"No need to get so worked up, Mother. You know we're proud of you and what you do, even if some of the parishioners do give Dad a hard time about it."

No doubt the casserole makers and dessert bakers trying to prove their own piety.

"All right, dear." Having made her point, Faye was eager to patch things up. "Shall I come to your house tomorrow or do you want to drop Becky off here?"

They worked out the details and rang off. And then, because she already had the phone in her hand and couldn't think of a good excuse, Faye dialed Calvin Aims's cell phone.

9

*The cat sat on the mat is not a story. The cat
sat on the other cat's mat is a story.*
—JOHN LE CARRÉ

If you got to the Downhome Diner in south St. Petersburg on a weekday before 8:00 A.M., you could get a man-sized breakfast for $2.08. Weekends it cost a good bit more, but that didn't stop folks from piling in and spilling out the front door to wait at the concrete picnic tables or peruse the ancient motorcycle sculptures made from scrap metal and old parts that dotted the parking lot.

On Saturday mornings like this one, bikes and expensive choppers sat cheek to jowl with minivans and late-model sedans, just like the leather-clad bandana wearers sat up close and personal to other patrons in khaki shorts and Hawaiian shirts.

Tanya reported to work at 4:45 A.M. six mornings a week, including Saturday. The doors opened at 5:00. The stream of waiting fishermen would come in first to take their seats at the counter. After them came the day-shift cops followed by a batch of old men who'd allegedly been coming there every morning since the doors first opened, which was almost as long as Tanya had been alive.

Belle Whalen, who'd been one of the original waitresses, had bought the place in the midseventies and had owned it ever since. She was pushing seventy now and had tough, leathery skin from an ill-advised love affair with the sun and decidedly feminist leanings. Pigs, which represented the male chauvinist kind, came in every form from stuffed to glass and occupied shelves, walls, and corners. Behind the cash register and all over the walls were plaques and posters that declared the supremacy of the female sex. Almost none of them were politically correct. "Give a man an inch and he'll call himself a ruler," proclaimed one. "If assholes could fly, this place would be an airport," read another.

Here the waitresses were competent and sassy, and fools, especially of the male variety, were not handled gently.

"How's Trudy doin'?" Red Thomas, a big bear of a man with a gray ponytail that had, in fact, once been red and a voice almost as big as his forearms, had been the head cook and Belle's main squeeze, for most of the last thirty years. He was a legendary speed cooker, having been clocked at forty eggs cracked in sixty seconds and claimed to go through 1,200 eggs, 140 pounds of potatoes, 50 pounds of sausage, and 40 pounds of bacon on a busy day.

"Same as usual," Tanya said, as she stowed her purse and tied an apron over her jeans and T-shirt. Tanya's shift had once belonged to her mother. In fact, they had shared the shift during Tanya's high school years, long before forward-thinking corporations had sanctioned the idea. One day when Trudy couldn't get out of bed after a night of partying, Tanya, knowing just how nonexistent their finances were, had simply shown up for her mother's shift. When no one threw her out, she worked it right up until she had to leave for school—when her mother had straggled in to take over.

Without discussing it, they'd fallen into the pattern—Tanya starting the shift at 4:45, Trudy taking that extra two hours to sleep off her hangover. Or enjoy her latest man.

Today it would have been called enabling, but then it had been a matter of survival and Tanya had been grateful that Belle, who'd had her own issues with alcohol, had let it pass as long as one of them was there to carry the shift.

Tanya had come back eight years ago when Kyle bailed

out on them and she and the girls had been forced to move in with her mother.

Theoretically Trudy stayed home to get the girls up and out to school and be there when they got home in the afternoon. The truth was that Loretta and Crystal mostly did for themselves, but Trudy's presence allowed Tanya to take the early shift at the diner and the afternoon shift at the Laundromat. No one was getting rich, but the jobs and her book earnings meant they could pay the bills and put a small bit aside each month for emergencies. It was the best she could do right now and if she was always tired and more irritable than she'd like to be, then that was the price of survival. One day, she hoped, her girls would understand.

Stifling a yawn, she retrieved her order pad from a drawer and lingered in the kitchen to pour herself a cup of coffee.

Beside Red at the griddle, Brett Adams, the latest in a long line of aspiring assistants, was doing his best to imitate Red's one-handed crack and release. Somewhere in his late thirties, he was well over six feet with broad shoulders and dark waves of hair. Dark stubble covered angular cheekbones and a squared jaw.

He shot Tanya a cocky grin as he cracked an egg one handed in a pretty fair imitation of Red's motion and dropped the shell directly into the trash in one smooth move.

"Not bad, boy." Red gave him an approving nod and then guffawed and shot Tanya a wink when Brent's next crack sent rivulets of yolk running down his hand.

"Damn," Brett swore. He looked up and saw Tanya watching him. "Pretend you didn't see that." He tried again with the same result. "Or that!" He shook his head and picked up a rag to wipe off his hands. "I'm blaming that one on you," he said, pointing a finger at Tanya. "How's a guy supposed to concentrate with such a good-looking audience?"

"Oh, be still my heart!" Tanya dismissed him with an exaggerated bat of her eyelashes. Brett was very nice to look at, but he was an outrageous flirt with enough charm to be dangerous. There was already a restaurant-wide pool as to who would sleep with him first. Tanya had placed a bet but had no intention of competing for the privilege. She'd already been married to a man with too much charm and not enough follow-through. She didn't intend to make that mistake twice.

Tanya left the kitchen and began to work her way around her section. The regular customers knew whose tables were whose and were careful to sit at their favorite waitress's table. Two waitresses had once come to blows over a big tipper who came in still blitzed at five one morning and accidentally sat in the wrong spot. The atmosphere might feel slightly bawdy, but it was also highly competitive. The waitresses were here for the tips, pure and simple. And they knew they had to earn them.

Tanya poured a cup of coffee for Jake Harrow, a former navy captain with tattoos of women's names running up and down his arms, one of which was Trudy's. Graham Andrews, a long-haul trucker who had also once dated her mother, sat with him. For a while, Tanya had wondered if one of them might be her father—Trudy absolutely refused to discuss Tanya's conception—but although they always asked after her mother and made a point of sitting in Tanya's section, neither had ever left a tip large enough to be construed as child support.

By ten, Tanya had made what felt like a thousand trips between the dining room and the kitchen. Her back hurt and her right knee ached, but she continued to flash her smile freely and squeeze a shoulder or laugh at a joke where appropriate. It was this personal touch as much as her efficiency that made people choose her section and up the tips. It was a point of pride with her that some customers would pass up an empty table in somebody else's section to wait for one in hers.

"Hey, Red, what's going on with my order?" she called now through the pass-through. "You're making me look bad."

"Hold your horses, girl!" Red snapped, not looking the least bit harried or put out. At the Downhome a certain amount of sniping and return fire was expected. "The kid's got your order and he just ain't a full-fledged speedster yet."

"But I will be." Brett flashed a smile at her as he began to plate the order. Lord, the man liked to show his teeth. "I figure in another ten years or so, Old Red here is gonna be eatin' my dust."

As if he'd be around that long, Tanya thought. Red had been here for an eternity, as had most of the waitresses, but Red's assistants were a more transient lot. They came, caused a bit of a stir sleeping their way through the waitstaff, and then they were gone. Not exactly something worth investing in.

"Who're you callin' old?" Red pointed to his still thick head of hair. "I got every one of these gray hairs from this place. Workin' with all these women will drive a man insane. Made me old way before my time!"

Tanya's phone vibrated in her pocket and she pulled it out to check the caller ID. It read "home."

"Make it quick," she said, bringing the phone to her ear. "I'm on the clock." Belle had a real short fuse for waitresses who yacked on their phones when they were supposed to be waiting on tables. Tanya didn't blame her.

"Crystal is being such a big baby," her older daughter whined. "All I said was . . ." A long-winded explanation followed.

Tanya cut her off. "If you are not bleeding or on your way to the hospital, Loretta, I do not want to hear from you again. Do you understand?"

"Yes, Mama, but Crystal . . ."

"No. Stop right there. I have customers to wait on. Where is your grandma?"

"In bed."

Of course she was. Tanya didn't know why she would have expected otherwise. A shriek reached her over the line. "You go take care of your sister right now," Tanya said. "And you two start behavin' yourselves. Do you hear?"

"But . . ."

Tanya did not have time for "buts." She flipped the phone closed and slipped it back in her pocket. She managed another pass through the dining room, took orders from two newly filled tables, freshened coffees, presented three checks, and then headed back to the pass-through. Her phone vibrated. Again.

Ducking back into the kitchen, she whipped the phone out and put it to her ear. "What?"

"Mama, Loretta is being a big old meanie. She won't let me watch what I want ever. Tell her to let me or . . ."

Tanya didn't even bother to answer before she hung up this time. Looking up, she caught Brett watching her with a slight smile on his lips.

"You think I'm funny?" she demanded, fisting her hands on her hips. "That's cause you don't have children plaguing you about every little thing." Or a mama who could sleep right through it.

He grinned right out at her for about the fifth time that morning. "Now how do you know that?"

She looked him up and down. "Doesn't take a rocket scientist to figure these things out. I know your type. I have completely got your number."

"Is that right?" He continued to crack eggs and flip hash browns, but his brown eyes held on to hers. He jammed his other hand down on the bell to announce the order was ready and flipped his spatula for good measure. "You do not have my number, girl. I can promise you that. You don't even have the first digit."

She heard her name called and turned to see Jake trying to catch her eye. She was off this morning, not her usual competent self, and her daughters' calls were not helping.

Her phone vibrated again. This time Tanya yanked it out of her uniform pocket, flipped it open without looking at the caller ID and practically shouted, "What in the hell do you want this time? Can't a woman work in peace anymore?"

There was a moment of silence and then she heard Mallory's voice. "Sorry. I should have realized you'd already be at work," she apologized. "Faye wanted us to have a conference call to talk about Kendall."

"Oh."

"Yeah, we're both here, Tanya," Faye's voice chimed in. "Sorry we caught you at a bad time."

Tanya could picture them in their silent offices in their beautiful homes. She was backed into the corner of the ancient kitchen trying to avoid being seen. She looked up and saw Brett watching her again. One of the other waitresses came back to her corner. "Your natives are getting restless. A couple of them want their checks," she said.

"Thanks," Tanya said. "Can you tell them I'll be right with them?" Into the phone she said, "What's wrong?"

"Cal said he and Kendall have split up. He claims he doesn't know where she's gone."

"Do you believe him?" Tanya asked. None of them were big Calvin fans, having heard one too many stories that demonstrated just how clearly Calvin Aims's life revolved around Calvin Aims. "I mean, you don't think he's *done* anything to her do you?"

"You mean like stuffed her in a trunk or tied a concrete block to her foot and dropped her in the closest body of water?" Mallory's tone was dry. "What are you, a writer or something?"

"No," Faye said, "We're not going to be seeing old Calvin on *America's Most Wanted*. He sounded too irritated to have done her in."

They all digested the "irritated" part.

"So what do we do?" Tanya asked, over the clatter of dishes and the clank of silverware. Out on the floor Belle poured coffee at two of Tanya's tables. Any minute she'd be back here looking for her.

"Well, both Faye and I think she's got to be at the mountain house," Mallory said. "And we think one of us needs to go there."

"Oh." Tanya wished she could volunteer to go, but she couldn't even stay on the line much longer. "I could maybe go next weekend if that would help," she began. "You know, maybe drive up Saturday and come back Sunday night." It would be ten hours each way from St. Pete to Kendall's mountain place, a weekend spent mostly driving, but Kendall and Faye and Mallory had always been there for her.

"I could probably go by midweek," Faye said. "Steve and I have a fund-raiser Monday night and I've got to get my proposal in by Wednesday. But after that I could . . ."

"No, I'll go," Mallory said. "I can go first thing in the morning."

Tanya was surprised at Mallory's offer. It wasn't that Mallory wasn't one to help; it was just that her offers normally came in the form of money or a gift—something that didn't eat into her writing time. She was the most prolific of all of them and other than when she was on a book tour or making an appearance, she seemed to spend most of her time working. "But you never . . ." Tanya began.

"Are you sure you can take the time?" Faye asked, getting to the words faster than Tanya. "I know you have a deadline coming up."

"I'll just take my work with me," Mallory said. "Maybe I'll even stay a few days once I make sure Kendall's OK. Just stay and write there for a while with Kendall."

Was that a wistful tone Tanya heard in her voice? No, it couldn't be. Mallory could write all day every day already if she wanted to. She didn't have Trudy or Loretta or Crystal or two jobs and a double-wide to take care of. She just had herself and that good-looking husband of hers who waited on her hand and foot.

Tanya tried to picture that, someone else taking care of her—fussing over her—but she just couldn't imagine it. Not even a little bit. If Tanya had a setup like Mallory's she'd never leave it. She'd bury herself in that beautiful office and write nonstop forever.

"My flight gets into Atlanta late tomorrow morning. I've reserved a rental car so I can drive up to Kendall's. I, um"— she cleared her throat—"found the directions in the bottom of my desk."

Was that a note of embarrassment in Mallory's voice?

"I'm not stepping on anybody's toes, am I?" Mallory asked uncharacteristically. "Is someone else able to go sooner?"

Than tomorrow? Tanya bit back a flip comment about her private jet waiting outside the diner to fly her up there.

"No," Faye said. "I'm glad you can go. But you have to promise to call us as soon as you get there and tell us what's going on."

"Yeah," Tanya added, popping her head out to scope out her tables, while trying not to let Belle see her on the phone. "After you give her some shit about avoiding us like she has."

She saw Jake raise a hand and make the scribbling motion for a check. Another one of her customers got up to take a container of artificial sweeteners from another table. She needed to get back on the floor.

"Don't forget to let us know how she is and what has to happen. It would be hard for me to get away right now," Tanya said. "Unless it's an emergency."

In which case, she'd put her kids on her back and walk through Florida and Georgia to get there if she had to. As far as she was concerned, she owed Kendall, Faye, and Mallory pretty much everything. And she didn't intend to ever forget it

10

Contrary to what many of you may imagine, a
career in letters is not without its drawbacks—chief
among them the unpleasant fact that one is
frequently called upon to sit down and write.
—FRAN LEBOWITZ

Kendall lounged on the deck, her feet propped up on the railing, and stared out at the distant peaks. It was Sunday right
around 1:00 P.M. and she was still wearing her pajamas and
drinking coffee in hopes the caffeine might somehow jolt her
out of her reality and into some kinder, gentler universe. It was
beautiful here, soothing, contemplative even, but if she allowed her inner voice to have its say, she'd have to admit that
she'd done little more than trade the family room couch for the
strapped outdoor chair she was sitting in and the television for
a breathtaking mountain view.

The thing was, no matter what she fixed her attention on,
the shards of her broken life kept poking through: Calvin's
defection, the need to tell the kids, the demise of her career,
the triumphant face of husband-stealing Realtor Laura Wiles,
the book she had to write. Like Pig-Pen from the Charlie
Brown comic strip, her cloud hovered over her, dark and
daunting and devoid of a silver lining.

She yawned and waited for the caffeine to kick in, hoping
it might at least propel her inside to her laptop, but she was
tired, so tired. She had sat up all night flipping channels on
the satellite TV—as always amazed that there could be so

many options and so little to watch. Exhausted, but unable to sleep, she'd been drawn inexorably to HGTV, where she'd watched episode after episode of people fixing things, thereby changing their lives. Flip that house and prove how smart you are; change the water heater yourself and improve your self-esteem; redecorate your neighbors' living room for under a thousand dollars and cement that friendship. The channel was filled with thirty-minute programs that could pave your way to happily-ever-after.

She'd nodded off in her deck chair when a stray sound broke the quiet and nudged her out of sleep. A car came up the drive, its tires crunching on the gravel road, and stopped at the side of the house. The engine went off, and a car door opened and closed. Footsteps sounded on the gravel and then on the kitchen steps. Kendall sat frozen on the deck, unsure what to do. There was no time to go inside for a robe and no-where out here to hide.

"Kendall?" A female voice rang out in the silence, and for a split second, she was afraid that Cal had given Laura Wiles a key for the mountain house, too. She had vowed that if she ever saw that woman again she would be wearing clothes.

There was a loud rapping on the kitchen door. "Kendall?"

Kendall considered her options. This took about one second because she had none.

"Kendall Aims, I left my house at 5:00 A.M. this morning and have spent most of this day traveling to get here. You damned well better answer your door!"

Certain she couldn't be hearing the voice she was hearing, Kendall crossed the deck and entered the kitchen.

"Kendall, I'm not kidding! Open up! Or I'll huff and I'll puff and I'll . . ."

Kendall pulled open the kitchen door and there stood Mallory in her low-slung designer jeans and high-heeled boots. "Blow my house down? Right now that would be completely anticlimactic."

"Would this be the time to mention that it's afternoon

and you're not dressed?" Mallory stepped through the open door. "I'm pretty sure even the three little pigs would have pulled on their little clothes by now."

Kendall stepped forward and into Mallory's open arms. Her friend smelled of the big city and expensive perfume; Kendall most definitely did not. "I'm so mind-bogglingly glad to see you!" She clung to Mallory in the doorway, not wanting to let go. "I don't even care that you just called me a pig!" She stepped back and swiped at the tears on her cheek with the back of her pajama sleeve. "How did you find me? What are you doing here? Oh, my God, I'm so glad to see you!"

She was crying freely now, all the tears she'd been holding on to so tightly pouring out of her like a damned waterfall. When she'd finally sniffled to a stop, Kendall led Mallory into the house. "I just can't believe you're here," she said, swiping once more at her face.

"One of us would have been here sooner if you'd let us know where you were and what was going on." She leaned against the kitchen counter and folded her arms across her chest. "Speaking of which, what *is* going on, Kendall?"

Mallory looked her up and down, and Kendall became fully aware of the picture she must be presenting: the wrinkled, ill-fitting pajamas; the greasy hair; the dark circles under her eyes that attested to her HGTV nights.

Mallory sniffed pointedly. "Is there something wrong with your plumbing?" She winced. "You do still have indoor plumbing, don't you?"

Kendall gave a final swipe at her tears. She felt as if she'd been toting a full set of emotional baggage around on her shoulders and someone had offered to carry some of it. "Let's go out on the deck. And to start with your last question first, nothing's wrong with the plumbing, though I think I could probably fix it if there were after all the HGTV I've been watching. And to your first question?" She pulled a second chair next to her old standby and motioned Mallory into it. She drew the mountain air into her lungs and tried to order her thoughts. "Everything's wrong. It's like I slipped when the Zelda didn't happen and then I started rolling down the mountain and everything I thought I could cling to ripped out of my hands."

She told her then about her conversation with Sylvia Hardcastle and her need to leave New York, her desperation to get home only to be forced to confront the truth about Calvin. She described the call from Jane's assistant and Cal's B-movie dialogue, his Realtor girlfriend and demand for a divorce. It all poured out of her along with another stream of tears.

"I don't know what to say to Jeffrey and Melissa. When they went away to school a month ago everything was fine. Suddenly their father has a girlfriend, their mother doesn't have a career, and their parents are getting a divorce. I don't understand how all of this happened. How can they?"

Mallory stared out over the deck railing, listening without comment.

"It's all so overwhelming I can't seem to clear my head long enough to think. I keep telling myself I don't have to *do* anything about Calvin right now. There isn't really anything to do, anyway. But I am supposed to write a book and I don't see how that can possibly happen. Definitely not now. Maybe not ever."

Mallory turned and looked at her but the "That's ridiculous, of course you'll write" that Kendall was expecting didn't come.

"I mean, what's the point?" Kendall asked. "Even when I thought my personal life was OK, my career was dying. In fact, of all the writers I know, you're one of maybe two handfuls I can think of who have real, big-time, name-recognition careers. You know?"

"But, I . . ."

"No, I don't hold it against you, Mal. That's not what I'm saying. I'm saying what are the odds of really making it? What if I somehow, miraculously, got my life back together and managed to write a really incredible book? What are the chances that something major would happen? A billion to one? A trillion?"

"I . . ."

"You know, the writer who most inspired me, other than you guys, is a woman who helped found the local writers' group I belong to. She wrote for years, one book after another, just trying to get somewhere. At one point, despite all the roadblocks her publisher put in her way, she hit the *New York Times* list and got a multimillion dollar contract with another publisher."

Mallory listened, her attention rapt, but she didn't interrupt.

"When I was trying to get published, she once said to me, 'The published people are simply the last ones standing.' And I believed her. I put the line on a Post-it note and taped it to my computer screen and on my bathroom mirror. I looked at it every day. I repeated it to other aspiring writers who were getting tired and wanting to give up.

"I understood what she was saying. The publishing business is brutal but if you just keep at it you can beat it. You just have to stay on your feet, never give up. That's what she said and I believed her."

"That's good, Kendall. That's right. It's all in the head anyway. Sometimes it's hard, unbelievably hard. You just have to—"

"That woman is selling houses now, Mallory," Kendall said quietly. "She's in real estate!" She grimaced. "And I'm not feeling too kindly about that field right now."

• • •

Mallory had thought she'd toss and turn all night, distraught over Kendall's situation, but she'd slept like the proverbial baby; a result no doubt of the crisp mountain air. Or the two bottles of wine that she and Kendall had consumed.

She'd heard the TV on during the night, little snippets of what sounded like "cornice mouldings" and "router," but her sleep had been deep and untroubled. For the first time her own problems weren't front and center clamoring for attention. Her first order of business needed to be getting Kendall back on track.

Pulling on her robe, Mallory followed the smell of coffee out to the kitchen. There she found Kendall dressed and smiling and writing something on a legal pad. Her gaze strayed to the clock on the kitchen wall. It was 8:30 A.M.

"Wow, you're already dressed." She sniffed. "And showered, too. I may change careers and become a counselor."

"What can I say?" Kendall said. "You've inspired me." She gestured Mallory to the empty mug on the counter near the coffeemaker.

Mallory poured herself a cup of coffee, mixed in creamer and sweetener, then took a long sip. "What are you writing?" she asked. "An outline? Character notes?" Maybe this wouldn't be the emotional ordeal she'd been anticipating. She'd offer to brainstorm or help solidify plot points to get Kendall started and then she'd do the same. Just the change of scenery should be a solid shot in the arm. How could a view this beautiful fail to inspire?

"Actually, it's a list for Home Depot."

Mallory dragged her gaze from the view to consider her friend. "Home Depot?"

"Yeah, all those HGTV shows I've been watching have inspired me to take care of some things around here."

"But you don't have a *renovation* due." Mallory felt compelled to state the obvious. "Scarsdale is expecting a completed manuscript, not photos of a room remodel."

"Oh, I'm not planning anything major," Kendall said. "But one of the back steps is loose and so is part of the deck railing. We wouldn't want either of us to fall through now, would we?"

"No, of course not. But . . ."

"And there's something wrong with the toilet handle—it's starting to drive me crazy. I'm sure I can fix that in no time.

"Why don't you run and get dressed and we'll drive down. We can have breakfast at the Clayton Café while we're down there and we can hit the grocery store on the way back. It shouldn't take us more than two or three hours."

"But I thought we'd work this morning," Mallory said.

"We both have books due. We could just bring our laptops out here on the deck and—"

"Look, Mal, you can stay here and work if you want to. I need to get these supplies and some groceries. Trust me when I tell you I'm down to my last bag of Doritos."

"But I came here to help you. . . ."

Kendall smiled and pushed her hair back off her face. "Mallory, this is the first time I've showered or had clothes on in the last three days. As far as I'm concerned you're already a miracle worker.

"But I can't even think about the book until I take care of these small repairs and we have some food in the house." She looked at Mallory, her expression both grateful and innocent, but Mallory had become a first-rate procrastinator in her own right and she knew an evasive move when she saw one.

She took another sip of her coffee, trying to decide how best to handle Kendall. The truth was that although she had never held a hammer or driven in a nail, that being Chris's bailiwick, she didn't think she could face the computer screen right now, either. Maybe breakfast and an outing would put them in the right frame of mind.

Besides, if she let Kendall go by herself, she might blow off the entire day. If she went along, she could keep their joint procrastination to a minimum. They'd have breakfast, pick up some supplies and sustenance, and get back here and down to work.

"All right," Mallory finally said. "Give me fifteen minutes to get ready." She looked up and caught the expression of relief that washed over Kendall's face, as if she were a death-row prisoner who'd just received a last-minute reprieve from the governor. "But we're going to stock up so we don't have to keep running into town. And then we're going to come back and start fleshing out your story idea."

Kendall didn't respond; she just carried her coffee out on the deck, the relieved smile still on her face.

Mallory started toward her bedroom wondering how

dressed up people here got for a trip down to Home Depot. And whether the abject relief she felt at not having to sit down and work yet was as clearly etched on her face as it was on Kendall's.

11

What I would say to a young person trying to become a writer is 'Don't.' It won't make any difference because they'll do it anyway, but they really shouldn't.
—A. L. KENNEDY

After practically licking their plates clean at the Clayton Café, Kendall and Mallory strolled Clayton's tiny Main Street to try to work off some of what they'd eaten.

"God, I'm full." Kendall tugged at the waistband of her jeans, trying to create more room.

"It was good," Mallory agreed. "Although I can't quite get comfortable with the idea of brown gravy at breakfast. And I do not understand the appeal of grits."

"Shh," Kendall admonished. "Don't say that so loud. Around here it's enough to get you tarred and feathered and run out of town on a rail."

"I don't know about that, but I do know this town isn't big enough to work off all the calories we just consumed. We're going to have to take a hike later today."

Anything that didn't involve assessing her life or sitting down in front of a computer sounded good to Kendall. After all, she had that new family motto to live up to. *Avoidus, avatas, avant.* Having Mallory here made her feel less alone and isolated, but she didn't see the fear and emptiness roiling inside her disappearing anytime soon. And she couldn't imagine how she was supposed to turn all that turmoil into a book.

"Sounds good," Kendall said, as they meandered past a row of antique stores and a carefully maintained garden that fronted a historic stone building now operating as a museum.

When they came to the town's lone bookstore, Mallory stopped, turning to Kendall. "God, do you remember when our first books hit the shelves?" She smiled at the memory. "How many stores did we go into when you came up to New York that first time? Twenty? Thirty? Remember how we cabbed from store to store and raced back to the fiction section as fast as we could without actually running?"

Kendall nodded, but for her the memory was tainted by her present reality.

"Do you want to go in and see if they're carrying us?"

Kendall looked into Mallory's face, with its almost dreamy look of nostalgia and felt the need to erase it. "I'm sure it would be fun for you, Mallory. Everybody stocks plenty of your books. But if they *do* have my books, they probably won't have enough of them to make me feel better. And if they *don't* have my books, I'll just feel worse. Which is kind of hard to imagine at the moment."

Mallory let go of the doorknob. Her hand dropped to her side.

"The thing is, Mallory, even in a tiny bookstore like this, there are thousands of titles vying for a reader's attention. And I have to ask myself, what are the chances that someone wandering in off the street is going to choose one of mine? And if they *do* buy one of the few copies of mine the store *might* have in stock, what are the chances the store will bother to reorder?

"For me, walking into a bookstore is a reminder of what I'm up against. It's too depressing."

"All the more reason to write this next book," Mallory countered. "Increase your backlist and your name recognition. It can never hurt to get your name out there."

Kendall shook her head, trying to suppress the surge of irritation at Mallory's response. "It seems pretty pointless to me."

"Now you've got me depressed," Mallory said, turning away from the store.

"Well, I try to be an equal opportunity depressant," Kendall replied. Her tone was purposely flip but inside she felt like a dark cloud bulging with rain.

"But, of course, you have no reason to be depressed or worried. You're prolific, your publisher has been pushing you from day one, your numbers are great." She tried to swallow her resentment at the unfairness of it all. "You have a husband who worships you."

Her voice broke on the last accusation and she hated herself for letting loose all over Mallory's parade. At the moment she simply couldn't seem to get past the fact that Mallory had absolutely everything she had ever wanted. "I'd be eager to write, too, if I were in your situation."

Turning on her heel, Mallory began to walk toward the car. She moved so quickly that Kendall, who had been focused on her own misery, was taken by surprise and had to scurry to keep up.

"So you think I have no problems? No stress?" Mallory bit out as she increased her pace. "You think that I don't have a care in the world and that when I sit down to write I just snap my fingers and out it comes?"

They reached the car and took their positions on either side of it, the lazy comfort of the morning blown to smithereens. "Is that what you think?" Mallory demanded.

Their gazes locked, Kendall told herself to choose her words carefully. She was grateful that Mallory was here and disgusted at the little pity party she'd just thrown. But that little green monster continued to egg her on. "Well, yeah, pretty much," Kendall said, popping the door locks. "You've certainly never indicated otherwise."

Mallory snorted and slid into the passenger seat. Kendall climbed in behind the wheel.

"You know what the real pisser is?" Kendall asked, as she turned the key in the ignition and backed out of the parking space. "The pisser is you're such an incredibly good friend I don't even have the luxury of hating you for it."

• • •

Mallory kept her mouth clamped shut and her retorts to herself as they crossed the Home Depot parking lot and entered the massive box of a building.

The angry part of her wanted to inform her friend that she'd assumed wrong; that every word was a battle and every moment spent in front of her computer a hard-won victory. And that she couldn't even remember why she hadn't called the husband who worshipped her to tell him she'd arrived safely.

But Kendall was smiling for the first time since Mallory had arrived and seemed to be contemplating the Home Depot with the same reverence and excitement with which Mallory approached the couture departments of Neiman Marcus or Saks Fifth Avenue. The part of her that had come out of friendship tamped down on the hurt and kept those truths to herself.

"Do you smell that, Mallory?" Kendall asked as they halted inside the store. "That's the smell of possibility."

Mallory drew in a breath but got only a whiff of wood chips, insect spray, and an underlying hint of fertilizer. The place was a hotbed of activity though; clearly an outing to the new Home Depot was a "do not miss" up here.

Mallory had her doubts that a home repair of any kind was going to make Kendall feel appreciably better about her life, but she was not about to say so now. Nor was she going to unburden herself. Kendall was right; she was in an enviable position. No one wanted to hear how hard it had become to maintain it. Or that no matter how much she had she couldn't block out the memory of what it would feel like to lose it.

Mallory took a step forward, trying to shrug off her ill humor. Kendall reached out a hand to stop her. "I am so sorry for attacking you," she said. "I had no right to do that. You're a fabulous writer and you work hard and you deserve what's happened to you." She smiled wistfully. "I don't normally envy you. It's just hard for me to be positive right now, you know? It's not just that I think the grass is greener on your side of the fence, Mal. I'm deathly afraid all the grass is brown." She squeezed Mallory's hand and then let go. "Do you forgive me?"

Mallory felt some of the tension seep out of her. "Yeah," she said. "And if there was ever proof of how much I value our friendship, being here is it."

Mallory waved a hand at the endless aisles of power tools and widgets and who knew what else. "We gutted and reno-vated a five-thousand-square-foot brownstone, and I never once set foot in a place like this." She'd left all of that, like most everything to do with the day-to-day running of their lives, to Chris. "I'm in foreign territory. And I don't speak the language. What do we do first?"

"Good question." Kendall pulled her list from her purse and perused it like a tourist trying to place his location on a map.

"You ladies look a little lost. Can I help you find some-thing?"

The deep male voice took them both by surprise. Their rescuer was of average height and build with hair that was more salt than pepper. His face was smooth and angular, his eyes a faded blue, as if they'd seen all kinds of things and gotten a bit washed out in the process.

Kendall looked down at her list, then at him. Then she just handed the slip of paper to him with an apologetic smile.

"Let's see now," he said as he perused the list. "Fix toilet thingy. Replace rotted plank. Install motion detector. Some-body's got her work cut out for her. Are you planning to do these things yourself or did your husband send you down to pick up supplies?"

Mallory looked up, surprised at the question beneath the question. Then she stole a peek at their rescuer's ring finger. There was no wedding band although there was a light circle as if he'd worn one for a long time. His name badge said his name was James.

"I'm it," Kendall said, not quite meeting his eye. "And I'd, um, like to do these things myself."

"Well, good for you," James said.

Mallory glanced up again, looking for any sign of calculation. His features appeared as sincere as his tone.

"But we're going to have to define 'thingy' a little more precisely." He smiled at Kendall. "If you come with me, I'll take you over to the plumbing department and we'll try to figure it out."

He got a cart and escorted them first to plumbing, where with great patience and what seemed like a hundred questions, he determined that the thingy on Kendall's list was actually a "flapper," which was not, he said with his quiet smile, to be confused with the dancer of the 1920s.

This was followed by a trip to the lighting and lumber departments where he made sure she had the tools and supplies that she needed to complete her tasks. Near the checkout area, he plucked a big orange book, titled *Home Improvement 1-2-3*, from a shelf and placed it in the cart. "This should get you through just about anything you might need to do." Then he pulled a business card from his shirt pocket and pressed it into Kendall's hand. "I give a do-it-yourself workshop on Saturday mornings if you ever have the time. And even if you don't, you can call me if you get stuck or have a question." He cleared his throat and scribbled an additional number at the bottom of the card. "Here's my, um, cell phone number. I'd be glad to help in any way I can."

"Thank you," Kendall said. "Thank you so much for everything."

"My pleasure, ma'am." He smiled again at Kendall then tipped his head to Mallory.

They watched him walk away.

"Wow," Mallory said, as they wheeled the cart into the checkout line. "That's what I call personal attention. I didn't think *anybody* made a house call anymore."

Kendall blushed, but her gaze stayed on James's retreating back. "He was nice, wasn't he? But I'm sure they do that for everyone."

"Right," Mallory said as they wheeled through checkout. "I'm sure that's why he asked whether there was a husband involved. And gave you his cell phone number."

Kendall blushed again, but Mallory noticed that her friend's shoulders seemed slightly less rigid and her step appeared noticeably lighter as they pushed the cart through the parking lot then loaded her purchases into the back of the SUV.

Mallory glanced down at her watch and was surprised to see that it was already close to one o'clock. By the time they hit the grocery store, made it back up to Kendall's, and took the hike she'd already suggested, it was going to be awfully late in the day to sit down and get to work. And, of course, Kendall was probably going to want to actually *use* some of the things that the sweet-smiling James had just sold her.

She hunched down in her seat casting about for the willpower she needed to get both herself and Kendall on task.

But the truth was she didn't feel like writing or pushing Kendall. Come to think of it, she'd rather rip out a toilet with her bare hands and read *Home Improvement 1-2-3* from cover to cover than do either of those things. Which didn't bode well for either of them.

12

*For those who can do it and who keep their
nerve, writing for a living still beats most
real, grown-up jobs hands down.*
—TERENCE BLACKER

"Lacy!" Jane Jensen didn't bother with the phone or intercom, but simply shouted from her office on the other side of the hall. "Bring me that cover the art department sent down."

Lacy stopped what she'd been doing for the tenth time that morning and picked up the large manila envelope that had been delivered earlier.

As she carried it into her boss's office, she realized that she was bracing herself much like a puppy faced with a rolled-up newspaper. It was just that she never knew which Jane she was going to be dealing with: the calm, yet condescending Jane, or the whacked-out, off-the-wall Jane. Lacy had discovered it was best to be prepared for the whack job and then rejoice when presented with the seminormal version.

In the corner office, Lacy handed her boss the envelope and turned to leave.

"Wait a minute." Jane extracted the cover mock-up from the envelope and held it out toward Lacy. "What do you think of this for Kendall Aims's next book. . . . What's it called again?"

"The working title is *Sticks and Stones*."

Jane frowned, the lines etched on either side of her mouth

creasing deeper. "I thought it was about a writer or a group of writers."

"It is," Lacy said, taking the cover and cautioning herself to be careful not to appear to be correcting or disagreeing with Jane. "You know, as in 'Sticks and stones may break my bones, but names will never hurt me'?"

"Oh, right." Jane's facial expressions seemed flat today, her body movements slow. Lacy suspected the catty comments about medication were more than just gossip.

"I think the title's really catchy," Lacy said, unable to hide her enthusiasm completely. "But it foreshadows at the same time, telling us there'll be problems, too, you know?"

When Jane didn't comment, Lacy dropped her gaze to the cover and studied it carefully. She could feel Jane's gaze on her, and her discomfort grew as she struggled to conceal her true reaction. The cover was attractive enough. It was cherry red, with a glossy sheen. A black line drawing of a tall, curvy woman in a miniskirt and stilettos drew the eye. A briefcase sat at her high-heeled feet.

For a long moment, Lacy debated her response. She knew what Jane wanted her to say, but a writer's career was at stake here—*her* writer's career. "But this is Carolyn Sinclair's cover," she said, stating the obvious since Sinclair's name took up the top third of the page. "I thought it was designed for her next book."

Jane settled back in her chair, but her body remained stiff and unyielding, just like her stare. "She rejected it. The art department's working on something else for her. But we can stick Kendall's title on the top and fit her name on the bottom just under the briefcase. It's a good clean women's fiction look." Her jaw tightened further. "We spent quite a lot of money on it."

Lacy swallowed as she once again felt compelled to point out what to her was even more obvious. "But it has nothing at all to do with writing or . . . or anything. Given Kendall Aims's situation, shouldn't we be trying to come up with something really strong to try to help sell the book?"

Jane considered the cover. "It's got a woman and a briefcase on it. We could maybe add a manuscript page sticking out of the top of the briefcase or something." She shrugged as if it couldn't have mattered less. "There's no reason to throw away a perfectly good cover when we can recycle it. One cover isn't going to salvage Kendall Aims's career."

"But if we just write her off she has no chance. It becomes a self-fulfilling prophecy. Wouldn't it be in everybody's best interest to try to sell more of her books?"

Lacy braced herself for the smack of the newspaper, but Jane remained strangely benign. "How did I end up with such a Pollyanna?" Jane *tsk*'d and dropped the cover on her desk. "Publishing 101," she said to Lacy. "You have to know when to cut your losses. Kendall Aims's numbers suck. We're not going back to contract with her. All we have to do is put the book out there. We have no obligation to throw good money after bad."

"But . . ."

"Trust me on this, Polly," Jane said, with a bit more edge. And that was the end of the conversation.

. . .

Steven Truett stood at the podium in the bright spill of a spotlight. His face flushed with emotion, his eyes aglow, his voice rang throughout the hotel ballroom as he exhorted his well-heeled audience to do better, to be more.

"God didn't create us in order to live our lives on the sidelines. He doesn't want us on the bench, afraid to get into the game."

There was a hush in the room and yet there was a buzz, an almost electric energy that gathered the crowd in its embrace and turned the air thick with hope and possibility.

"Don't fall into the negative. Don't take the easy way out. God is in control, he's there for us, but he lets us choose."

Had it been a different crowd, there might have been a chorus of amens, some heartfelt hallelujahs.

Faye scanned the tables of ten that filled the massive room. This audience wore ball gowns and thousand-dollar suits.

They'd paid $250 apiece, all of which would go directly to the Rainbow House Shelter for abused women and children and its new after-school program, to hear Pastor Steve's message.

Rainbow House was Faye's passion, a safe place for women and children fleeing abuse. She'd begun raising funds for it ten years ago, when Steve's ministry had become self-supporting and all three kids were finally out of college.

She'd drafted church members as volunteers and hired a trained staff to run it. She worked intake there once a week and in lean times she kept it afloat with her own earnings. These twice-yearly fund-raisers allowed them to add services and programs and garnered attention outside of the Clearview congregation. Sometimes they brought in outside keynote speakers, but Steve was always their biggest draw.

All eyes were on Pastor Steve as he preached his message of wonder and possibility. He made them feel good about doing good and reassured them that God was there for the affluent as well as the poor.

There were those that dismissed his message as "gospel lite" and Steven as a spiritual rock star, albeit an aging one. But Faye knew that his message came directly from his heart and a deep abiding faith and that despite the twelve thousand plus who came to church services each Sunday, the eighty countries that watched him on television, the money that poured in, unsolicited, from all over the globe, his goal remained the same: to inspire and help.

"Men and women of God are full of strength and wisdom; they are full of can-do power. There is nothing in your future, your life, that you cannot accomplish."

Faye felt her husband's certainty and conviction well up from that place inside him and infect the audience. Even these people who had achieved worldly success wanted to hear his message, needed something larger than themselves to believe in.

She told herself that his polish didn't diminish the importance of his message. That he was the same person he'd always been. She was proud of all that he'd achieved and of her role in his success, but dismayed by it at the same time. It had become so much bigger than she'd ever imagined.

She looked down at the remains of the dessert on her plate and then once again into the faces of his audience. The men nodded occasionally in agreement, comfortable with the message and themselves. But there was a special edge in the women's eyes, a wanting, a hint of worship that she had to look away from. That kind of adoration carried its own danger.

She thought, not for the first time, how easily that emotion could be turned against the recipient. How much pleasure some felt at watching the mighty fall. How little it would take to destroy all that had been built.

She shifted uncomfortably in her seat and turned her gaze back to her husband. Once there had been nothing about one that the other did not know. But that had ended when Faye had decided that nothing was more important than keeping her family and her husband's dreams afloat.

She didn't know what detours along their joint journey Steven might have taken. But Faye had set her feet down a path many years ago out of a necessity that would be close to impossible to explain today and which, if exposed, could threaten the very foundations of the church that Steven had built.

Her husband stilled for a moment and then raised his arms in benediction. "God knows what is in our hearts and souls," he said gently. "He understands our motivations. And no matter how far we may stray from *His* path, He loves us anyway."

The applause was instant and deafening as the audience sprang to its feet. Faye rose with them, love and pride propelling her.

Steven bowed his head as if receiving a benediction in return. But as the applause thundered throughout the ballroom, Faye felt a now familiar stirring of unease. Bowing her own head, she prayed that Steven's concluding remarks were true and that God was, in fact, all-knowing and all-loving.

Because she no longer knew whether Steve's love for her was as unconditional. Or whether he would pick her over his pulpit if he were ever forced to choose.

. . .

The Liberty Laundromat was quiet in the early part of the afternoon. Wash-and-fold customers usually dropped off their dirty clothes in the morning on their way in to work then picked up around 5:00 or 6:00 P.M. on their way home. Do-it-yourselfers drifted in and out throughout the day but came in bigger numbers in the early evening after dinner. Tanya did the drop-off loads all afternoon and stayed until most everything had been picked up at 6:30 P.M.

During the afternoons Tanya worked on her manuscript between loads. The steady tumble of the dryers and swish of the washing machines served as a gentle sort of background noise to her forays into her own fictional worlds. The buzz that signaled the end of a drying cycle or the bell that jangled when the front door opened pulled her back to reality as needed.

At the moment she was struggling over how to keep her heroine, Doreen, out of bed with her older brother's friend for at least another twenty pages. She'd built their sexual tension to a point where it was going to have to happen soon, though she didn't know exactly how or where. At this point of her life, the sex, just like everything else in the story, would be a product of her imagination; she had absolutely nothing in recent memory to draw from. Three jobs, two children, and a difficult mother didn't leave much time to look for a relationship. Or the energy to do anything physical if she had one.

The cursor blinked at the start of a new page and she closed her eyes, trying to insert herself into the scene. The front doorbell jangled when she was almost there.

"Hey, sweet thing." There was a louder ding, this time of the bell that sat in front of her on the counter. "Belle told me you worked here, and I have to say you're a mite easier on the eyes than old Juan Carlo over at the Washaroo. You got some quarters for these dollar bills?"

Her eyelids sprang open at the bell and the familiar voice. Sure enough there stood Brett Adams, aspiring speed cooker, with a shit-eating grin on his face and a bulging duffel bag in his hand.

"Sorry to wake you. I've never actually seen anyone type and sleep at the same time before." He nodded down to the laptop keyboard where her fingers still rested.

"I wasn't sleeping, I was just thinking with my eyes closed." Not to be confused with the times she was so tired her head actually fell onto the keyboard. "How many do you need?" She purposely ignored the warmth of his gaze, the muscles straining against his white T-shirt, and the impudent curve of his lips.

He slid three dollar bills across the counter. "Watcha doin'?"

"I've got a book due. These are my only daylight working hours."

He nodded sagely, but the smile stayed in place. "I heard you were a writer. Romance novels, right?"

"Yeah." She braced herself for the usual joke or ignorant comment. At the very least, most men felt compelled to offer to help her research the love scenes.

"That's cool. My mother used to be a Masque junkie; she bought a whole new batch every month. We had stacks of them all over the house. She never could bear to throw one away. I used to sneak 'em into my room and look for the racy parts." His grin broadened. "I'm more of a fan of Nelson De-Mille and Stuart Woods these days, but, hell, I think the world can use as many happy endings as it can get."

She closed her mouth on the automatic acid response she'd been about to deliver as she digested what he'd said. Brett Adams was not only a reader but a supporter of romance? Perhaps the world was about to go on ahead and freeze right over.

Brett shot her a wink then took the quarters she held in her hand. "I told you not to judge this book by its cover. Don't want to fall into those easy stereotypes, now do we?"

He whistled merrily as he walked over to a nearby folding table, dumped out the dirty laundry, and started sorting, which was pretty unusual in and of itself. In Tanya's experience, most men who came in here weren't anywhere close to whistling. And they were more likely to throw everything that would fit into one machine and hope for the best. Colorfastness and water temperature were not a part of their known universe.

Tanya wanted to ignore Brett and get back to her manuscript, but she couldn't seem to tear her gaze from him. He'd yanked her right back into the here and now and even when she turned away, she caught herself watching him out of the corner of her eye.

He slipped the quarters into the slots of a nearby machine, set the knobs like a pro, and emptied a packet of detergent into the water. Then he began to drop clothes into the sudsy water, making quick work of the chore until he paused and groaned aloud. Unable to stop herself, Tanya turned to see the item dangling from his finger. It was a black silk thong, a mere scrap of fabric, clearly designed to titillate rather than cover.

Why was she not surprised?

"This is not good," he said as he considered the triangle of fabric.

Tanya crossed her arms over her chest and gave him the look she normally reserved for diner customers who crossed the line and touched or pinched. "Most men would say just the opposite," she replied, not even trying to hide her disapproval.

He met her gaze. "Most men wouldn't be forced to discover that their teenaged daughter was wearing something this skimpy."

"Oh."

"Yeah," he replied. "That's what I thought when I saw it."

"How old is she?"

"Sixteen."

Tanya let that one sink in for a minute. "And you're doing her laundry." It was a statement rather than a question.

He dropped the thong into the washing machine and closed the lid then began to sort through the whites still sitting on the table. Now that she was blatantly looking, she noticed other girl clothes go by, some that probably belonged to the teenaged daughter, others that looked more appropriate to Loretta's and Crystal's ages.

"Yep. I surely am."

He turned to put the quarters into the second washing machine slot without offering any more detail and Tanya's interest was piqued. Nothing about Brett Adams would have made her peg him as a single father, nothing. But she knew if there was a wife and/or mother in the picture, he wouldn't be here measuring and pouring detergent with that air of competence.

He started whistling again as he stowed the empty duffel bag under the folding table and checked the clock on the wall. "The washers go about thirty minutes?" he asked.

She nodded, pretty much floored by the afternoon's revelations.

"I'm gonna run over to the Publix then to pick up some groceries. I'll be back in time to put them in the dryer."

"OK." Tanya couldn't think of a thing to add so she just watched him stroll out the door and climb into his beat-up Jeep Cherokee. As he peeled out of the parking lot, she found herself trying to imagine what the girls over at the diner would say if they knew what kind of baggage Brett Adams carried with him. And how many of them would still be competing to be the first one to sleep with him.

13

"Mallory, here, will you read me the directions as we go?" Kendall held out the *Home Improvement 1-2-3* book, which was already looking somewhat dog-eared.

"You want me to . . . what?" Mallory made a face as the tome filled her hands.

"Come on, it won't take long if you help," Kendall promised. "It slows me down when I have to read while I do the repair."

"Kendall," Mallory said, "this is ridiculous. You've already fixed the flipper—"

"That's flapper."

"Whatever. The porch railing, the back step." She ticked the projects off on the cover of the manual. "Cleaned out the showerhead, and if I'm not mistaken, spent a good part of the morning memorizing the anatomy of a toilet."

"And your point is?" Kendall asked, though it sounded somewhat bizarre even to her.

"My point is, it's Tuesday afternoon and we've already been back to the Home Depot twice. Your friend James undoubtedly thinks we've got the hots for him."

"Do you really think so?" Kendall both hated and loved the idea. Just having a male look at her and really see her was worth the trip into Clayton, though that wasn't the reason she'd been going.

"Good grief!" Mallory snapped the do-it-yourself book shut and slapped it down on the kitchen counter. "I think the larger concern is that no matter how often I bring up *Sticks and Stones*, you find a way to put me off. And I don't know if you've noticed or not, but I haven't written a word yet, either!"

"Ah," Kendall said, as understanding dawned. "Now I think we've gotten to the crux of the matter."

Mallory closed her eyes and blew out a breath.

"Look, Mal," Kendall said to her friend. "I really appreciate that you're here. Really. I don't know what I would have done if you hadn't shown up on my doorstep. I can't even let myself think about it."

"Kendall, I didn't mean to complain. I just—"

"No, no, you're right. I don't want to keep you from working. For some reason that I don't understand, I just feel sort of compelled to fix things here. It feels good. I don't know, maybe it's just a need for immediate gratification. Fit part 'a' into part 'b,' turn on switch. Voila!" She reached for the bright orange book and picked it up, hugging it to her chest. "But that doesn't mean you shouldn't be working. You don't have to hold my book for me. Or my hand. You go ahead and get to work. I'll keep the noise down, no hammering, I promise. Do you want me to set you up on the deck?" She nodded to the sliding doors, which had been left open to the afternoon breeze.

"Kendall, I only meant . . ."

"No, no, don't apologize." She could only imagine how fragile she must appear if outspoken Mallory was afraid to criticize. "I'm glad you were honest with me. I can always count on that from you."

Mallory winced as the phone rang. But Kendall was intent on getting Mallory to work. "Come on." She reached for Mallory's arm. "I'll get you set up."

"Aren't you going to answer the phone?"

"No," Kendall said. "We don't have caller ID on this phone. The last times I answered a phone without knowing who was on the other end, it was bad news. I can't handle any more of that right now."

"But Kendall, it could be—"

"Whoever it is can leave a message on the machine." She nodded toward an oversized metal box that belonged on the shelves of an antique store. There was a mechanical beep and then, "Kendall, it's Calvin. Pick up."

Kendall and Mallory looked at each other. Kendall shook her head slightly, oddly afraid that if she moved too noticeably Calvin might somehow hear her.

"Jesus, Kendall. You can't just run away from everything. My attorney wants to know who's representing you."

Kendall continued to imitate a statue, but her heart was beating so loudly she was afraid Calvin would hear it.

"Shit, I can't believe I'm having this conversation with a machine." A pause. "I know you have to be up there, Kendall. Although why you ever liked that place, I'll never know."

He waited and she wondered if he actually thought he could goad her into picking up. Clearly he was unaware of their new family motto. *Avoidus, avatas, avant.*

"All right, so maybe you're not there. I don't know. I left a message on your cell phone, too. You need to have your attorney call Josh Lieberman at . . ." He recited an Atlanta phone number area code first.

Kendall didn't move; she couldn't. Even the breathing thing was becoming more difficult.

"I need to know whether you've spoken to the kids. I didn't really want to surprise them with Laura. I thought maybe you'd already let them know?"

Kendall blanched as his girlfriend's name left Calvin's lips and echoed menacingly in the kitchen. Her husband had apparently shed her and their life together as easily as any snake might shed its skin, and still he expected her to pave his way with the children, to run interference so that he didn't have to confess to his bad behavior.

Kendall snuck a look at Mallory, who looked every bit as horrified as Kendall felt. Without breaking the silence, Mallory mouthed the word "Asshole," overenunciating each syllable.

Evidently out of bombs to drop, Calvin finally hung up.

Kendall stared at Mallory. Mallory stared back.

Kendall opened her mouth, closed it, then opened it again, searching for the words that would allow her to vent the Vesuvius of emotion boiling up inside her. But no matter how hard she tried, how deep she dug, she couldn't seem to come up with a single sentence scathing enough to offer the slightest bit of relief.

Certain that she would erupt—or possibly implode—if she didn't take action of some kind, Kendall reached over and pulled the answering machine plug out of the wall socket. Then she lifted the offending instrument off the counter and dropped it into the garbage can, wishing with all her heart that there was a trash compactor handy so that she could flatten the metal to the size of a Frisbee and hurl it off the side of the mountain.

"How in God's name did I end up married to such a jerk?" she shouted.

Her eyes blurred as the tears welled and then squeezed out to slide down her cheeks, so hot and heavy she was afraid they'd sear her skin. Each rounded drop was weighted with hurt and humiliation, a visible testament to the end of life as she knew it.

She felt completely pathetic as she stood in the middle of the kitchen and cried. Mallory watched her with a baffled and helpless expression that made Kendall cry harder.

And then she was racing for the bedroom, slamming the door behind her and throwing herself down on the bed, where she buried her face in her grandmother's chenille bedspread and sobbed.

She had no idea whether she was crying for Calvin. Or her marriage. Or her children. Or her lost career. If this were a multiple choice test, she'd be forced to check "All of the above."

All she knew for sure, as the sobs tore through her, was that everything she'd built her life on had been yanked out from under her. And she didn't see how she'd ever find her footing again.

. . .

Feeling helpless and out of her depth, Mallory stood in the center of the kitchen listening to the sound of Kendall's sobs fill the house. Though she'd known great despair twice, Mallory had spent most of her life since determined not to feel it again, and she'd never tried to help another person through it. She wasn't sure she had it in her.

Quietly she retrieved the answering machine from the garbage can, wiped it off, and set it back in its place on the counter. For some time she paced the house, trying to decide what to do, finally coming to a stop outside Kendall's bedroom door. She wanted to help, but didn't want to intrude. Oh, who was she kidding? She was afraid to go in there because she might say the wrong thing and somehow make Kendall feel worse. Or give something away.

Finally she pushed open the door slightly. The shades were drawn and it was difficult to see; she could just make out Kendall's limp body angled across the top of the old-fashioned bedspread. "Kendall?"

"Y-y-yeah?" Kendall rolled onto her side and curled into a fetal position, facing Mallory. Her face was streaked with black mascara and tears.

Mallory stepped inside the room and inched toward the bed. "Can I get you a cold drink? Or a wet rag for your head?"

"N-n-no," Kendall stammered, and looked at her expectantly.

Still uncertain how to offer comfort, Mallory took another step toward the bed and said the first thing that came into her head. "I hate that Calvin is such an asshole."

Kendall smiled weakly and sat up. She sniffed. "Me too. He's a major, big-time asshole."

"The biggest," Mallory agreed, casting about for some

extra adjectives to throw into the pot. "Calvin Aims is a gargantuan, King-Kong-sized, we-should-throw-him-off-the-Empire-State-Building-and-watch-him-bounce-sized asshole."

Kendall smiled and this time the smile curved her mouth upward and even reached her reddened eyes.

"Do you want a glass of wine?" Mallory asked, encouraged. "Maybe two glasses of wine?"

Kendall shook her head. "Not now. I think I'm going to take a little nap or something."

"OK." Mallory stepped back toward the door.

"But when I get up we'll have a drink, OK?" Kendall said.

"Absolutely," Mallory promised. "In fact, I'm going to stick a couple extra bottles of white in the refrigerator in case you wake up parched." She reached behind her for the doorknob.

"Thanks, Mal," Kendall said quietly.

"No problem." She swallowed and prepared to leave. "I'll be out on the deck."

"OK."

Mallory closed the bedroom door softly and walked out to the kitchen where she retrieved her cell phone from her purse and walked outside. Shaken, she stared out at an array of distant peaks for a time and then she carried the phone to the only spot from which it seemed able to retrieve a signal.

Chris picked up on the third ring.

"Hi," Mallory said, her voice still trembling. "How are things in the large apple?"

"Are you OK?"

Mallory almost sighed aloud at the quick concern in his voice. "Yeah. I think so."

"How's Kendall?"

"Not so good. Her husband is in a hurry for a divorce, and she, she doesn't even have an attorney."

"How's her book coming?"

"It's not. Not at all. She won't even talk about it. She's become obsessed with fixing things."

"What?"

"Yeah." Mallory smiled. "You'd be in your element here. I've been to the Home Depot down in this little place called Clayton three times now."

"You? No way."

"Way. Yesterday I helped Kendall pick a router."

She could picture him shaking his head in disbelief. She didn't want to think about the fact that she'd braved Home Depot for Kendall, but had refused to stop working long enough to share in the nuts and bolts of their own major remodel. Another man would have stuck it to her about that now, but Chris didn't have a malicious bone in his body.

She waited for him to ask how her own work was going, but he didn't. Of course, he would assume she was writing away regardless of what was happening around her. She'd never stopped for him, why would he assume she'd stop for Kendall? Not that it was actually Kendall she'd stopped for.

"Patricia's left several messages," he said, mentioning her agent, Patricia Gilmore. "And so has Zoe. I wasn't sure if you wanted them to call you down there?" Chris said. "Or whether they could reach you on your cell phone?"

Hearing her agent's and editor's names caused a moment of actual panic, followed by a sharp stab of guilt. For the briefest moment she considered admitting to Chris the stress she was feeling, how frightened she was of her inability to get anything on the page, hell, to even sit down and try. She refused to even consider it writer's block, let alone call it that. As if somehow admitting it would make it more real, give it more power over her.

She forced a laugh. "The only way you can use a cell phone here is to press yourself into the corner of the deck and lean to the left, hard. But, truthfully, I'd rather not talk to them right now. I'm trying to focus on Kendall."

"So shall I call and let them know that you'll be in touch when you get back on Thursday?"

Mallory stared out over the mountaintop, looking for the right words. "About Thursday . . ."

There was a silence on the other end of the line.

"I, um, don't feel like I can leave Kendall so soon. I thought I was just coming in for a quick check and maybe a pep talk, but she's in a really bad way."

"We're supposed to leave for the beach house on Friday. It's Labor Day weekend."

This time she was the one who remained silent largely because she didn't know what to say.

"We've been planning this for months, Mallory."

She didn't speak, couldn't really.

In the silence, his voice hardened, became very un-Chris-like. Underneath was the hurt and anger but on the top was a steeliness she'd never heard before. "*I've* been planning this for months. We agreed we'd take the time off and spend it together."

"I know," she said quietly. "I'm sorry."

She waited while he absorbed what she'd said. She'd promised to take the time off when she cancelled the last trip he'd planned and she had had every intention of going.

She heard Chris let his breath out on a big gush of air and could picture him running his hand through his hair. "I'm such an imbecile," he said. "I keep thinking that once you finish a manuscript, or a tour, or whatever the hell you're onto next, you'll make some time for *us*. Give a shit about *us*. But it never seems to happen."

"Chris, I just can't leave her right now." Mallory heard the urgency in her own voice, the need to make him understand. "I thought I'd get Faye and Tanya to come in for the weekend so we can help Kendall brainstorm her book. She hasn't written a single word and its due December first. This has nothing to do with us."

"I've tried to understand, really I have." He almost seemed to be talking to himself now, which sent a chill down Mallory's spine. "I think it's commendable that you want to help your friend. Somewhat surprising considering how self-absorbed and driven you generally are, but commendable."

No, she wanted to say, not self-absorbed, just scared. Not just driven but terrified of failure. But, as usual, she said nothing.

"The thing is, Mallory. I can't wait forever for those occasional slivers of your attention. And you're completely wrong if you think blowing off our time away has nothing to do with us."

He hung up without waiting for a response. A gentle click and then he was gone. Even pissed off, Chris was admirably polite and restrained.

But that didn't keep Mallory's heart from pounding or her head from ringing with all the things she might have said.

14

*Technique alone is never enough. You have
to have passion. Technique alone is just an
embroidered pot holder.*
— RAYMOND CHANDLER

The sun had begun its swan dive behind the mountains when
Kendall finally padded out onto the deck, her bare feet slap-
ping on the aged wood. She held a bottle of wine in one hand,
two goblets threaded through the fingers of the other.

Plopping down on the deck chair next to Mallory, she set
the opened bottle and glasses on the small table between
them. Without asking she poured two generous glassfuls,
placed one in Mallory's hand, and clinked hers against it.

They sipped the dry white wine in silence as the last of
the daylight faded. Kendall's brain was still slightly numbed
from sleep, the overweening sense of worry cushioned by the
clean mountain air she drew into her lungs and Mallory's
companionable silence. She wished she could sit here like this
forever with nothing more pressing than watching the lights
blink on down in tiny Dillard, Georgia.

"You need an attorney," Mallory said.

Kendall took a long sip of wine. "That would be admitting it's really over."

Mallory turned from the view to look at her. "That call
today wasn't an attempt at reconciliation."

Kendall remained silent, clinging to her new family
motto. *Avoidus, avatas, avant.*

"Avoiding it isn't going to make it go away."

Kendall sighed. "If you're going to remain my friend, you're going to have to stop reading my mind."

They sat in silence again as the dark gathered around them and the temperature began to drop. There was a rustle in a nearby bush. The faint tap of a woodpecker echoed somewhere not too far off.

"Seriously, Kendall. You need representation. You can't just let him proceed without having someone looking out for your interests."

Kendall closed her eyes against the whole idea. She was far from the first of her friends or neighbors to get dumped for someone younger; in her neck of the suburbs, it was practically a cliché. The fact that it had happened to her made her long for her bed and a darkened room. *Avoidus, avatas . . .*

"And I think we should get Faye and Tanya to come in for the weekend so that we can brainstorm your book for you."

"Jesus, Mallory. You're like the self-help Energizer Bunny. You just keep right on pushing."

Mallory remained silent but Kendall could feel her intention like a palpable force, so at odds with the serenity that surrounded them.

"Besides, what makes you think they can just drop everything and come running here? It's a holiday weekend." She turned to face Mallory. "Don't you need to get back to New York? I thought you and Chris were going on a vacation or something."

"You wish." Mallory took a sip of her wine. "I'm not going anywhere and if we get Faye and Tanya here we can plot out your whole book, maybe even do a detailed outline."

"You are something, aren't you?" She studied her friend's face. "Was Chris upset?"

"A little." Mallory shrugged, but when she spoke her voice didn't match her nonchalant air. "We can go away some other time. He'll get over it."

"Do you really think Tanya and Faye will come?" Kendall asked.

"Well, we won't know unless we call and ask them. But I'm guessing yes. Steve'll be too busy to care. And Tanya's probably already exhausted again. I can't figure out how she keeps up the pace—*she's* the Energizer Bunny in the group. I'm just the pushiest bunny."

Kendall didn't dispute the comment, nor did she mention how grateful she was that someone had the energy to push at all. Every action that needed to be taken would set off a whole slew of potential reactions, most of them negative. Just thinking about them made her tired.

"You know if I see an attorney I'm going to have to tell Melissa and Jeffrey. I just don't see how I can face them."

"They're not children anymore, Kendall," Mallory said quietly. "And I think you'll be surprised by how much they already know or suspect." She looked away for a moment and then back at Kendall. "But if you're not ready to face them yet, just see the attorney and talk to the kids later when there's something concrete to tell them. All you really have to let them know is that you're strong enough to deal with this, that everything will be OK."

"But I'm not strong. And I can't promise that everything will be OK. Everything is such a mess."

They sat in silence for a few moments, listening to the sounds beneath the quiet: the hum of an insect, a faint echo of a waterfall across the valley floor.

"The one thing I know is that you have to break the big black cloud hanging over you down into small manageable parts so that you can deal with things individually, one step at a time," Mallory said. "I'll give you a few more days on the referral to a kick-ass attorney, but I think we need to get Tanya and Faye on the phone right now and ask them to come. I'm willing to bet you a trip to Home Depot that they'll be here by Friday. That'll give us almost three full days to work on your book together."

• • •

"Look at all these fan letters!" Steven carried a corrugated box full of mail into Faye's office and dropped it on her desk. "And these are just the ones that came to the church." He leaned over her to give her a buss on the cheek, his tone jubilant. He'd gone directly from work to dinner with several church board members and was just now getting home. Faye had elected to stay home and work and had been hard at it for the last three hours; being able to work in a robe and slippers was one of the greatest perks of being a writer. "Where did you go?" she asked.

"Gibson's and I'm stuffed to the gills. I always tell myself I'm going to eat healthy there, but I never can resist their bone-in sirloin." He perched on the side of her desk and motioned to the box of mail. "If this continues, pretty soon I'm going to be known as Faye Truett's husband, that minister who's married to the famous writer."

Faye smiled at the pride in his voice. He took her success almost as personally as his own.

"We can have some of our volunteers read and reply to them if you don't have the time," he said. "We've had hundreds of hits on the link from our site to yours and vice versa. The switchboard keeps fielding inquiries from fans wanting to know where they can buy your books."

Faye considered the box, pleased. The quantity of reader mail had been growing steadily. She was still surprised when people not only emailed her through her website but took the time to compose and mail a handwritten note. There was nothing quite like knowing that something you'd created from nothing had affected someone strongly enough to make them want to communicate with you.

Faye had started writing inspirationals long before the market for them had begun to mushroom. It was only in the last five or six years that the genre had begun to take off, translating into larger advances and royalties.

Of course, being Pastor Steve's wife didn't hurt. Faye knew it was a big promotional advantage.

Faye smiled at the irony: Fifteen years ago she'd been forced to write anything that would produce the smallest trickle of income. Now her inspirational backlist was about to be repackaged and reissued, which was bound to increase her name recognition and reader base even further.

She reached for a letter on the top of the pile and slit it open, reading the letter aloud to Steven. "Dear Ms. Truett, I've been having a hard time with my son, Jackson, ever since his father left us. I could barely bring myself to get out of bed in the mornings, let alone deal with him. But then someone loaned me a copy of your book *In His Name* and I read about what Molly went through and how her belief in God got her and her family through their troubles. I loved that she found a man who could honor and respect her even after everything she'd gone through."

Faye's voice slowed. She could feel Steve's gaze on her. "It gave me hope," she continued. "I read all about you on your website and I've seen you on Pastor Steve's church service. I've read four of your books now, and I'm going to read the rest of them as soon as I can afford to. I almost feel like your book saved my life."

"It's something, isn't it?" Steve asked. "Having that kind of impact on a stranger's life?"

She rose and moved toward him, slipping her arms around his neck.

"It's a blessing," he mused, his breath warm against her ear. "But it's a big responsibility, too. You have to be so careful not to let them down."

He smelled of the cigars they'd probably smoked after dinner. His cologne was light and woodsy. His arms around her waist were strong, familiar. His hands, clasped together, rested at the small of her back.

She breathed him in as she asked, "Don't you worry that they may expect too much? That they might want you to be more than you are, or I don't know, think you should be something you're not?" Faye tried to keep the question casual, but she could hear the slight tremor in her voice.

"Well, I do think they hold a man of God to a higher standard. And they should. I don't have any problem with that."

"And what about the people connected to that man of God?" Faye asked. "Do you think they should be held to that standard, too?"

He left his arms around her but leaned back against her desk so that he could look into her eyes. "Is there something you want to tell me?" His eyes glimmered with amusement, certain there could be nothing of importance about her that he didn't know. "As you know, confession isn't one of the cornerstones of our church, but if there's something you need to get off your chest . . ."

For the briefest of moments Faye considered telling her husband the only secret she'd ever kept from him, could practically taste the relief she would feel if only she could share her mounting worry with him. But as she hesitated the amusement left his eyes and was replaced by something else entirely.

Their eyes remained locked as he pulled her belt loose and slipped his hands inside her robe. She had a flash of what they might look like to an observer, an older graying couple actually contemplating sex in the middle of a home office, but then the image was gone and all she saw was herself in his eyes.

"I'll miss you while you're gone." He helped her shrug out of the robe and tightened his hands on her waist to pull her closer.

"You don't mind that I'm going to Kendall's, do you?" Faye's body pressed against his. Her pulse quickened and her skin warmed to his touch. She imagined she could feel the normally sluggish blood in her veins speeding up its flow; there was a loosening inside her. "I figured you'd be busy with the revival, and Kendall needs . . ." Faye's voice trailed off as his hands moved higher.

"It's not a problem," he murmured as he stared down into her eyes and the tips of his fingers brushed lightly against her breasts. "I understand. She needs you."

He kissed her for a long time then, slowly and thoroughly as if they had all the time in the world. Her knees actually grew weak as she thought back to all the times they'd done this together and what a miracle it was that this could still be so good between them.

Without discussion they sank to their knees beside her desk, their clothes coming off in a hurried jumble, both of them eager to consummate their love for each other.

. . .

Tanya didn't know exactly how she'd ended up on Brett Adams's doorstep with a store-bought chocolate cake in her hands and a daughter on either side, but there it was. Stranger still, Trudy stood slightly behind her in a low-cut top and hip-hugging jeans.

"Why are we here again?" Loretta asked.

"Because we were invited for dinner." Tanya tried to say the words as if this was some sort of everyday occurrence, but of course it wasn't.

She made a point of getting along with the other waitresses at the diner and she'd known Belle and Red since she was a kid. But outside of the yearly Christmas party and the cupcake with a candle that Belle organized for each of their birthdays, there was little socializing outside of work. Everyone had families and responsibilities and too little money. So while they pitched in and helped out when someone was in real need, they didn't exactly hang out together. And certainly no one had ever offered to cook an entire meal for her and her family.

She'd been stunned when Brett had suggested it that morning as he'd handed her an order of corned beef hash and eggs. Standing on his welcome mat now didn't make the whole thing seem any more real.

"Not exactly fancy digs." Trudy sniffed at the cinder-block ranch-style house with its peeling white paint and the chipped decorative metal trellis. What looked like an original 1950s jalousie window was inset into the front door.

"Yeah, your double-wide is so much fancier," Tanya said as she waited for Loretta to push the front doorbell. "You better behave yourself, Mama. I'm not kidding. Whatever happens, it was nice of him to invite us and I'm not turning my nose up at a home-cooked meal."

"Seems like a lot of effort to get into somebody's pants." Tanya figured she should be grateful her mother had whispered the observation so that the girls couldn't hear.

"It does, doesn't it?" Tanya taunted right back. She was pretty sure the most Trudy had ever held out for was a double scotch. "I don't think that's all bad."

The door was opened by two girls somewhere in between Loretta and Crystal's ages. "They're here!" the taller one shouted back over her shoulder. The other, a mirror image of long dark hair and eyes, maybe a year or so younger, just stood, staring at them.

"OK, already." An older girl, also tall and dark haired, approached, and Tanya pegged her as the thong-wearer. Unless Brett had still more daughters hidden somewhere in the tiny house. "Stop staring and let them in," the girl instructed. And then to Tanya and crew, "I'm Valerie. This is Andi and Dani."

The three Adams girls stepped back as Tanya ushered Loretta and Crystal inside. Trudy followed on their heels.

"I'm Tanya." She stuck her hand out toward the older girl. "This is my mother, Trudy, and this is Loretta and Crystal." She waited for her girls to offer their hands as they'd been taught.

"Wow, cool! Like the singers!" Dani said.

"That's right," Tanya said. "Their daddy had a real thing for country music."

"That's way better than our names," the other young girl said. "Our dad kept hoping for a boy."

The older girl laughed. Teetering on the brink of womanhood, she had a bright, friendly smile exactly like her father's and legs that went on and on. She turned to her sisters. "You're ten and eleven already. Get over it!"

Tanya handed the cake to Valerie and stole a look around. The living room was small and dominated by a wide-screen

TV, but someone had made an effort to coordinate fabrics and there were some scattered throw pillows and an afghan neatly folded over the sofa arm. A few framed travel posters hung on the walls and a vacuum had been run before they'd arrived; you could still see the tracks on the harvest gold shag carpet.

A dining room table, lengthened by the addition of a card table at one end, was set for eight. The sound of clattering pots came from somewhere beyond.

Tanya breathed in the heady scent of furniture polish and cooking meat. She held it in her lungs and savored it; it smelled like a home. A scratch and sniff right out of the pages of *Southern Living*.

"Hey, there!" Brett came toward them from the back of the house, wiping his hands on a dishtowel tucked into the waistband of his jeans as he approached. "You're right on time."

They stood in a huddle in the center of the living room, but within moments Brett had taken charge, clearly unwilling to allow any awkwardness. "Trudy, you're lookin' especially lovely tonight. I hope you're up for a beer or a glass of wine. I wasn't sure which you'd prefer."

Trudy perked right up. A smile replaced the more usual downturn of her lips.

"Did you girls introduce yourselves?" he asked.

"They did," Tanya assured him. "Brett, this is Loretta and Crystal."

"Just like the country singers, Dad!" Tanya wasn't sure if it was Andi or Dani who'd spoken; at the moment they seemed virtually interchangeable except for their height.

"Maybe we'll get 'em to do a little number for us later," Brett teased. "Or maybe we should make 'em sing for their supper."

It wasn't exactly an original comment—Tanya doubted there were any comments about her children's names that they hadn't heard—but Loretta and Crystal giggled. Brett

Adams had that effect on women. Tanya reminded herself there was no way on God's earth he could be as good natured as he seemed, but she caught herself smiling nonetheless.

"I swear we've got almost enough for a girls' softball team," he continued. "If you and Trudy were willing to play and I put on a pair of Soffes . . ."

Tanya laughed out loud at the very idea of it. He smiled at her laughter, clearly pleased that he'd produced it.

"You don't do that near enough," he said, "not nearly. But I intend to work on that."

Before Tanya could answer, he turned to her mother. "I've been meaning to ask, Trudy. How old were you when you had Tanya here? Ten? Twelve? I figure you musta been a child yourself cuz you all look more like sisters than mother and daughter."

Trudy harrumphed, but the smile hovering on her lips and the flush on her cheeks made it clear she wasn't immune to Brett's charm.

Tanya wanted to laugh again at the blatant flattery, but she had to admit the man could probably charm paint off the wall.

"Val"—Brett turned to his oldest, still spinning his parental magic—"why don't you take the girls into your room and teach them some of your modeling techniques?"

"Val's on the high school teen board," he explained as the girls turned and left without a lick of protest. "She gets to do runway modeling at the Macy's fashion shows."

"Wow, that was smooth," Tanya conceded, as the bedroom door closed behind the girls and Brett led her and Trudy past the dining alcove and into the small U-shaped kitchen. A small ceramic bowl of nuts and a board with cheese and crackers sat on one counter, individual Caesar salads sat on the other, ready to be served.

"When you're outnumbered three to one on a daily basis, you have to develop some skills," he said.

Deftly he poured them each a drink and when they insisted on helping, he asked Trudy to put the salads out at each place and let Tanya fill the glasses with ice water for the adults and milk for the girls. Then they nibbled on the appetizers while Brett pulled the roasting pan out of the oven and lifted the lid with a flourish to reveal a pot roast laced with potatoes and carrots.

Tanya got a warm, fuzzy feeling in the pit of her stomach, which she identified as hunger and then resolutely pushed away. Just because the man could cook and do laundry didn't mean he didn't have a whole passel of faults. Still, she had to admit that the evening flowed effortlessly.

With Brett as ringmaster and buffer, the meal flew by. And when dinner was over, Valerie led the girls—even Loretta and Crystal, who normally whined at the slightest sign of housework—in clearing and doing the dishes while she and Brett and Trudy, who had miraculously confined herself to only two beers, sat at the table and talked over their coffees, both of them basking in the attention Brett seemed so willing to bestow.

"Y'all have any special plans for the holiday weekend coming up?" he asked as he poured them another round of coffee.

This of course had been a major source of contention between her and Trudy. Tanya snuck a look at her mother, but Trudy had all of her attention focused on their host.

"I wanted to go up to North Carolina to help a writer friend, but I think it's too much for Mama to take care of the girls again so soon," Tanya said, trying not to gag on the enormity of the understatement. Trudy had pitched a first-class hissy fit at the mere mention of the idea. "And I don't think Belle's wantin' to give me any more time off after the days I took to go to New York."

Brett studied her intently for a moment and then he turned to address her mother. "Why, I bet Trudy could manage your girls with one hand tied behind her back," he said.

So much for Brett Adams's grasp on reality. Tanya was about to set the record straight when he turned slightly away from Trudy and sent Tanya a wink; sure confirmation that he had no idea what he was up against.

"Oh, I'm sure she could," Tanya said, somehow managing to keep a straight face, "but I wouldn't dream of asking her to do it." She leveled a gaze at her mother. "She does so much already." *Especially if you counted drinking and complaining.*

Trudy simpered. She may have actually batted her eyelashes at Brett. "Oh, I never mind watching the girls. I opened my own house up to them when Tanya left that no account excuse for a man she was married to."

Tanya bit down on her lip, hard, to stop herself from pointing out that she, at least, had been married when her children were conceived. And that she'd tried her best to turn Kyle Mason into a responsible human being before she'd finally given up.

Brett sent Tanya a bracing look; a glint of humor lit his eyes. "It would be a shame not to be able to help a friend," he said. And then, as if the idea had just occurred to him, "You know if you were to go, Valerie could help Trudy out. She's used to managing the younger ones and despite her unfortunate choices in lingerie . . ." He raised his voice on this and got an, "Oh, Dad!" from the kitchen in return. ". . . she's really pretty responsible."

His oldest huffed into the dining area apparently prepared to defend her taste in lingerie further if necessary.

"Oh, I couldn't ask Valerie to—" Tanya began.

"I could do it, Miz Mason," Valerie said. "If I have all four of them together it'll keep Andi and Dani from killing each other."

Tanya had begun to feel the tiniest ray of hope, but unlike Brett, she knew her mother. Every concession required begging and negotiating with a heavy emphasis on answering Trudy's question of "What's in it for me?"

"I really don't think Belle's gonna want me traipsing off again so soon anyway," Tanya said. "So . . ."

But Trudy, clearly basking in the glow of Brett's attention, evidently craved his approval, too. "If Valerie'll be helping out with the girls, I could probably take Tanya's shifts."

Tanya's mouth dropped open as she contemplated the

woman who had temporarily taken over her mother's body. "But you'd have to get out of bed early, you'd—"

"If you're thinking about saying anything besides, 'Thanks, that sounds great,' you might want to reconsider," Brett interjected.

"But . . ."

He raised an eyebrow at her and cocked his head to one side. He flashed her a conspiratorial grin, which he managed to hide from Trudy.

And just like that Tanya discovered she was going to Kendall's mountain house to help her brainstorm. She could hardly wait to e-mail Mallory to accept the airline ticket she'd offered.

15

*A woman must have money and a room
of her own if she is to write fiction.*
—VIRGINIA WOOLF

"Are you almost ready?" Mallory called through the bedroom door.

"Five minutes," Kendall called back. "I just need to finish dressing."

"Well, hurry up. If you want to stop at your house for more clothes before we pick up Faye and Tanya at the airport, we need to get going."

Kendall took a deep breath and tried to steady herself. She'd had a day and a half to prepare for this little venture back into Atlanta, but she wasn't anywhere near ready. Her fingers actually trembled as she buttoned up her blouse and pulled on a pair of black slacks. She'd washed and blow-dried her hair and put on makeup for the expedition, like a knight drawing on his armor.

She was hoping to avoid seeing Calvin, or God forbid, his girlfriend, Laura Wiles, but she was determined to be prepared for the worst-case scenario. Which would entail discovering the two of them living and sleeping together in *her* home with a For Sale sign firmly planted in the front yard.

In the kitchen Mallory handed her a cup of coffee in a to-go mug and poured one for herself. "You ready?"

Kendall drew another deep breath and told herself it would

only be a matter of hours before she'd be back. And she'd have her posse with her. "As I'll ever be."

"There's nothing to be afraid of," Mallory said. "We're just going to stop by your house, pick up some things, see about getting a referral to a lawyer, and then we're on to the airport."

"But what if they're there?" Kendall gave voice to her fear, afraid even as she did so that speaking it aloud might summon it into being.

"Then we'll do what we came to do and make them feel like the shits they are while we're doing it," Mallory said. "You're the injured party here, Kendall. And don't you forget it."

On the drive into Atlanta, they made desultory conversation. Kendall's hands clutched the wheel too tightly and her gaze stayed straight ahead. By the time the office towers of the Perimeter area appeared, she'd gnawed off most of her lipstick and imagined a hundred horrible scenarios.

The traffic grew lighter as she exited Highway 400 and turned onto Roswell Road. It was Friday morning in the northern suburbs; the school drop-offs had already been completed and the afternoon carpools and after-school activities not yet begun. Those women who worked were already in their offices; ditto for those who shopped and/or played tennis.

Kendall held her breath as she made the left into her subdivision and took the first right onto Dahlia Lane. "Please, God," she prayed silently. "Don't let them be there." She drove down the street slowly. If she could have done it with her eyes closed, she would have.

Turning into the driveway, she thanked Him for the lack of a Realtor's sign. Her last prayer was answered when the garage door went up and she found it empty. Almost giddy with relief, and possibly from holding her breath, Kendall pulled into the garage and turned off the car. She leaned her forehead against the steering wheel and breathed deeply in an attempt to restore her equilibrium.

"Are you OK?" Mallory asked.

Kendall lifted her head and nodded. "I think so. But I don't want to stay here any longer than we need to."

"Got it." Mallory was the first to open her car door. "Let's roll."

Together they entered through the garage door and paused for a moment to survey the kitchen and family room.

"Wow!" Kendall exclaimed.

"No kidding," Mallory agreed. "It looks like a bomb went off in here." She did a 360 as they both took it all in. "If the lovely Laura's been here, she's a really sucky housekeeper."

"I'd say Cal's been on his own. I can't believe anyone with an ovary would leave this big a mess," Kendall concluded.

They surveyed what surely qualified as a natural disaster area. Dishes were piled high in the sink and on the kitchen counter as well as on the coffee and end tables. At some point a move had been made to paper plates and these dotted the landscape, too.

The garbage can was stuffed to overflowing with empty beer bottles, food wrappers, and take-out bags. A pizza box with nothing but crumbs and clumps of cold cheese in it sat on the floor beside it.

Kendall made a move toward the pizza box.

"Don't you dare pick up a thing," Mallory said. "This is not your mess. Go get your things. I'll wait in your office."

Kendall climbed the front stairs to the master bedroom, which was also covered with debris and puddles of clothing, clearly left wherever Calvin had stepped out of them.

The bed was rumpled and unmade and Kendall turned her head away, unwilling to think about who might have shared it with him. Pulling a suitcase from the closet, she emptied her dresser drawers into it, then scooped an armful of hanging clothes together. It took them three trips to get everything down and into the car. Back in her office she considered what calls she needed to make.

At Mallory's urging she dialed two recently divorced friends who she'd heard had come out well. Both of them offered sympathy and gave her the same name.

"Call her right now," Mallory said. "See if you can get an appointment for early next week after Faye and Tanya leave."

She didn't mention her own travel plans and Kendall didn't ask. Right now she couldn't imagine doing any of what had to be done on her own.

Knowing she couldn't cop out with Mallory right there she picked up the phone and dialed Justiss, Delaney, and Tannenbaum, Attorneys at Law, and asked for an appointment with Anne Justiss. "I don't suppose she has anything free for next week?" she said to the secretary who took her call.

"Why yes, actually, we've had a cancellation at eleven thirty Wednesday morning. Can you spell your name for me?"

In disbelief, Kendall did as requested. With a pen and a piece of paper Mallory shoved in front of her, she jotted down the date and time and copied directions to the office in midtown Atlanta.

"See?" Mallory said, after she'd hung up. "Not so hard. We just take one small step at a time." They were sitting in Kendall's office, the one room in the house that didn't bear the signs of Calvin's bachelorhood. As they talked, Kendall cleared her desk and stuffed nonessential files into the filing cabinet. She found a box in the closet and filled it with office supplies, a few reference books and business-related files, as well as her favorite knickknacks and photos of her and the kids. "I feel like a longtime employee who's just been sacked."

Mallory smiled and shook her head. "I prefer to think of you as a budding entrepreneur about to go out on her own." She hefted the box into her arms. "It'll be OK, Kendall. Really. Most of the time the really horrible stuff turns out, in the end, to be for the best. It just takes a while to realize it."

"Spoken with the voice of experience," Kendall said, but any hope that Mallory might elucidate was dashed when she carted the box out to the car, leaving Kendall alone.

Before she could lose her nerve, Kendall dialed Melissa's

cell phone number and waited while it rang. When she was just about to hang up, her daughter picked up, apparently short of breath.

"Melissa?"

"Hi, Mom. What's going on?" Melissa asked, breathing heavily. Kendall sincerely hoped she was . . .

"I'm just jogging, trying to get in shape for that 5K I'm doing." A few more huffs and puffs followed. "You OK?"

Grateful that her daughter seemed happily occupied, Kendall focused on presenting a front of normalcy she wished she could feel. "Sure," she lied, crossing her fingers over the falsehood. "Mallory's here." She sent a weak smile to Mallory, who'd just come back in and now stood in her office doorway. "And we're just, um, getting ready to go to the airport to pick up Faye and Tanya. We're going to be doing some brainstorming up at the mountain house." She paused for a moment, but kept the smile firmly on her face. She'd heard once that shaping your lips into a smile whether you meant it or not made your words sound happier. "And then I'll probably stay on to work on the book I have due."

"Wow, that's great, Mom. I guess now that we're gone you don't really have to be at home if you don't feel like it."

"No, no, I don't," she said, shutting her mind to the fact that she was already a stranger in her own home.

"Maybe we'll surprise you one weekend. I'll tear Jeffrey from his girlfriend and we'll both come up."

"Jeffrey has a girlfriend?" Kendall asked dully. The fact that her shy sports-fanatic son was seeing a girl was yet another breach in the Aimses' status quo.

"Oops, I don't think I was supposed to tell you that." There was some more heavy breathing as Melissa attempted to run and backpedal at the same time. "Don't tell him I said anything, OK?"

"No, no, of course I won't." Kendall was getting pretty good at not telling things. And she was pitifully glad that Calvin hadn't felt compelled to tell the kids about their breakup. Mallory was right about that; there was nothing to be gained by upsetting them until there was something more concrete to tell.

Still, the fact that her children were so obviously living their own lives was bittersweet. Their independence was what you hoped for and worked toward, but the reality was you just weren't that critical anymore.

That realization hit her squarely in the gut. She had become superfluous to her husband as well as her children. They had moved on with their lives. And what had she done? She'd run to the mountains to hide, and she would still be there feeling sorry for herself if Mallory hadn't come and dragged her out.

"Hey, Mom?" Melissa said, panting. "I'm glad you called. I hope you're not too lonely without us."

"I'm OK, sweetie." Maybe if she said it enough times it would simply be so. "I miss you, but I'm going to have my 'peeps' with me all weekend. It's hard to feel too lonely with the whole gang filling up the place."

Melissa giggled. "Glad your people are flying in. I gotta go, OK? I'll call you soon."

Then Melissa was gone and Kendall was standing in the middle of her office once again feeling lost and unsure.

"Are you all right?" Mallory stepped toward her, a worried look on her face.

Kendall nodded, focusing most of her energy on holding off the tears that threatened. "Let's go pick up Faye and Tanya," she finally said, turning her back on her office and heading toward the garage. "Then let's treat ourselves to a really huge lunch."

• • •

"I have to admit I was picturing something slightly more . . . elegant," Mallory said with a sigh as she crumpled her napkin and tossed it onto her empty plate.

They were sitting around a table in the center of the Clayton Café, the remnants of their afternoon feast surrounding them.

"Well, it does remind me a bit of the Downhome Diner,"

Tanya conceded, "and I wouldn't say this to Belle, but that's some of the best fried chicken I've ever had."

"You can't get black-eyed peas and collard greens like that in Chicago," Faye added. "I'm going to have to let the waist-band out on these pants. And I know I shouldn't have had that piece of peach cobbler."

They left a hefty tip and paid their checks on the way out. Practically waddling from all they'd consumed, they stepped out onto the sidewalk two abreast and decided to walk off some of what they'd eaten.

Faye hesitated in front of the bookstore, but Mallory shook her head. "Don't even think about it. Kendall has a whole slew of reasons for not setting foot in there right now, which I'll explain when I'm not so close to exploding. But I bet you big money she'd be glad to show you the Home Depot."

Kendall blushed slightly. "Well, I did think we might stop off just for a minute so I could pick up a few supplies. There are a few things up at the house that I'd like to take care of."

"That's because the store manager's a real hottie and has a thing for Kendall," Mallory teased.

Kendall blushed again. "And I thought we might stop off at the grocery store, too, so we can lay in some food."

"Now that's a great idea," Mallory said. "Let's buy enough so we don't need to come down the mountain until it's time to go back to the airport."

"Damn straight," Tanya said. "I say we give ourselves to-night off and then get up early tomorrow morning and get right to work on Kendall's idea."

"Absolutely," Mallory said.

"I'm with you on that one," Faye added.

Kendall just stared at the three of them, trying to keep the panic out of her eyes. "I hate to disappoint you when you've gone to such effort to come visit. But I don't know how much I'm capable of right now. I mean I'm thrilled to have the com-pany and the support, but I don't feel even the tiniest germ of creativity at the moment. I can't even concentrate long enough to *read* a book right now; I can't imagine trying to write one."

She saw the quick look the other three exchanged and she held her hands up in surrender. "Hey," she said, "I'm not saying I wouldn't love to be writing, and I know for a fact I *need* to be writing. I just don't think there's much of anything you could say or do right now that would make that possible."

16

Writing a novel is like driving a car at night. You can only see as far as your headlights, but you can make the whole trip that way.
—E. L. DOCTOROW

Mallory sat propped up in bed, her laptop, appropriately enough, in her lap, as she stared at the view through the sliding glass doors of her basement-level bedroom. She'd been sitting in this position since just before 6:00 A.M. when her alarm had gone off so that she could start writing.

So far she'd spent most of the last hour and a half either watching the sun's rise through the layer of clouds that hovered over the valley floor or staring at the cursor blinking its *nyah nyah nyah nyah nah* at the top left corner of the blank page. In between these two time wasters, she'd checked her e-mail, which was full of communications from her editor and agent, but displayed not a single message from Chris.

Tired of looking at the blank screen, Mallory closed her eyes, took a deep breath, and tried, once again, to place herself inside the mind of the character from whose viewpoint she'd intended to write this scene. But her own mind raced, lighting briefly on everything from what they'd have for breakfast to getting Kendall started on her book to her agent and editor's queries about her progress. Chris was there, too, yet another member of the crowd in her head vying for her attention.

The only person who didn't seem to be there was the character she was supposed to be writing.

With a groan, Mallory pressed back against the pillows and closed her eyes more tightly, but she could barely remember what Eleanor Rafferty looked like let alone what she thought or felt.

Above her head, footsteps sounded on the wood floor of the kitchen. Soon the scent of coffee reached her nostrils. She was debating whether to admit defeat or soldier on when the dinner triangle clanged loudly and Tanya's voice pierced the morning quiet.

"Rise and shine!" Tanya yelled. Another clanging of the triangle followed. "It's time to get out of bed and get to work!"

Mallory thought a rooster would have been both kinder and gentler, but Tanya seemed to be taking her role as alarm clock and personal motivator seriously.

"Don't make me come in and pull you all out of bed!" she threatened, after several more clangs failed to produce the desired result.

Mallory pulled on her sweats and tied her hair back in a ponytail then took the stairs up to the main floor. Within fifteen minutes they all sat around the kitchen table with steaming mugs of coffee in front of them. Some of them looked more compos mentis than others. Tanya was the only one who seemed not only completely awake, but eager to get started. "Boy, you all are pathetic," she said. She hadn't bothered with makeup but was fully dressed in jeans and a long sleeved T-shirt. Her hair had been tied on top of her head with a scrunchie. Her face bore a look of determination.

"I would've already waited ten or twelve tables by now." She looked at the three of them then focused on Mallory. "I bet Mal's already done her twenty pages."

"I wish," Mallory mumbled into her coffee. Maybe she should hire Tanya as her personal motivator.

"You wanna go ahead and finish them up while I whip these two into shape?" she asked, as she pointed toward Faye and Kendall, who still looked half asleep.

"No!" Mallory sat up too quickly and came close to knocking over the sugar bowl. "I mean, we're, um, here to get Kendall started. My work can wait."

All three of them looked at her as if she had just offered to tear her clothes off and run naked through Times Square. But focusing on Kendall's panic had allowed her to minimize her own and she still believed—or at least desperately hoped—that applying their combined creativity to Kendall's idea would not only get Kendall going but also somehow unstop her own logjam.

"Well," she challenged. "Isn't that what we're here for?"

"Absolutely!" Faye roused and raised her mug in agreement.

"Without a doubt!" Tanya added vehemently.

The three of them now turned to Kendall, who looked as if she were trying to hide behind her ceramic coffee cup. "Yeah, um, right." She got up and walked to the coffeemaker, where she took her time pouring and creaming another cup of camouflage.

"So, why don't we cook a real country breakfast—eggs and bacon and the whole nine yards," Tanya suggested. "Get lots of protein up to our brains."

"And fat to our arteries," Mallory couldn't help adding.

"And then we can set up on the deck and get started," Tanya concluded as she began to open cupboards. "I'll cook if you all want to set the table and brew some more coffee."

Faye joined Kendall at the coffeemaker. "Do you want to take care of the coffee while Mallory and I set the table?" she asked.

Kendall turned to face them. "I'm not quite ready to eat yet, but you all go ahead." Then she walked over to the hall closet and retrieved a large rectangle of canvas, which she buckled around her waist, just above the drawstring to her pajamas. "I thought I'd go ahead and try to replace that bad section of baseboard in the living room."

Tanya, who'd already started removing eggs and bacon from the refrigerator, stopped what she was doing to take in

Kendall's attire. "She's got a tool belt on over her pajamas," she said to Faye and Mallory, as if they couldn't see this for themselves. "I didn't even think they let suburban women wear those things."

Mallory noted the odd clothing combination but was even more concerned by the anxiety etched on Kendall's features. The woman would rather work with power tools than think about her manuscript. Mallory understood all too well. She herself would rather have her fingernails pulled out one at a time than be forced to sit down and try to write at the moment.

But they had limited time together. And none of them wanted to leave Kendall until she was back on track with her manuscript under way.

"Honey," Tanya said, moving in on Kendall. "The only tools you need today are your brain and a pad and pencil. I really don't think—"

Unable to bear the panic on Kendall's face any longer, Mallory cut Tanya off. "Why don't we let Kendall go ahead and take care of that baseboard?" she suggested. For some reason Mallory didn't understand, working with her hands seemed to calm Kendall; right now she didn't think they should rip away a security blanket of any kind.

Checking the kitchen clock, Mallory proposed a compromise. "It's eight right now," she said. "It'll take us about thirty or forty-five minutes to make breakfast, eat it, and clean up. Maybe another thirty minutes for those of us who want to shower and dress. So why don't we get to work on *Sticks and Stones* at nine thirty out on the deck?"

She looked first at Kendall, who nodded in relief. Faye and Tanya agreed, too.

"Good, we've got a plan." As always Mallory preferred to be proactive rather than reactive. "Since you all have the cooking and table setting covered, I'm going to go down and take a shower and dress so that I can handle cleanup while you two get ready."

Faye and Tanya set to work on breakfast while Kendall

headed to the living room to tackle the allegedly rotted base-board. Mallory took the stairs down to her bedroom silently thanking God for allowing Faye and Tanya to come for the weekend. She wasn't a religious person and there weren't a whole lot of things she believed strongly in. But the combined force of their creativity was one of them.

. . .

By 9:35 they were all assembled on the deck. They sat at the round Plexiglas-topped table with yellow pads and ballpoint pens in front of them. Kendall also had an egg-and-bacon sandwich that Tanya had made for her plus an extra large glass of orange juice, neither of which she could bring herself to touch. She still wore her pajamas and tool belt because the baseboard project wasn't quite finished when Tanya had come to drag, er, escort her out onto the deck. But at least she was here. And so were her "peeps."

"Why don't you start by telling us the basic premise," Faye suggested.

"Well." Kendall thought for a moment about the story she had once been so excited about; something she hadn't been able to do in a long time. "It's about four writers at varying stages of their careers who became friends before they ever got published and who help each other deal with the ups and downs of publishing."

"So you're writing about us," Tanya said.

"Well, in a sense. I mean, I didn't plan to write about our real lives—although I was envisioning a *New York Times* Best-seller." She glanced at Mallory. "And an author who writes inspirationals." Faye raised her hand, "Present."

"And I did sort of have a category writer who was a, um, single mother as a primary character."

Tanya stood and took a bow.

"But what I wanted to capture was the connection we felt, feel, for each other. And how it enhances our work and, well, um, our lives." Saying it out loud it sounded as if she'd been too lazy to imagine something and so had decided to rip off their lives. "Originally I thought one of the writers would have a real problem and the others would come to her aid." Kendall looked around the table and smiled sheepishly. "I had no idea I'd be the one needing help so desperately. I'd pictured a car crash or an illness that kept the protagonist from being able to write, not an evil editor and a disappearing husband."

"How much of a plot do you have?" Faye asked.

"Not much. I'd seen the main POV character suddenly unable to write the book she had to write and her friends somehow stepping in and helping, but that was as far as I got." She shook her head at how closely her life seemed to be mimicking her idea. "Weird, huh? I feel like I'm stranded in the middle of a Stephen King novel—you know, a writer gets an idea and all the sudden she's living it. Maybe if I'd never come up with *Sticks and Stones* Calvin wouldn't have left me."

"With all due respect to Stephen King, I think we can rule out your idea being the impetus for Calvin's being an asshole." Mallory's tone was dry. "But I really like the idea. There aren't that many books about writers. And whenever I do a signing or a talk, people are really curious about the business and the whole creative process. It could have real appeal."

"Yeah," Faye added. "There is a whole mystique attached to being a writer even though it's probably the least glamorous profession on the planet. All those hours alone in front of a computer; the self-doubt that sneaks in; the flukiness of the business."

Mallory grinned wickedly. "The lack of showers and grooming during that last patch when you don't leave your computer for days as the end of a book pours out of you."

"Or what's even worse," Tanya put in, "when you're so close to typing 'The End' that you can taste it and you can't think about anything but finishing. But you have to keep stopping to go to work. Or take your kids somewhere." She grimaced. "Or deal with your mother. It's like being in labor and ready to push and having the doctor say, 'Wait, don't push right now. I need to go deal with something. We'll get back to this in a couple of hours.'"

"You know if you can capture all of that, if you can intertwine the realities of being a writer with the personal stories and relationships of each of these characters, you could have something major," Faye said. "And if you put enough insider information in it, it could be huge with readers *and* other writers. You could generate a real buzz within the industry."

Kendall looked at her friends and saw the genuine enthusiasm reflected on all their faces. They weren't hyping her just to get her started. This was a great idea and could really be something out of the ordinary, a true breakout book much larger than what she'd done before.

For a moment Kendall felt the possibility, imagined the satisfaction of writing such a dynamic story. But in the next moment she realized the futility of it. Because even with such a strong premise, even with her friends here to help her think it out, she didn't see how she could possibly summon the energy to write this book and do it any kind of justice. Not with the state her life was in and not in the time she had left.

She shook her head. "I'm sorry, guys." She swallowed, trying to rid herself of the lump that had risen in her throat. "I really appreciate you being here and all your fabulous brainpower. You're the best." She looked away for a moment, out over the deck railing to the world beyond, hazy through the sheen of tears she was trying not to shed. She wished she could respond in the way she knew they wanted her to, but there was no point in pretending she was going to do something she couldn't. If nothing else, she owed them complete honesty.

"It could be an incredible book," she said carefully. "But I can't write it." She blinked back the tears that threatened. "Not right now. I just don't have it in me."

No one spoke right away, for which she was grateful. But she could practically see the wheels turning in their heads, could see them marshalling their arguments, trying to figure out what it would take to turn her around.

"There's just no way," she said, wanting them to understand. "There's no way I could write a four-hundred-page manuscript in less than three months. Not with my whole real life falling in around me. I can't even think straight right now. How in the world could I write?"

In the silence that followed Kendall's pronouncement, Tanya considered her friends. No one really had an answer but all of them wanted like hell to make things better for Kendall.

She had never had to deal with the inability to write, thank you, God. From the time Tanya had started, writing had been the one consistently bright spot in her life.

But she completely understood the horror of having your whole world cave in around you. For Kendall it had been sudden and cataclysmic; Tanya had spent her entire life like that little Dutch boy she'd once heard about who had to keep his finger in the dike. Since childhood she'd been an active participant in adult realities. For a very brief time after she'd married Kyle, she'd thought she could let up and let someone else take over, but this had proved a bad case of wishful thinking. When the dust settled she'd still been all that stood between herself and disaster, only then she had two babies to protect, too.

She looked at the others, trying as always not to be resentful of the easier lives they seemed to lead and reminding herself that Kendall's life had appeared pretty cushy from Tanya's perspective and look how that had turned out.

Faye had struggled when her husband had first started his ministry, but they seemed to be doing really well now. There was something in the back of Faye's eyes that didn't quite jibe with her role as inspirational author and wife of the charismatic Pastor Steve, but Tanya was not one to pry into even a close friend's personal life.

And Mallory? For all her outgoing personality and celebrity status, *there* was a closed book for you. Tanya could count on one hand and maybe a couple of toes the personal things Mallory St. James had ever shared. Up until recently, she'd seemed pretty much like a bestseller machine, cranking them out one after the other, accepting it all as her due. But something was off there, too. For someone who had it all, she didn't seem all that happy.

And not to look a gift horse in the mouth, but Mallory's self-sacrifice in rushing to Kendall's aid also seemed a bit off. If Tanya had been writing a story and had a character who acted so out of character, she had no doubt these very people would have called her on it.

But whatever her motivations, Mallory had brought them all together to help Kendall and that's what they needed to do. If Kendall Aims thought the three of them were just going to let her slide down the publishing drain, she didn't know who she was dealing with.

Mallory was the first to make it clear that the conversation was not over. "Why don't we start with your character's growth arc? Where does she need to get to emotionally? What does she have to deal with to get there?" Mallory said. "Once we have her set, we can figure out the other writers' journeys."

Faye jumped in next. "Maybe you should use what really happened to you, from the time your editor left and things started going downhill," Faye suggested. "Include a husband who does the wrong thing. Maybe even the kids leaving for college. They always say it's best to write what you know. And it might be cathartic."

Tanya watched Kendall process the fact that they weren't going to let her off the hook. A whole boatload of emotions washed over her face, but at least when she finally spoke the tears that had been welling in her eyes had dried and her tone was both sharp and sarcastic.

"Do you think it would be too obvious if my main character was named Kendall and her lying, cheating husband was named Calvin? And do you think it would be OK to kill and dismember him by chapter two?"

Faye and Mallory laughed in relief, but Kendall's words smacked Tanya right between the eyes and cleaved right through to her brain. She had what she thought of as a "duh" moment, the kind that practically walks up and clops you on the head and says, "Don't be stupid, just do this."

Trying to work it out, she stood and began to pace to the edge of the deck and back. The others' conversation stuttered to a halt as they watched her. Faye took her feet off the deck railing and sat up straighter. Mallory stopped scribbling on her yellow pad and Kendall stopped fingering her tool belt.

"OK," Tanya said, turning to face them. Her thoughts seemed to be outpacing her ability to communicate, and she made a conscious effort to slow them down. "Kendall's story is supposed to be about four writers, loosely based on us." She paused to make sure she had their full attention and then emphasized each word carefully. "But what if they *are* us?"

"What?" they Greek chorused.

Again she tried to slow herself down so that she could be as clear as possible, certain that if they only understood, they would be as excited about her idea as she was. "What if Kendall's character *is* Kendall. And Faye's is Faye. And yours is yours, Mal? And the beautiful, yet driven, single mother is me?"

Kendall's brow furrowed. In fact, all of them stared back at her as if she'd somehow taken a nose dive over the edge of reason. But Tanya could see it all clearly now; she just had to make them see it, too.

"Kendall's right. She's in no shape to write a four-hundred-page manuscript from multiple points of view right now. But what if each of us wrote our own character?"

The shocked silence continued, but Tanya was determined to push through it.

"We could each write from our own character's point of view and then we could meld the pieces together." She paused a moment to gather her thoughts. "That way each of us would only be writing about a hundred pages—a quarter of the book." She paused once more to let this part sink in; a hundred pages was nothing compared to a complete manuscript—another twenty-five pages a week over the course of a month. "And just think of how genuine each of those characters' voices will be. We could really create something great."

Still no one spoke, but at this point Tanya couldn't have

stopped talking if they'd wrestled her to the ground and taped her mouth shut, which they looked somewhat tempted to do. She just kept spewing out her thoughts, reforming and restating them, trusting that if she talked long enough her message would get through.

"It'll be labeled fiction," she explained, "so we can make up our characters' backstories or we can write the absolute truth and let people think it's fiction—whatever's easiest or most interesting to us. Of course, we've got to figure out the plot and what it is that threatens their careers and their friendship—but that should be fun if we do it together."

She paused for breath and to scan their faces for clues to their reactions. She'd explained her idea as best she could. Now she was going to have to ask them point-blank whether they were willing to consider it or were just trying to figure out how to tell her "no."

17

*The only important thing in a book is
the meaning it has for you.*
—W. SOMERSET MAUGHAM

It took Kendall some time to absorb what Tanya was suggesting. Faye and Mallory also seemed to be stuck in the processing mode; the idea was so staggering that it was hard to take it in right away. Still no one had jumped up yet and said, "That's ridiculous," although, of course, it was.

The minutes ticked away in the late-morning silence as the sun inched up farther and each of them tried to navigate her way through the alien territory Tanya had invited them into.

"You're offering to write this book for me." Kendall wanted to be certain she hadn't misunderstood.

"Well, I'm actually thinking of it as more of a collaboration. You'd be writing the primary point-of-view character. And, of course, your name would be on the cover. We'd just be helping you finish out your contract so that you could get the hell out of Scarsdale."

"I want to help and I have no problem with doing the pages," Faye said. "But it feels a bit . . . unethical. Kendall would be putting her name on something she didn't write alone. I mean, even James Patterson admits when there's another author on the project. And we're all under contract to other publishers. I don't even know if we can legally contribute to a book that someone else has contracted to write."

"We'd just be like ghostwriters," Tanya argued. "There are lots of projects where one person's name is on the cover and the real author doesn't get cover credit."

"But in those situations the publisher *knows* who wrote the book," Faye pointed out.

Kendall listened to their points and counterpoints, all of them valid. It felt so odd to be the subject of discussion, to have her life and career debated in front of her as if she'd died and been invited to the postmortem.

"And what if it becomes a runaway bestseller. Makes the lists. Lands Kendall on *Oprah?*" This from Mallory, who'd done all of those things.

Tanya snorted. "Hell," she said, "we all know Oprah only picks stories about dysfunctional families and somebody has to die in the end; these would just be dysfunctional writers. I don't think she's gonna be interested."

Some of the tension dissipated as they laughed in agreement.

Kendall was still trying to gather her thoughts. "The truth is I'm not sure we should even be considering this, but I think the chances of that kind of attention are remote." She ticked off her points on her fingers. "Lacy Samuels has never done this before. Plain Jane is going to slap some crappy cover on it, print the smallest amount of copies possible, and stick it on some shelves. And nothing with my name on it right now is likely to end up anywhere but on the remainder table."

They all stared at each other, considering.

"But more importantly," Kendall said, "I can't ask you to do this. You're all on deadlines and don't need to take on mine. And I wouldn't feel comfortable taking credit for your work. Whether it was a hit or a flop, I'd know it wasn't really mine."

"You didn't ask, Tanya suggested," Faye said. "And the more I think of it the more I think, 'Why shouldn't we?' I don't believe anyone here, with the possible exception of Tanya, would be snowed under by another hundred pages. And I think there'd be a great energy from doing this together. We could create something more than any of us could create on our own. There's lots of work out there done under other names and for different reasons. And besides, no one would ever know. We'd have to make it our secret."

Kendall looked at her friends and a flood of love for them coursed through her. "You guys will never know what even having this conversation means to me. You make me feel like I'm not alone. That somehow getting through all of this . . . shit . . . is possible." She paused to regroup, amazed that she could be this close to tears all the time. "I don't know if what Tanya's suggesting is the right thing to do. I hate feeling this needy but frankly, the idea of not having to write this book alone makes me almost weak with relief."

Kendall paused, wanting to make sure she put it all out there. If they did do this, their whole group dynamic would change; just the act of writing this book together—a book about themselves—could open them up in all kinds of ways, and that wasn't even taking into account what might happen after it had been published.

"But we don't really know what to expect from this; it's completely uncharted territory. And we could end up wandering in the wilderness. I love Tanya for suggesting it and both of you for considering it. But I don't want to do anything that might jeopardize our friendship. I could probably find a way to live without money or a publishing contract. I don't think I could live without my 'peeps.'"

"All right, all right," Tanya said. "We are not going to get all weepy about this. Kendall, if we decide we want to write this book with you, do you want us in on the project?"

Kendall gnawed at her lip. Her pride told her to hold her head up and tell them thanks, but she'd be fine on her own. Except, of course, that would be a big fat lie. Even with them here propping her up it was taking everything she had not to run and curl up in bed. Or buckle on her tool belt.

Slowly she nodded. "I can completely understand if you choose not to do this. I won't be hurt or offended." She paused, wanting to make sure there would be no misunderstanding.

"The whole idea is definitely on the funky side, but working together would take a huge weight off my shoulders."

She could see that Tanya was ready to press for a decision, so she stood to leave, not wanting to know who might be in favor and who might not. "I'm going to go in and make us some lunch. Let me know when you're ready to eat."

"No," Mallory said. "Don't leave." She raised a quizzical eyebrow to Faye and Tanya, both of whom silently nodded their heads. "It looks unanimous to me," Mallory said.

They all broke into smiles as Tanya pumped a triumphant fist in the air. "Let's all go in and make lunch together," she said. "Then we can start seriously brainstorming while we eat."

They trooped inside chattering about *Sticks and Stones* and the logistics of writing the book together. The brainstorming started over tuna sandwiches and sweet tea and continued well into the evening when they had to stop because their jaws ached and their brains were reeling.

On Sunday they woke up early to hammer out the basic plot points then sketched out a cast of characters, knowing that each of them would flesh out her own.

Just for fun, they added an evil and highly unattractive editor as well as a well-intentioned but naïve young editorial assistant. Then they placed bets on how long it would take Jane and Lacy to recognize themselves.

When their brains were once again completely fried, they went for a hike. After showers they broke open the wine, tossed a salad, and threw a frozen pizza into the oven.

Kendall's home-improvement project that day was a small one—just a new latch for the screen door and a fluorescent fixture that she attached under one of the kitchen cabinets; a definite sign of progress that everyone noticed but was careful not to comment on.

On Monday afternoon Kendall and Mallory drove Faye and Tanya to the Atlanta airport. They stood on the curb and hugged each other fiercely. "Thank you," Kendall whispered as she threw her arms around Tanya and then Faye. "I can't even begin to tell you how much I appreciate . . ."

"Don't." Tanya hugged her back, holding on tight. "I can't wait to work on your book. *Sticks and Stones* is going to be killer."

"She's right," Faye added. "We're going to write a knock-out of a book. You just wait and see."

There was a final round of hugs and then Mallory confirmed their plan. "We'll e-mail detailed character sketches to each other as soon as we can and Kendall's going to start on the first chapter. We'll aim for a conference call at the end of the week to discuss what's been completed and lay out the upcoming chapters. Kendall and I'll join the scenes together and handle all the transitions. When it's complete we'll all do a read through and make notes. After Thanksgiving we'll get together again to tweak and produce a final."

Kendall stood with Mallory and watched the other two disappear into the terminal. If she didn't have a meeting with a divorce attorney the day after tomorrow, she could have convinced herself that things would be fine. Trying to sidestep a nosedive back into the negative, she got behind the wheel of the Pilot and worked her way out of Hartsfield-Jackson Airport then headed north on Highway 85, fairly certain the car could make the trip without her by now.

They passed the first few miles in silence, Kendall trying to imagine what Anne Justiss, attorney-at-law, might look like and how much she would charge, Mallory thinking about . . . Kendall had no idea what.

"Have you been in touch with Lacy Samuels since she first made contact with you?" Mallory asked.

"No."

"Well, I think it would be a good idea to send her a quick e-mail updating her on where things stand with the book."

"You mean like, 'Dear Lacy, Just wanted to let you know that I haven't actually started the book yet due to a small emotional breakdown. However, even though my husband has left me for a much younger woman, there's nothing to worry about because when my friends realized how incapacitated I was they volunteered to help me write it?"

"Very funny," Mallory said, a pained expression on her face. "But I think we should make sure something from you is waiting for her when she gets into the office tomorrow morning."

Kendall shook her head. "If there's going to be something in Lacy Samuels's inbox in the morning, it's going to have to come from you. I was sort of hoping my level of interaction with Scarsdale would fall somewhere between little and none."

"Actually," Mallory said. "I think it needs to be just the opposite. Our goal should be to get her hyped. It can't hurt to have someone excited about the project."

"She's an assistant, Mal," Kendall pointed out. "An insult delivered by Jane Jensen."

"But she's also a resource," Mallory argued. "And whether we like it or not, at the moment she's your conduit at Scarsdale. It can't hurt to try to get her on your side."

Kendall shrugged, not even close to believing that Lacy Samuels could be any kind of asset. She was more than likely a chip off of Jane Jensen's block. And if she wasn't, she was probably some sort of timid little mouse, who'd never question an executive editor.

Back at the mountain house, Kendall went to her room to take a nap. Mallory retrieved her laptop from the downstairs bedroom and carried it upstairs and out onto the deck.

With only occasional glances out to the view, she scanned e-mails and responded to both her agent and her editor, staying as vague as possible without sounding any alarm bells. She wasn't quite ready to find out whether she could force herself to focus on her own work, but felt a strange stirring of excitement about Kendall's project, which she already thought of as a gift to a friend and not an obligation. The fact that no one but her closest friends would even know she'd written it was incredibly freeing.

The warm feeling in her belly dissipated when she found

no sign of a message from Chris. She debated what to do about it and settled for sending a chatty e-mail filling him in on all that had transpired and apologizing once more. She stopped short of committing to a return date because she'd already decided to let Kendall's state of mind be her guide, but she vowed to herself to make things up to Chris just as soon as *Sticks and Stones* was under way and she had her own project back on track.

Her next order of business was to initiate contact with Lacy Samuels. Using the password Kendall had given her, Mallory logged on to Kendall's e-mail account and pulled up the Write Mail screen. With her fingers poised above the keys, she thought for a moment, and then, attempting to capture Kendall's tone and personality, she began to type.

> *Hi Lacy, thanks so much for your call. Just wanted to touch base to let you know that I'm up in the mountains and am now completely focused on* Sticks and Stones. *Am very excited about this book and look forward to working with you to make it all that it can be. The story is developing really well and I see no problem in meeting my December 1 deadline.*
>
> *In the meantime, I do have some thoughts about the cover.*

Here Mallory gave very specific input. She knew that Kendall didn't have cover approval like she did, and that the "cover consult" written into many contracts consisted of an editor sending the completed cover to the author as little more than an FYI. Still Mallory thought it better to give direction than to sit back and wait for the bad news. Everyone knew a cover could make or break a book and yet so often the really great covers were lavished on authors who were so big they no longer needed them while those who would most benefit got covers that could actually hurt them—like the author they knew whose hero had been depicted with three hands. And another whose heroine, shown in a revealing clinch with the hero, could have been the author's double.

I look forward to working with you and to hearing Scarsdale's plans to promote this book, which I think should appeal to both insiders and those outside the industry.

Here she went on to suggest several promotional ideas that had occurred to her before she realized that Kendall would have never done such a thing—having never been given any reason to believe that her publisher would appreciate these kinds of suggestions. After some internal debate, she deleted those sentences and then before she could rethink it to death, she pressed Send.

18

Lacy Samuels got back from the Hamptons, where she'd taken a share in a house for the Labor Day weekend, late Monday night. She was suitably sunburned and happily tired, having discovered that the attraction to a friend of a friend was reciprocated.

On Tuesday morning she took the subway to Penn Station and despite the state of semidread she always felt until her boss's mood was known, she walked eastward to Scarsdale with a jaunty step.

The truth was, she'd always been a glass-is-half-full kind of person and she'd taken plenty of grief from her friends over the years for her eternal optimism. But there was a chance that Jane Jensen had also gotten laid over the holiday weekend. Or that she'd be relaxed and rested after the long weekend. Or at least up-to-date on her meds.

In the Scarsdale lobby Lacy ran into Cindy Miller, an assistant in the publicity department, and her friend Shelley in marketing, and they compared weekends in the elevator on the way up to their respective floors. In her cubicle, Lacy booted up her computer and skimmed down her e-mails, most of which were either companywide memos or terse directions from her boss.

An e-mail from Kendall Aims speared her attention and

she held her breath while she clicked it open, afraid it might carry a demand that Lacy be taken off her book. She breathed a sigh of relief when she read the pleasantly innocuous missive, though the query about the book's cover gave her pause. She wasn't looking forward to having to show the recycled cover to Kendall. She sent off an equally pleasant reply, saying that she looked forward to reading *Sticks and Stones* and inviting Kendall Aims to be in touch if she could be of assistance in any way.

She had just pressed Send when Jane Jensen appeared in her cubicle, looking neither sunburned nor satisfied.

"There's an editorial meeting in five minutes," she said, wasting no time on pleasantries.

Lacy nodded, unsure what this had to do with her; her boss had never bothered to inform her of the timing of any such meeting before. "That's great," Lacy said tentatively.

When Lacy made no move to move or respond, Jane motioned for her to get up. "That means we need to go to the conference room," she said, her tone impatient.

"You want me to come to the editorial meeting?" It was embarrassing, but Lacy could actually feel her face light up with excitement.

Afraid Jane might change her mind, Lacy jumped up and grabbed a yellow pad and a pen, though she had no idea whether either of these items would prove necessary. Then she fell into step beside Jane, unable to tamp down her excitement over this unexpected opportunity.

Jane brought them to a stop just before they reached the boardroom. "I don't want you embarrassing me, so there are a few things you need to understand."

Lacy nodded. She could already imagine the insights into publishing she would glean. Maybe she'd come up with a great idea and be noticed by the associate publisher, Brenda Tinsley, whom she'd heard referred to as "the hand of God."

"You will not sit at the conference table. There's a row of chairs around the outside of the room. You will sit in one of those behind me in case I need you to do or go get something."

Lacy looked more closely to see if Jane was joking, but although her eyes were clear and focused, which was not always the case, there was no humor in them.

"You will not make eye contact with anyone actually sitting at the conference table, except me."

Lacy resisted the urge to look around for the *Candid Camera* crew. Surely Jane couldn't be serious.

"Most importantly, you will not speak during the meeting."

Lacy blinked, certain she'd misunderstood or that despite the grim look on her face, Jane was joking. "You're not serious."

"That's the way it is. If you can't follow these simple directions, you can go back to your desk."

The conference room was beautifully decorated, the mammoth table in its center an oval of shiny mahogany. The associate publisher sat at the head of the table with the heads of production, art, sales, and publicity, as well as others Lacy didn't recognize, radiating out around her. She had no doubt they were arranged in some sort of pecking order that she didn't yet understand.

As she followed Jane in and around the table, Lacy glanced longingly at the empty seats, but Jane, who clearly had eyes in the back of her head, turned and gave one menacing shake of her head. Jane drew out the empty chair next to Cash Simpson from sales, and settled herself into it. Realizing eyes were on her, Lacy hurriedly took the empty seat behind her, a much narrower, less padded affair pressed up against the wall.

As Tinsley called the meeting to order, Lacy's breathing slowed and she began to recover her equilibrium. OK, so maybe she wasn't an important part of this meeting, maybe she couldn't participate or speak. But she was here, privy to all sorts of things. She'd finally know, firsthand, what happened at the weekly editorial meetings. It was a first step. She owed it to herself to learn as much as she could.

She watched as each of the editors present gave status reports on the books they were already responsible for and then pitched manuscripts they wanted to buy. It came down to a vote on each of those, with the editorial director having final say. The books pitched with the most enthusiasm and by those able to build consensus generally seemed to get approved. She also noted that in some cases, the pitching editor had already gotten others at the table to read the manuscript so that they could introduce their favorable feedback as well.

Lacy's interest was piqued by the careful dance at the table. She noted the alliances that existed, who had the most power, who bowed to whom.

Hannah Sutcliff seemed especially well liked and respected. A polar opposite to Jane, Hannah was tall and blond with an innate sophistication that made her look as if she could have spent her days lunching and shopping on Fifth Avenue rather than nursing books into the world. She was rumored to have a trust fund or a wealthy patron, though Lacy had no idea if either of these things were true. Others claimed she'd had an affair with the publisher, but this also was unsubstantiated.

What was known was that she had come to Scarsdale as Jane Jensen's intern and had taken an incredible amount of abuse at Jane's hands. And had never forgiven her for it, despite the fact that she and Jane were now equals.

About thirty minutes into the meeting, Lacy began to notice how often Jane turned to Cash Simpson, how often she stole looks when he was speaking or looking elsewhere. Cash Simpson was one of the most dynamic at the table and one of the best looking. As one of the few males present, he drew plenty of eyes. But no one studied him as frequently or with as much interest as her boss.

Lacy filed this bit of information away for future examination.

When it was Jane's turn to speak, Lacy had to admit, she came across well. She was clear and precise with no hint of the turbulence that Lacy often saw bubbling beneath the surface.

Lacy stilled when Kendall Aims's book was brought up. Jane managed to sound coolly professional and yet somehow dismissive as she indicated that they would not be going back to contract with the author and that the book was due December first and slated to come out the following December. When someone asked about cover art, Jane said they already had the cover and held up the rejected Carolyn Sinclair cover, which now had a manuscript page sticking out of the briefcase and Kendall Aims's name squeezed underneath. She then explained that the author's numbers were in the toilet and that she had already been informed they would not be going back to contract. There was no need for promotion or anything else. They simply needed to get it out on the shelves to fulfill their obligation. No mention was made of Lacy editing the book.

In moments they'd moved on to a new author another editor was interested in acquiring. This was her first manuscript, the editor explained, and would help fill Scarsdale's hole in the still popular paranormal category. Best of all, the author could be gotten cheap and appeared to be quite prolific. She suggested a three book contract locked in at a shockingly low advance per book. There was a show of hands and that was it.

Lacy imagined the aspiring author's excitement when she received "the call" informing her of her first sale and the celebration that would follow. But Lacy's glass, which she generally saw as half-full, was looking more like a dribble glass at the moment and she couldn't shake the sense that she'd just witnessed the purchase of a "widget" as opposed to the beginning of a publishing career.

• • •

When Mallory awoke late Tuesday morning and went upstairs for coffee, she found Kendall already sitting at the kitchen table making notes on a yellow pad. A peek over her shoulder confirmed that it was not a to-do list.

The house felt emptier and quieter without Tanya and Faye, but it was nonetheless imbued with an air of expectation and possibility as well. For the first time in months, Mallory was actually looking forward to sitting down in front of a computer screen. She savored the sweet sense of anticipation as she poured herself a cup of coffee from the pot.

"Good morning," she said, as she added creamer and sugar substitute then brought the cup to her lips for that first wonderful sip.

"Morning." Kendall looked up from her notes. "How'd you sleep?"

"Good." Oddly enough it was the truth. She'd slept through the night and had awakened with this unfamiliar sense of well-being.

"Me, too," Kendall said. "I'm just making some character notes. It's kind of interesting to try to figure out how close to the truth I can come without turning *Sticks and Stones* into an autobiography."

"Well, at least the names will be changed to protect the innocent."

"Yeah." Kendall smiled. "But it'll feel so good to vent. I realized this morning that the book will give me the opportunity to point out the arbitrariness and brutality of the publishing business without appearing to be whining."

"That's true," Mallory said, her own mind also whirling with just how much she might reveal. She'd become so used to sidestepping and deflecting. Maybe this was her chance to tell all the things she'd kept so carefully to herself. And if Tanya, Faye, or Kendall, who would be the only ones who ever knew she created the character of Miranda, ever called her on it, she could simply claim "fiction." After all, they were writers; they made things up all the time. That's what they were supposed to do.

Humming under her breath, Mallory took an apple from the fruit bowl and carried it and her laptop out to the deck. She arranged herself at the table where she could see out over the valley and took a generous bite of her breakfast. Before long she wasn't seeing the valley or the mountains or even the deck itself. She was remembering that first conference where she'd met Faye and Kendall and Tanya, when her dreams were just that. And her writing was a means of escaping the past that still haunted her.

She roughed out a first scene through Miranda's excited eyes, drawing on the remembered emotions of that first day of the conference when she'd found herself surrounded by a thousand other writers who wanted what she wanted, and dreamed what she dreamed.

From the beginning she'd realized that many of the attendees were more excited about calling themselves writers than actually being one. They would spend years cleaning and polishing the first chapters of a manuscript, never persevering on to the end. The act of writing was hard and lonely; talking about writing was just the opposite.

Mallory's fingers flew over the keyboard as she tried to put the reader in her character, Miranda Jameson's, point of view. For Miranda, becoming a novelist was an emotional escape and a way to get back the security and comfort that had been taken from her. No one bothered to tell her how stacked against her the odds of success were. And she wouldn't have listened if they had.

"Miranda Jameson was not her real name, of course," Mallory typed, "but a name she'd adopted long ago. Her clothes were expensive, though not the latest style, and her air of confidence was mostly bravado. She surveyed the gaggle of authors waiting to make their fifteen-minute pitches to an editor or agent and felt a surge of panic assail her. Miranda shrugged it off and walked with her head held high to the place where she'd been told to wait, rehearsing her pitch in her head, refusing to mutter it aloud like some of the others.

"A twentysomething young woman with big blond hair and clothing, which might have been stolen from Daisy Dukes's closet, glanced up from the couch on which she was seated and looked Miranda up and down. 'Lordy, me, look at you,' she said in a Dogpatch sort of accent, 'You don't look one bit scared. I'm so damned nervous I can hardly keep my teeth from chattering.'

"Two other women standing nearby turned at her comment. One was near fifty and had a face that looked vaguely familiar. She introduced herself as Faith. The other was midthirties and said her name was Kennedy. When she spoke Miranda could hear a trace of the South in her voice, though her accent was both more affluent and educated than the blonde's."

The sound of an electric drill brought Mallory back to the present and she debated for a few moments whether to go check on Kendall. She'd already rejected the idea of getting up when Kendall came back to the kitchen table with her laptop. Soon she heard Kendall's fingers tapping on computer keys.

Mallory closed her eyes and drifted back into the scene. As the truth flowed out of her in its fictitious disguise, Mallory stopped judging and tried not to edit. She sketched a scene between all four of them, trying her best to capture the feeling of comfort that had come from the unexpected bonding between them.

Mallory wasn't sure how these scenes would go together or which of them she'd keep, but when she finally looked up from her computer screen, Mallory was surprised to see the sun high up in the sky. She'd been completely unaware of the passing time or her page count or anything except the feelings of the character she was intent on bringing to life.

Now she heard Kendall moving around in the kitchen, heard the refrigerator open and shut. She felt a faint stirring of hunger and noted with surprise that it was already 2:00 P.M. Had she really been writing for almost six hours without even realizing it?

Mallory saved what she'd written on her hard drive and then on the jump drive she always carried with her. She stretched, trying to work out the kinks from sitting so long, but despite the physical aches and pains, she felt fabulous; she couldn't remember the last time she'd written so freely or for so long.

She would not think about the book she had due or the

husband she still hadn't heard from. She intended to rejoice in the flow of words and leave it at that.

Her step was light, and her spirit lighter, as she headed inside to join Kendall. And if she was going to allow herself at least one cliché today, she'd have to say that she felt as if the weight of the world had been lifted from her shoulders.

19

Tanya made it through her shift at the Downhome Diner without actually speaking to Brett. She turned in orders, picked them up, and fenced mechanically with Red, but felt awkward and uncertain around Brett, knowing she needed to express her gratitude but uncomfortable with feeling beholden to him.

She'd come home the night before, braced for Trudy's complaints and her daughters' whining, and instead found them content and happy—or as close to both as Trudy could get. The three of them couldn't seem to stop singing the praises of the Adamses and the whole thing had Tanya completely off-kilter.

And so she waited her tables, flashed her smile, poured countless cups of coffee, all the while so busy trying to figure out what to say and how best to say it that she ended up saying nothing at all.

Now it was time to clock out and it was clear she couldn't leave without acknowledging what Brett had done for her. She wouldn't have been at Kendall's if he hadn't handled Trudy so beautifully.

Resolute, she untied the pocketed apron she wore during her shift and walked slowly toward him, crumpling the fabric in her hands. He cracked eggs, tossed the shells, flipped, fried, and plated up with an impressive economy of motion, never once taking his eyes off her as she approached; the man had come a long way under Red's experienced eye.

He smiled and raised an eyebrow as she came to a stop before him, but he didn't stop working and he didn't speak.

"I, um, wanted to thank you for what all you did for my family over the weekend." Tanya's gaze didn't quite meet his; she kept it aimed just over his left shoulder.

"It was no problem. Valerie and the girls had a good time."

With great difficulty she shifted her focus to his face and saw the amusement on it. She continued to mangle the apron with her hands. "What is so dumned funny?"

"You." He flipped an egg and plucked two slices of whole wheat bread from the toaster. "You look like somebody made you walk through fire barefoot. It's not such a big thing. I was glad to help out. You say, 'Thank you.' I say, 'You're welcome.'" He shrugged as he plated two meals and rang the bell for pick up. "No big deal."

"It is to me," she said. "I haven't had a lot of people wanting to help over the years. It's kind of foreign, you know?"

"Well, I'm real sorry to hear that," Brett said. "Everybody needs help now and then." And then he shifted the conversation in that effortless way he had. "So how'd the brainstorming go? Did you figure things out?"

"Good, real good. I was really glad I could be there."

Other waitresses came, picked up their orders, and went, and every one of them gave Brett some kind of once-over. She noticed Red eavesdropping. She also knew that she should offer something in return. But she wasn't about to invite the Adamses into Trudy's shabby mobile home, and even if she'd wanted to, she was no match for Brett in the kitchen. And she sure as hell wasn't going to sleep with him just because he'd done her a good turn, no matter how attractive he was. That was Trudy's way, not hers.

"So, uh, like I said. I do appreciate what you did." Pulling the apron out of the ball she'd smashed it into, she pulled out a wad of bills and counted out $25 in ones and laid the stack on the counter next to him. "Please give this to Valerie and tell her thanks."

"There's no need," he began. "It wasn't a babysitting job. It was just—"

But Tanya didn't want to feel in debt, not even to a teen-aged girl. And she wasn't planning to let herself get too used to Brett's charming ways or his white knight complex; if she let herself enjoy either too much she'd feel worse than she did now when he was gone.

"I'm sure there were lots of things Valerie would've rather been doing than taking care of Crystal and Loretta," she said. "Or humoring my mother."

Brett opened his mouth clearly about to offer an argument, but Tanya wasn't having any of it. "You give it to her, you hear? And when you do, you tell her not to waste that on those thongs she's been buying. In my experience, the only thing they're good for is attracting a whole passel of trouble."

• • •

It was late and the house was silent except for the loud tick of the grandfather clock in the living room and the faint rhythm of Steve's snoring from the master bedroom. Alone in her study, Faye typed in the combination of letters that would al-low her to open the password-protected file. Scrolling down, she read the chapter she'd roughed out the night before, her eyes skimming over the words and phrases she'd used to de-scribe and establish Faith Lovett, the character she'd created for *Sticks and Stones.*

When she reached the end of what she'd written, Faye went into Edit, chose Select All, and hit Delete. Faith Lovett was so "her," she might as well have named her Faye.

For a few long moments Faye watched the pulse of the cur-sor on the blank screen and contemplated her options. If she wrote the public version of herself she'd bore the readers to death. If she wrote the truth about herself, and it was recognized as the truth, she could end her husband's ministry and her own career, not to mention the charitable works her income funded. Confessing to her husband was one thing—not that she'd even come close to working up the nerve to do that yet—a public admission of the secret she'd guarded so closely was something else entirely.

So what was she to write? How could she contribute a compelling character and plotline to Kendall's work without destroying life as she knew it in the process?

Faye sat for some time weighing the possibilities. If ever she'd needed to think outside the box, it was now. But as she knew from her fifteen years of writing, the brain was an ornery organ. The heart might be required to beat regularly and predictably, but the brain took circuitous paths and had its own way of solving a problem or creating an idea. It rarely produced on any schedule but its own.

Faye closed her eyes and tried to direct her brain in search of inspiration, but it kept coming back with her own life and what would happen if she exposed it. After a time, her eyelids began to feel heavy and her head fell forward, pressing her chin into her chest. In midthought, she fell asleep. When her eyes fluttered open it was 2:00 A.M. and a glimmer of an idea teased at her consciousness. She breathed slowly, afraid to make any sudden moves, lest she lose it.

In this half-awake state she summoned up Faith Lovett and attempted to see her more clearly. A scene began to unfold in Faye's head and she realized, as it spun out, that she could place her character in a similar background and give her a surprisingly damaging secret without revealing her own.

Slowly she began to type, carefully picking and choosing the words that would create a multilayered character that would surprise the reader, as each layer was first revealed and then stripped away.

The words came faster as the first meet scene unfolded in Faye's mind. She held her breath as she felt the strange and wonderful surge of power that took her thoughts and ideas and transformed them into something even greater than what she'd imagined. She didn't know where this power came from, whether it was a gift from God or was something even more ancient that was buried within. But it was the reason that she wrote; it was what compelled her to continue to put words on a page, even when those words weren't what others might expect from her.

An author possessed the kind of power others only dreamed of. The writer created both the characters and the worlds they inhabited. A writer decided who lived and who died, who found happiness and who tragedy. Her husband spent his ministry in an effort to revere and communicate with God; Faye, in her role as writer, got to play Him.

· · ·

The appointment with divorce attorney Anne Justiss was both better and worse than Kendall had expected. Mallory had had to drag her out of bed Wednesday morning, rush her to get dressed, and then drive them into Atlanta; Kendall had no doubt that if she'd been on her own she simply wouldn't have gone. At the moment she could completely identify with the ostrich and his predilection for sticking his head in the sand.

Anne Justiss didn't look like the man-eater Kendall was expecting. She was petite with stylishly cut blond hair and bright blue eyes. In the right kind of light and through the right sort of filter, the attorney might have passed for Cameron Diaz.

"So," she said, without preamble. "Tell me what's going on."

Kendall did, cringing inwardly as she explained that Calvin didn't want to be married to her anymore and describing, in way more detail than necessary, her encounter with his Realtor girlfriend who'd had the nerve to show up expecting to list their house.

"And he's represented by Josh Lieberman?" Justiss asked.

Kendall nodded and handed over the sheet of paper on

which she'd copied the name and contact information for Calvin's attorney. "Is that bad?"

The attorney shrugged. "Look, none of this is good. Typically after a divorce the man's standard of living improves. The ex-wife and children's standard of living drops dramatically. I do my best not to let that happen to my clients."

Kendall swallowed, wishing her neck was longer and a patch of sand readily available.

"I know it's a lot to take in and it's always worse when the divorce isn't your idea," the attorney said. "But you won't be in this alone, Kendall. I can promise you that.

"As soon as we get your deposit and paperwork on file, we'll sue for subpoena and get hold of all the relevant financial information. We want to move quickly so that we can freeze your joint assets."

Kendall's lips were so dry now she could barely find the saliva required to swallow. She hadn't even let herself think about money or who would get what. She just didn't want Calvin selling the house out from under her. And she really didn't want to have to tell Melissa and Jeffrey.

"I don't know if the friends who referred you mentioned it or not, but I subscribe to the Green Giant School of Divorce."

Kendall looked up into the bright blue eyes, certain she must have misunderstood. "Green Giant?" she asked. "As in the packaged vegetables?"

Anne Justiss smiled, but there was no humor in it. "There's an old joke that asks, 'What do you have when you've got one large green ball in one hand and a second green ball in the other?' "

Kendall shook her head, thrown by the insertion of veggies into the conversation.

"Complete control of the Jolly Green Giant!" The attorney's bark of laughter was disconcerting, as was the glint in her eyes. Her features hardened. "That's my goal: to get your husband by the balls."

Kendall told herself that this was good. She'd come here because she needed someone strong and unafraid—someone who could squeeze on her behalf—and it appeared she'd found her. Now was not the time to turn squeamish or question Anne Justiss's taste in jokes. Calvin should be glad she was hiring Anne Justiss to squeeze his financial balls and not Lorena Bobbitt to remove them.

20

Kendall stewed all the way back from Atlanta. She shook her head when Mallory slowed in front of the Home Depot and waited in the car while Mallory ran into the grocery store for more wine. At the moment neither wine nor her tool belt offered the least bit of comfort.

As they wound their way up the mountain road, she kept her gaze glued outside the window, trying to still her panic and wishing she could throw it over the side of the cliff or hide it behind a curtain of Kudzu. By the time they reached the house she was slightly calmer but no clearer.

Mallory turned off the motor and they sat in the car on the gravel drive. Only the whistle of the wind through the branches of the trees broke the silence.

"I know this is really hard," Mallory said.

"I keep thinking I'm feeling better," Kendall said. "And then something reminds me that everything's come apart and it's not going back together again."

"It'll go back together," Mallory said. "It just might fit together in a different way."

Kendall's gaze was still riveted out the windshield. The quiet, normally so reassuring, clamored with her own fear and uncertainty.

"It's like when you move to a new place and at first every-thing seems so alien—the stores around it, turning into the neighborhood, where the windows in the bedroom are," Mallory continued in her most soothing tone. "And then all the sudden one day it's the most natural thing in the world; the mind just makes that adjustment and it becomes home."

"Well, I haven't moved in twenty years," Kendall said, absolutely hating the whiny note in her own voice, but un-able to stop it. "And I haven't dealt with any men besides Calvin. I can't imagine how I'm going to do any of that."

"I know. But you will. We can do all kinds of things we can't imagine when we have to." Mallory turned to Kendall, her eyes both certain and unbearably weary. "That's when we find out who we really are. Or who we want to be."

They sat a little longer, both of them staring out the wind-shield as the afternoon sun began to slip in the sky. One day she'd have to ask Mallory how she'd learned all of this, but right now it took every ounce of energy to contemplate her own reality.

"So how do I start?" Kendall asked.

"We get out of the car. We go inside and pour ourselves a glass of wine." Mallory looked Kendall in the eye. "And then we spend exactly one hour free writing any scene we choose for our characters. No plotting, no editing, no deleting, no conscious thinking.

"Just get it all out, Kendall. Kill Calvin, maim him, give him a lisp. It doesn't matter. Just write. No one will see it but you. Tomorrow morning we'll both get up bright and early and see what gems exist and throw the rest away."

"An hour, huh?"

"We can set a timer, if you want. And we won't write a second more. Even if we want to."

OK, Kendall thought. An hour was a manicure and pedi-cure. A shower and a blow dry. A trip through the grocery store including checkout. She could vomit her feelings onto paper for an hour. She'd worry about what came next tomorrow.

And that's exactly what they did. Sitting side by side on the deck, their laptops perched on the table in front of them, the bottle of wine at the ready. Each of them turning off the internal censor and putting whatever came to mind down on the page.

. . .

Over the next few days Kendall and Mallory fell into a pattern. They got up in the morning, nodded at each other over the coffeepot, then headed to their respective spots—Mallory out on the deck and Kendall at the kitchen table with its view of the woods and the bird feeders.

To Mallory's knowledge, Kendall hadn't actually started the first chapter yet, but she seemed to be putting ideas down on paper, working on scenes and character sketches. The words continued to flow for Mallory—as long as she was working on notes and ideas for Kendall's book. The same was not true for her own manuscript, which came out in the barest of trickles no matter how long or how hard she tried.

E-mails from Tanya and Faye promised in-depth character sketches by Saturday morning. The parameters they'd set had left a lot to each writer's discretion, and Mallory could hardly wait to see what they sent; she hadn't felt this eager about anything in years.

Most days she and Kendall broke for lunch around one, making sandwiches or heating up leftovers while they sounded out ideas. Then Mallory worked for another hour or so on *Safe Haven*—trying mightily to turn the trickle into something closer to a torrent—while Kendall puttered around the house or strapped on her tool belt to tackle some kind of project.

Then they'd head out for a hike or drive into Franklin or Highlands or some other quaint town with a tiny square and a stretch of dust-filled antique stores.

The hour before dinner was spent napping or reading. In the evenings they watched an old movie together in the living room or retreated to their own rooms. In this way one day began to blend into the next in a soothing rhythm that both of them came to rely upon.

On the negative side, it was Friday and Chris still hadn't answered any of Mallory's e-mails and Mallory hadn't answered any of Patricia's or Zoe's. Mallory knew she couldn't duck dealing with either situation any longer.

She waited until Kendall left to drive into town for some household supplies and went out on the deck to place her calls.

"Mallory?" Patricia Gilmore's voice indicated both surprise and relief. "Where on earth have you been? I've never known you to disappear like—"

"I'm in the mountains," she said. "Visiting a, um, sick friend." She sent a silent apology to Kendall, though in truth she didn't think it a complete lie. "Cell phone reception is spotty—I'm leaning out over a balcony right now, risking falling down a cliff to reach you."

"Well, be careful," her agent replied. "I wouldn't want to have to tell Zoe she'd lost you to the wilderness."

The mention of her editor was not a coincidence, Mallory knew. She had no doubt Patricia had already heard from Zoe about Mallory's lack of responsiveness.

"No, we wouldn't want that," she said.

"So, I don't know if you've had a chance to check your e-mail or not," Patricia said delicately. "But Zoe wants to bring out *All That Glitters* ahead of schedule to capitalize on the buzz on *Hidden Assets,* which means they'd need *Safe Haven* completed ahead of deadline.

"*People* magazine called *Hidden Assets* a 'must read' and ran a photo of Paris Hilton carrying a copy to the beach last weekend."

"I didn't realize Paris Hilton knew how to read," Mallory replied.

"Well I suppose she has to do something when she's not shopping. Maybe she has someone on staff who reads it to her." Patricia's tone was droll. "I don't care if she never cracks the spine; the photo alone has sent *Hidden Assets* back to print and as you know the first print run was substantial. Universal Studios is inquiring about movie rights."

Mallory stared out over the deck railing, enjoying the feel of the breeze stirring her hair. The afternoon sun shone through the leaves and cast a sway of shadows on the deck.

It took her a moment to realize that she felt next to nothing about the whole Paris Hilton thing. Kendall's book and career felt much more pressing and immediate; so did the alarmingly absent Chris.

She'd always been afraid to say no to a request or suggestion from her publisher. Always at the back of her mind was the fear of being penniless again, without the simplest of resources. This fear had done great things for her. It had driven her to harness her talent, to maximize her opportunities, to put out two books a year for the last eight years. It had kept her writing even when she didn't feel like it, when she felt she had nothing left to say.

But now the fear had begun to strangle rather than motivate. It had always compelled her to write rather than question. But now she asked herself the questions she'd shied away from: What would happen if her next book came out a little later, after she helped Kendall finish her book and then took a much-deserved break? Would that really mean the end of her career? Would her backlist suddenly disappear? Would her fans desert her?

The fear said, "Yes, don't take the chance; you'll be sorry." But she was so damned tired of the pressure and sick to death of the fear.

"That's great, Patricia." Even Mallory could hear the lack of enthusiasm in her voice. "About the movie thing."

She paused when she realized what she was about to say, shocked at the words that she didn't think she could hold back. "But I need a break. I can't write *Safe Haven* any faster. In fact"—she told herself that once the words were out she wouldn't be able to retract them, but even that didn't stop her—"I'd like my deadline extended." She drew in a breath, let it out. "I need some time off."

There was a shocked silence.

"But you've never asked for an extension before. And now's the time to jump on the—"

"Patricia," Mallory said, still trying to process what she'd just said, trying to stay calm. "It's always the time to jump on something. I just can't do it right now. I think after all the books I've sold for Partridge and Portman I have the right to take a break. Don't you?"

There was a prolonged silence, which Mallory decided to interpret as agreement. After all, she reminded herself, Patricia Gilmore had gotten wealthy off her and did, in fact, work for her, though it was easy in all the craziness to forget it. "I appreciate your support," Mallory said, eager now to end the conversation. "I trust you'll call Zoe and let her know."

Mallory hung up the phone and stared out over the deck. Relief didn't exactly flood through her, but God, she hoped she'd done the right thing. Without thinking it through she dialed Chris's cell phone, wanting to share her news with him.

The phone rang so many times that she was ready to hang up. When he came on the line, his voice carried none of its usual warmth and enthusiasm and she realized he must have been debating whether or not to answer. "Hello, Mallory," he said.

That was it. Not once in the twelve years they'd been married or the year for which they'd dated had Chris ever offered so little of himself to her.

"Hi." Mallory cast about for what to say but it was almost as difficult as filling a blank page had become. "How was your weekend? Did you go up to the beach house?"

"Nope."

"So you stayed in the city?"

"Yep."

She felt a horrible stab of guilt as she pictured him alone

in New York, when everyone who could would have fled the city for the final hurrah of summer. She felt even worse when she thought about how she'd spent the weekend. True, most of her time had been spent working, focusing on Kendall, but she'd been surrounded by people who cared about her. Chris had been alone.

His silence reached out to engulf her but it was far from the companionable silence they normally shared. She felt an urgent need to fill it, to keep him on the line. "I just spoke to Patricia and I've asked for an extension. I'm going to take a break."

"Really?" His interest level rose a notch. "That's great. Does that mean you're coming home?"

Too late, she realized she should have prefaced her announcement with an explanation. Worse was the realization that her decision had had almost nothing to do with Chris and almost everything to do with Kendall and her own need to write Miranda's story.

"Of course," she hedged, trying to think how she could present this to minimize the damage. "I'm, uh, just going to stay here a little longer. Until I feel like Kendall's OK and on track."

Silence again.

"So you took time off to be with her, to help her." It wasn't a question.

"Yes," Mallory admitted. "But that wasn't the only reason. I've been having a problem with . . ." She gathered steam as she finally found herself dying to tell him about her inability to write and how badly it had frightened her, but Chris was still following his own train of thought.

"You haven't taken a break for the thirteen years I've known you. No time off. No anything. But now that your friend needs help, it's not a problem to take that break. How do you think that makes me feel?" The pain in his voice was palpable.

"But it's not like that, Chris. It's just that I needed . . ."

For the first time since she'd met him, Chris simply wasn't

interested in what she needed. His love and automatic concern, both of which she now realized she'd always taken completely for granted, were completely absent.

"You . . . Kendall . . . your publisher . . . everyone but me, that's what matters to you."

"No," she said. "That's not . . ."

"I never really noticed it before; I guess I never wanted to notice it. I loved you so much and was so—honored—to be supporting your creative process that I just kind of tuned out how one-sided everything was."

She noted his use of the past tense and hastened to counter it. "It's not one-sided, Chris. I love—"

"I can't really have this relationship all by myself, Mallory," he continued, as if she hadn't spoken. He spoke so quietly she had to strain to hear him. "If I wanted to be alone and rely on myself for everything, I would have stayed single."

"No, you're not alone. I . . ." Mallory heard the pleading note in her voice, but Chris seemed oblivious to it.

"I don't know, Mal. You're there, I'm here. It feels pretty alone to me."

And then he hung up the phone on her for the second time, leaving her alone on Kendall's mountaintop with nothing but the breeze and the distant tree-topped peaks for company.

21

*The last thing one knows in constructing
a work is what to put first.*
—BLAISE PASCAL

"Mallory, have you seen my tool belt and my *One-Two-Three* book?" Even from downstairs, where she'd just printed out the detailed notes and character studies Faye and Tanya had e-mailed, Mallory could hear a note that sounded perilously close to hysteria in Kendall's voice.

Mallory gathered the pages and added them to her own then went upstairs, where she found Kendall digging through the kitchen drawers and shelves.

"I can't seem to find my tools or my how to book." She stopped pawing through her possessions to look anxiously at Mallory. "Have you seen them?"

Mallory set the pages down on the kitchen table and studied her friend. Kendall's eyes darted about furtively as she frantically cast about for another place to look.

"Yes," Mallory replied.

"Oh, thank goodness." Kendall closed the drawers and cupboard doors she'd left hanging open and moved toward Mallory. "Where are they?"

"I, um, put them away."

"Away?" Kendall asked, her brow furrowing.

"Yes. You know, as in . . . somewhere else. Where they won't distract you from your writing."

Kendall's eyes narrowed. She looked less frantic, but more incredulous. "You *hid* my things?"

"It's for your own good, Kendall. I—"

"Go get them." There was a tic in Kendall's cheek; a glint of combat stole into her eyes.

"I will," Mallory promised. "Just as soon as you've written the first five pages of *Sticks and Stones.*"

"You're holding my tools hostage?"

"Kendall, it's Saturday morning," Mallory said reasonably. "Faye, Tanya, and I have delivered everything you need to get started." She picked up the pages from the table and holding onto one corner, rifled through them to demonstrate their completeness. "Much as I'd like to, I can't stay indefinitely and I'm not leaving until I know you've got at least the first chapter or two under your belt."

"You don't think I can control my urge to . . . remodel?"

The answer, of course, was no, but Mallory suspected that might sound a bit abrupt, even from her. "I think you have a severe fix-it fixation that you're using in order to put off starting this book. And believe me, I know all about procrastination."

Kendall folded her arms across her chest. Her eyes, with their combative glint, got even narrower.

"I'm looking at this as a form of incentive," Mallory explained, "a carrot if you will. You write the first five pages. I give you your tools and book and you can spend the rest of the day hammering your little heart out."

"You're kidding."

"We have a conference call tomorrow with Faye and Tanya to discuss the second and third chapters so that they can start their scenes, but this first chapter is all yours."

Kendall continued the flinty-eyed stare thing; Mallory soldiered on. "I figure we do this for the next few days until you've made a good, strong start, and I know you're comfortable with how we're all going to interface and where you're going with the story."

Kendall uncrossed her arms, but she didn't surrender. "This is ridiculous."

"No," Mallory said, equally determined. "This is tough love."

"Tough love!" Kendall snorted. "Like I'm some sort of addict or something."

Mallory raised an eyebrow, but she didn't back down. "Well, I'm not aware of any halfway houses or twelve-step programs for rabid remodelers, but if the shoe fits. . . ."

Kendall turned her back on Mallory and huffed over to the coffeemaker, where she poured another cup of coffee. "You can't just snap your fingers and expect me to write something brilliant."

It appeared arguing was also preferable to writing, but then Mallory knew all about that, too.

"It doesn't have to be brilliant, Kendall," she said, when her friend finally turned around to face her. "Not yet, anyway. That's what polishing is for. You just have to get it down on paper so we can all move forward." She met Kendall's glare. "I'm going to have to go by the end of the week."

Kendall's features shifted from belligerent to stricken.

"I promise I won't leave until you're ready," Mallory hastened to reassure her. "I'm completely committed to your project. In fact, I've asked for an extension on my deadline so I can focus on it. But I have to get back to New York." She looked away, not wanting Kendall to see the panic in her own eyes. "Chris is kind of upset about how long I've been gone."

"Oh, Mal. I'm sorry." A lot of the fight went out of Kendall. "I didn't realize. . . ."

"I'm sure it'll all be fine. And I'm really into *Sticks and Stones*. I think it's a winner, Kendall. But I'm going to have to get back and I don't want to leave you until I know you're back on track."

Kendall cast a last longing look over Mallory's shoulder toward the hall closet where her tool belt normally resided.

Mallory shook her head. "Don't bother. You could spend

the rest of the morning looking and still not find it." Sensing Kendall's capitulation, she smiled and took her friend by the shoulders to lead her to the kitchen table. Gently she pulled out a chair and pressed Kendall into it. "Or you could sit right here and get to work and be finished with your pages in a couple of hours. What do you say to that?"

There were a lot of things Kendall could have said to that, none of them civil, Kendall thought as she settled into her seat ready to grumble some more. *Or suitably grateful.*

The thought filled her head, cutting off the complaint before it left her lips.

Mallory had left her husband and her own work to come rescue her. She'd already been here for ten days, she'd gotten Faye and Tanya to come, too, had set up the brainstorming, had forced Kendall to see a lawyer. If it weren't for Mallory, she'd still be curled up in a fetal position in her bed or sitting like a zombie on the deck. Or, possibly, gutting and remodeling this house with no hope of ever making her deadline.

"OK," she said, not wanting to appear to give in too easily. "You win. You want five pages, you get five pages. But there's every chance they're going to suck."

"I'll take my chances." Mallory gave her shoulders a final squeeze and took her coffee and laptop out onto the deck, where Kendall saw her settle into her favored position.

For a time Kendall just sat. Her mind swirled with too many thoughts to put into any recognizable order: the blue jay on the far branch; the sun streaming through the morning fog to reflect off Mallory's hair; Anne Justiss and the Green Giant's balls, Calvin and his Realtor, the kids, Plain Jane, Lacy Samuels.

"Enough." Kendall pushed all of these fragments of worry from her brain. She actually spent some time visualizing them leaving, wiping out one image at a time until she reached a blank slate on which she could write.

They had discussed where the story should begin when they were together. It was the most critical choice an author made. Start too soon with too much backstory and you could lose the reader. Start too late without any backstory at all and you ran the same risk. The writer had to pull the reader in with the first sentence and then hang on for dear life.

Kendall had spent the week laying out her character, Kennedy Andrews, in her mind and on paper. Kennedy had a cheating husband, a close circle of writer friends, twins who'd just left for college, and a career that was crumbling, unexpectedly, around her. She had come as close to her own reality as she possibly could without having to label this an autobiography.

To make Kennedy the primary point-of-view character, Kendall would have to set her up, get into her head, and stay there long enough to give the reader a chance to identify with her. Faye, Tanya, and Mallory's characters would also appear in the first chapter, but it was Kennedy who would have to draw the reader in, Kennedy's eyes that she'd have to make sure the reader could see through.

Kendall sighed. It was generally accepted that to grab the reader right away, it was important to begin just before the moment of change. For Kendall this had happened at the WINC conference the night she failed to win the Zelda Award on which she'd pinned all her hopes. But she couldn't start at the awards ceremony because the reader wouldn't understand who Kennedy was and why the award was so important. This meant backing up to Friday night when she was worried but still hopeful.

Kendall lifted her fingers above the keyboard but was afraid to hit the first key. There was nothing more important than the first line. Nothing.

Quickly, before she could chicken out, she typed a sentence, read it on screen, then backspaced it into oblivion.

Her stomach churned with anxiety. What if she couldn't do this? What if she couldn't even come up with a first line worthy of the story? What if . . .

No!

She tried again, typing more tentatively, but when she read the words they were too self-conscious. The next were too clever, not at all capturing how she'd felt or who she'd been. Things had not been good, but there had still been that glimmer of hope.

"Just write it," she whispered to herself. "Stop being such a wuss and just write how it felt."

Kendall drew a deep breath and with her gaze fixed to the screen, she began to type. She watched the words appear, letter by letter, as if by their own volition.

"Kennedy Andrews's writing career was about to go down for the count on that Friday night in July as she hurried down Sixth Avenue toward the New York Hilton."

Yes, she thought. *Yes.* Enough to grab on and draw someone in without giving everything away. And the boxing analogy felt right. Kendall typed on, playing with the imagery. As she typed she saw herself at the New York Hilton waiting at the lounge entrance, saw Mallory moving toward her, saw her friends waiting to toast her.

And then she stopped seeing and began feeling as her fingers moved with growing assurance over the keyboard.

22

The most essential gift for a good writer
is a built-in, shock-proof shit detector.
—ERNEST HEMINGWAY

"Good God, Trudy, why is it that you can act like a responsible adult when you're dealing with Brett and as soon as I'm back, you turn into a damned pain in the ass?" Tanya's disappointment pressed down like a load of concrete, infusing her words with a bitterness she normally kept in check. She felt stupid, too, because despite a lifetime of evidence to the contrary, she'd actually allowed herself to hope that her mother might actually be changing.

Trudy just looked at her, though Tanya wasn't sure how much she could see through the bloodshot eyes she peered through.

"He expects me to," she slurred. "You know me better."

"Well, I wish to hell I didn't," Tanya muttered as she dumped the empty whiskey bottle into the trash can and shoved the other garbage over the top of it. "Why don't you go on to bed?"

It was 1:00 A.M. and the girls were asleep. Tanya had been making notes on her laptop, having just finished reading Kendall's first chapter, when Trudy staggered out of her bedroom with the empty bottle in her hand, looking for more. The chapter was good, damned good, and Tanya had jotted down some thoughts for the conference call Mallory had scheduled for the four of them.

"I can't sleep," Trudy whined.

"You know that alcohol is a stimulant, Mama. Drinking it before you go to bed is a bad idea." She glared at her mother as she went back to the kitchen table to shut down her computer then tidied up her notes and files and put them where she could grab them to take with her in the morning. "Oh, wait. Seems to me I've mentioned that before. Though I have lost count of how many millions of times we've had this exact same discussion."

"You don't know shit." Trudy sat in a heap on the couch, her chin on her chest while Tanya bustled all around her. "You just don't know."

"Oh, Mama." Tanya groaned. "I've been watching you do this to yourself my whole entire life. Thirty-five years of watching you destroy yourself. You've got to be as tired of it as I am."

"I am tired. But I can't sleep."

Tanya sighed and rubbed her eyes. If she didn't get in bed right now she'd be a basket case in the morning and Belle had already cut her all kinds of slack.

"Come on. I'll tuck you in." Tanya reached down and slid her hands under Trudy's armpits then lifted her up from the couch like she'd done a thousand times before. There wasn't a lick of meat on her mother's bones.

"No point. Can't sleep," Trudy observed, though she didn't resist.

"Well then, you'll just lie there and rest your eyes." Tanya propelled her toward the back of the mobile home, though propel was maybe the wrong word; it was sort of like herding a wet dishrag.

In Trudy's bedroom, Tanya pulled back the ancient comforter and smoothed the rumpled sheets. She plumped her mother's pillows then helped Trudy down into a sitting position.

"You don't want to let Brett get away. He's a good man," Trudy said as Tanya tucked her under the covers.

"Oh, Mama. How would you know that?"

"Just 'cause I ain't ever had one don't mean I don't recognize one when I see him. I ain't never had a million dollars either, but I'd recognize all them zeros if I came acrost 'em."

Tanya pulled the covers up to Trudy's chin and turned off her bedside light. Despite her protests, Trudy's breathing was already turning shallow and even. "I been wrong a lot, Tanya, I admit it," she said.

Tanya snorted at the understatement.

"But I'm right about him. You be careful you don't run so fast that he can't catch you."

"Oh, Mama." Despite all the heartaches and disappointments that were part and parcel of being Trudy's daughter, Tanya still felt a wallop of love when she looked down at the battered shell of her mother. By most standards Trudy had failed miserably as a parent, but she'd done far better by Tanya than her own mother had done by her. Trudy might have sidestepped much of her parental responsibility, but she'd never abandoned her daughter. Mess that she was, in her own way she'd soldiered on.

"I don't have the time or energy for running. Or for playing any other games for that matter." Another understatement, Tanya thought. She was weary deep down into her bones. In just a few hours she'd have to jump on the treadmill that was her life and start up all over again.

Trudy's eyelids fluttered shut and she began to breathe noisily through her mouth.

"I'm right in the middle of my very own reality edition of *Survivor*, Mama," Tanya said as she tiptoed out of the room, "and I can't figure out how in the hell to get myself voted off."

• • •

Faye spent the morning making notes for the upcoming conference call with Kendall, Mallory, and Tanya, then finished a chapter of her own work in progress and roughed out the first scene of the next chapter before breaking when Sara dropped off Becky for the afternoon, fresh from kindergarten.

For a treat, they strolled hand in hand along Central Avenue, the tree-lined two-lane main street of Highland Park, walking west, away from the lake toward the shops and restaurants, while Rebecca explained her plans for famous ballerinadom.

Promising Rebecca an ice cream from the Dairy Queen for the walk home, Faye paused outside the Borders bookstore and noticed a window display of Mallory St. James's latest hardcover, *Hidden Assets*. "My friend wrote that book," she said to Rebecca. "She's gotten really famous."

"Cool!" Rebecca peered through the window. Her head turned slightly toward a display of historical romances by another author Faye had met at conferences.

Rebecca scrunched up her nose in concentration as she sounded out the words on the cover. "*One Night with You.*" She looked up at Faye, her brown eyes wide. "Is that one of those porn-io-graph-ic books my mommy tole me about?"

Faye squeezed Rebecca's hand and knelt down so that she could look straight into Rebecca's eyes. "No, of course not."

"But that lady has her lips poked out to kiss that man." She pointed at the cover, her finger unswerving. "And his chest doesn't have any clothes on it."

This was true, Faye thought as she searched for the right words of explanation. In her mind, a clinch cover did not pornography make.

"It's a book about a man and a woman who fall in love and try to live happily ever after," she said. "There's nothing wrong with that." She continued to look into Rebecca's eyes, not wanting to undermine her daughter's authority, but once again disappointed by and irritated with her daughter's narrowmindedness. She and Steve had gone out of their way to try to instill empathy and open generosity of thought in their offspring, yet with each year, Sara aligned herself more and more with the ultraconservative faction of Steve's congregation. She seemed to spend much of her time in judgment of others.

"Let's go in and pick out some books. Then we'll see how Gran Gran's new release is selling."

Inside they went to the children's section where Rebecca immediately found two Junie B. Jones books, one she couldn't live without and one for the children's library at Rainbow House. On their way to the religious fiction section, where Faye's inspirational romances were shelved, they passed a table display of books by the now notorious erotica author Shannon LeSade. Faye clutched Rebecca's hand more tightly in her own, intending to simply speed past it, but Becky must have felt the urgency in Faye's grasp. She stopped right in front of the display and began to gawk.

"I bet *that's* porn-i-ography," the child said, with absolute certainty. "What are they doing on that cover?" She moved closer, practically sticking her face into a stack of books.

Faye pulled her away. "That's not exactly porniog . . . pornography," Faye said, at a loss as to how to continue. She didn't particularly want to add the word "erotica" to her granddaughter's vocabulary. Sure as she did, it would be the first word Becky shared with her mother when she got home. "But it is for adults, not children."

"Why?"

"Because it's too . . . grown up for kids." This she knew for a fact.

"Why?" Rebecca's trusting brown eyes stared up at her waiting for an explanation from the one person who up until now had always told it like it was.

"Because it is!" Despite attempts to stop it, Faye could feel her face flushing. She knew she was handling this badly. Overreacting would impress the book even more strongly in Becky's mind, but she couldn't seem to help it.

She was tugging on Becky's hand in an effort to move her away from the display when the store's customer relations manager, Judy Winslet, approached, an enthusiastic smile on her face.

"Mrs. Truett!" The manager stopped next to them. "We've been hoping you'd stop by to sign some stock." Her gaze moved from Faye and Becky to the table display in front of them. "It's amazing how big LeSade's gotten," she said. "Erotica's so hot right now—pun intended—but I think part of it's how reclusive she is. Have you ever met her?"

Faye cleared her throat and shook her head no. She was growing increasingly uncomfortable with their proximity to the display and to their conversation. She could practically see Becky's ears growing larger, the better to suck in their conversation for repetition later.

"I heard her publisher is getting ready for a big publicity push. Maybe that will bring her out of hiding."

Faye could have told her exactly why this was not going to happen, but since she wanted only for this conversation to end, she didn't say so. Instead she widened her eyes and tried to use them to motion toward Becky in warning, apparently a much too subtle form of communication for the woman.

"Maybe not though," the young woman chirped, now not only asking questions, but answering them. "They say her agent doesn't even know her real identity."

Faye took a firmer hold of Rebecca's hand, intent now on changing the topic of conversation as well as their location. "Judy," Faye said, "this is my granddaughter Rebecca. I was just explaining to her that these books are only for adults." She shot the manager a final look of warning then turned her back on the display and began to move toward the religious fiction section, pulling Becky with her. Judy followed.

"Becky's five and she loves Junie B. Jones." Faye was the one chattering on now as she led her granddaughter by the hand and the manager with her voice.

"I'm getting two of them," Rebecca chimed in, mercifully distracted. "One for me and one for Rainbow House."

"Junie B. is very cool," Judy said to Rebecca. "And so is your grandmother."

They came to a halt at the information desk. "In fact," she said, "if you all wait here, I'll go get the copies of *In His Image* off the shelf so you can autograph them."

She and Becky waited for the manager to return.

"How's it doing?" Faye asked, when Judy returned with a stack of books balanced against her chest.

"Great. We have two book clubs reading it and a third has expressed interest. One of them wanted to know if you'd be willing to come speak to their group." Judy stacked the books on the counter in front of Faye and pulled out a Sharpie and autograph stickers.

Faye felt a flush of satisfaction as she handled the books, carefully signing her name and a personalized message on the front title page of each book then handing it to Judy who put an autograph sticker on each cover.

Having booksellers excited about your work was critical. In the end a book purchase often came down to a salesperson's recommendation. Some store personnel loved books and were excited about having personal contact with the authors who wrote them, and would then go to great lengths to hand sell an author they knew and liked.

Others had no interest in knowing or meeting you. Faye had once had a bookseller disdainfully refer to her mass-market paperback as one of those "little books."

From early on Mallory was sent on multicity tours where crowds of readers queued up to buy her books. Faye's first few book signings had generated much less fanfare and had consisted of her alone at a folding card table in the back of a bookstore. Selling books in this situation required either attracting the buyers to the store or somehow convincing someone already browsing to buy a copy, which left an author feeling like a Girl Scout hawking cookies in front of a grocery store.

All too often the only thing an approaching customer wanted was directions to the restroom.

Fortunately Faye was no longer unknown and this bookstore was on her home turf. As she signed the books a small knot of customers wandered closer, turning the stock signing into an impromptu event. Faye smiled encouragingly at them. She might not do the numbers or generate the same level of excitement as Mallory, but she knew how important one-on-one contact could be.

"I loved *In His Name,*" one woman said. "I can't wait to read this. Can you make that out to me? And I think I'll take one for my sister, Claire, too."

Faye finished signing and then stayed to chat with the

women now vying for her attention. When she felt Becky growing restless, Faye offered her good-byes and led Becky up to the checkout line to pay for their purchases.

"Wow, you must be famous, too! Will you just keep getting famouser and famouser?"

Faye smiled at her granddaughter's enthusiasm. "I'm nowhere near as famous as my friend Mallory," she said, as she handed her credit card to the clerk. "But I'm famous enough for me."

They stopped at the Dairy Queen as promised then walked toward home, Rebecca greedily licking her ice cream cone while Faye reflected on the pros and cons of both fame and notoriety. At Central Park, opposite the house and overlooking the lake, Becky played happily on the equipment while Faye watched from a shaded spot on a nearby bench, her mood still reflective.

A certain amount of name recognition was necessary to build a career. But too much exposure could be a dangerous thing. Especially if you were married to a prominent televangelist who had no idea his wife was the notorious Shannon LeSade.

. . .

Lacy was beginning to feel like a mailman. Despite the fact that Scarsdale had interoffice mail and many other mechanisms for communicating with and sending things to others in the building, Jane Jensen, who would probably be using the Pony Express if it still existed, appeared to believe that everything, really, every little thing, would be better delivered and/or communicated by her lowly assistant.

Actually, compared to the mindless errands that took her out of the building—to Jane's dry cleaner, the corner newsstand, the nearest Starbucks, the not-so-nearby theater box office to pick up Jane's tickets—the time she spent going floor to floor and department to department on Jane's behalf had become the best parts of Lacy's day.

She took her time as she made her deliveries and pickups and as a result got to know people throughout the publishing house that she might not have otherwise met. Happily, almost all of them were more pleasant and accommodating than Lacy's own whacked-out boss.

Lacy especially liked editor Hannah Sutcliff, whose office was located as far as one could get from Jane Jensen's office, without leaving the editorial floor. Although it was about half the size of Jane's, it had a small reading nook anchored by a brightly patterned wool rug and a chenille-covered love seat. Framed posters for several of Hannah's authors' works filled one wall. Family photos dotted her desktop. A vase of fresh-cut flowers sat on a small end table next to the love seat.

"Hi, Lacy." Despite her seniority, Hannah always made a point of being friendly and seemed to consider their punishment at Jane Jensen's hands as a common bond. "You ready for more reading material?"

Unlike Jane, Hannah encouraged Lacy's interest in the editorial process and had allowed Lacy to read several recently purchased manuscripts and then taken the time to explain her acquisition criteria. Today she handed Lacy a sealed packet for Jane and a copy of a partial she'd received. "I thought you might like to read this and tell me why I won't be requesting the full manuscript. Sometimes knowing why someone doesn't buy is more important than knowing why they do."

"Thanks." Wishing for about the thousandth time that she'd been assigned to Hannah rather than Jane, Lacy moved on, taking the elevator up to the art department where she found the art director, Simon Rothwell, dealing, rather badly, with his recent nicotine withdrawal.

"Hi, love," he said, in his lilting British accent. "You don't happen to have a smoke with you, do you? Not that I'd smoke it, of course. I'd just like to smell it. Or maybe I could hold it between my fingers and caress it for a while?"

Lacy took the manila envelope he handed her with a slightly shaky hand. She eyed him fondly, glad she'd come prepared. "There will be no caressing of cigarettes, Simon; it's way too dangerous. But I did bring you something that might help."

From her jacket pockets Lacy pulled out the miniature candy bars she'd stashed there. With a flourish, she piled them on his drafting table in an impressive mound.

Simon's face lit up. "Bless you, love. Those should see me through the afternoon." He unwrapped the first candy and popped it in his mouth, then smiled in mock ecstasy. "I'm going to weigh ninety kilos before this is done and my dentist will probably kill me. But you, my girl, are a wonderful human being."

His grandiose expressions of gratitude followed her down the hall. In the publicity department she stopped to pick up a copy of an interview that had run in *Library Journal* and an itinerary for an upcoming book tour from Cindy Miller, who'd just been named an assistant to publicity head Naomi Fondren.

"Hi, Cindy, how's it going?" Lacy and Cindy lunched together on occasion and shared in-house gossip whenever the opportunity arose. They chatted while Cindy got the things together for Jane.

"I'm good, just busy," Cindy said. "Lots to do before the sales meeting."

"Any news?" Lacy asked.

"I heard Carol Lloyd in marketing is hot for Cash Simpson."

This was not exactly a news flash. Much time was frittered in the halls of Scarsdale discussing Cash, who was not only the head of the sales department, but the best-looking heterosexual male at Scarsdale, not to mention a former winner of the Gawker's "Hottest Straight Guy of Book Publishing" title.

"I'm headed up to the sales floor next," Lacy said. "I plan to keep a sharp eye out."

"Good luck with that." Cindy giggled. "And if you get anywhere near him, be sure you have a big stick with you so you can fight off all the other women."

As she traversed the sales floor Lacy did in fact keep an eye out for Cash Simpson. Despite the company policy forbidding cross dating and/or mating there were lots of in-house romances currently under way.

Beginning to realize just how long she'd been away from her desk, Lacy headed for the elevator and pushed the down arrow, slightly disappointed that she hadn't had a single Cash sighting. She'd stepped on and was already reaching for the floor button when a male voice called out, "Hold that elevator."

Lacy looked up to see none other than the hunky Cash Simpson covering the carpeted floor in long unhurried strides. His layered blond hair moved with him and he had a stylish-looking five o'clock shadow, even though it was barely 11:00 A.M.

"Thanks." His voice was a baritone saved from complete cockiness by a note of warmth.

"No problem." Lacy held the Door Open button as he stepped onto the elevator and promptly filled it up. Having been compared unfavorably to a string bean, Lacy's height had always been an embarrassment, but next to the NFL-sized Cash, she felt practically petite.

"What floor?" Her voice came out in an embarrassing squeak of longing and attraction.

He gave her a closer look and she thanked God for making her wash and blow-dry her hair that morning. "Ground please."

She pressed the appropriate button then turned her gaze on the numbers, waiting for what felt like an eternity for the doors to close. His cologne was masculine and compelling; his shoulders were as wide as a doorway and triangled down to a trim waist. She wouldn't be a bit surprised if washboard abs lay hidden beneath the cotton oxford shirt. For the first time since beginning at Scarsdale, she was in complete agree-ment with her boss: Cash Simpson was a great-looking guy with charisma oozing from every pore.

When nervous, Lacy felt a compulsion to babble. She fought this off valiantly for several floors, but didn't hold out great hope for making it much longer without humiliating her-self.

"Aren't you going to a floor?" His question, with its underlying hint of amusement, got her attention.

"What?"

"I think you need to choose a floor or you're going to end up on the ground floor with me."

As if this would be a bad thing.

"Oh!" Lacy exclaimed in embarrassment. "Right!" She reached forward and pressed the four for editorial, only realizing after she'd done so that they'd already passed the fourth floor.

He was studying her openly now and with a surprising level of interest. Despite her height, Lacy tended to think of herself as easily overlooked. (Who really looked at a string bean?) But his appreciative gaze made her feel giddily attractive.

"You look familiar, but I don't think we've met," he said as another floor sped by. "I'm Cash Simpson. What department are you in?"

"Editorial." She shoved her hand out toward him like some overly zealous business type. "I'm Lacy Samuels. I'm Jane Jensen's assistant," she said, wishing she had a title that would make her sound more experienced or important. Her hand in his conducted way more electricity than she was used to, and she hurriedly removed it.

"So you're Jane's new slave." He smiled and there was a teasing note of sympathy in his voice.

"That's me." She looked into his eyes, trying to assess his allegiance to her boss. "I've learned a lot from her already," she said carefully. *How to gauge her mood . . . how to duck . . . how to . . .*

"Well, you're still standing," he said. "So I'll take that to mean you come from sturdy stock." The eyes were glittering now and she wondered if he knew Jane had a crush on him.

The elevator's free fall slowed as the numeral two for the second floor lit briefly then went out. Soon he'd be walking off the elevator and she'd barely done more than stammer out her name. Say something, you dolt, she commanded herself;

something that will set you apart and make him remember you.

"I *am* from sturdy stock," she said, as the elevator yanked to a halt on the ground floor. "Good old Russian peasant stock. Why, we'd work the fields until it was time to drop our babies right there, and then get right back to tilling the soil without missing a beat."

His look of surprise was close to comical and inspired her to blunder on. "Of course, we don't do that nearly as often as we used to." She swallowed, suddenly aware of exactly what she'd just said. "Give birth in the fields, I mean."

She barely bit back her groan of embarrassment as the elevator doors slid open, but unexpectedly, miraculously, he threw back his head and laughed, a great unselfconscious guffaw that somehow made him even more attractive.

"I'll remember that, Lacy Samuels," he said as he prepared to step off the elevator. "And I'll tread very carefully the next time we're in a field together."

He was still chuckling when he exited the elevator and strode out into the marbled lobby. Lacy rode the elevator in humiliated silence. All the way back up to the floor from which she'd begun.

23

*You don't write because you want to
say something, you write because
you've got something to say.*
—F. SCOTT FITZGERALD

For Kendall the remainder of the week both flew and dragged. She'd completed the first chapter of *Sticks and Stones* and e-mailed it to the others for their critique and to help set them up for the scenes they would write. Tonight they'd have a conference call to discuss the book in more detail now that everyone's character sketches and backstories were complete—all of them much more intriguing than Kendall had expected.

Chapter two, like chapter one, would be written from her character, Kennedy's, point of view, and would cover the day of the awards ceremony. All Kendall had to do was close her eyes to remember the dread and panic coupled with that tiny ray of hope that had lain like a dead weight in her stomach.

What she needed to do was mine the pain, but it wasn't easy to find the strength required to relive such unpleasantness. The more she thought about it, pictured it, tried to frame the best words to describe it, the more she longed for the feel of a hammer in her hand and the distraction of directions to follow.

Mallory sat outside on the deck checking e-mail and preparing for tonight's conference call, though Kendall couldn't help noticing that this was interspersed with long sessions spent staring out over the valley.

Kendall sat at the kitchen table dreading what she had to write. Normally the personal things that found their way into her work had been processed over time; the pain already deadened to a manageable level. But Kendall was still living this story and she had no distance or perspective to cushion or protect her.

And what would happen when Mallory left tomorrow? Who would make her sit down and work? Who would withhold her tool belt until her page quota had been met? Who would commiserate with her? Who would sit next to her patting her hand ineffectually while she cried?

She calmed herself with a replay of her recent conversation with Calvin, once again taking great pleasure in his bellows of outrage over Anne Justiss's opening salvos.

"What do you think you're doing?" he'd shrieked when she answered the phone. "That woman is a total ball buster!"

"That's ball squeezer," she'd wanted to retort, but she'd kept quiet, enjoying his discomfiture too much to interrupt it. "You told me to hire an attorney, Calvin," she said reasonably, knowing this would irk him even more. "You didn't really expect me to hire someone your attorney could walk all over, did you?"

He'd sputtered and raved for a while afterward, but Kendall knew that was exactly what he'd expected. He'd believed she'd simply step back and expedite what he wanted, like she'd always done, but as he ranted incoherently Kendall had vowed that her doormat days were over.

"I've invited the kids up here for the weekend," she said, once he'd sputtered to a halt. "And I'm not planning to say anything about . . . us . . . until more of the details are worked out. I don't see any reason to jeopardize their finals or ruin the holidays for them."

There was more cursing, but she realized that while she still disliked the language, it no longer had the power to move her. And neither did Calvin.

"If you want to tell them you can go ahead," she said. "And while you're at it, maybe you should explain Laura and her plans for the only home they've ever known."

This suggestion was greeted with a stony silence, as she'd known it would be. Calvin would expend considerable energy trying to push her to do the dirty work, but he didn't have the courage to do it himself. Especially if it would make him look bad.

"You might want to get the house picked up in case either of them wants to come home. Or maybe you can talk Laura into doing it." She realized with some surprise that she was beginning to enjoy herself. Not caring what Calvin thought was wonderfully freeing. "If they come home and see that mess, they'll know something's wrong."

"And you don't think the fact that we're living in two different places might clue them in to that?" he'd sneered.

"Suspecting and knowing are two different things," she said, with a certainty born of experience. "I mean, look what it took for me to accept the truth about you."

• • •

That night Kendall and Mallory sat at the kitchen table, each with a phone pressed to her ear, their notes spread out in front of them as Mallory punched in Faye's and Tanya's phone numbers. Within minutes the conference call was ready to begin.

"Are we all on the line?" Mallory glanced over to Kendall, who nodded.

"I think we're all here," Kendall said. "Can everybody hear all right?"

Tanya and Faye answered in the affirmative and then everyone started talking at once.

"OK," Kendall said. "Now I really feel like we're all here. But I think we're going to have to speak in some sort of order or figure out the verbal equivalent of raising our hands."

Now no one spoke, each afraid of talking over the other. "All right," Kendall said with a laugh. "Faye, why don't you go first?"

"OK." Faye cleared her throat. "First of all, I want to say how great I think the first chapter is. I know it couldn't have been easy to write, and I think it was dead on. You let everyone know exactly what you were feeling and still managed to set up our characters without detracting from that."

Kendall breathed a small sigh of relief. Even when something felt right, it helped to have validation.

"I agree," said Mallory, not waiting to be called on. She flashed a smile at Kendall.

"Me, too," said Tanya. "Kendall, the first chapter was first rate. But the character sketches? Some of them were plum full of surprises."

"I'd ask you to explain," Mallory said. "But I've never known you to need an invitation for that."

"Well, since you *asked*," Tanya said. "I wasn't all that wild about your character describing mine as a big-haired blonde with a Dogpatch accent who stole clothes from Daisy Duke's closet."

There was laughter.

"I don't know," Faye teased. "I thought it was pretty dead on."

"Oh, yeah?" Tanya retorted. "And what about your character, Faith? A preacher's daughter who rebels and writes super sexy romances in secret? Does that feel dead on, too?"

Faye's voice when it came over the line carried an odd note that Kendall couldn't identify. "Are you saying you don't think that could happen? Or that you don't think I'm capable of writing a sex scene?"

There was a brief pause before Tanya answered. "I think Pastor Steve's flock would be shocked and horrified to discover that you even know what sex is!"

"You're right about that. And I don't intend to ever tell them. But do you actually think that just because I'm married to a religious leader and write inspirational fiction I can't write sensual?"

"Well, not exactly," Tanya backpedaled a bit. "But it does seem like a stretch."

"That tells me you need to be careful not to judge all the books you know by their covers," Faye said, her voice tight.

Tanya laughed. "Next thing you'll be telling me is that the backstory Mallory created for her character, Miranda, shouldn't have surprised me, either."

Across the table Mallory stiffened.

"She has a father who loses the family fortune and then commits suicide? And then, just a few years later, her mother does the same? I couldn't stop bawling."

A look of embarrassment passed over Mallory's face and Kendall figured it had been a long time since anyone had questioned anything Mallory had written. Mallory didn't respond, but Kendall could feel the intensity with which she was following the conversation.

"I was under the impression that since this was fiction and no one is ever going to know who wrote it that everyone could do whatever she chose with her character as long as it worked in the story," Kendall said, eager to defuse the situation. Of all the things she feared at the moment—and there were many—jeopardizing their friendship terrified her most. "I like Faith, and I can't wait to see how Faye handles the sex scenes. And I think Miranda's backstory gives her character the perfect motivation and makes her rise to *New York Times* Bestseller all the more impressive."

Kendall snuck a peek at Mallory, but Mallory was staring out the window, her thoughts seemingly a million miles away.

Faye added another note of conciliation. "That's right. *Sticks and Stones* is going out under Kendall's name. No one's going to be asking themselves why Pastor Steve's wife is writing sex. Or why Mallory St. James would create such a grim background for herself."

Mallory continued to stare out the window.

"And they're not going to ask who the short-order cook in Tanya Mason's life is, either," Kendall added, reaching for their earlier teasing tone. "Or why the big-haired blonde in the Daisy Duke clothing isn't snapping him right up."

"And that's a good thing," Tanya declared, "because that's nobody's damned business. Like I keep trying to tell my mother."

There was a silence in which Kendall felt them all trying to regroup. There had been an undercurrent to the conversation that she didn't understand and that no one seemed inclined to examine too closely.

"When you offered to help me write this book, I had my doubts that we could do this," Kendall said. "I mean, you offered me a lifeline and I grabbed on and I'm not letting go. But now I see what we can create together and it's even bigger than what I'd originally envisioned."

Mallory turned to look at her and Kendall could feel Faye's and Tanya's presence as if they were in the room.

"I love what you all have come up with, *including* the surprises," Kendall said. "Although I don't see why they're such big surprises. We're professional liars, aren't we? It's our job to keep the story interesting. Until we decide to stick the word autobiography on the spine, I say we continue to write what we're writing. No one ever has to know how real or imaginary our characters are."

Then they were talking all at once again, debating, tweaking each other's ideas, arguing good-naturedly. They roughed out the first five chapters, noting whose character's point of view each scene would be written from, agreeing on a timetable for getting the chapters to each other, deciding when they would have their next conference call.

After they'd said their good-byes and hung up, Kendall and Mallory continued to sit at the kitchen table. The sun had slunk down behind the mountains and the remaining daylight was seeping slowly out of the sky.

"I wish I didn't have to leave tomorrow," Mallory said.

"Yeah, me, too." Kendall studied her friend as she gathered her notes and tucked them into her laptop case.

"Will you be OK?"

Kendall gazed out the window thinking about her answer, gently testing her emotional cuts and scrapes, relieved to discover they'd begun to scab over. "I'll be fine," she said. "Not great, you know, but definitely OK."

She would have said this regardless of her true feelings.

Mallory had held her hand long enough and it was time for Mallory to get back to her own life. But Kendall was relieved to realize it was the truth. She was healing, slowly—somewhere near the speed of a glacier—but healing nonetheless.

Mallory nodded. "Good. I was getting tired of kicking your butt anyway."

Kendall smiled. "Well you're even better at it than your characters are. I'll be glad to write you a reference anytime. Maybe I should post something on one of the writer's loops: Mallory St. James is a first-rate butt kicker."

They laughed companionably and Kendall tried not to think about how much she was going to miss Mallory.

"Funny how much easier it is to kick somebody else's rear end," Mallory said, smiling. "I'm counting on you to control your fix-it habit. You just call me whenever the urge to use a hammer gets too strong and I'll talk you out of it."

"Thanks, Mal." Kendall stood and went to the wine rack where she picked out a bottle of red. "In the meantime, what do you say we take this out on the deck and drink to the success of *Sticks and Stones*?"

"I'm with you on that." Mallory took two wine goblets out of the drain board while Kendall scooped up the corkscrew. Together they trooped outside, settled into their favorite seats, propped their feet up on the deck railing, and contemplated the universe.

24

*Beyond talent lie all the usual words: discipline,
love, luck—but, most of all, endurance.*
—JAMES BALDWIN

Fewer than three hours after Mallory left for the airport, Kendall's kids arrived. They came in Melissa's car, she and Jeffrey bounding out almost before it came to a stop. Jeffrey's girlfriend advanced more slowly.

"Mom." Jeffrey beamed after squeezing her mightily. "This is Deeana; Dee for short." The look of adoration in her son's eyes was almost painful to see. He had always been the quieter of the twins, the more reflective. While Melissa had dated her way through high school, Jeffrey had hung with the guys, only asking a girl out when absolutely necessary.

"Hi, Mrs. Aims." Deeana's voice was soft and wispy like the girl herself. She extended her hand and Kendall relaxed a bit, whatever she'd been afraid of, it wasn't this shy young girl who was practically trembling in fear herself and whose glances at her son were equally adoring.

"Hi, Dee," Kendall said. "I'm so glad you could come for the weekend. The kids have been spending time here since before they were born, and I know Jeffrey must be looking forward to showing you around."

And with that they came in and filled up the house with their youth and warmth and laughter, which Kendall, who needed exactly that more than she'd realized, drew in and hugged close.

For the most part Kendall managed to dance around the fact that she was living here and Calvin, well, wasn't. Melissa cornered her in the kitchen on Sunday morning and, as was her way, called her on it. "What's going on between you and Dad?"

Kendall shrugged. Somehow she managed to look her daughter directly in the eye and lie, as she had now and again over the years when she'd felt it was in her child's best interests. "It's just this horrible deadline, sweetie," she said. "I realized the only way to meet it was to lock myself away until I finished." And then a sliver of the truth: "I just couldn't seem to write a word at home; there were too many distractions." Including a blond-haired Realtor determined to take her place.

She was certain that Melissa would report back to her twin and she knew she was right when Jeffrey joined her out on the deck later that afternoon.

"Mom," he'd said tentatively, as they stared out over the valley together. Melissa and Deeana were in the kitchen preparing dinner. "I'm really glad you and Dee are getting on so well. Do you really like her or are you just being polite?"

She looked into her son's eyes, shaped and colored like his father's but brimming with a sincerity and gentleness of spirit that even at their best Calvin's had never possessed, and was grateful no lies were required this time.

"I think she's lovely, sweetheart. I really like her and I'm glad you've found someone you want to be with."

She saw the relief on his face. Oh, God, had she ever been that young? That in love?

"But she's your first real girlfriend. I want you to enjoy it and make the most of it. But don't be too upset if it doesn't turn out to be forever."

"It is though, Mom. I can tell. Just like you must have known when you met Dad."

Kendall was very careful not to react; she didn't even blink. "I hope that whomever you end up with that you'll be even happier than your Dad and I have been." And for longer, she added silently.

They were sitting, once again staring out at the view, when Melissa and Dee came out carrying a tray of cheese and crackers and some other predinner nibbles.

"Did you tell her about Thanksgiving?" Melissa asked her brother as they settled themselves.

Kendall's sense of well-being evaporated. She hadn't yet figured out how to pull off Thanksgiving without either being forced to sit across from Calvin over turkey and stuffing and pretend all was well or tell the truth to her children, who might look like and think of themselves as adults, but who were certain to be shaken by the news.

She was so busy casting in her mind for potential options—could she get Calvin to declare a truce in honor of the holiday? Would he come and pretend there was no Laura? What were the chances she could make it through the first course without plunging the carving knife into his tiny Grinch-like heart?—that she at first missed Jeffrey's stammered statement.

"What?" she asked. "What did you say?"

He looked to Dee for moral support and then repeated himself. "I hope you and Dad won't be upset, but Dee's parents invited me to Savannah for Thanksgiving."

"Oh."

"And I'm planning to go home with Todd," Melissa added. "Will you and Daddy be all right on your own?"

If she had been Catholic she would have been shouting, "Hallelujah!" As it was she was so flush with relief she could barely find her voice. The children interpreted this as disapproval.

"If it's a problem, Mrs. Aims, I'm sure my parents would understand."

"Yeah," Melissa added. "I could go to Todd's over spring break instead."

"Oh, no. No, I won't let you do that." Kendall found her voice and hurried to reassure them before her escape hatch slammed shut. "I have so much work to do it would almost be a relief not to worry about Thanksgiving this year."

"But you will have one, right?" The idea of it not existing, even if they weren't going to be there, seemed to upset both of them. Which reinforced Kendall's decision not to trouble the children with the divorce for as long as possible.

"Don't you worry about a thing," Kendall said. "You go and enjoy yourselves. Your father and I will do exactly as we please on Thanksgiving." This, happily, was completely true. They just wouldn't be doing it together.

Kendall smiled at her children and the lovely Dee and intentionally changed the subject. For now, half-truths and sins of omission seemed the lesser of evils. She only hoped that if her prevarications were ever discovered, Jeffrey and Melissa would understand that she'd had their best interests at heart.

. . .

Mallory returned to New York full of apologies and eager to deliver them, only to find the intended recipient gone and the brownstone empty.

Chris's note, which she found propped against the toaster, was short and to the point; a client had asked him to supervise a project in Phoenix personally, and he had accepted. Perhaps some time apart for reflection would be good for both of them.

Now as Mallory roamed the silent rooms of their home, she saw his hand everywhere: in the gloss of the hardwood floors that he'd refinished himself; in the dark sheen of the dining room wainscoting that he'd rescued from a nearby demolition and artfully installed; in the window seat in her office underneath which he'd carved a bookcase for her favorite oversized tomes. Everything he'd designed and/or installed was both functional and beautiful in a subtle and undemanding way, very much like Chris.

In her study, Mallory dropped onto the velvet-covered window seat and stared out at the walled garden, yet another of Chris's creations. The house settled around her, the silence so profound that she could count the number of cubes disgorged by the automatic ice maker. The muted sounds of traffic from Sixth Avenue were much too distant to include her. Chris's absence carried an accusing silence all its own.

The great irony of course was that the words, and her command of them, which had deserted her so capriciously, had returned. Each time she sat to write Miranda Jameson's part in Kendall's story, they gushed out of her and onto the screen in a steady, eager stream. She had not yet found the courage to go back to her own work in progress, but the fact that she was writing at all was a relief she desperately wanted to share. With Chris.

Moving to the computer, Mallory held her breath while she scrolled through her inbox. There were numerous entries from her agent and her editor, which she could tell from the subject lines she didn't want to open. She also saw updates from Faye, Tanya, and Kendall, which she'd look at shortly. The head of her fan club, her publicist, and her masseuse had all sent her e-mails. But there wasn't a single missive from her husband.

Mallory picked up the phone and debated whether to call him. But she'd already apologized to Chris via voice mail, e-mail, and text message. It didn't look like she was going to get to do it in person.

After another fruitless, pathetic turn through the house, Mallory stopped in the kitchen, where she spent several minutes contemplating the blank stainless-steel face of her refrigerator. A load of ice landed in the bin and she counted four cubes. A new number flashed into the minutes' column on the digital clock above the microwave.

The last time she'd felt this alone had been the day after her high school graduation, the day her mother, who had hated being poor even more than being without Mallory's father, had chosen to follow him into the hereafter.

Somehow she'd clabbered together a series of student loans to get her undergraduate degree at Boston College. Her graduation gift to herself was a new name and a new city.

Her first job in New York had been as a receptionist for a

brokerage firm, which had exposed her to a series of "high-net-worth individuals" who reminded her of her father—none of whom wanted to leave his wife for her, but all of whom helped her enjoy a lifestyle well beyond her means.

A decade and a half out of school she had nothing but a co-op she couldn't afford and a salary that never made it to the end of the month. The clients who'd panted after her began to pant after younger women. The specter of poverty loomed, calling to mind her father's demise and striking fear in her heart.

And how did she deal with it?

She read novels. One book after another, sometimes at the rate of one a day, for a solid year. An acceptable form of escape that didn't leave a hangover. She read every author she could get her hands on who wrote a strong female protagonist who triumphed in the end. Patricia Cornwell, Nora Roberts, Terry McMillan, Sue Grafton, Sandra Brown, Olivia Goldsmith; she read them all and more, haunting the library and the used book stores until the day she realized that what she really wanted to do was *write* a novel. And what set her apart is that she actually did.

She was thirty-six when she started her first manuscript; thirty-seven when she met Chris and finished the book; thirty-eight when they got married.

She'd been almost forty and desperate to make something happen when she attended the WINC conference where she met Faye, Tanya, and Kendall. And during her agent appointment, on the strength of the one book she'd actually written, she somehow landed Patricia Gilmore as her agent. The rest, as they say, was history.

By the time she hit the *New York Times* list she was an obsessive write-aholic afraid to let up lest she lose all that she'd managed to accumulate and be forced to return to the lonely, poor little girl she'd been and hated.

She had created a brand and real wealth, which she was determined to hold on to. Chris had given her his love and support. In many ways he'd built their life with his own two capable hands. And she had been too busy writing, and too afraid to stop, to thank him for it.

"Get out now," she said as she caught herself counting the ticks of the digital clock. "Get out of this house before you end up out in the garden watching the grass grow."

Without further internal debate, Mallory grabbed a windbreaker, her cell phone, and a set of house keys and let herself out of the brownstone. With no destination in mind, she took a left, then a right, deciding to follow the sidewalk wherever it wanted to take her.

. . .

Things were quiet in the Liberty Laundromat that afternoon, for which Tanya was grateful. Her editor at Masque, Darby Hanover, had just called to tell her that her last book had come in first in sales for the month, which Darby saw as a win for her team. Then she told Tanya that she'd put her name up for inclusion in an upcoming anthology with two bigger-name authors. The very possibility made Tanya vibrate with excitement.

A dryer buzzed and she left the front desk to get the clothes and put them in a basket for folding. She was rolling it toward the front desk when the bell above the door jangled. Before she looked, Tanya knew that it was Brett. Apparently despite the amount of time she'd spent trying to stay away from him, she'd developed a sixth sense that tingled whenever he got within range.

Out of pure orneriness, she took her time getting back to the desk, schooling her thoughts and her features as she moved toward him. He didn't need to know that her first response to his presence was a swift kick of excitement. Or that her heart actually sped up whenever he was near.

Her mouth was already open to offer some sort of glib comment when she noticed that he wasn't carrying dirty laundry but copies of her latest Masque release, *The Rookie Gets Revved.*

"Hey," he said, his face creasing in a grin that could only be called shit-eating. "How's it going?"

"Fine," she said, though, in fact, what she felt was off balance. "What's going on?"

"I brought these copies in to get them autographed." He held up a stack of four triumphantly. "I tried to buy more, but all the stores are sold out. I practically had to duke it out with a white-haired woman in the aisles of the Tyrone Barnes and Noble to get its last copy."

"But, why would you . . ."

"Do you remember when I told you my mother was a romance junkie?"

She nodded numbly. "Well, yeah, but . . ."

"When I told her I knew a real live Masque author, I swear you coulda heard her scream clear across the state." He grinned, seeming to enjoy her confusion. "She couldn't believe her no-account, good-for-nothing son knew a celebrity. My stock went up almost as high as it did the years when Valerie and Andi and Dani were born."

Tanya smiled. "So I earned you some points with your mama?"

"Girl, she told me if I didn't send her an autographed copy of one of your books pronto that I didn't need to call again."

Tanya laughed.

"Then she called me back and told me everybody in her book club wanted autographed copies, too."

Tanya no longer cared how much of this might be BS. She was absolutely enjoying herself.

"So I went out and tried to corner the market on Tanya Mason novels, but it seems like a bunch of people beat me to it."

"Yeah, my editor just called and told me I was the top seller this month."

"Well that sure sounds like something to celebrate."

"It's pretty great," Tanya admitted. "I may be invited to be a part of an anthology they're planning. It's a definite step-up."

"You deserve it. I thought the book was great. It had lots

more character development and more powerful emotion even than your earlier releases, but then I guess there's room to build more of that in a Masque Xtraromance than a Masque Appeal."

Her mouth dropped open at the realization that he not only knew the difference between the two Masque lines but had obviously read not only her current but earlier releases.

He set the books on the counter and pushed them toward her. Tanya felt a warm glow in her chest that she couldn't seem to shove away. The fact that this man liked her children and put up with her mother was a good thing; the fact that he had not only read but understood her work—Tanya figured that was a flat-out miracle.

"Yep," he said. "All this good news definitely calls for a dinner out. Some place with white tablecloths and fancy service."

"Oh." Tanya stopped glowing and remembered that her goal here was not to get drawn in. "No." She shook her head. "I don't think . . ."

He whipped out a pen and started to direct the autographing. "OK, this one's for my mother, LindaLee." He spelled her name and waited while she signed the book. "And this one's for her best friend, Lila."

He talked her through the rest of the signatures and then asked where she thought he could get four more copies.

"I can check with the Borders at the mall," she said. "I know the buyer there. But about the dinner . . ." She was flattered and deeply touched, but that didn't mean getting involved was the right thing to do.

"Why don't we plan on a Saturday night?" he said, not really asking. "I may need some time to get the right reservation."

"Oh, I don't think . . ."

"I can get Valerie to sit if that would help."

"It's not that, it's just . . ."

"It's settled then," he said, as if they were in complete agreement. "Definitely a Saturday night. That way we won't have to worry about what time we get in or how hard we party." He waggled his eyebrows at her and her heart flip-flopped down into her stomach. "I'll make sure that neither of us is on the schedule for that Sunday morning."

25

*Truth may be stranger than fiction, but
fiction is truer.*
—FREDERIC RAPHAEL

Kendall didn't want to jinx anything by feeling too good, but
the truth was that with each day that passed and each page she
wrote, she felt a corresponding lightening of the dark cloud
that had been hovering over her since the WINC conference in
New York.

After months of being beaten down and stomped on, Kendall felt the universe conspiring to lift her up.

Her children were happy at college and blissfully unaware of
their parents' impending divorce, her attorney had taken over
the onerous job of communicating with Calvin and his equally
onerous attorney, and her friends continued to rally around her,
sending scenes as they wrote them and calling often to discuss
the book and check on her well-being.

Even from a distance she could feel their love and support
and she fed on it hungrily, using it to keep her going as she
wrote the book that had evolved from punishing task to welcome therapy.

With October well under way, the air turned crisper and
sharper as the mountains exploded into color, drenching her
in infinite shades of red and gold.

Today she sat in what she now thought of as Mallory's spot
on the deck while she worked on chapter eight and her character's flight to her haven in the mountains. When she was

satisfied with the scene, she stood and stretched. Leaning against the deck railing, she stared up into a cloud of claret-colored leaves and allowed her thoughts to wander to the second bathroom, where she'd decided to install bead board.

Inside she showered and dressed then took final measurements of the bathroom. She was pretty sure James would be working this afternoon and though she didn't allow herself to think about the correlation, she spent more time than usual on her hair and makeup.

Highway 78, which was a winding two-lane affair, was choked with cars bearing Georgia license plates. It was prime leaf season and it seemed that half of the Atlanta area's four million inhabitants had driven up to gawk at the scenery. She called Mallory from the car, expecting an admonition or irritation when she admitted where she was headed, but Mallory sounded very un-Mallory like when she came on the line.

"Are you all right?" Kendall asked, when Mallory didn't raise a single objection to the bead board project or the trip to Home Depot. "You don't sound like yourself."

"I'm fine," Mallory said. There was a hesitation. "I'm just trying to figure a few things out."

"Do you want to brainstorm?" Kendall asked. "I've got a good twenty-five minutes in the car."

There was another weighty pause. "Well, it's not actually a plotting issue. Miranda's scenes in *Sticks and Stones* seem to be pretty much writing themselves."

"Glad to hear it," Kendall replied, afraid to push for more. Mallory was notoriously closemouthed about her personal life. But after all the help Mallory had given her, Kendall wanted to return the favor. "How's Chris?"

The silence was so profound that for a few moments Kendall thought the call had been dropped—not an unusual occurrence up here where the mountains and their towering treetops played havoc with cell reception. But a glance at the face of her cell phone indicated that she and Mallory were still connected.

"Has something happened?" Kendall asked.

"Not really." Mallory's voice carried none of its usual certainty.

"So, something's sort of happened?"

"Chris has been on a project in Phoenix for the last three weeks. And it just feels a little strange here without him." The admission was grudging.

"Oh. So he's just home on the weekends?"

"Um, no. Not exactly." Another pause. "He hasn't been home at all."

Kendall wanted to offer sympathy, but she knew Mallory would hate that. "When will the project be over?"

"That's a bit unclear," Mallory said. "The project appears to be remarkably . . . open-ended."

"Awww, Mallory." Kendall took the shortcut that would allow her to avoid Dillard's Main Street where she knew the tourists would be barely chugging along in the mountain version of rush hour.

"No 'awwwing,' Kendall. He's just upset that I haven't made enough time for us. And now that I have made the time, he's upset that he wasn't the reason I made it." She sighed. "And they call women irrational!"

Kendall cut back onto 441 just past the garbage and recycling center and headed south toward Clayton. "Well, I'm here if you need me. And you're welcome to come back and write with me anytime. The Mallory St. James Memorial Bedroom stands ready and waiting. I just finished repainting it and the floors are all buffed up and shiny. Pretty soon the bathroom will have beadboard and molding."

"I knew you wouldn't be able to control yourself without me." Kendall was relieved to hear a teasing note in Mallory's voice.

"You'd be proud of me, Mal. I haven't exactly kicked the habit, but the pages do come first. When it gets really hard, I stop and ask myself, 'What would Mallory do?' And the compulsion usually passes."

Mallory laughed, which Kendall took as a personal victory. "I'm glad to hear I'm hanging over your head even when I'm not there."

"Believe me," Kendall said. "You're almost as big a pain in the ass long distance as you are in person."

"Good." There was another pause, but not as weighty. "Tell James I said hello. And don't let him sell you any more power tools."

"Will do," Kendall said as she signed off. "Though I can't imagine what makes you think I expect to see James there."

• • •

James's face eased into a smile when he spotted her. "There's my best customer!" he said as he came up to greet her. "What perfect timing. We just got in those pneumatic power nailers I was telling you about. I put one aside for you."

He led her over to the information desk and stepped behind it to hunt on a bottom shelf. "Take a look at this beauty."

He pulled out the power nailer, which Kendall had to admit was gorgeous. Reverently she reached out to take it from him and their hands brushed. Both of them pulled back at the same time.

When she looked up, he was studying her out of those faded blue eyes that had intrigued her from the beginning. They made her think of old blue jeans that had been washed a million times and the sky on those perfect summer days at the beach. Her writer's mind had already created a thousand backstories to explain the things those eyes had seen.

"You must know I've been wanting to ask you out since the first day I met you," he said.

Kendall nodded tentatively, her hand still tingling from the unexpected contact.

"So I was wondering." He paused for a moment as if to gather himself. "Would you like to have dinner with me one night this week?"

Her sharp intake of breath surprised both of them.

"We could just make it coffee." He looked into her eyes, trying to gauge her reaction. She wished him luck, because she didn't fully understand it herself. "In a public place," he added.

She took a half step back.

"Have I made a mistake?" he asked quietly. "Have I been reading interest where none was intended?"

Still she didn't speak and so he began to apologize. "If I've presumed, I'm sorry. I . . ."

"No, no." Her mind was tiptoeing through the potential minefields his invitation seemed to carry. She had been attracted to him from the first and flattered by his attention. But was she ready to actually date someone right now?

"We can just pretend I never asked," he said. "Really, it's not . . ."

"Shhh," she said. "Please don't apologize." She looked down for a moment and realized she was cradling the power nailer in her arms like a baby. She had to smile. "You're completely right. I've been interested in you from the beginning, too. And you've fueled my fix-it mania, which, frankly, I think has helped to keep me sane."

He waited while she spoke, his whole being calm and comfortable, just like his eyes. She had the sense that nothing would shake or surprise him and one day she wanted to know what had made him this way. But not today.

"It's just that I'm going through a really difficult patch right now. I'm separated from my husband, and I'm on a book deadline, and . . ." She took a deep breath before plunging on with her disclaimer. "Anyway, it's not at all about you. I mean you're . . ."

She paused a moment to search for the right adjectives and this time he shushed her.

"It's OK." His quiet warmth seemed as far from Calvin's bluster as it was possible to get. "I understand," he said, and she could see in his eyes that he did. "It's not a problem. I'm here and I'm not going anywhere." His smile was as gentle and as full of wisdom as his words.

"You just go on about your business. And when and if you feel ready to get better acquainted, you just let me know."

Kendall felt a soft flush of gratitude along with a sharper pull she hadn't felt in a long time. "Sounds good," she said, still holding the power nailer in her arms. "I'll be looking forward to that." She set the power tool in an empty cart and pulled her list out of her purse to show him. "I'm thinking bead board for the second bathroom. And some kind of molding just above it. Do you have any of that in stock?"

• • •

Faye might have benefited from some do-it-yourself instruction. Or a power tool that could take the threads of her life that had begun to unravel and twine them back together.

As she drove toward Rainbow House, Faye reflected on the previous night's conference call. It had gone well. They were all making good progress on their parts of *Sticks and Stones* and Faye had noticed that the love scenes written by her character, Faith, were now garnering more compliments than surprise.

Still she hated keeping yet another secret from Steve, though her involvement in *Sticks and Stones* was nothing compared to her secret career writing erotica, the weight of which seemed to grow heavier each day.

At the front desk, she signed in wondering, yet again, how Rainbow House would survive if she were ever exposed as Shannon LeSade.

As she passed through the administrative offices on her way to the day care center, the irony of the situation smote her. It was her earnings from the very thing she was now afraid to admit to that had brought Rainbow House and its myriad services into being. It was her continued monetary support, much of it derived from her secret career, that kept it growing and attracted other large donors.

Once Faye had believed that the source of the money was insignificant in comparison to the good it achieved, but the world was a different place today. And she'd come to realize that if the true source of Rainbow House's funding were ever revealed, Rainbow House and those it served would suffer. As would her husband.

That was what she knew. What she didn't know was what to do about it.

In the shiny new library a group of preschoolers sat in a semicircle around a Rainbow House volunteer. The children's eyes shone with excitement as they listened to a spirited reading of Maurice Sendak's *Where the Wild Things Are*. Faye watched for a few moments, breathing in the heady smell of new books and remembering when she'd first read the story to her children and then to her granddaughter, Becky.

After the story there'd be a snack and supervised play followed by nap time; for most of these kids this would be the closest to a normal life they'd ever gotten.

Faye shelved the books she and Becky had chosen and then checked "the closet" where new arrivals, who often fled their homes with little more than backpacks or belonging-stuffed pillowcases, were brought to "shop" for clothing and accessories.

Beside "the closet" was the computer center where women could formulate resumes and do class assignments. Those who wanted to improve their skills got on-site computer training.

How could she pull the plug on all that she'd worked so hard to create?

How could she not when every day the chance of exposure and scandal increased?

Her last stop was the office, where she met with the administrator and her assistant to go over the plans for a playground expansion. And then she was on her way to meet Steve for lunch, something they hadn't been able to work into their schedules since she'd gotten back from Kendall's last month.

As she waited for him at a favored table at Café Central, a small French restaurant near home, she realized how much she wished she could discuss her dilemma with her husband. In the past he'd been her most reliable sounding board and she had been his. But every time she imagined the relief she might feel in telling him the truth, that happy picture was wiped out by the vision of his shock and dismay.

A stir near the doorway halted her internal debate. Faye glanced up to see her husband striding toward her.

"You look . . . elsewhere," he observed as he leaned down to kiss her cheek then took the seat opposite her. In one smooth motion, he unfolded his napkin and placed it in his lap. "Is everything OK?"

As opportunities went, Faye thought, it didn't get much better than this. All she had to do was open her mouth, explain the situation, and ask for his input. Simple. Clear. Like they'd always done.

Despite the trappings and the fame, she reminded herself, this was still Steve. Her husband. Who'd known her since her freshman year of college and with whom she'd had three children and . . . OK, built an evangelical television empire.

Others, like those checking them out over their own lunches, knew him only as Pastor Steve, font of patience and wisdom with a pipeline to God. But Faye had been in love with him before he became a pastor. When he was just Steve Truett, the best-looking guy in her comparative lit class.

She looked into her husband's eyes trying to gauge his mood, imagining his reaction, looking for some sort of sign.

Was this the time and place to tell him that she was not only Faye Truett but Shannon LeSade? Would there ever be such a time or place?

"Oh, I'm fine," she began when his gaze began to cloud with concern over her continued silence. She drew a deep breath. "But you see I . . ."

"Welcome, Monsieur and Madame Truett," the waiter, who'd apparently materialized from thin air, said. "What may I get you to drink?"

And that easily, the moment, if it had been one, was lost. They placed their drink orders and Steve's gaze fell to the menu. The next thing Faye knew, she was telling him about the new library at Rainbow House, her plans to go back to check on Kendall after Thanksgiving, and the funny thing Becky had said to her on the phone that morning.

A flashbulb went off and Faye realized that a shot of them

dining at Café Central would most likely end up in the next morning's *Chicago Tribune,* or at least that week's *Highland Park News.* She had no doubt that those who saw the photo or paused now in their own lunches to observe them would see Pastor Steve and his wife, Faye Truett, the novelist, engaged in a steady flow of what would appear to be intimate conversation.

But Faye knew just how lacking in intimacy their conversation really was. Because as far as she was concerned, there could be no true intimacy without an underlying foundation of truth.

26

The first e-mail took Lacy completely by surprise. It was waiting in her in-box when she got to work, just another communication in a long line of interoffice directives that ended in scarsdale.com. It was only when she noticed the c.simpson, which stood for Cash Simpson, that preceded it that her pulse sped up and the blood began doing a strange sort of happy dance in her veins.

"Hope things are good in the fields," it read. "Don't toil too hard." It was signed, "Cash."

Lacy had spent a full fifteen minutes trying to come up with a clever response, checking surreptitiously over her shoulder for any sign of Jane Jensen as she did so. Unfortunately between her excitement at hearing from him and the performance anxiety that struck at the mere thought of him, she'd finally settled for, "Birthing no babies today. But toiling mightily." She signed it "Tillie the Toiler" and hit Send before she could chicken out.

His reply came almost instantly. "Dear Tillie, Can't wait to find out how old you actually are! First Russian peasant girl now WWII toiler." This time he signed it, "Intrigued, but unfortunately out of town."

At this admission, Lacy began to relax and enjoy herself.

Without thinking she typed. "Taking secret to grave. Only plastic surgeon and devil with whom bargain was made know for sure!" Without rereading or editing she hit Send.

"Devising top-secret plan to discover truth," came the speedy reply. "On way out now to purchase trench coat and secret passwords. Heard of special store on Miracle Mile."

This had gone on for a week now and although he remained in Chicago and she therefore knew she wouldn't run into him at the office, Lacy could hardly wait to get to work each morning to check her e-mail.

Cash Simpson's attention had gone straight to her head and, if she were honest, to other body parts as well. Somehow this simple flirtation made her feel entirely different about herself. Where before she'd looked in the mirror and seen too tall and too awkward, she now saw statuesque and exotic. Her already half-full glass of optimism got fuller and then began to spill over. She caught herself smiling at the oddest times and for no reason at all.

Lacy Samuels had always prided herself on her intelligence so even as she enjoyed Cash Simpson's e-mail flirtation, she realized that someone only got this good at something with lots and lots of practice. Still she was thrilled that out of all the women who lusted after him, he'd chosen her as the recipient of his attention. And she wasted a great deal of time imaging what else he might have had lots of practice at.

Jane was already in a meeting when Lacy arrived that morning and so after getting herself settled at her desk and positioning her double latte just so, Lacy logged on eager to see what waited for her.

The first e-mail was from Kendall Aims offering an enthusiastic update on *Sticks and Stones*. Lacy took a long sip of her latte and read the e-mail; she'd expected some resistance or negativity given the situation and adversarial relationship Jane Jensen had created, but Kendall's e-mails were consistently positive and upbeat. Lacy e-mailed back that she was looking forward to reading it, and she let herself imagine the thrill of editing her first real manuscript.

The next e-mail was, happily, from Cash. She opened it, smiling even before she read it.

"Dear Tillie," it read. "Still awaiting arrival of trench coat. Must resort to plying you with drinks to ascertain secrets in meantime. Due back in NY tomorrow. If willing to participate in alcoholic interrogation, meet me at Grand Central Oyster Bar at 6:00 P.M. tomorrow after work. Cash."

Lacy smiled and took a sip of her latte. She was trying to come up with something a little less obvious than "YES! YES! OH GOD, YES!" when she realized that someone was standing behind her.

Jane's gasp of outrage startled her so completely that she didn't even move to delete the incriminating e-mail.

"Is that Cash as in Cash Simpson?" Jane demanded, as if there might be a thousand men with that name currently employed by Scarsdale Publishing.

Lacy didn't like the idea of lying outright, but one look at Jane's mottled face told her that the truth was not going to be her friend. She remained silent.

"You know that fraternization between employees is not allowed at Scarsdale." Jane said this with a straight face, as if she or any other female in the organization would have turned down Cash Simpson's attention on these or any other grounds.

Lacy nodded.

Jane Jensen stared at her for a long moment. When she finally spoke again, her voice was cold and hard-edged. "I'd like a cup of coffee," Jane said. "And be sure to make a fresh pot."

Not expecting or awaiting a reply, Jane turned on her heel and went back to her office. Lacy practically ran for the break room, where she dumped the used grounds and washed out the pot while she tried to think of what she could say that might smooth things over without constituting an admission of guilt.

Fifteen minutes later she was standing in Jane's office, trying to keep her hand from shaking as she placed the cup of coffee on her boss's desk.

Jane didn't even look at the coffee that Lacy had placed in

front of her and from which steam was still rising. Her attention was focused on her assistant and it didn't take a rocket scientist to tell that what was going to come out of her mouth was not going to be good.

"Since you seem to have so much time on your hands, I want you to begin working your way through this pile of unsolicited submissions." She pointed to a chest-high pile of manuscripts stacked in a far corner of the office. In all the times Lacy had been in Jane's office, she'd never seen anyone even look at them. "This is just the first stack; the rest are in the sixth-floor storage room."

Lacy took a step toward the pile and peered down at the cover page on the top manuscript. "But the return address is a correctional institution." She lifted the top manuscript and sneezed as a puff of dust rose to meet her nostrils. She leafed through the next few, her horror growing. "And this one's from the state mental hospital." She looked into Jane Jensen's eyes—wondering briefly if they'd been submitted by Jane's previous roommates.

"Yes."

"I, um, thought the rule of thumb was not to read or respond to these, um, kinds of submissions," Lacy said.

"That's normally true," her boss acknowledged. "But that's primarily because we don't have anyone with the time to do it." She stared directly into Lacy's eyes. It took every ounce of willpower Lacy possessed not to look away. "Now we do.

"I want you to read, write a report for, and then respond to every one of them. Maybe that will leave you with less time for personal e-mails on company time."

Lacy had always considered herself more competent than competitive; she was much more interested in getting a job done well than in competing just for the sake of besting someone. But this was a punishment pure and simple, personal retribution for Cash Simpson's interest in her. As she stared into her boss's vindictive gaze, Lacy vowed then and there that if Cash Simpson could, in fact, be had, she was going to have him.

"Is there anything else?" Lacy asked carefully.

Jane Jensen smiled a tight-lipped smile. "Not at the moment," she said. "But I'm sure I'll come up with something."

. . .

Through late October and early November the vibrant color that set the hills and mountainsides aflame began to fade. The deep wine colors became a mottled red and the heavenly golds turned a paler yellow-brown. As they dried and stiffened, the leaves' grip on their branches loosened and strong autumn winds pried them loose and sent them spiraling to the ground. By mid-November they lay in piles and drifts all over the forest floor.

As the temperatures dropped, Kendall no longer ventured out onto the deck to write, preferring the cozy warmth of the kitchen where she spent her mornings, her notes strewn across the kitchen table. Her gaze occasionally strayed out over the increasingly barren landscape, but her attention remained focused on Kennedy Andrews and her frantic attempts to salvage her life and her career.

In the afternoons, when the day had warmed as much as it was going to, Kendall bundled up and went out for a hike, her boots crunching through the piles of leaves, the sun glinting through the bare branches to places it never reached in spring or summer.

Her work on the house continued, but she could feel the compulsion lessening. Now she chose a project because it needed to be done or because she knew she'd enjoy doing it—not because she couldn't stop herself.

She and Calvin communicated through their lawyers in a complex and sometimes unfathomable language that had everything to do with their things and very little to do with them. The negotiations dragged out interminably, but Kendall was not inclined to rush them, because once the divorce was final, Kendall knew she'd have to tell Melissa and Jeffrey. And start thinking of herself in a whole new way.

When the vision of her soon-to-be single self became too real, Kendall calmed herself by thinking of only the next step. Just do this now, she'd tell herself, and then you'll worry about that. Do five pages now, two more this afternoon. One conversation with Anne Justiss today, a trip to Home Depot tomorrow.

In this way Kendall inched through the days doing what had to be done, relying on Faye and Mallory and Tanya to see her through when even the smallest bite seemed too much to chew.

The unexpectedly bright spot in all of it was *Sticks and Stones*. She'd originally agreed to Tanya's idea of a group effort because she'd been so lost and afraid she would have agreed to most anything that would allow her to fulfill her commitment. But she hadn't really stopped to think about what their involvement would do to the project.

A talented and imaginative writer could put herself into numerous characters' heads and do a credible job of presenting their points of view in noticeably different ways. It was not only possible, writers did it all the time. But having those points of view written by different people added a dimension that she'd never experienced before. The book was good, better than good. In fact, it was far beyond what she'd originally envisioned—much bigger and of greater depth than she could have dreamed up or written by herself.

Kendall tried not to think about what Jane Jensen would do with this book. How wasted it would be.

That night they rendezvoused on the phone to discuss the recently completed chapters. They'd completed almost three hundred fifty pages and were nearing the black moment, where everything would appear to fall apart for all of the key characters. Then would come the resolution that would reflect the characters' growth and pave the way to the end.

The call began, as they all did, with teasing and chatter.

"I just want to know when Tanya's character, Tina, is going to go ahead and have sex with that cook," said Faye. "I mean what is she waiting for?"

"And I'd like to know when Faith is going to stop writing about it!" Tanya replied. "Just reading those scenes gets me all steamed up."

"I agree," Kendall said. "I think Faye's missed her calling writing inspirationals. She writes some of the best sex I've ever read. Frankly the sex she writes is better than most of the sex I've *had*!"

"Amen to that," Tanya chimed in. "Maybe we should warn that Shannon LeSade to step out of the way and make room for Faye Truett."

There was laughter all around, though Kendall thought Faye's sounded a bit forced.

Mallory was unusually quiet and Kendall sought to put her at ease. "I think your Miranda Jameson is a fabulous character," she said. "It would have been easy to make an automatic *New York Times* Bestseller seem unsympathetic. But giving her that traumatic past to overcome makes us all root for her." And then she asked what she'd wanted to ask since she'd read Mallory's first scene. "But why wouldn't she share her past with her closest friends? Or at least with her husband? Why would she keep everything to herself that way?"

The question hung in the air, filling the sudden quiet on the line with an almost electrical charge.

When Mallory finally spoke, she sounded unusually tentative, as if she were hearing the words for the first time along with them. "I'm not sure. I think she'd been through so much she just wanted to pretend none of it had ever happened. I mean, two parents blowing their brains out—that would leave a person feeling pretty unworthy, don't you think? She'd have to believe that neither of her parents thought she was important enough to stick around for. If people knew, they'd look at her differently. They'd pity her." Her voice trailed off. "She'd be vulnerable."

There was a pause and then Mallory cleared her throat. "I decided it would be easier for her to be strong and act strong if nobody knew. It would give her the chance to re-invent herself."

They were all silent as they weighed what Mallory had said.

"But to not even tell her husband? Or her best friends?"

Kendall just couldn't grasp it. If she hadn't had the three of them, she never would have survived the last months.

Mallory spoke quietly but with a growing intensity. "But those would be the last people she'd tell. Because of how important they are to her. Because if she lost them—well, it would be like losing her parents all over again, wouldn't it? Only worse. She'd be alone again. With no one to rely on but herself."

There was a heavy silence as they absorbed what Mallory had said. Then Mallory laughed, breaking the somber mood. "See how bad you feel? How sorry for her you are? *That's* why she doesn't tell anyone. Because then she couldn't be who she wants to be!"

Mallory's tone lightened even further. "Pretty good, huh? I spent a long time coming up with Miranda's rationale and it works, doesn't it? All the pieces fit for the character. I love when that happens!"

Faye was the first to recover. "You're right, Mallory, it's brilliant." She paused as if searching for the right words. "Some things are better kept to oneself. And that applies to people and characters. Because the information colors everything. And it changes how people react to you, I mean, the character."

"Too true," Tanya added. "And to go back to our earlier conversation about my character, Tina? I think having sex opens you up too much, too. Even when you say it's just going to be sex, it never really is." Her voice faltered for a moment. "Especially when it's with someone who's acting like they want more." She cleared her throat. "That's why I, um, don't think Tina should cave to the cook."

"Well, I have a question for you," Mallory said, earning gratitude from all of them with the change of subject. "How inept do you think we should make Plain Jane's assistant, Lucy Simmons?"

They debated this briefly, enjoying themselves but not really deciding.

"I have a more pressing question," Kendall said. "I'm not

at all clear about how this book is going to end. We're awfully far down the road not to have committed to that."

Everyone spoke at once, their ideas spilling out on top of each other's, but it was Mallory who had the final say. "I don't think there's any question how the story has to end."

They all waited to hear what Mallory thought because while they all had their own opinions and could argue them with complete conviction, no one could ignore the fact that Mallory had been the most commercially successful of them all.

"I just don't think there's any question," she said again. "If we've done our job right, the reader is going to be rooting for Kennedy and her friends all the way through the book. *Sticks and Stones* is going to hit the *New York Times* list and become a runaway bestseller. And its author is going to live happily ever after."

27

*Writing is like getting married. One should
never commit oneself until one is
amazed at one's luck.*
—IRIS MURDOCH

Tanya spent the night starring in a fairy tale, though it was hard to tell which one. Brett picked her up at 7:00 P.M. in a washed and waxed Jeep that shone almost as brightly as his eyes did when he spotted her.

"Wow!" That was all he said when she opened the front door and struck a pose for him in the red satin cocktail dress that made her feel like Marilyn Monroe. She teetered slightly on the red stiletto heels and one hand fingered the strand of faux pearls nervously, but he seemed not to notice. His gaze slid slowly down the form-fitting red silk, over her bare legs to the dyed-to-match shoes, and back up again. The girls giggled behind her; they'd spent the day watching her primp and dress and were as thrilled as she was by the end result. Even Trudy was breathless with excitement over the mystery date.

Almost as much for them as for Brett, Tanya let the fake fur stole slip further down her bare shoulders and shifted her weight slightly so that she could jut out the other silk-clad hip. Her lips, which she'd painted a matching shade of red, curved into a pouty smile, in her best Marilyn imitation.

"Did I say 'wow' yet?" Brett's smile was warm, his voice thick with admiration. Chill bumps rose on Tanya's bare arms and they had nothing to do with the night air.

Without a backward glance at her audience, she stepped out onto the front stoop and closed the door behind her, suppressing a smile at the collective groan of disappointment that arose from inside the trailer.

She had to admit that Brett had cleaned up pretty well himself. He had on gray pants and an open-necked white dress shirt and blue blazer. His blond hair looked freshly cut and his face newly shaved. A hint of something male and spicy clung lightly to him.

"Yes, I think you've got 'wow' covered," she said.

He leaned down to kiss her hello, a simple brush of his lips across her cheek that made her goose bumps goose bump.

"Ready?" He gave her his arm and escorted her down the rickety aluminum steps to the hardscrabble lawn as if leading her down a marble staircase onto a ballroom dance floor.

Her heart twisted in her chest as he helped her into the car.

"Where are we going?" she asked as he put the Jeep in gear and headed out of the trailer park. He'd refused to answer this question for a full two weeks, saying only that she'd want to dress up and that she should save her appetite for the meal he had planned.

"It's a surprise," he said. "I think I mentioned that before."

No one had ever gone to such effort for her—no one. The fact that he'd spent weeks planning and building up to a surprise just for her was inconceivable. All day the excitement and anticipation had simmered inside her, stoking her imagination, lighting her internal furnace. There was a fine tightening inside her, an ache that began deep at her core and vibrated outward. She'd written this kind of intense physical desire many times, but had never actually experienced it. She'd had sex many times before, too, but had never felt this keening want that had begun in her brain and somehow taken over her body.

Sexual energy filled the space between them and it wasn't all coming from her. She imagined it pinging off the dashboard and ricocheting through the car. She wasn't sure how to control it, but she knew if they didn't do something about it soon, she was going to pull him into the backseat, have her way with him, and end up at a drive-thru.

Tanya clenched the evening bag between her hands and dug deep past all the humming and tightening, searching for the one thing that might save them: her sense of humor.

"I'm going to feel real silly in this getup if we end up at Ci-Ci's all-you-can-eat pizza bar or the China King Hunan Buffet," she said in as flip a tone as she could manage.

Brett smiled, and she thought it might have been from relief. "Trust me when I tell you you're perfectly dressed for the evening." He slowed to a stop as the light turned red then faced her. "The only thing I can imagine you looking better in is nothing."

So much for the elimination of sexual tension. Tanya groaned as her entire body went warm and liquid; of its own accord and without a speck of permission from her, it strained toward his.

She didn't answer because her mouth was too dry to form words. They stared at each other, their gazes frighteningly hungry, until the light finally changed. It took the honking of horns behind them to turn Brett's attention back to the road.

Tanya gave herself a stern, if silent, talking to.

Sex with Brett was *not* a foregone conclusion, she reminded herself, and not a particularly great idea either. This . . . humming and tightening   was a result of her overactive imagination. A culmination of all the sex scenes she'd written. And all of Faye's that she'd read. She'd simply let Brett's interest in her become something more than it was. They were just going out for a nice dinner; it didn't have to lead to anything else.

Her body, which was still tingling and straining and hadn't had sex for longer than she cared to remember, told her to shut up.

They crossed the Gandy Bridge to Tampa in silence then turned onto Bayshore Boulevard. Stately homes and high-rise condos whizzed by on their left; the concrete balustrade framed glimpses of Tampa Bay on the right.

By the time Brett pulled into valet parking at Bern's Steak House and she was handed out of the car like a piece of delicate china, Tanya had resolved to stop analyzing and start enjoying.

Brett was Prince Charming as he led her into the famous restaurant's red velvet and brocade lobby and she was Marilyn and Dorothy and Cinderella all rolled into one. With Brett's hand pressed lightly to the small of her back, Tanya floated behind the maitre d' to a linen-draped table in an intimate corner.

They chose from twenty-six types of caviar to start, had their dry-aged chateaubriand for two carved table side, and washed it all down, if such a phrase could be used for such a place, with one of the fifty-five hundred available bottles of red wine from the Bern's wine cellar.

The meal passed in a haze of pleasure. The food and wine were miraculous, the service flawless, and the prices, at least in Tanya's menu, blissfully nonexistent. Afterward they lingered over chocolate soufflé and French brandy in the dessert room upstairs and Tanya knew that somehow Brett's Jeep had turned off of Bayshore Boulevard not onto South Howard Avenue as she'd thought, but onto the superhighway that led to Oz.

Tanya, being the practical, responsible, thinking mother of two that she was, was very careful during the longest and most wonderful evening of her life so far not to click her ruby slippers together. If there was anywhere she didn't want to go right now, it was home.

• • •

It was the Saturday evening before Thanksgiving, and Mallory, who still hadn't heard from her husband, resorted to subterfuge. Using the caller ID block on her cell phone, she dialed Chris's number. He picked up on the second ring.

"Hi, Chris, it's me. Mallory," she said.

Mallory had a brief, horrible flash of him taunting her

with "Mallory who?" But Chris remained politely Chris-like, though his "Oh. Hi," carried an underlying tone of detachment that made her want to cry.

He left a silence that she hurried to fill. "I just wanted to see how you were," she said.

Chris didn't respond.

"And, um, how the project's going."

"Fine," he said. "It's going fine."

She waited for him to continue, but he didn't.

"That's good," she said.

She waited for him to ask how she was doing so that she could admit how much she missed him, but he didn't do that, either.

"Will you be home in time for Thanksgiving?" Mallory asked. In the past Chris had invited his parents, his brother and his wife, and a few friends from work and then created a feast that included what she'd dubbed their trifecta of turkey—one roasted, one fried, and one smoked. Mallory had no family and it had never occurred to her to invite Faye, Kendall, or Tanya, who all would be having Thanksgiving with their own families.

"No," he said. "I'm planning to go to my parents' for Thanksgiving. They've been after me to come home to visit for a while now."

She waited for him to ask her to meet him in Akron, where he'd grown up and his parents still lived. Or to say that he'd come back to New York first so they could fly there together. Once again she waited in vain.

There was another long silence during which she debated what to say; the whole time she was afraid that he'd hang up before she figured out what the right thing was.

"When do you think you'll come home?" she asked carefully, fighting back the urge to beg him to come back to her now, this minute. It hadn't escaped her notice that he'd referred to Akron as home. "It's so empty here without you," she said, trying to keep the quiver out of her voice. "So quiet."

"Yeah," he said. "I know exactly how that feels."

Mallory closed her eyes and tried to still the panic. She was completely alone and he wasn't coming home. She did feel guilt at how she'd treated him, but she felt the panic of being alone even more.

"Chris," she said. "I *am* sorry. I've apologized so many times I don't even know what else to say. I will do better. As soon as I've finished this project I'll—"

"I know, Mallory. You always mean to do better. And I think you actually mean it when you say it. But not to 'diss' what you do for a living, but actions really do speak a whole lot louder than words."

In the silence, she imagined she could hear him thinking, which was really weird because she could barely think at all. When he spoke, she latched onto each word, wanting desperately to turn them into the words she wanted to hear.

"I'm planning to fly into Akron the day before Thanksgiving and stay for the week," he said. "If you want to meet me there . . ."

Mallory was so relieved at the invitation she didn't even let him finish issuing it. "That would be so great," she said quickly. "I could come in Wednesday night and be there all of Thanksgiving. I just have to fly back to Atlanta Friday morning. It could work though, I could . . ."

His sigh stretched all the way from Arizona, across the telephone wires, to stop her. It was filled with regret and resignation and other things she did not want to identify.

"Forget it, Mallory," he said. "I'm not open to one of your quick in and outs. You're invited to spend the week with me and my parents." He paused. "Or not at all."

"Oh, Chris, I want to be with you. Really, I do. It's just that Kendall needs me and I promised that I'd—"

"No, Mallory," he said, sounding horribly weary. "Not this time. When you're ready to put us first we'll have something to talk about."

Mallory's heart pounded and the blood whooshed in her ears. She couldn't let this happen, couldn't let him hang up on such a final note, but she couldn't find the words to stop him.

"Until that happens, I'm just not interested," Chris said. "And I wouldn't wait too long, Mallory," he added as he prepared to hang up. "I've already waited for what feels like forever."

. . .

Tanya's eyes flew open at 5:00 A.M. out of habit. The bedside clock confirmed the time but a quick scan of her surroundings told her something else: She was no longer in Oz. Or her own bed for that matter. And from the feel of things, the warm body tucked tightly against her was not one of her daughters.

Shit. She wished herself back asleep, but she appeared to be all out of wishes. Her ruby slippers and Marilyn dress lay strewn across the bedroom floor. The fairy tale was definitely over.

"Morning." Brett's voice was warm and rumbly on the back of her neck. His arm was folded around her waist and his hand cupped her breast. His erection pressed against her bottom. They were both naked.

She didn't respond, choosing to feign sleep while she tried to figure out her next move. She had a vague memory of driving home in what she might have referred to as a pumpkin-turned-coach. And she remembered their clothes coming off in a mad race to this bed once Brett had assured her the girls were spending the night out. And the sex? She swallowed now as it came flooding back to her. She'd made love to him once wearing nothing but the red stilettos. And another time on the floor with the faux fur stole spread beneath her. The other intimate details remained mercifully hazy, but her limbs were weary and she felt a pleasurable ache between her thighs.

She closed her eyes more from embarrassment than any real hope that she could go back to sleep. She held back a groan.

"Are you OK?" Brett's hand tightened slightly on her breast and his thumb brushed across her nipple. She felt an answering tug between her thighs, but resisted the impulse to press her bottom tighter against him. She needed to go home and back to her own reality. Fairy tales simply weren't built to stand up to the light of day.

"Yeah. Sure." The words were hollow even in her ears. She felt oddly cheap and stupid, though she thought cheap wasn't exactly the right word since last night's extravaganza must have cost him a week's pay. She didn't understand why he would have gone to so much trouble. Or spent so much money. Or why she had let him.

Uncomfortable with her thoughts, she pulled away to sit on the side of the bed, keeping her back to him. "I need to go."

Brett swung his legs over to sit beside her. Like naked bookends they sat for a moment staring at their clothes, which littered the bedroom floor.

"I thought I'd make omelets." His smile was crooked and charming and it promised things she no longer believed in. "Or we could eat junk food in bed."

Tanya got up to retrieve her dress. She slid it over her head, not bothering with the push-up bra or matching thong, and bent in front of him, holding her hair out of the way so he could zip her up. She didn't know why she felt so compelled to get out of here, but she did.

Following her lead, he pulled on a pair of jeans, buttoning the fly as she scooped up her underthings and smashed them into her evening bag. The red stilettos dangled from her fingertips; so much for their homing properties.

"Wait a minute." Brett stopped in the living room and waited for her to turn and face him. "What's going on? We had a great time last night. An incredible time. And I know it wasn't just me having it."

His cheeks were covered in morning stubble. His shoulders were broad, his chest bare. Tanya's gaze got caught in the mat of dark hair that arrowed downward. She forced herself to look away.

"I did not imagine that we talked without stopping all through dinner. Or how good we were together afterward." Brett raised a hand and pushed his hair back with it. "I think you owe me at least an explanation for why you're practically running out the front door."

It was the words "owe me" that struck her. They jumped right out of everything else he'd said and commanded her complete attention.

Trudy had given her love for as little as a bar tab and as much as a month's rent. Tanya had held out for marriage with Kyle Mason, but that hadn't gotten her anything but knee deep in debt.

Last night had been a fairy tale night. But she was not Marilyn or Cinderella or Dorothy. She was a thirty-five-year-old writer/waitress with four mouths to feed. Her mother had taught her the folly of depending on the kindness of others and Kyle had reinforced the lesson. As long as she stayed strong and took care of her own, she'd be OK.

"It was a great night," she conceded. "It went way beyond my imaginings. I couldn't have invented one that was any better."

He took a step toward her, clearly intending to take her in his arms. She shook her head. "But I don't know what you want from me. I'm not sure you even do. And I can't afford to owe anybody anything; I'm not willing to take the chance. Not even with a guy who seems to have a Prince Charming complex."

"That is one of the stupidest things I've ever heard," he said. "You're not going to let something good happen because . . . What? It might not last forever? Are you kidding me?"

He turned his back on her and went into the bedroom. When he came back out he had on a T-shirt and was carrying his car keys. He led the way out to the Jeep and this time he didn't open the door or hand her into her seat.

He drove efficiently and quickly, much like he cooked at the Downhome Diner. Tanya tried not to look at his profile or think about how good he'd been in bed.

When they pulled in front of Trudy's mobile home, the sun was up, but the streets were still quiet. The newspapers hadn't yet been delivered. Tanya gathered her things.

"Thank you for everything," she said politely, as if he'd

just handed her something across a counter or passed her the salt and pepper. "I'm sorry I . . ."

"You're welcome," he said, in the same polite but impersonal tone. And then as he prepared to pull away, "I guess I'll be seeing you around."

28

A book is so much a part of oneself that in delivering it to the public one feels as if one were pushing one's own child out into the traffic.
—QUENTIN BELL

On Thanksgiving afternoon, after more than twenty consecutive hours attempting to do Kennedy Andrews's emotional journey and the last chapter of *Sticks and Stones* justice, Kendall Aims typed, "THE END."

Numb and weary, she sat in the kitchen chair staring intently at the monitor, as the tension that had consumed her during the weeklong push toward completion seeped from her body.

She was done. Finished. The manuscript, all 135,240 words of it, was complete.

Sticks and Stones existed in its own right, wrestled from the germ of her idea into flesh and blood and, as soon as she printed it out, paper.

Slowly Kendall pulled herself out of Kennedy Andrews's head and slipped back into her own. She saw her kitchen for the first time in hours and smelled the comforting smell of the turkey breast she'd put in the oven earlier.

Her knees were stiff as she stood and stretched, her body tight from the hours spent hunched in the chair. Her eyes ached from the strain of all those hours staring into the computer screen.

It was done. Finished. As the numbness wore off, the relief

coursing through her began to turn to joy. Straightening, she gave a great shout of happiness that echoed through the silent kitchen.

Despite Jane Jensen, despite Calvin, despite the emptiness of her nest, despite all the obstacles thrown in her path, she'd done it.

She froze in the midst of the thought, the joy and happiness spraying up inside her like a Magic Kingdom fountain halted in midspike as she reminded herself this wasn't exactly the case.

She had not done it, at least not all of it. *They'd* done it.

Kendall paced the kitchen trying to distance herself from the thought. But there was no getting away from it.

Even before the final read through and tweaking they would do over the weekend, Kendall knew that *Sticks and Stones*, with its five viewpoint characters and gentle lifting of the publishing industry veil, was the best book she'd ever written.

Except she hadn't really written it.

Her name was going on the cover of a book she hadn't written alone.

Looking for a distraction, Kendall pulled the turkey breast out of the oven and set it out to cool. She mixed a packet of instant mashed potatoes and put the bowl into the microwave. She fitted a can of cranberry sauce onto the can opener then took the store-bought pumpkin pie out of the refrigerator so that it could get to room temperature.

She had planned her little feast as a celebration of finishing the manuscript on time, but the rush of pleasure had already fled in the face of reality. She was going to be a liar, a fraud. She was going to claim sole credit for a book she hadn't actually written alone. It had seemed such a simple fix for all her problems when they'd first agreed to it and the manuscript had benefited enormously. She wasn't at all sorry that the manuscript existed or that she'd be able to fulfill her contractual commitment. But she hated the idea of pretending to have created something she hadn't. Or at least not all the way.

For the first time in weeks, she felt an almost irresistible urge to slip her hand around the handle of a power tool. She tried to think what materials she had around but she'd finished her last serious project two weeks ago. And even if she could think of something to work on, today was Thanksgiving. Home Depot wasn't going to be open. James and all the other employees were undoubtedly sitting around Thanksgiving tables with family and friends right now, enjoying beautiful meals and spirited conversation. Or sitting comatose on couches watching football together.

For the first time that day Kendall felt sorry for herself. She was alone on a major holiday about to eat a Thanksgiving meal of instant dishes and store-bought food. How pathetic was that?

Once she allowed the self-pity in, it grew and multiplied. The next thing she knew she was imagining Laura prancing around her kitchen in Atlanta cooking a feast for Calvin and all their new friends. She sniffed and swiped at her nose. Now both angry and pathetic, she walked back to the computer and hit print so that she'd have a hard copy of the manuscript to make copies from in the morning on the way to the airport.

Soon the whir of the printer filled the silent kitchen, which she reminded herself was, in fact, a very good thing. Determined to banish her bad mood, Kendall shook a mental finger at herself. She should be celebrating the positives, not dwelling on the negatives.

Sticks and Stones was finished and it was first-rate. Tanya and Faye and Mallory would be here all weekend to help tweak and revise it. After she did a final pass, she'd send the manuscript to Lacy Samuels and to Sylvia. Then it would be time to finalize things with Calvin and find some way to move forward.

She was beginning to look at her holiday meal with a little more appetite when the phone rang. She picked up on the second ring.

"Mom?" Melissa's voice rose over a hum of voices. Kendall could hear a television commentator in the background. "I've got Jeffrey on the line, too. We're having a turkey-themed conference call."

"My, aren't we sophisticated?" Kendall said, responding to the pleasure in her daughter's voice.

"That's us, totally high tech, Mom." Jeffrey's voice also sounded happy, though this was the first Thanksgiving the twins had spent not only without their parents but without each other. And this, she realized, was only the beginning of their independence. How long until one of them really found "the one"? Good God, in the not-too-distant future she could become a grandmother!

"So tell me all about your Thanksgivings. Are you both having a good time?"

They chatted easily, sharing vignettes of their visits, debating the relative merits of stuffing versus dressing, which Melissa had just tasted for the first time. Someone had brought a sweet potato casserole that Jeffrey thought she should try next year. One of them, she thought it was Melissa, was expounding on the wonders of Krispy Kreme—doughnut bread pudding. "It was to die for, Mom," her daughter said. "I told Todd's mother I'm not leaving here without the recipe."

Kendall felt herself calming as they talked. Her relationship with her children was solid. They were beginning lives of their own, but she would be a part of them. She wasn't alone today; she was just somewhere else.

"How about you, Mom? What's happening with the book?"

She'd told them in advance that she was going to be holed up here over the holiday finishing and made Calvin call and tell them that he'd been invited to friends.

"I just typed my two favorite words," she said.

Both of them chimed in without prompting. "The end!"

"Yep." Kendall laughed. "It's finished. And I think it's really, really good." She kept her reservations about the joint authorship to herself, just as she had the pending divorce. She loved picturing them happy and surrounded by friends; she saw no reason to taint their holiday with things beyond their control.

"And are you OK?" This came from Melissa, who always cut to the chase.

Without thinking the affirmatives began to spring to her lips. But as she began to reassure her daughter that all was well, she was pleased to discover that she really meant it. "I'm good," she said, with conviction. "My critique group is coming up tomorrow to help me tweak, but I'm absolutely thrilled to have this book done. And I'm looking forward to taking some time off."

"That's so cool, Mom," Melissa said as they prepared to say their good-byes. "Todd's mother can't believe you're an author. And she said she's read all of Mallory's books."

There was a loud roar in the background and Jeffrey groaned. "Oh, man! That touchdown just cost me twenty bucks!"

Melissa giggled and gave her brother some grief over backing the wrong team and then in a flash they were gone, leaving Kendall feeling immeasurably better.

The printer continued to whir out the pages. The scent of turkey reached her nostrils and penetrated her thoughts. Without further internal debate, Kendall dished up a heaping plate and carried it into the living room, where she settled herself in front of the television.

She ate her feast while she watched Bing Crosby and Danny Kaye hamming it up in the season's first showing of *White Christmas*. She finished her piece of pumpkin pie as costars Vera-Ellen and Rosemary Clooney sang the number "Sisters."

Which reminded her she'd better pick up the guest bedrooms and make a grocery list before she headed into the Atlanta airport the next morning to pick up her "peeps."

• • •

Faye, Tanya, and Mallory had coordinated their flights as closely as possible, and after a late breakfast at an Atlanta Waffle House, they'd driven back up to the mountains with only a grocery stop and a hurried walk through Home Depot to delay them.

An unseasonably warm day put them in their favorite chairs on the back deck by 2:00 P.M., where they began to read their copies of the manuscript. They read through the afternoon, the silence interrupted only by the chirp of a bird or the scratch of a pen on paper as one of them or another jotted a note in a margin or paused to take a sip of sweet tea.

As dusk and then the early dark of winter descended, they came in to make sandwiches for dinner and then settled inside to continue their reading.

Occasionally someone laughed out loud or shook her head or murmured her approval, but no one interrupted the concentration of the group. Speed readers all, they'd agreed to finish their read throughs before they went to bed, intending to let their thoughts simmer overnight so that they could begin the discussion and revision work first thing Saturday morning.

Kendall was the first one up. She'd slept fitfully, her dreams vague and ill formed. Faye and Tanya and Mallory appeared in them but their actions were unclear and their motivations even murkier. It was still dark when she padded into the kitchen to make a pot of coffee.

The temperatures had dropped overnight and she pulled on a sweatshirt over her pajamas and watched the sunrise through the kitchen window, her grogginess evaporating like the fog before the sun. Growing impatient, she laid a fire in the fireplace and went into her bedroom to pull on a pair of sweat pants and an extra pair of socks. If the others didn't show up soon, she would wake them. She could hardly wait for the day to begin.

As if sensing her vibes, they appeared in rapid succession. And although all of them needed coffee, no one seemed inclined to linger over it. Kendall pulled out a box of sweet rolls they'd bought the day before and set out the remnants of the pumpkin pie. The conversation about *Sticks and Stones* began at the kitchen table and would last all day.

"OK," Kendall began. "I've been reading your chapters as they've come in, so I've watched the story taking shape. My biggest concern was how our voices would blend." She smiled. "But I think it's the fact that they *don't* blend that kicks it up another level."

"I agree," Mallory said. "The characters are completely different from each other yet they're drawn to and held together by the bond of their writing. And their determination to survive in a brutal business." She looked around the table. "Just like we are."

"Of course," Tanya added, "I've wasted lots of hours trying to figure out how much real life everybody's written into their characters. I mean I've never seen Mallory experience one second of writer's block. And we all know Chris is pretty much her love slave."

Everyone but Mallory joined in the laughter. Seeing the stricken look on her face, Kendall shifted uncomfortably in her chair.

"And, of course, I catch myself wondering about Faye's love life," Tanya said.

"Tanya!" Kendall yelped.

"Well, I can't help it," Tanya said. "Where did all that great sex she's writing come from? And does Pastor Steve know he's married to a Sex Goddess? I mean my imagination's nowhere near that highly developed." She winced at the look on Faye's and Mallory's faces. "Even though my mouth apparently is. Sorry." She made a zipping motion across her lips.

Faye stepped into the resulting silence. "Well, fact or fiction, I like that all the characters are flawed and surprising in some way."

Her eyes behind her glasses glinted with mischief. "I mean Tanya's character, Tina, is so afraid of being disappointed, she runs away from the best thing that's ever shown up in her life. Not to mention the best sex." She smiled as her point hit home. "None of our characters are perfect. And they've all got secrets that they're trying to hide."

All four of them were silent for a moment as they digested Faye's words, but Kendall noticed that no one stepped forward to clarify how much of what they'd written was fact and how much was fiction, herself included.

"We've all put ourselves out there in different ways," Faye continued. "And before we get into the nitty-gritty of corrections, I, um, want to make sure we're all still in agreement that we'll never reveal that anyone besides Kendall wrote this book." She looked into their eyes, her gaze intent. "I felt free to write what I did because I was counting on anonymity. My husband's pulpit and a lot of what I've worked for could be damaged if my part in this were ever revealed."

"Well, I'm with you, Faye," Tanya said, her unzipped lips once again in movement. "Darby says my sales figures are still climbing and it looks like I'm definitely going to be a part of that anthology. I don't want to do anything that might mess things up. My contract gives Masque the rights to pretty much everything I've created, including my kids." She grinned. "I'd feel a lot better if I could trade 'em Trudy for Loretta and Crystal, but I don't think that's gonna be happening."

"OK, then," Mallory said. "We're all in agreement that the book is Kendall's. And that no one else will ever lay claim to it except in the direst of emergencies."

"We could put our pact in writing," Kendall said. "But then we'd have to rig the document so that it would self-destruct if it were ever discovered."

Somebody hummed the *Mission Impossible* theme song as they adjourned to the living room, where they spent the day camped out in front of the fire with occasional breaks for food and drink.

They went through the manuscript page by page, discussing anything that dealt with character or story, knowing that the typos and miscellaneous corrections they'd noted could be addressed in a final pass.

Mallory thought Lacy's and Jane Jensen's characters should be given a little more page time. Kendall wanted Miranda's husband to realize his life was empty without her and come back of his own accord.

"No way," Tanya said. "This is women's fiction. Everyone's not necessarily going to end up living happily ever after."

"I agree," Faye said as she settled into a more comfortable position on the couch. "These women are facing serious choices and making decisions with real ramifications. We have to be careful not to wrap everything up too perfectly."

"Well, I don't want Kennedy's kids finding out about their father until she's ready to tell them," Kendall said. "I know we discussed this before but couldn't we let him realize a lifelong dream to run away and join the circus?"

There was much eye rolling over this suggestion, but mostly they hashed things out, generally coming up with a solution everyone could live with. When they couldn't, they handed the final decision to Kendall.

Tired and with their jaws aching from talking, they finished just after midnight and were in bed within minutes. On Sunday morning they staggered out of their beds with the sun and set to work on the revisions they'd agreed to.

By the time they left the house for the drive to the Atlanta airport that afternoon, all four of them were pretty much numb. Kendall dropped them at curbside, hugged them all tightly, and watched them disappear into the throng of holiday travelers. Somehow she made it back to the mountain house and threw herself into bed just about the time the sun made its exit behind the mountains.

Three days later after a final pass through the manuscript and the inputting of all the agreed-upon changes, Kendall Aims typed a brief e-mail to Lacy Samuels, which she copied to her agent, Sylvia Hardcastle, attached the file that contained the completed manuscript of *Sticks and Stones*, drew a deep breath, and hit Send.

It was exactly 10:35 P.M. on November 30. One hour and twenty-five minutes before her December 1 deadline.

29

Lacy Samuels was writing a rejection letter to a current resident of the Florida Correctional Center, hoping that FDOC
#85762 wouldn't be released and therefore able to come after
her anytime soon, when the e-mail from Kendall Aims that
contained *Sticks and Stones* landed in her inbox.

She knew the instant it arrived because the *click* of an arriving
e-mail signaled a reprieve from her struggle to find the appropriate words to tell a convicted felon not to give up her day job. She
left the grueling task in midword to see what had come in and
found Kendall's e-mail, which made her even more eager to finish the rejection letter so that she could get a first glimpse at the
manuscript.

Lacy cautioned herself not to rush through the onerous
task. It was bad enough running into rejected writers at a conference or writers' meeting—she'd discovered that many editors were very careful not to mail out rejections until *after*
they'd come back from these events. Rejecting aspiring prisoners seemed even more terrifying; one had to believe they were
at least a little more volatile than the average writer. And they
had a lot more time on their hands to commit that rejection
letter to memory and plot their revenge.

Lacy made a note to find out whether the prisoner's ID
number gave any clue as to the severity of their crime or their

possible release date and then downloaded and opened Kendall Aims's manuscript.

Her eyes skimmed the first line then went back and read it again. More slowly she read the first page on screen then scrolled down to the next. A chill ran up her spine.

"Holy shit!" she whispered, unable to drag her gaze from the screen. "Ho-ly shit!"

In a matter of minutes she inhaled the first chapter, all eleven pages of it, and felt a mad rush of excitement. It was like stumbling on a gold mine completely by accident. Or discovering a website that sold designer shoes for $9.99. That no one else knew about.

"OK," she said to herself "Calm down. It can't be this good all the way through."

She read the second chapter, trying to tamp down her excitement, looking for flaws, and then the third. But they were even better than the first.

Lacy sat in her chair staring at the screen trying to come to terms with the treasure before her. Even if the rest of the manuscript was only half as good as the first few chapters, Kendall Aims had created something undeniably special. Something that deserved to be read. Something that could make both their careers.

Lacy wasn't sure how she was going to fall asleep, given the way her heart was pounding and her brain was racing, but she nonetheless set her alarm for two hours earlier than usual and slid into bed. She wanted to get into the office early so that she could print out the full manuscript before Jane got in.

By the time Jane buzzed to demand her first cup of coffee, Lacy had already printed out a full copy of *Sticks and Stones* and stashed it in the bottom drawer of her desk.

All day, in between answering phones, fetching coffee, going floor to floor to deliver and pick up items that could easily have been sent via interoffice mail, running out for Jane's tuna on wheat bread and then once again for her dry cleaning, Lacy scurried back to her desk, pulled out the next chapter and read. And was stunned anew by how good it was.

The characters were both unique and complex, their voices entirely different. Kennedy Andrews was clearly the main point-of-view character and the one the reader would most readily identify with. Her pain and devastation were achingly real, the language used to paint her skillfully textured. But Miranda and Faith and Tina were also richly drawn. Their stories received a little less page time but were equally compelling.

As an industry insider Lacy was intrigued by the writers' view of the business and the brutality of the industry as a whole that emerged in the story. But she sensed that others, whose only contact with publishing might be the purchase of a book or membership in a book club, would absolutely love this inside peek. It spoke not only to the vagaries of the industry but to the act of writing and the often uncontrollable desire to create that could both nourish and destroy.

When the character of editorial assistant Lucy Simmons appeared, Lacy got her first vision of herself through Kendall's eyes. She winced at the reference to the naïve assistant's breathy voice and the depiction of her assignment to the book as an insult, but had to laugh at the tattoo and nose ring Kendall gave her. Kendall's portrayal of evil editor June Jankowitz was scathingly funny, but Lacy doubted that Jane Jensen would appreciate the humor. Assuming she ever actually read the manuscript.

With each chapter Lacy's excitement grew. Because instead of falling off after the first establishing chapters as Lacy'd expected, *Sticks and Stones* just got better and better. Even as she raced through her work so that she could get back to the manuscript, Lacy was completely enthralled by the women's friendship and the lengths they went to for the friend in need. She caught herself wondering what would happen to the book the four of them labored over; whether Miranda would overcome her writer's block; if Faith would tell her husband her secret; how Tina might tear down walls to open herself to the cook at the diner.

Lacy did what work she absolutely had to, and kept a wary

eye out for Jane, but mostly she read. Not because she wanted to, but because she simply couldn't stop.

At 5:30 she looked up from the manuscript and realized that the office had grown quiet. Tiptoeing out of her cubicle toward Jane's office, she was relieved to see that her boss had already gone. Lacy had agreed to meet Cash at six for drinks near Grand Central Station and she hurried now to stuff the manuscript into her briefcase and clear her desk.

Even in the darkness of the bar Cash Simpson was the best-looking man there. Lacy could feel the stares from other women and even some men and she imagined they were trying to fathom what it was about her that had merited his attention.

Lacy still hadn't figured it out herself, but not too long after the flirtation began she'd decided she didn't have to understand it; she just had to enjoy it for however long it might last.

Cash Simpson was not prone to delving into thoughts and feelings, but he was fun to be with and the sexual tension building between them made her feel like the heroine in a really great romance novel. So far she'd managed to avoid doing the actual "deed," which she suspected would be highly enjoyable, but would most likely signal the beginning of the end of his unflagging pursuit.

"You look about a million miles away," he said as the waitress brought their drinks and took her time setting them down on the table. The woman made a point of leaning over as she served, giving both of them a look at the benefits of investing one's tips in plastic surgery.

Lacy dropped her gaze and took a sip of her martini, her lips puckering at its dryness. She'd started drinking them in an effort to raise her sophistication quotient and had discovered that they allowed her to be in Cash's presence without turning tongue-tied and pathetic.

"Hmmm?" She looked up and into his inquiring gaze, realizing he was right. The real subject of her thoughts was tucked into the briefcase sitting at her feet. What did it say about you when the allure of a book was greater than that of a hunky and interested flesh-and-blood man?

"Just thinking about work," she admitted, though she was reluctant to say too much about *Sticks and Stones*. She had no idea if it was normal for an assistant to be given the job of editing a manuscript and she didn't want to say or do anything that might take the manuscript currently in her briefcase out of her hands. Especially not before she'd finished reading it. Which she should be doing right now.

"Tough day with Jane, huh?" He gave her a sympathetic look and signaled the waitress to bring them another round. "How many convict manuscripts have you read now?"

Lacy sighed. "I lost count somewhere after thirty and I haven't even made a dent in the stacks." She raised an eyebrow at him and took on an injured air. "I think it's a pretty steep penalty for the offense of a small flirtation with the infamous Cash Simpson."

"Well, I hope you're finding me worth the price." He took her hand in his and lifted it to his lips. The move was incredibly corny; anybody with an ounce less looks and charm—or without such a sexy first name—could never have pulled it off.

"I don't know," she teased, as a ripple of lust shot through her. "I have personally pissed off a boatload of felons. Depending on their release dates, I may have only a short time to live."

"Well then," he said, taking her other hand in his so that both of their hands were joined across the table, a move that was undeniably sappy but that he somehow managed to make unbelievably cool. "That would make you like a soldier going off to war not knowing when he might fall in battle." He smiled wickedly, aiming the even white teeth and sparkling blue eyes at her. "Or to a maddened aspiring author with criminal tendencies."

She smiled, enjoying the joke. Then he leaned in closer, burying her senses in a hint of lemony aftershave and warm skin. "I'm betting you need what every soldier headed off to war needs," he murmured. "I can send you off with a smile on your face." An eyebrow cocked upward. "And a song in your heart."

Their drinks arrived, but this time neither of them looked at the waitress.

"You didn't really just say that." She wanted to laugh out loud, but she knew that despite the humorous come-on, Cash wasn't joking about making their relationship physical. "I know you didn't just offer to put a smile on my face and a song in my heart."

She was smiling as she took a sip of her drink and let the gin-vermouth combo swirl down her throat.

"Ah, but I did. I can pretty much guarantee you a trip to the moon and back."

She could see all the other women in the bar straining to hear what Cash was whispering to her. Their envy was almost as big a turn-on as Cash's attention. But despite the martini haze, his lines were a tad too rehearsed and she caught herself wondering if he carried a list of satisfied partners in his pocket. Or had testimonials recorded on his cell phone.

He leaned forward to brush his lips across her cheek and nibble on her earlobe. Her breathing grew shallow and her body actually tingled in response. But her brain pointed out, yet again, that nobody got as polished as Cash Simpson without massive amounts of experience. She'd been playing at this since the day in the elevator, dancing closer and closer to having sex with him, but she was way out of her depth here. Could she handle having sex with Cash Simpson? Did she really want to?

"I don't live far from here," he whispered against the ear he had just nibbled. "Let's skip dinner and get right to dessert."

She realized with some surprise that part of her would be just as happy if people just thought she'd slept with him. Actually doing it seemed fraught with potential embarrassment and unnecessary complications. She'd had two brief college affairs—barely more than an introduction to what went where. The childish phrase, "Let's not and say we did," floated through her subconscious.

Lacy eased back in her chair, pulling away from him. Her foot grazed her briefcase.

Her briefcase.

The alcohol haze began to dissipate as Lacy stole a quick peek at her wristwatch. She had intended to stay for one drink and then go home to finish reading *Sticks and Stones*. It was already almost eight o'clock.

"I'm sorry," Lacy said. "I really have to get home." She pulled the weighted briefcase from the floor and set it in her lap where he could see it. "I have a manuscript to read. One from a writer not incarcerated or mentally incapacitated."

A look of surprise crossed Cash's face at her refusal; Lacy suspected he had little experience with rejection of any kind and so didn't know quite how to handle it.

She hadn't ruled out sleeping with Cash Simpson, but it wasn't going to happen tonight. Cash's blue eyes, even filled with all kinds of physical promises, were no contest for the manuscript that was once again calling out to her.

"I hope you'll forgive me," she said as she stood, the briefcase now clutched to her chest. "I really appreciate the drinks. And the, um, offer."

He was watching her intently now, with an odd kind of smile on his lips, like a benevolent spider watching a fly that had somehow managed to wiggle free from its web.

"But I really have to get home and get this thing read." She hefted the briefcase in front of her, exhibit A. And then she scampered out of the bar as gracefully as she could. Cash Simpson, and all the lovely women now getting ready to pounce on him, watched her go.

• • •

Lacy finished reading *Sticks and Stones* at 3:00 A.M. When she was done, she lay in bed staring up at the pockmarked ceiling of her bedroom, stunned by how the manuscript had made her feel. As she'd read, turning the pages faster and faster as the story progressed, she'd waited for it to fall off, for her interest in the characters to flag. But it never happened.

Nor did she feel the urge to skim so much as a line of dialogue or a paragraph of description.

Sleep completely eluded her as she sought a solution to the problem she faced. The manuscript was simply too good to be left in her hands. It needed to be edited by someone who knew what they were doing and then nursed through the publishing process by someone who could make sure it got what it deserved: a standout cover, prime positioning in bookstores, and a serious publicity campaign. She didn't have the experience or the clout to achieve any of these things.

Kendall Aims had been right when she'd had her character Kennedy Andrews call the assignment of a young assistant to her book an insult of the highest order.

But now, having read what Kendall was capable of, Lacy wanted to make it up to her. The only way she could do that was to get *Sticks and Stones* its due.

This, of course, would be much easier said than done.

30

*When in doubt, have a man come through
the door with a gun in his hand.*
—RAYMOND CHANDLER

In the morning, Lacy took her time in the shower, trying to come up with some means of convincing Jane to do right by *Sticks and Stones.* As she dressed and tucked the manuscript back into her briefcase, she had to admit that if she'd ever had the slimmest hope of influencing her boss in any way— and this was a big question mark—she'd forfeited it when she started dating Cash Simpson. Her part in making Kendall's already bad situation worse made Lacy all the more determined to get Kendall's book its due.

She dragged her feet on the way to the office, debating how to best handle Jane. But as she rode the elevator up to the editorial floor, she realized that Jane Jensen was not now, and had probably never been, "handleable." Even if her boss hadn't already written off Kendall Aims, even if she hadn't been completely pissed with Lacy, convincing the executive editor to do anything she didn't want to belonged in the category of "not gonna happen."

Could she convince Jane that she *wanted* to do something for Kendall Aims's book? This, too, seemed highly unlikely and better suited to a plot in a television sitcom than the harsh reality of Scarsdale Publishing.

In her cubicle, Lacy pulled the manuscript out of her briefcase and set the big mound of paper, now slightly dog-eared, on her desk. It consisted of some hundred and something thousand words double-spaced across four hundred and something pages. It contained the journeys of four unforgettable female characters and it deserved to go out into the world under the best possible circumstances with all the resources that a big New York publisher like Scarsdale could put behind it.

She went and made coffee, using the time it took the hot liquid to pool in the carafe to sort though possible strategies. She came up with nothing. Not a single argument that might convince Jane Jensen that Kendall Aims and her book were worthy of attention.

Lacy knew in her heart that Jane, who was erratic and ruled by her emotions, which appeared constantly conflicted, was never going to accept Lacy's analysis of the book. She would never act just because Lacy urged her to.

Lacy poured a cup of coffee for herself and one for Jane, which she lightened and sweetened the way her boss liked it. In her cubicle she set her cup down on the warmer and, once again, contemplated the manuscript. She could practically hear the book calling out to her, begging for her help. But how was she supposed to convince Jane to do anything for a book she hadn't even read?

Lacy's head jerked up as realization dawned.

The only thing she really had to do was get Jane to read *Sticks and Stones*. Because then, regardless of her personal feelings, Jane Jensen would have to recognize how commercially viable *Sticks and Stones* was. How much could be done with it.

Surely Jane Jensen, vindictive as she was, wouldn't squelch a potential moneymaker; surely even Jane Jensen cared about doing her job and making money for her employer.

Surely.

Lacy left her coffee at her desk and scooped up the manuscript, hugging it to her chest as she carried Jane's coffee to her office. At the open doorway, she waited for Jane to acknowledge her existence and wave her in. Lacy set the cup of coffee on her boss's desk and waited to be invited to speak. Although she hadn't yet figured out her pitch, she was determined not to leave this office with the manuscript. She was going to pass it on to Jane.

Finally Jane looked up. "What?" she demanded.

Lacy felt a stammer coming on. She banished it. This was not about her. It was about *Sticks and Stones* and getting it what it deserved.

"Kendall Aims's manuscript came in."

"So?"

"So. I read it and it's . . ."

Jane's gaze sharpened.

"It's fabulous. More than fabulous really. It's one of the best books I've read in ages."

Jane shook her head. "Maybe in comparison to the slush pile. Perhaps you've read more of the slush than you should have." She sniffed and turned away in dismissal. But Lacy didn't move.

Jane turned back to her. "You're still here," she said, clearly unhappy about it.

Lacy drew a deep preparatory breath. She'd been taught to stand up for what she believed in; she couldn't let a little derision from Jane Jensen stop her from trying to do what needed to be done. "You have to read it."

Jane's face registered her shock. "Are you trying to tell me what to do?" she asked, her tone incredulous.

"No. Of course not."

"Good." She turned her back on Lacy again. "You can go."

Wanting more than anything to do as she'd been told, Lacy nonetheless stood her ground. "I can't." Once again she drew a breath and then plunged in where she knew she shouldn't go. "I think if you just read the first few chapters you'll be as excited about the manuscript as I am."

She had Jane's full attention now. And not in a good way. But she'd committed to a course of action and there was no going back. "It's too good for me to handle. It deserves an experienced editor. You need to read it." She swallowed. "And edit it. And put Scarsdale's resources behind it."

Jane's face turned an ugly red. Lacy had a bad feeling that the part where her head did a 360 on her neck was going to come next. She prepared to duck before the green bile began to blow. But instead of shouting as she usually did, Jane's voice turned icy. Which was even scarier. "So your vast experience with the submissions of convicts and mental patients qualifies you to recognize a great manuscript. And to somehow tell me what to do with it."

"I'm just trying to make you see that this is a manuscript you need to read. I'm sure that once you do you'll see—"

No longer trying to mask her anger, Jane sprang from her chair and moved toward Lacy. "What I see is an assistant who has stepped way over the line." She came closer until they were virtually nose to nose, or given the disparity in their heights, nose to neck. "I have exactly *no* interest in anything that Kendall Aims has written. And the fact that a 'fraternizing nobody' with a thimbleful of experience is telling me I should be, makes me even less interested. If that were possible." Her eyes were flinty. Despite the icy delivery, her whole body quivered with rage.

Lacy felt like a lion tamer facing a wounded king of beasts without so much as a chair. She fell back a step, but knew that if she betrayed the extent of her fear, she'd be torn to bits. "If you could just let go of your anger and consider reading the first few—" she began.

"That's enough!" Jane bit out. "If you want to keep your job or ever have another in this business, don't say one more word."

Closing her mouth as instructed, Lacy clasped the manuscript to her chest and watched her boss struggle for control. Jane drew a deep breath then exhaled and some of the tension seemed to seep out of her.

"Now you're going to take that manuscript back to your desk and you're going to do whatever you can for it editorially."

Jane's tone grew more reasonable, but Lacy was afraid to trust it. "Then we're going to put the cover we already have on it and it's going to be released next December as scheduled. End of story."

She gave Lacy a level look, as if they hadn't just hurtled toward some emotional precipice and only pulled back at the last possible moment.

"Got it?" Jane asked.

Lacy nodded, but she was still afraid to speak. When it appeared that Jane wasn't going to say anything else, Lacy backed out of her boss's office and hightailed it to her cubicle.

. . .

Back at her desk, Lacy reached for the cup of coffee, but her hand shook so badly the milky brown liquid sloshed all over her desk. She put it down untasted and tried to calm herself.

Although she would have liked to deny it, the truth was she was afraid of Jane and her roller-coaster emotions. And of losing her job. But at the same time, she just couldn't let the book die. Even though she had no idea how to save it.

Her brain raced down every path it could think of, but her experience and knowledge were so limited that the paths were few and led only to dead ends.

When she was certain that Jane had left for lunch, Lacy dialed the phone number Kendall Aims had included in her e-mail. She waited nervously for the author to answer the phone.

"Hello?"

Lacy heard what sounded like the whir of a power tool in the background. "Is this Kendall?" she asked, having only heard the author's voice once before.

"Yes." The whirring noise stopped.

"This is, um, Lacy Samuels." She paused. "At Scarsdale. In New York."

"Oh. Hi." A pause. "Did you get the manuscript?"

"Yes, in fact that's why I'm calling."

There was another pause. She could actually feel the author's wariness. "Oh." Another long beat. "Is there a problem?"

She'd realized when she read Kendall Aims's description of her that Kendall had automatically assumed the worst about the person assigned to edit her book.

"No!" Lacy said, consciously trying to lower and "debreathalize" her voice. "There's no problem. I actually called to tell you how much I loved it."

There was an even longer pause.

"You've already read it?" Kendall Aims's tone conveyed her incredulity.

"I printed it out early the morning after it arrived. And once I started reading it, I couldn't put it down. I finished reading it about three A.M."

"You're joking."

"No. No joke. I just couldn't get over how individually compelling the four main characters were. You have one of the most incredible commands of point of view I've ever read."

There was another pause, longer this time.

"I've never had anyone read a manuscript this quickly," Kendall said. "Even before Mia left to have her baby, she sometimes took as long as a month. I haven't even heard back from my agent yet."

"Well, I may be a little bit on the new side," she said. "But you're my only author. So I have a lot more time to focus on you than a more experienced editor might." Except of course for the felonious slush pile.

"About the description of the editorial assistant . . ." Kendall began.

"No, it's OK," Lacy said. "Now that I understand more, I can see why Jane assigning me to you would feel like an insult." She paused a moment, unsure how much she could safely reveal. But the truth was, at the moment Kendall had no more power than Lacy. Somehow it felt important to let her know that although it might not translate into action, she was at least on Kendall's side. Or rather on the side of her book.

"It's true that I don't have much experience or clout. But I love *Sticks and Stones* and . . ." Should she say this when she was still waffling about how far she could stick her neck out? Yes, she thought. She had to do whatever she could for this book. Even if it meant losing her position. "And I'm going to do everything I possibly can for it."

"Oh." The one word carried a wealth of amazement.

"Of course, I don't know how well I'll succeed. Jane is, um, not inclined to rethink her plans for it at the moment."

"No, I don't suppose she would be."

"But I'm not a quitter. I've just got to learn how to work within the system on your behalf."

There was another weighty pause. And then. "Well if there's anything I can do to help, please let me know," Kendall said.

"I will."

And then as they said their good-byes, a last remark from Kendall: "Thanks, Lacy. For your interest, I mean. Sometimes when you have to eat an elephant, the biggest problem is finding someone to take that very first bite." A smile took over her voice, the first Lacy had ever heard from her. "Bon appétit!"

· · ·

Lacy left the building for her thirty-minute lunch break. She picked up a hot dog and Coke from a vendor then wandered up Fifth Avenue looking into shop windows, heading, as she so often did, toward the New York Public Library and Bryant Park behind it.

The sun shone above the skyscrapers and filtered down through the concrete and glass, diminished, to the street. People streamed around her, all of them apparently in a hurry, their hands crammed in their pockets or clutched around their cell phones. Like her, they were warmly dressed but not yet bundled against the coming frigid temperatures.

As she walked and ate, the questions circled in Lacy's

mind. What could she do on Kendall's behalf? Was there
any way to get around Jane Jensen? And, if so, was there any
way to salvage her job at the same time?

In front of the library, she paused to contemplate the Beaux
Arts building's grand Corinthian columns and its three immense archways. Two majestic marble lions served as bookends. Mayor Fiorello LaGuardia had named them Patience and
Fortitude during the depths of the Great Depression in an effort to inspire his beleaguered New Yorkers, and Lacy had
adopted them as her personal mascots. She looked to them
now for the answers she sought, but Patience and Fortitude
weren't talking.

In the park she threw her crumpled wrapper and empty
drink cup in a trash can and ambled along a walkway that
took her past the French-styled carousel then headed toward
The Pond to see who might be twirling across the ice.

Her cell phone rang and she saw Cash Simpson's cell number appear on her caller ID. He was somewhere in the South-
east on business and wouldn't be back until the weekend. She
answered, holding the phone to her ear as she approached the
skating rink, entering easily into their normal opening ban-
ter, realizing as they spoke that Cash had much of the experience she lacked. He'd know how things worked and, unlike
Jane Jensen, might be willing to explain them to her.

"Cash, I need to understand how to get a book noticed.
You know, how to get it the right kind of cover and in-house
backing."

"Well, that would start with the editor who wanted to purchase it. You were at that editorial meeting when the books
got pitched. The editor starts building excitement for the book
then. By the time they get to the sales meeting, if they've done
their job right, they can get the sales force pumped, too, along
with the publisher."

Lacy stopped near a vacant table that overlooked the rink
and plopped down onto its chair. "Well, what if the editor
wasn't at all excited about the book, maybe had passed it off

to some underling who knows it's fabulous but can't even get the editor to read it. What if this editor is whacked out and erratic and has told the underling to drop the whole thing or she'll make sure the underling never works in the business again?"

"Then the underling should listen," Cash said.

"But what if the underling would like to listen, but her conscience won't let her? What if she knows the book is incredible and that it's a moneymaker. And she just can't let it die. What then?"

"Lacy, you're a very bright girl. And I think you need to use your very bright brain to do what your editor told you."

"Well, I'd like to," she admitted. "But I can't. I owe this book—and its author—my best shot. I mean, that's why we're here isn't it? To publish the best possible books?"

He groaned. "This is what happens when you hire children. They think they're invincible and that they don't have to follow the rules."

"Just tell me how I can get around her," Lacy said with a wheedling tone. "I won't drag you into it if you don't want to be involved."

There was a silence in which she could feel his internal debate, could practically feel him weighing what his chances of sleeping with her might be if he turned her down. She should be heading back to the office, but she just sat and waited him out.

She was about to speak when he said, "You'd have to get other people within the publishing house to read it before the sales meeting that's scheduled for two weeks from now. I'd find another editor—someone who's not a fan of Jane would be best. Someone from PR, who could work up some ideas about its promotability, should read it. And maybe a marketing person. Then I'd see if I could get someone from the art department who could bring in some rough cover sketches." He paused. "And of course you'd need somebody relatively high up in sales to speak for it."

Lacy smiled to herself, but managed not to speak.

"Look, Lacy," Cash said. "I'll read it, but I'm not promising anything. If the book doesn't warrant it, I'm not going to stick my neck out."

"Fair enough."

"But I just want to warn you one more time. This is overstepping. And if you don't achieve your goal, you'll be out." He snorted. "Hell, you could be out anyway. Jane's not stupid, and as you know, she's not particularly kind or understanding."

"Point taken," Lacy said. But in truth, despite her fear, she'd already made up her mind. "I'll have a copy waiting on your desk when you get back." She lowered her voice and added a teasing tone, unwilling to dwell on the danger of her actions. "I'll make sure it's wrapped in plain brown paper."

She hung up, satisfied. Hurriedly, because she was already over her thirty minutes and still had to walk back, she pulled a crumpled piece of paper from her purse and made a list of who she knew in the various departments Cash had mentioned.

Cash was the only really influential person at Scarsdale that she knew well. But she had a good rapport with Hannah Sutcliff, who was a staunch enemy of Jane's. And Cindy Miller in publicity might have enough experience to work up a plan that made sense. The art director, Simon Rothwell, had declared himself eternally grateful for the candy bars she'd been supplying. Maybe she could cobble together enough of a team to make something happen.

As Lacy walked briskly back to Scarsdale's building, she planned her line of attack. She'd spend today and tomorrow making copies of the manuscript while she contacted everyone she thought might be willing to help. The next day, while she made the rounds doing all of Jane's grunt work, she'd drop copies with the people she'd recruited. And she'd stay on top of everyone to make sure those copies got read or passed upward.

Lacy felt almost giddy with excitement as she neared the

publishing house. But she also felt a serious sense of intent and purpose, like a general preparing to marshal his troops for an assault. She, Lacy Samuels, was about to unleash her version of "shock and awe." All over Jane Jensen's head.

31

Pen names are masks that allow us to
unmask ourselves.
—C. ASTRID WEBER

For the first few days after her conversation with Lacy Samuels, Kendall walked around in a daze. There was the utter relief of being done with the manuscript and fulfilling her contractual obligations. And her surprise at the young assistant's reaction and response to it.

Now that the manuscript was literally out of her hands, she tried to put it out of her mind as well. It was time to regroup and face the future. And although that included a divorce from Calvin, in the meantime it needed to include some sort of Christmas for the twins.

She reached Calvin at the office, bullying her way past the secretary, who was apparently new and who seemed not to have been informed that Calvin Aims still had a wife.

"Hello, Kendall." His tone was neither hostile nor welcoming; she might have been a stranger he'd once sat next to on a plane. Or a second cousin on his mother's side twice removed.

"Hello, Cal." She made a point of matching his level of disinterest. "I'm calling to discuss Christmas."

"Oh." It was clear that despite this being the beginning of December the idea of the upcoming holiday had not penetrated his consciousness. Not too surprising since she'd always handled the holidays and just about everything else that required any thought or planning. Or emotional investment.

"I think we need to come up with a plan for the holidays."

"A plan?"

"Cal, Christmas is only three and a half weeks away. The kids went elsewhere for Thanksgiving, but they're bound to expect to come home for the holiday."

"Oh. Right."

Kendall closed her eyes as she sought to hold on to her patience. "I think we should book a trip," she said. "Maybe to a ski resort. Or a beach somewhere. It would be a lot easier for us to pretend there's nothing wrong in another environment where there are lots of things for the kids to do." She paused. "In fact, I think we should include Todd and Dee for that very reason."

"Todd and Dee?"

"Melissa and Jeffrey's boyfriend and girlfriend. You remember that they invited the twins to their homes for Thanksgiving?"

"Right," Calvin said, though Kendall doubted he remembered. "But this might not be the best time to be spending that kind of money."

Kendall suspected Calvin was reluctant to display any portion of his net worth for fear it might lead a judge to question Calvin's recent assertions of poverty, but that was too damned bad.

"Maybe there's a better way to handle this. . . ." he began.

"Well," Kendall said. "Although I don't personally think the kids are ready for it, we could just go ahead and tell them about Laura and your plans to start a new life now. You know, as a kind of an early Christmas present."

She paused to let him envision it as she had so many times. "Then you could explain your rationale for breaking up our family." This was said calmly and was followed by another pause to let it sink all the way in. "Then there'd be no need to keep up the charade over Christmas. We could just have separate celebrations—maybe you and Laura could host the kids on Christmas Eve. And then they could drive up here to spend Christmas Day with me."

She didn't push either scenario, but just let them hang in the air. He was the one who had to make the choice: confessing and upsetting the kids right before the holiday. Or taking everyone, except Laura, on a vacation and sidestepping the whole confession.

Despite his bluster, Calvin was a coward at heart. And although he obviously no longer cared about her opinion of him, he did want his children's love and approval, something he was going to forfeit as soon as they found out that he'd not only had an affair, but was planning to bail out on their family.

"All right," he said finally, sighing. "A ski resort is probably the best idea. Will you see if we can get a condo in Beaver Creek or, I don't know, maybe Park City?" He named two places they'd been before, assuming, as always, that she'd take care of the details of their life. "Try to use frequent flyer miles for the flight though, will you?"

Kendall felt her eyes narrow at his assumption that despite all that he'd done, she would simply drop what she was doing to make his life easier. "I'll e-mail you our frequent flyer numbers and the name of the hotel in Park City. I've been arranging our lives for the last twenty-three years, Cal. I think it's your turn."

"Laura's not going to like this at all," he muttered.

A potent mixture of hurt and anger bubbled in the pit of her stomach. "That's such a shame," she said, her smile grim. She'd pushed for this vacation to protect her children from some of the pain she was feeling; upsetting Laura Wiles was just a happy by-product. "I can't imagine how I'll live with the knowledge."

Kendall ended the call. Phone still in hand, she dialed Mallory's number.

"Kendall?" Mallory sounded much too happy to hear from her.

"It's little ole me, all right," she said, wanting to entertain.

"Little ole Machiavellian me." And then she launched into the details of her conversation with Calvin.

"But won't that be awkward for you, too?" Mallory asked. "I mean the kids'll expect you to share a room and actually speak to each other whether you're in Atlanta or somewhere else."

"Nope," Kendall replied, with assurance.

"Because?"

"Because I'm not actually going to be there."

"Obviously I'm missing something," Mallory said.

"I'm not going," Kendall explained. "Oh, I'll let Calvin make a reservation for me and I'll be in the conversation right up until it's time to go. But then I'm going to have this horrible, unbearable sinus infection. Or bronchitis. Or some other yucky contagious something that simply won't allow me to fly."

"OK, I get it," Mallory said. "But I still don't get it."

"Well, I figure that way Calvin and the kids will have the holiday together. Maybe they'll forge some sort of something without me in the picture that'll help them make it through what lies ahead. You know I'm completely pissed off at Calvin for what he's done, but it has occurred to me that part of the reason he's done so little on his own with the kids is because I've always been there to do it for him."

"Interesting."

"Yeah. We just sort of fell into a pattern when the kids were little and it never occurred to me to try to change it. He made money and I raised the children and ran our life. Calvin participated when he felt like it or I made him." It was funny how clear it had all become to her now that it was about to end. Why hadn't she complained or at least asked for what she wanted?

"Hopefully something good can start between them." Kendall smiled. "And my plan has the added benefit of leaving Laura Wiles out in the cold over Christmas. And not the good, ski-resort kind of cold."

"You're right. Very Machiavellian," Mallory said. "I'm

proud of you. You stopped being a victim some time ago. And now you're becoming proactive. Good for you."

"Thanks," Kendall said. "It's funny how much better I feel. I'm even kind of charged about starting a new project. I mean, I know we just wrote *Sticks and Stones* to fulfill my contract. But I have this idea for a sequel. I may use the holiday to try to get a proposal down on paper."

Kendall stopped, realizing how she'd been going on. "And now, as they say, 'enough about me.' How's everything with you?"

"Well," Mallory said. "The writing is good. I'm flying through *Safe Haven* and the news is good about *Hidden Assets*. I'm thinking about calling Paris Hilton's mother and thanking her for teaching her to read."

Kendall laughed. "And how are things with Chris?"

There was a silence on the other end of the line.

"Not quite so great," Mallory finally admitted.

There was another pause and Kendall thought Mallory was going to change the subject. But the normally closed book of Mallory's personal life had apparently fallen open a crack.

"It seems as if I can only have one or the other: my career or Chris." She cleared her throat. "He's waiting for me to prove that 'we' come first, but I have no idea how I'm supposed to do that. I think I can write less than I have, slide my deadlines back a bit, but it's such a fluky business, Kendall. You really have to take advantage of your opportunities while you're hot. I love Chris and I miss him more than I can say. But I'm not going to give up financial security or jeopardize my career just to prove my love to him. I don't really think it's fair for him to ask me to."

* * *

At home in Chicago, Faye was absolutely dying to tell the truth. She'd been feeling the weight of her secret for far too long now and there was something about the approach of Christmas and its miraculous story of Jesus' birth that made Faye want to unburden herself and start anew.

As she'd decorated the Christmas tree, when she'd taken

Becky to Macy's to sit on Santa's lap, when she'd shopped for gifts for the Rainbow House moms and kids, and gotten the spare rooms ready for her sons and their families' arrival, the certainty that now was the time had grown. No matter what she was doing to prepare for the holiday, the imagined relief of unburdening herself was never far from her thoughts.

On a Thursday morning two weeks before Christmas she decided she couldn't let another day go by without telling Steve. Whatever his reaction, however surprised or hurt he might be that she hadn't confided in him sooner, she would tell him today.

Quickly before she could lose her nerve, she put on a skirt and blouse that he'd commented on favorably then applied her makeup and smoothed her hair with extra care. A last glance in the mirror confirmed what she knew: She looked like a well-kept sixty-year-old wife and mother; no one looking at her would ever suspect that she'd helped fund the Clearview Church of God writing erotica. Too bad *What's My Line?* was no longer on television; she doubted Bennett Cerf or Arlene Francis could guess her secret occupation in a bazillion years.

She took a few extra minutes in front of the mirror to rehearse what she wanted to say then continued to rehearse mentally as she gathered her coat and purse in the kitchen and as she slid behind the wheel of her car. Over and over she told herself that if she just explained it clearly enough everything would be OK. Maybe she'd just start with, "Hello, dear. Have I mentioned that I've been writing erotica under the name of Shannon LeSade?"

The sky was a pewter gray and the air thick with the promise of snow as Faye traveled west on Central, which ultimately became Deerfield, and then continued to wind her way south and west. Some thirty minutes later she was in South Barrington where land had been more plentiful and less expensive when they'd first begun purchasing land for what would one day be the Clearview Church of God. Spotting the church's spire in the distance, Faye marveled, as she always did, at what the years and Steve's faith and determination had wrought. Like the area around it, the church had mushroomed over the last two decades, growing from one simple structure with a broadcast antennae into a hundred-thousand-square-foot star-shaped complex.

She continued to rehearse what she would say, using the calm, rational tone she intended to use to say it, as she pulled into the massive parking lot that surrounded the complex, parked behind the administrative wing, and walked into the reception area. She was still mentally rehearsing as she approached the front desk.

"Hello, Mrs. Truett," the church receptionist said. "Are you ready for the holidays?"

"Almost, Evelyn. The boys and their families are due in on the twenty-third, right after the kids are out of school. How about you?" Evelyn Holloway had been manning the desk almost since Clearview Church and Steve's mission had existed. She had permanent-waved steel gray hair and Coke-bottle glasses, which gave her a somewhat quizzical air, as if she were peering at the world from a great distance.

"Oh, Harry and I don't fuss too much anymore. I already sent out the kids' and grandkids' gifts. I always get Harry something golf related. And he gets me a gift certificate for Barnes and Noble." She shrugged surprisingly hefty shoulders. "We've become awfully predictable. Sometimes I wish he'd surprise me with, oh I don't know, maybe a little black lace nightie." She winked. "Or even a big black lace nightie."

Faye smiled, wishing, not for the first time, that Evelyn Holloway's open-mindedness was more prevalent among the Clearview congregants. "Is he in?" She nodded toward Steve's closed office door.

"The pastor's on the phone, but there's no one waiting. He's probably still trying to get his bearings after his meeting with the delegation that stormed his office a little while ago," she said.

Before Faye could question the receptionist further, Evelyn asked, "Do you want me to hold his calls?" Evelyn raised her eyebrow suggestively and Faye had to bite back a smile. Despite Evelyn's apparently wild imagination, Faye wasn't planning to seduce her husband on the office couch. Although, now that she thought about it, she did, in fact, plan to ambush him.

Please, God, she prayed silently, as she moved toward Steve's office, *help me find the right words to explain.* She stopped in front of the closed door but didn't yet knock as she framed her second request. *And please help him understand.*

She knocked lightly on the door, hoping that God was in fact not only on her side, but ready to answer her prayers. When there was no answer, she pushed open the door and entered the room.

Pastor Steve was seated behind his desk, the phone pressed to his ear. His face registered surprise at seeing her and then transformed into a welcoming smile. He motioned her closer and held up a finger to indicate he'd be off the phone momentarily. Trying to remain calm, she perched on the side of his desk, facing him. For a few moments she just watched him talk while she gathered her nerve. She'd brought one of her books, hoping it would help her ease into her explanation, and she drew it out of her oversized bag and began to leaf through it. She was still flipping pages when he hung up and half rose from his chair to give her a kiss.

Faye kept a finger wedged in the paperback to hold her place as she leaned down to accept his kiss. His lips were firmly familiar, his scent, which mingled with the light lemony flavor of the cologne she'd been buying him forever, was subtly masculine.

He scooted his chair closer and looked up into her face. "Did I forget lunch?"

"No," she said, pushing back her nervousness. She had planned to just plunge into the topic without too much preamble, but now she found herself once again reluctant—make that afraid—to begin.

"I just stopped by to see if we could talk about . . .

something." Her voice trailed off uncertainly under his regard. So much for all the mental rehearsal.

"Is something wrong? Are you ill?" He sat up straighter, his expression turning to one of alarm.

So far nothing had gone at all as she'd practiced or planned.

"No!" She hated that her cowardice had sent his thoughts in a completely wrong direction.

"Are you sure?" He'd lowered his voice, but she could still read panic in his eyes. His tone carried a touch of suspicion that she was keeping something from him. Boy, did he have that right. She only hoped that when she finally spit out what she'd come to tell him, they'd be able to laugh over her secret's insignificance in comparison to the life-threatening illness he was now imagining.

"I'm positive." She spoke with all the certainty she could muster given how uncertain she felt. "There's nothing wrong with me." She smiled down at him as she emphasized her words with her hands, one of which still clutched the book she'd brought.

He'd begun to relax back into his chair when his gaze landed on the paperback. His smile disappeared. "What are you doing with that book?"

Puzzled at the tight-lipped intensity of his reaction, Faye held the copy of *Spiraling Seduction* up to examine the cover more closely. She looked back at Steve. "What do you mean?"

"I spent an hour this morning listening to a delegation of church ladies demanding that I speak out against the author, Shannon LeSade. Our daughter led the delegation."

"Sara?" Faye couldn't quite take in what he was saying.

"Yes. It seems she and her group are outraged by the ready availability of erotica, which they have decided, though I'm not sure how without actually reading it first, is pornography."

"But why? What does this have to do with them?" Faye's heart had sunk somewhere around her knees and was pounding madly.

"Apparently Borders has a large display of the author's books in the center of the store where, and I quote, 'anyone might see them.' And there's talk that the author may be coming here on a book tour, which has them completely incensed."

Faye shook her head, trying to clear it. None of her rehearsal had prepared her for this.

"They're planning to picket the store and organize other protests at bookstores around the country."

Faye's limbs felt heavy, her brain was moving too slowly to take it all in.

"It's apparently smut," Steve said. "I can't imagine what you're doing with it or why you would have brought it here. But frankly, after the uproar this morning, I don't ever want to see that book or that author's name again. And I don't want you seen carrying it around, either."

"But that's ridiculous. That's censorship." Everything Faye had intended to say, everything she'd been so desperate to say, flew right out of her head. The look on Steve's face made it clear the conversation she'd envisioned was not going to take place. "That's—"

"That's just the way it is." Her husband completed her sentence for her. "And after all we've gone through to build this ministry together, you more than anyone should know that sometimes perception carries more weight than reality."

Faye's thoughts swam in a murky sea of disappointment. She saw no way now to use her book as a springboard to the conversation she'd hoped to have. Even more troubling was Sara and her delegation. How had they raised a child who was so judgmental and unforgiving? Who thought she could stipulate what others should and should not be allowed to read? To think? And how could Steve condone it?

"Did you agree to speak out against LeSade?" *Oh, God.* She tried one last prayer despite the fact that none of her earlier entreaties had been answered, *Please don't let him say yes.*

"No," he said. "I'm not a fan of this sort of . . . trash. But I don't believe it's up to me to pass judgment on others' reading material."

He sighed as Faye tried to come to terms with it all. "Sara has a mind of her own, though," he said. "And she's got it set down a path that we never imagined."

Faye eased off the side of the desk and stood, tucking the book back in her bag and slinging the bag over her shoulder. She had accomplished nothing she'd come here to accomplish, but she no longer had the heart to try.

"I think I'd better go," Faye said, the taste of disappointment bitter on her tongue.

"But I don't even know why you came," Steve said. "Wasn't there something you wanted to talk about?"

"No, not really," Faye said, the lie tinged with her regret. "I just thought I'd stop in and say hello."

"All right," he said as he walked with her toward the door. "I guess it's hello *and* good-bye then." He leaned over to give her a peck on the cheek then pulled the door open for her. "I'll see you later at home."

"OK" was all Faye could manage. Her attempt at honesty had been feeble and inadequate. Despite all the rehearsing and the determination with which she'd arrived, she hadn't come anywhere close to confessing.

She left her husband in his office doorway staring after her. And as she waved good-bye to Evelyn and walked out into the parking lot, she realized she was going to have to set the idea of unburdening herself aside. She'd simply have to continue to live with her secret. And hope against hope that no one else ever revealed it.

32

*You can't wait for inspiration. You have
to go after it with a club.*
—JACK LONDON

Tanya stood in the center of the trailer's living room, trying
to get her family into the Christmas spirit. "Come on, Loretta, open up some of that tinsel."

The colored lights were already strung. The boxes of tinsel
and ornaments sat ready to be placed on the white artificial
tree she'd bought at the after-Christmas sale at Walmart last
year.

Tanya had tuned Trudy's radio to a station that had started
playing holiday music the day after Thanksgiving. She even
had two refrigerator rolls of cut-and-bake sugar cookies, with
Christmas designs already on them, sitting in the refrigerator
to be sliced and popped in the oven later: green Christmas
trees for Loretta, red Santa Clauses for Crystal.

"I bet they're singing carols over at the Adamses' house,"
Crystal whined. "Instead of listening to the stupid radio."

"And I guarantee you they're going to make their Christmas cookies from scratch," added Loretta. "We could be over
there doing it with them right now."

Trudy shot Tanya an "I told you so" look, but mercifully
refrained from saying it.

"Well, I am tired to death of all this whining and complaining," Tanya said. "We've been decorating a tree and getting ready for Christmas just fine on our own for years." She

turned the radio up higher in an effort to muffle the sounds of bad temper. "We can sing along while we do this if you all want. We don't need the Adamses to be . . . festive!"

Loretta huffed out of her seat and stomped over to the boxes of tinsel. Glaring at Tanya, she grabbed two of them, ripped them open, and carried them to the tree. Tanya winced as Loretta began to hurl clumps of tinsel at the branches, but held her tongue. She might be able to control her preteen's actions; controlling her attitude was a whole other matter.

"Come on, Crystal, baby, why don't you hang these ornaments?" Tanya placed one of the boxes of brightly colored balls in her nine-year-old's hands.

The first bars of "Silent Night" played from the radio's tinny speaker, but no one seemed interested in chiming in. Desperate to lighten the mood, she offered Trudy an olive branch. "Mama, why don't you pull those cookie rolls out of the refrigerator so they can soften up a bit and then ladle us all up some eggnog?"

Trudy didn't complain about the eggnog being store bought and in exchange Tanya didn't complain about the large tot of rum Trudy poured into the adults' glasses. In fact, she could hardly wait to drink hers.

Tanya opened the box of homemade ornaments and pulled out the angel Loretta had made in kindergarten. "Hey, Retta, will you put this on top?" Her daughter took the much-handled decoration, white gossamer wings glued over a triangle of white silk tied onto a used cardboard toilet roll, and held it carefully in her hands. This, at least, she wouldn't hurl at the tree.

"Do you remember the year you made it?" Tanya prompted. "When you were so little we had to put you up on Daddy's shoulders to reach the tip of the tree?"

It was dangerous ground, bringing up their mostly absent father, but at least it brought back more pleasant memories and hopefully reminded them that they had a few traditions of their own. "Look, Crystal," she said, pulling out another ornament. "Here's your Snoopy. I always did love his ears."

She took the generous glass of eggnog Trudy brought her and took a long sip of it, making no comment on the strength of the rum or the hot trail it burned down her throat even though it was encased in the cool creamy eggnog. The two of them watched the girls hang the remainder of the ornaments. Without being asked, Loretta pulled apart the clumps of tinsel she'd hurled earlier and took her time hanging the strands more evenly around the tree.

"That's looking great, don't you think, Mama? It's nice to have our *own* tree-decorating ritual."

She kept her gaze level with Trudy's and actually saw her mother consider and then discard possible comments. She'd already voiced her displeasure over Tanya turning down the Adamses' invitation and had not been shy about her disapproval of Tanya's handling of Brett in general. She'd told her in no uncertain terms that if she'd been ten years younger she would have already married him herself.

But for once Trudy seemed prepared to think before she spoke. Instead of stirring up trouble as she normally did, she seemed willing to help keep the peace.

"Well, now," Trudy said, still sipping from her own drink, which was bound to be twice as strong as Tanya's, which meant nigh on to melting paint. "I do think it's nice to have a family tradition of our own." She rolled the creamy drink around in her mouth for a time, clearly relishing it. "What with the girls' homemade ornaments. And the cute little tree. And making cookies and all."

Relieved, Tanya began to turn away. However, it appeared that Trudy wasn't quite done. "But I don't think there's anything wrong with sharing the holiday, either. It was right nice of the Adamses to ask us. And I think we could have found a way to work it out."

"Thank you for sharing your opinion, Mama," Tanya said carefully. She drained the rest of her glass and held it out to her mother. "Do you think you could get me a refill? And then we'll go on ahead and make those cookies."

"The Little Drummer Boy" came on with its gentle *pa-*

*rump-a-pum-pum*s, but despite the relative calm that surrounded her and the rosy little internal glow the eggnog had created, Tanya didn't feel at all peaceful. She was very afraid of how much her children and her mother wanted a relationship with the Adamses, how convinced they seemed to be that whatever was happening at the Adamses' house right now had to be better than anything they might do here.

Tanya understood that everything seemed more fun with Valerie, Dani, and Andi. She would even concede their home was nicer than the trailer and Brett's cooking better than her own. A part of her would have liked to be there right now, too.

But it was far safer not to need anything from anyone else, including the Adamses. Tanya knew, like she knew her own name, just how dangerous and foolish it was to hang your happiness on others.

· · ·

The morning of the Scarsdale sales meeting, Lacy woke at 5:00 A.M., having spent most of the night tossing and turning from an alarming mixture of fear and excitement.

She had not been invited to the fancy cocktail party Scarsdale threw the night before at the InterContinental Hotel, where the sales meeting was being held. The biyearly sales meetings were used to present and hype important books to the Scarsdale sales reps, who in turn would sell them to their accounts. The editorial department knew that the more excited the sales force was about a title, the harder they would sell it to their bookstores and retailers. Hence the hotel venue and party atmosphere.

Lacy hadn't exactly been invited to the actual sales meeting this morning, either, at which individual books were presented by their acquiring editors and plans for their launches revealed. But she intended to be there when, unbeknownst to Jane Jensen, the outstanding insider novel *Sticks and Stones* would be presented to Scarsdale's sales force.

Her hands were sweaty as she dressed and applied her makeup. Her mind raced with all of the things that could go wrong. Because she had no power at all and Jane not only refused to listen to her, but was inclined to believe the opposite of whatever she said about Kendall Aims's manuscript, Lacy had been forced underground, where she had done everything Cash Simpson had suggested and more in her efforts to put together a cohesive presentation on the book's behalf. She'd entrusted the presentation of the manuscript to Hannah Sutcliff, who had loved *Sticks and Stones* almost as much as she hated Jane Jensen, and who had come up with an angle for presenting the book that Lacy hoped would neutralize the evil executive editor.

Simon Rothwell, who had become a friend and ally as she'd fed him chocolate to help him through his nicotine withdrawal, had read and loved the book, and on his own time—time he'd told her he used to waste going outside to light up—he'd designed a new cover that Lacy had had bound on the front of the manuscript copies that would be passed out. Cindy Miller, her friend in publicity, had managed to not only get publicity head Naomi Fondren to read the manuscript, but had asked to be allowed to plot out a publicity campaign for the book—a brilliant move that had called Cindy to her boss's attention and moved Lacy's plan a major step forward. Cindy's friend Shelley in marketing had laid out a plan for placement and co-op dollars after she, too, got her boss to read the manuscript.

Of course none of the many steps that had been taken would have been possible without Cash's enthusiasm for the book once he'd read it and everyone else's antipathy for Jane Jensen, who had apparently scrambled over one too many backs on her way up the Scarsdale ladder.

Lacy's plan was fairly simple, but depended more on luck than she would have liked. The biggest threat to its success was Jane herself. If Jane tried to evict Lacy from the meeting or convinced the publisher that the book was lacking, Lacy's plan could blow up in her face.

And since the only thing predictable about Jane Jensen was her unpredictability, Lacy knew that anything was possible.

Dressed in a black skirt and sweater and with her hair subdued into a businesslike chignon, Lacy gathered her materials and cabbed it to the InterContinental. In the lobby, with its black marble column and gold leaf pediments, she drew a deep breath to steady her nerves and followed the directions Cash had given her to the meeting rooms. In an atrium off the elevator, sales and editorial staff mingled over coffees and Danish. An omelet station and bagel bar had been set up for those requiring more sustenance.

Lacy spotted Jane in a distant corner talking with Scarsdale's associate publisher, Brenda Tinsley, with whom Jane had roomed in college. Cash was near the bagels, conferring with the editorial director and the head of marketing. Perhaps feeling her gaze on him, he looked up and spotted her and, without interrupting his conversation, sent her a bracing glance.

Wanting to stay out of Jane's sight until it was too late for her boss to get rid of her, Lacy cadged a cup of coffee and went to sit in a far corner with her back to the crowd. She bent her head over her notes, but was much too nervous to focus on them. She took a sip of coffee and realized she'd forgotten to add cream or sweetener, but was afraid to go back for it lest she be spotted. She sat where she was until the buzz of conversation lessened. When the sound of china being stacked reached her, she stood and, carrying her materials with her, strode into the large conference room as if she were supposed to be there.

She spotted Jane right away, interestingly enough, chattering away to Cash Simpson, who was seated on her right. Careful not to catch her eye, Lacy moved around behind them and took a seat against the wall just as Brenda Tinsley called the meeting to order.

The meeting began with short pep talks by the publisher and associate publisher, followed by one from the editorial director. Cash stood and spoke at his seat for a few moments, something generic and welcoming. Jane Jensen watched him the entire time he spoke.

Hannah Sutcliff, who sat opposite Cash, watched Jane Jensen, a small, not very kind smile on her lips.

Lacy drew another deep breath and tried to fade further into the back wall. She was very aware of holding Kendall Aims's fate in her hands, not to mention her own. Her anxiety built steadily and silently until she could hardly breathe. And then it was time.

Hannah Sutcliff stood to address the group assembled around the conference table. She looked at Jane Jensen, that small smile on her lips, and then she winked at Cash. "I'm here to talk about one of the best books I've read this year."

Everyone sat up a little straighter in their seats. A hum of excitement coursed through the room.

"It has everything the women's fiction market gobbles up right now—and we all know how hard it is in the present market for any book to do that." Hannah smiled and made eye contact with others around the table. "It's the story of four women's friendship and the lengths they go to for each other, expertly interwoven with their own personal stories." She paused for emphasis and the small smile grew larger, drawing everyone in. "And it's set in the publishing industry, a real insider story, though we aren't always the heroes we might like to be."

Lacy had noticed Jane Jensen's back grow straighter, had seen her head jerk up at the mention of the publishing angle.

"The title of the book is *Sticks and Stones.*"

Jane Jensen came half out of her seat. Lacy watched Cash put a hand on her shoulder and gently push her back down.

"It's actually written by one of Jane's authors." Hannah nodded to Jane now, her smile wicked. "Because it's so different from anything this author has written before, because it's so much bigger in scope"—her voice grew steely—"and because her relationship with the author was somewhat strained due to having informed the author that we would not be going back to contract with her, Jane asked a number of us to read the manuscript when it came in so that she could get some unbiased opinions on the manuscript. Because that's what it's all about . . . the work."

Jane Jensen's hands clutched the arms of her chair; her entire body appeared clenched.

At the head of the table the publisher and associate publisher had their heads together. Most everyone else was looking at Jane Jensen.

"The heads of marketing, sales, art, and publicity have all read the manuscript, and the consensus is that this is a book we need to get behind." Hannah smiled again, putting all of her lovely white teeth to use.

Lacy was certain Hannah Sutcliff wouldn't have taken these steps if she hadn't believed in the book, but there was no denying how much the editor was enjoying putting Jane Jensen in a corner. "I am recommending that we make this a hardcover release and put it out as quickly as possible; we have a slot that's opened up in April and although it will require a huge rush for both production and promotion, I'd like to put *Sticks and Stones* in its place.

"Cash has already had several key members of his staff read it and they have some very positive feedback from Barnes & Noble and two other of our largest accounts. Marketing and publicity have prepared plans that they're going to present to you today. The art department has designed a new cover, which is included in the packet that will be passed out to you now."

Her smile grew broader. "Lacy Samuels, Jane's assistant, has been instrumental in seeing this book through to this point. I'm sure she has a long and distinguished career ahead of her here at Scarsdale. Lacy?"

Jane gasped. Apparently following Hannah's gaze, which had come to rest on Lacy, she swiveled around in her chair so quickly she crashed into Cash's.

Without speaking, Lacy stood and walked unsteadily to the conference table, giving Jane Jensen a wide berth. She didn't know whether Hannah's attempt to protect her would prevent Jane from firing her immediately, but it was much too late to worry about that now.

With shaking hands, she passed out the packet of materials she had prepared, Simon Rothwell's fabulous new cover rendered in color as its cover. When she came to Cash she gave him two packets and let him pass one to Jane, who was now glaring at her with an intensity that would have had Lacy running for her life had they not been in a room full of potential witnesses.

Lacy took her seat and kept her eyes on her own packet as one department head after another stood and offered support of *Sticks and Stones* and gave specifics of what they and their departments would do to help drive initial orders and then, once the book was on the shelves, to help build sales quickly enough to get the book on the all-important bestseller lists.

Excitement built in the room, everyone clearly thrilled that they had somehow come up with an unexpected winner. It was then that Lacy began to believe this might actually happen, that her fumbling attempt to do the right thing for Kendall Aims's book had taken on a momentum that not even Jane Jensen could stop.

With all the reports done, gazes came to rest on Jane Jensen, who had remained silent throughout Hannah Sutcliff's presentation. Those not in on the coup were obviously aware of the unorthodox manner in which *Sticks and Stones* had been presented by an editor who should by all rights have had nothing to do with another editor's book.

Jane was going to have to speak; it was inconceivable that they could move on to the next presentations without hearing from her. Brenda Tinsley stood and looked over at her former college roommate. "Jane?"

It was breathtakingly quiet as Jane Jensen pushed back her chair and stood. In fact Lacy held her breath as she waited for her boss to speak. She didn't see how Jane could fly in the face of Hannah's carefully scripted presentation, but Jane Jensen was not always rational. Then again she hadn't gotten where she'd gotten without being able to adapt when necessary.

Lacy's view was of Jane's back and other than its rigidity there was not a lot of information to be gleaned from it. But when she began to speak, her voice gave no hint of the anger Lacy knew had to be bubbling inside her. Nor did she give any indication that everything that had just happened had occurred without her knowledge and certainly without her permission. "I have to thank Hannah for presenting *Sticks and Stones* so . . . diligently. As if it were her own."

Her gaze swept the rest of the table. "As to everyone else who's spoken up today, I'll never forget what any of you have done on behalf of this book. Not ever."

Hannah, whom Lacy could see across the table, nodded calmly, unperturbed. But others shifted uncomfortably in their seats. Those who were in the know knew a threat when they heard one.

"So now all that's left is to give *Sticks and Stones* and its author their due. And believe me I'm going to do that."

If Lacy hadn't known how pissed off Jane Jensen had to be, nothing in her words or actions would have alerted her. Nor would she have guessed that the woman had never read the manuscript or that she had so little regard for its author. Jane Jensen's ability to act calm and rational was even more frightening than her inability to do so.

The meeting moved on. Other books were discussed, their merits hyped. Lacy felt an odd mixture of elation and fear. She had no idea whether Hannah's recognition of her efforts would prevent Jane from firing her. Or whether if she was allowed to stay, she'd ever lay a finger on Kendall Aims's manuscript. But she didn't want to find out any of that today. For today it was enough that she'd accomplished what she'd set out to. Even if she found herself out on her ear and out of publishing forever, she'd have that satisfaction.

About thirty minutes before they were scheduled to break for lunch, Lacy got up and practically tiptoed out of the conference room. No one commented on her leaving, but as she closed the door she could feel Jane Jensen's gaze on her back. As if measuring it for the knife she planned to stick there.

33

Two days before Christmas Kendall sat alone in the living room of the mountain house staring into the fire. It had begun to snow early that morning and she hadn't left the house all day. She kept telling herself that this was fine, that she should be celebrating the opportunity to spend the day reading in front of her cozy fire, but what she felt was pitiful and alone.

Melissa and Jeffrey had called from Park City earlier to check on her and so she'd been obligated to pinch her nostrils together to achieve a nasal sound and throw in the occasional cough. They told her how much they wished she was there and how it wasn't Christmas without her, but they sounded happy. The conversation was brief because they were about to head out to the slopes. She should have felt good that her plan was working; this was, after all, what she had hoped for. But the fact that she'd orchestrated it didn't make her feel any less abandoned.

The Christmas tree she'd set up in the corner of the living room was scrawny, picked up at the last minute from the undesirable unchosens in the lot at the grocery store. She hadn't had the strength or interest to go up into the attic to find the few ornaments that might have been stored there. Instead she'd purchased boxes of candy canes and a couple of rolls of red velvet ribbon from Walmart, which she'd hung and tied to the branches of the tree. She suspected a fully decorated tree for one would have made her feel worse; she'd seen the articles encouraging singles to treat themselves to gourmet meals served on fine china, but had always thought the idea both pathetic and wasteful. She preferred to think of her tree decorations as "minimalist." And they had the added advantage of being partially edible.

Now she lay on the couch wrapped in an afghan with her head propped up on a throw pillow, a book splayed across her chest. She'd tried for more than an hour to lose herself in the story, but had been unable to concentrate.

From the kitchen the click of an incoming e-mail echoed through the silent house. E-mail had been sparse in these last days before the holiday; presumably the rest of the world was too busy getting ready for the holiday to communicate. Except, of course, for those touting penile implants and enlargements, who should have been too busy having really great sex to find the time to send e-mails.

After much internal debate, Kendall got up and headed to the kitchen by way of the tree, where she plucked a candy cane from a branch and peeled off its protective cellophane. Holding the crook of it in one hand, she slid the cane into her mouth and sucked on its sharp sweetness as she plopped down into the kitchen chair.

The sight of Jane Jensen's name in her in-box caused Kendall's fingers to freeze over the mouse. The subject line read, "Revision letter: STICKS AND STONES." If she'd had anything else to do, Kendall would have gotten up now to do it. Instead she sat and stared at the line of type on her computer for a good five minutes before she finally opened it.

The e-mail was brief but professional and revealed none of the enthusiasm for her manuscript that Lacy Samuels had conveyed. It specified January 2, which was barely ten days from now, as the deadline for the return of the revised manuscript. This was a fairly quick, but certainly not unheard-of, turnaround. Except, of course, for the fact that it would require Kendall to work through the Christmas break. No apology was offered for the intrusion into her holiday, and if Kendall had had anything at all to do for the next ten days, she would have been on the phone to Sylvia complaining about Jane's lack of respect for Kendall's private life.

But what would she gain from complaining now? Jane Jensen was not excited about this book, but she was at least editing it rather than sloughing it off on her assistant.

Perhaps Kendall should feel honored.

Oh, grow up, she mumbled to herself as she downloaded and opened the attached revision letter. This signaled the end of her relationship with Scarsdale Publishing and Jane Jensen. She would revise as directed and deliver those revisions on time. Once the revisions were accepted, the part of her advance due upon acceptance of the manuscript would be released and she would be free.

As she printed out the attachment, Kendall read it through on screen. Grudgingly she acknowledged that the suggested changes had come from an experienced professional. The direction was clear and well thought out and there had been no attempt to efface the author's voice or intent, which sometimes happened when an editor tried to impose her own style. Despite her personal dislike for Jane Jensen, Kendall was impressed. The editorial suggestions were first rate and would make *Sticks and Stones* even better.

With Jane's notes in front of her, Kendall began to read through the manuscript. In the margins she made notes about where and how she could strengthen the scenes that led to Kennedy's flight to the mountains as well as build the backstory and rapport between the four writers. Especially challenging would be capturing the point-of-view character's reactions and internal dialogue when her book took off. This was something with which Kendall had no personal experience and would have to rely on imagination. She made a note to herself to talk to Mallory about this. Then she pulled out a legal pad and started a list of page numbers on which she could drop in paragraphs and scenes to accomplish the changes. Then she began to make note of scenes she might revise or take out.

For the next eight days Kendall worked almost nonstop. She broke for a couple of hours on Christmas morning to cook and eat a breakfast of bacon and eggs topped off by a candy cane and a talk with the twins.

In the late afternoons when she had to get out of the house, she'd pull a coat on over her sweats and tromp a ways down the road and back. Or she'd go out for a drive. Or to the grocery store to pick up a few things.

But mostly she kept her head in the story, using the breaks she took to think through the areas that gave her the most trouble, and then hurrying back to the house once she'd figured them out.

On New Year's Day she e-mailed the revised manuscript to Jane Jensen and sent a copy to her agent. Then she slept for almost twenty-four hours, waking up just in time to straighten the house before the twins arrived.

· · ·

Melissa and Jeffrey stayed with her for the last three days of their winter break.

They were in great spirits, happy with their holiday vacation and looking forward to their return to school. Calvin had, it seemed, come through in ways that had surprised the twins during their ski vacation and they couldn't wait to share the details with their mother.

"You should have seen him, Mom," Jeff said the evening he and his sister arrived at the mountain house. "He only checked phone and e-mail messages once a day. He hung with us practically the whole time. It was really cool." Jeffrey had always worshipped Calvin, but sometimes that worship had had to come from afar.

"That's great, honey," Kendall said. And she meant it. Whatever happened, she wanted the twins to know that they were loved by both of their parents.

"Yeah," Melissa added over hot chocolate in front of the

fire, "the only thing that would have made it better would have been having you there." She gave Kendall a searching look. "Is everything all right between you guys?"

Kendall studied the twins in the glow of the fire. They had her dark, heavy hair, Calvin's green eyes. Other bits and pieces of her and Calvin poked through, an expression here, a walk there, but their sums were far greater than her and Calvin's parts.

They weren't children anymore, she reminded herself, and hadn't been for some time. The days of pretending about Santa Claus and the Tooth Fairy were ancient history. Nonetheless she had no intention of telling them about Laura. Or their father's decision that he no longer loved their mother. When the time came to talk about the details of a divorce, Calvin would have to be there. All four of them would sit down and discuss it together.

"Well, I guess you not answering is an answer, isn't it?" Melissa jutted out her chin and scrunched up her nose, as always, combative when threatened. "You're getting divorced!"

"No way," Jeff said, watching them closely. Kendall felt as if every ounce of pleasure had been sucked out of the room. "It's not true is it, Mom?"

Still she hesitated, unsure of what and how much to say. There was no reason to send them back to college worried about their family falling apart. Especially when things were still so up in the air.

"It's true that your dad and I made a decision to spend some time apart," Kendall said carefully. "We needed a . . . break."

Melissa's jaw jutted out even further. A lone tear managed to escape. Kendall watched it fall onto her daughter's sweater and darken the fabric.

"I just can't believe this. I thought everything was fine. What happened?" Jeffrey's voice quivered; his childish anguish was so at odds with the broad shoulders and grown man's body.

Looking into her children's panicked faces, Kendall knew

there was no way she could tell them the truth. Not now. Not without Calvin at her side. She'd simply have to force him to commit to a time and place for the four of them to talk. For now she'd resort to a few little white lies.

"Look," Kendall said gently. "I know we all want things to stay the same. It's human nature. But you're just at the beginning of your lives; everything's stretching out in front of you. And that's as it should be. Daddy and I have been together a long time. We're at a stage where it's not unusual to reassess and, er, reevaluate."

"Is it because we went away?" Jeffrey sat on the edge of the sofa, intent on understanding. "Is it that empty nest thing? Because I could transfer to Georgia Tech and move back home. Or take off some time to . . ."

"It's true, Mom, if it would help we could . . ." Melissa joined in. They'd always been of the same mind, their emotions finely attuned. It was only that Jeffrey was generally the one to express his first.

Kendall felt an overwhelming rush of love for her children. Their concern flowed over her, buoying her, helping her find the words she needed. "I appreciate your offer, but everything's OK. Your dad and I will work things out."

"But how are you going to fix this? How will you know if you're . . . reevaluating properly?" Always the more practical, Melissa was now looking for more concrete reassurances.

Kendall would have bet money that deep down Melissa suspected the truth. But the more important truth was that her son and daughter didn't want those suspicions confirmed.

Kendall drew a steadying breath and tried to find her way out of the maze without relying too heavily on deceit. "I've got the book done, which is a huge load off my mind. And now your father and I need to deal with our marriage."

Melissa and Jeffrey still looked miserable. Kendall continued to look for the right words to reassure them.

"Whatever happens between your father and me, you have to remember that we both love you very much—more than anything really. And that we always will."

"But what are you *doing* about it? How are you going to make things better?" Again Melissa demanded specifics. Jeffrey looked like he wanted to put his hands over his ears and pretend this conversation had never taken place. At the moment, she was with Jeffrey but it was clear she needed to offer some additional reassurance.

"We've been meeting with a marriage counselor," she lied. "She's trying to help us . . . sort through things."

"Who are you seeing?" Melissa asked. "What's her name? Are you sure she's reputable?"

Because her daughter seemed to need it, Kendall cast about for a specific, a name, something she could hold out. But because she also felt backed into an emotional corner by her children's panic, she couldn't think clearly. All she kept picturing was her attorney with her hands on the Green Giant's balls.

"Her name is Anne Justiss," Kendall said. "She's very well known in Atlanta." She managed a smile. "And now I think that's enough on this topic. You're going to have to trust your father and me to figure things out."

She stood, her legs shaky but her smile in place, and kissed them good night.

34

It took me fifteen years to discover I had no talent
for writing, but I couldn't give it up because
by that time I was too famous.
—ROBERT BENCHLEY

In the morning Kendall saw Melissa and Jeffrey off then busied herself stripping beds and changing sheets. Later she'd call
on Anne Justiss, divorce-attorney-turned-temporary-marriage-
counselor, to see where things stood. Maybe in the afternoon
she'd run down to Home Depot to pick up a few things.

When the phone rang, the shrillness cleaved the silence,
startling her. Caller ID showed it to be a New York number.
With some trepidation, Kendall answered, bracing for a complaint from Jane Jensen. Or a demand for more revisions.

"Is this Kendall Aims?" The voice was clipped and very
Upper East Side. Kendall searched her memory banks, but
she didn't think she'd ever heard it before.

"Um, yes," Kendall admitted. "This is she."

"This is Naomi Fondren at Scarsdale."

The name sounded vaguely familiar, but Kendall couldn't
quite place it. "Yes?"

"I've been asked to prepare for a mid-April lay down for
Sticks and Stones. Obviously this doesn't give us near enough
time to prepare for a major hardcover release."

Kendall said nothing. She'd worked with a low-level PR
assistant on her first few books, but the young woman had
left and after that Kendall had been forced to rely on what

self-promotion she'd been able to afford. Kendall's mind paused in midthought and went back as the realization hit: Whoever Naomi Fondren was she'd just referred to *Sticks and Stones* as a major release. A hardcover major release.

Kendall dropped down into the nearest chair. She may have stopped breathing.

"I'm planning to have advanced reading copies out for review by February first," Naomi said, referring to the bound copies of the book galleys that were traditionally sent out for review. "But obviously that doesn't give us near enough time for the major publications, with their longer lead times. *Publishers Weekly* has agreed to read a loose-bound manuscript. And I'm sending another over to *Ladies' Home Journal* right now; they've expressed an interest in serialization rights."

Kendall had to force air back into her lungs. The lack of oxygen was clearly impacting her ability to hear and think. Only two of her eight books had been reviewed by *Publishers Weekly*. And serialization in *Ladies' Home Journal*? That was normally reserved for authors of Mallory's magnitude. Hell, that sort of exposure was the very kind of thing that turned an author *into* an author of Mallory's magnitude.

"What, um," Kendall began. "What's your job title at Scarsdale?"

The woman laughed. "Oh, I'm sorry," she said. "Did I forget to introduce myself? I'm Scarsdale's head of publicity."

"Are you new?" Kendall asked. If so, perhaps Scarsdale had finally hired someone willing to promote *all* of their authors and not just the top sellers. Or maybe she simply had Kendall confused with someone else.

"Only to you, dear," the woman said, with some amusement. "I don't work personally with all that many authors."

Kendall had no doubt the few she did work with probably had sales figures equivalent to Stephen King and Tom Clancy. But she didn't have a chance to raise this question; Naomi was already on to the next item on her list.

"I've got someone working on a discussion guide right now. And I've called several of our top photographers to see who we can get down there to shoot a new color photo for your book jacket."

A book jacket photo? Kendall had been using the same black-and-white photo for the past eight years. She'd never considered a new one—she'd just been getting older and the photo on her mass-market paperback releases had become smaller and smaller until the picture might have been of anybody.

"I'm also talking to the people at the Margaret Mitchell House in Atlanta to see if we can do a launch party for you there. This will be followed by a book tour to include sixteen key cities with *New York Times*-reporting bookstores. It'll end in Chicago."

"A tour?" There was just too much information coming at her, all of it ranging from highly improbable to completely impossible. Kendall was certain she must have misunderstood.

"Yes, dear. A tour," Naomi said, as if speaking to a child. "Could you make yourself available for the last two weeks of April?"

Kendall surveyed the silent kitchen and the equally silent mountaintop. Then she looked down at her grubby sweats. There was a hole in the toe of her thick wool socks. Maybe she should tell Naomi she had to check her calendar to see whether she could squeeze the tour into her busy schedule. Did anyone ever turn this sort of opportunity down?

"We're going to end in Chicago because . . ." Naomi paused here as if waiting for a drum roll. "I had the chance to pitch a producer I know at *The Kristen Calder Show*." She named the nationally syndicated talk show out of Chicago, whose host had chosen to go head to head against Oprah. The publicity head laughed giddily—a really strange sound, given the sophisticated accent. "In fact I had a bound galley hand delivered to the show's production offices. And Kristen Calder has chosen *Sticks and Stones* as her next book club pick!" She paused again, as if waiting for applause.

Kendall batted her eyelashes, trying to blink back her surprise. Kristen Calder had not yet achieved one-name status, but she was very big and still growing. Kendall knew this had to be a dream and any minute she was going to wake up. She squinched her eyes shut then opened them, but she was still in her kitchen, still on the phone. And her sock still had a hole in it.

"Did you hear what I said?" Naomi Fondren asked. "*Sticks and Stones* is the next Kristen Calder book!"

Kendall swallowed back tears. Everything she had ever dreamed of, right down to the last detail, was being flung at her at the speed of light and she was deathly afraid she was imagining it. She glanced frantically around the kitchen, but there were no Daliesque clocks melting on the wall, no *Twilight Zone* theme music playing in the background. "But . . ."

"Lucky for us, Kristen is trying to differentiate her book club by doing less weighty books and focusing exclusively on new authors."

Kendall had to smile at the idea of being "new" after a decade of writing, but she didn't speak. She simply couldn't find the words.

"So then," Naomi concluded. "That's all I have for now. I'm going to e-mail you the name of a media coach I know in Atlanta; she'll help you put together a look and a wardrobe and teach you how to deliver sound bites and such. Plus we want to make sure you're ready to handle Kristen when you get to Chicago." She laughed again. Naomi Fondren was having a very good day.

Kendall still didn't know what to say.

"Do you have an author escort you prefer to work with?" Naomi asked.

This time it was Kendall's turn to laugh. All of this was so utterly unbelievable she was bound to wake up in her real life at any moment. The knowledge that she was probably asleep or having some sort of out-of-body experience loosened her tongue.

"Escort?" Kendall giggled. "Hmmm, let me think. . . ." As if she'd ever needed one to get her to the Borders at her local strip mall. Or the few other local chain stores that occasionally invited her in to sign her books—provided she sent out newsletters and flyers to bring in the people to buy them, too.

"I'll tell you what," Naomi said, possibly grasping what alien territory Kendall had just passed into. "Dana Kinberg is based in Atlanta and she's great. I'll give her a call when we hang up and see if we can book her at least for the prep and the southeastern leg. She knows absolutely everyone and she'll help you get comfortable with the whole thing."

"Thanks," Kendall said, even as she hoped Dana was the patient sort. Despite her eight books and a decade spent in publishing, Kendall felt as if she were being reborn. Dana Kinberg was going to have to teach her to crawl. She felt both fear and excitement at the prospect.

"So then," Naomi concluded brightly. "If you don't have any questions, I'll get back to work on all this. I'll keep you posted via e-mail whenever necessary. And I think you'd better give me your cell phone number."

She waited while Kendall gave it to her; then she insisted that Kendall take down hers and put her into her speed dial. "I'll send you an itinerary for the tour as soon as I have all the details worked out," Naomi promised. "Feel free to call me twenty-four/seven."

As Naomi prepared to hang up, Kendall forced herself to speak. "So," she said tentatively, not quite sure how to frame the one question she felt compelled to ask. "I guess Jane Jensen must have really liked the book."

There was a brief pause and then, "Jane Jensen?" Naomi pronounced the name with a sniff, as if it didn't mean much to her. "I don't know about her."

"Oh."

"But the publisher certainly loved it. And so did the associate publisher. And the head of sales. And pretty much everyone else who really matters at Scarsdale."

She laughed gaily while Kendall marveled at the absurdity of all of this happening now. How could it be that Jane Jensen, who cared so little for her and her work, had allowed this to happen?

"I don't know where you've been up 'til now, Kendall. But there's no question that at least as far as Scarsdale Publishing is concerned, you most definitely have now arrived."

• • •

The first phone call Kendall made was to Mallory, who hooked them up to Faye and Tanya.

"Are you telling me this woman just called you out of the blue?" Tanya had started shrieking when she heard the name Kristen Calder and hadn't stopped. The sound of washing machines and dryers roared faintly in the background.

"Yes!" Kendall replied. She was still quivering with excitement, her thoughts ricocheting in what felt like a million directions. "I was bracing myself for Jane Jensen and there was Scarsdale's head of publicity handing me the moon."

"Oh, my God! A Kristen Calder pick!" Tanya was still shrieking. "I just can't believe it!"

"This is so great." Mallory had said this five or six times now, but Kendall couldn't help noticing that the congratulations sounded a bit hollow. "We all knew how good this book was. I just didn't think Jane Jensen would ever admit it."

"Really," Faye agreed. "We all thought we were flying under the radar on this one." There was a tinge of something Kendall couldn't quite identify in Faye's voice. "I have to admit I never expected this."

Were they jealous? Kendall wondered but then dismissed the thought as quickly as it arose. They'd made this happen for her. Why wouldn't they be pleased? Still some of her excitement began to fade. Not wanting to let the thought fester, she put it out there. "Is this a problem for you guys?" Kendall asked. "I mean, obviously I'm incredibly excited, but I hate that you're not getting credit."

"Not to mention the royalties," Mallory observed, her voice dry.

Tanya stopped shrieking.

"Any idea what kind of print run we're talking?" Faye asked.

Kendall had been so shocked by Naomi Fondren's call she hadn't even thought to ask.

"Well," Mallory said. "You remember James Frey, the guy who wrote *A Million Little Pieces*, the Oprah pick that turned out to be fiction and not nonfiction as advertised? His book sold something like 3.5 million copies and sat on the *New York Times* Bestseller List for about fifteen weeks. Kristen Calder doesn't have as big an effect as Oprah, but her last couple of picks topped all the bestseller lists. We could be talking close to a million copies." Mallory's tone had gone from dry to grim. "You do the math."

Now Kendall felt like shit. Her friends had done her a tremendous favor; if it hadn't been for them there would have been no *Sticks and Stones*. Yet here she was about to reap monetary benefits and critical acclaim as well. "Look, you guys," she said, "we all know this wasn't how it was supposed to be. I mean, who ever thought we'd be having this conversation?" She stared out the kitchen window, trying to push the guilt far enough aside so she could figure out what to do about it. "We all thought the book would disappear and that would be that."

"Clearly we did way too good a job," Faye observed, trying for humor. "But once you're a Calder pick, making the *New York Times* list can't be far behind." She didn't sound at all excited about the prospect.

"Is anybody else still trying to do the math?" Tanya asked weakly, and Kendall thought about what this kind of money would mean to Tanya and her girls.

"We'll just split the money up," Kendall said. "That's the easy part. We did this together and we should benefit equally." She thought for a moment. "And when I go on Kristen Calder I can just tell her what really happened. If I put the right spin on it, she might like the story behind the story of four friends pulling together. Then you all could share in the credit, too."

For a minute, Kendall could see it. She'd want the three of them in the audience anyway—she couldn't imagine being there without them—she'd just introduce them and they could all confess together on national television. It would be a Kristen Calder exclusive.

"Absolutely not!" Faye put a halt to Kendall's little fantasy. "We talked about this before. My name can't ever be attached to this book." There was regret in her voice, but something that sounded like fear, too. "Not ever." She cleared her throat. "And as hard as it is to pass up *The Kristen Calder Show* and a spot on the *New York Times* list, I can't believe Mallory and Tanya want to be in breach of their contracts, either."

"I could sure use the money, Kendall," Tanya said. "And I'd love for people to know I had a hand in a bestseller." She gave a bitter sort of laugh. "But I can't let Masque know I had anything to do with *Sticks and Stones.* I checked my contract, and I'm definitely not allowed to work on any outside projects. It could give them grounds to drop me."

"I agree," Mallory said. "Admitting coauthorship could open us all up to trouble. I don't want anyone to know I wrote Miranda Jameson. She's not exactly a heroine I'm looking to claim. And I can promise you Partridge and Portman's legal department would have plenty to say about one of its golden geese collaborating on a book for one of their competitors."

"OK then," Faye said, her relief apparent even over the phone line. "We all agree that Kendall will split the royalties equally among us and that Kendall remains the acknowledged author of *Sticks and Stones.*"

Kendall agreed, but her earlier emotional high had given way to an uncomfortable low. She disliked dishonesty, yet submitting *Sticks and Stones* with only her name on it was one great big fat lie.

No matter how compelling her reasons, or how insistent Faye, Tanya, and Mallory were about keeping the collaboration secret, taking credit for their work left Kendall at odds with herself and undeniably diminished.

"Listen," Mallory added. "I know this is really great news for you. I'm sorry not to sound more enthusiastic. I've just got a few other things on my mind."

Kendall suspected her friend was referring to the standoff with her husband. Chris had finished his project in Arizona and accepted another up in the Pacific Northwest. Mallory was writing up a storm as usual, and had just found out that *Hidden Assets* had moved from number ten to five on the *New York Times* list. In a rare confidence, she'd informed Kendall that she wasn't going to drop everything and chase across the country after him.

"As exciting as it all seems, you need to be prepared," Mallory said. "All the touring and signing seems very cool at first, but it can get really old really quickly."

Kendall laughed. "Well, it's going to be quite a departure from sitting alone up on my mountaintop, but I figure I might as well enjoy it. Wouldn't it be a great irony to hit the list on my way out of Scarsdale?" Not to mention with a book she hadn't authored alone.

"One last warning," Mallory said. "Scarsdale might not be so quick to let you go now that you've delivered a book they can make real money off of," Mallory said. "If *Sticks and Stones* does as well as it looks like it's going to, they're going to want the sequel."

"But they've already terminated her contract," Tanya pointed out. "Jane Jensen told her to get lost."

"All I'm saying is in publishing you should 'never say never,'" Mallory replied. "If they think they can make money from Kendall in the future, they could offer her big bucks to stay. And Kendall wouldn't have to work with Jane if she didn't want to. Once you become valuable enough, you're in the driver's seat. And all the choices become yours."

"I'm still trying to deal with the reality of Kristen Calder and the possibility of the *New York Times* list." Faye sounded downright unhappy at the prospect. "That's going to call an awful lot of attention to a book we all agreed we didn't want to call too much attention to."

Once again, Kendall felt as if she'd strayed into completely alien territory. In a span of months she'd gone from being afraid she'd never sell again to full-fledged publisher support. Whether anyone else ever knew it or not, she'd be aware that she hadn't gotten there on her own merits.

For the first time in a month, her fingers itched for the feel of a power tool. She would have liked to have a project waiting for her when she hung up.

"I don't think we should worry about making the list before the book is even in print," Kendall said, trying to smooth things over and put everyone, including herself, at ease. "Besides, I have a much more pressing concern at the moment that I need your input on."

The murmurings of support began. Faye joined in, too, though Kendall was no longer sure who was rooting for the success of *Sticks and Stones* and who was rooting against it.

"I'm about to have an author photo taken and go on a sixteen-city tour," Kendall said. "And I don't have a thing to wear."

This stimulated the hoped-for change of topic as everyone piped in with suggestions that would help her minimize the amount of luggage while maximizing the number of outfits, but it didn't completely calm Kendall's nerves. She caught her attention straying to the hall closet where her tool belt hung. Maybe she should leave some room for it in her suitcase. So that she could strap it on if things got tense.

35

*Some writers take to drink,
others take to audiences.*
—GORE VIDAL

By the time *Sticks and Stones* came out on April 16, Kendall had pinched herself so many times her arms were black and blue.

She spent the day in Atlanta, where she went to a Buckhead salon for the works, coming out late that afternoon buffed and polished and professionally made up. She dressed in her room at the Ritz-Carlton where Scarsdale had booked her for the night. Tomorrow Dana Klinberg would escort her to bookstores all over Atlanta to sign stock and meet booksellers. Then she and Dana would fly to Miami, from where they'd begin their trek northward. Her last appearance would be in Chicago, when Kristen Calder would interview her about *Sticks and Stones,* with selected book clubs in the audience.

Hardly recognizing herself in the mirror, Kendall changed into one of the Travelers ensembles that she'd bought at Chicos—after being assured that all of the pieces were not only interchangeable and machine washable, but could be balled up in her suitcase only to pop out unwrinkled at each destination.

As she slid into the passenger seat of Dana's car for the drive to the Margaret Mitchell House, Kendall offered up a silent prayer of thanks for the petite dark-haired author escort that Scarsdale had provided and without whom she was certain she would now be bouncing off the walls. Or cowering in a darkened corner.

Somewhere in her early forties, Dana Kinberg was an unusual mix of calm and chutzpah, a champion hand-holder who remained unfazed by Kendall's fear of the unknown, the publisher's punishing schedule, or the bazillion details she'd be expected to handle on the road. Normally Dana only worked in and around Atlanta, but Scarsdale had arranged for the escort to accompany Kendall all the way through to the stop just before Chicago.

To date there hadn't been a single question Kendall had posed that Dana was unable to answer. If Dana wondered how Kendall could have written so many books and remained so ignorant of the touring process, she was too tactful to say so. Kendall was already growing dependent on her and they hadn't even left town yet.

"Oh, God." Kendall breathed heavily as they turned onto Peachtree and pulled into the parking lot behind the Margaret Mitchell House. "What will I do if no one shows up?"

"That's not going to happen," Dana said in her soothing matter-of-fact voice. "I checked in with reservations this morning, and the event is a complete sellout. You don't need to worry about a thing."

Kendall didn't see how this could be so, but rather than waste these last few minutes arguing, she spent them breathing deeply in an effort to calm down. On the front step, she paused in a final attempt to gather herself. With Dana at her right shoulder acting as her entourage and literary "wingman," Kendall entered the room.

The first familiar faces she saw were Melissa's and Jeffrey's. They rushed over to her, identical smiles creasing their faces, their arms already open for hugs. Calvin followed with a pleasantly neutral smile on his face. Todd and Dee flanked him on either side. Laura Wiles was nowhere to be seen.

"Look, Mom!" Melissa said. "The place is packed!"

Kendall looked around her and saw that her daughter was right. A well-dressed crowd milled about, drinks in hand, waiting to take their places at the cloth-covered tables. Many were friends from the suburbs—women she'd volunteered at school with, played tennis with, seen casually at church. There were a few people from Calvin's office that she'd known forever. Others were members of the local chapter of Wordsmiths Incorporated, to which she'd belonged for more than a decade, but a gratifying number appeared to be complete strangers who'd come to see her or at least to hear more about *Sticks and Stones*.

Surreptitiously she pinched herself yet again. Once she was certain that she was awake and not in the midst of a lovely dream, Kendall began to circulate. She chatted with the Margaret Mitchell House staff as well as several reporters that Dana led over to meet her. Then she made the rounds of all the familiar faces; she was so grateful that they'd come, she hardly knew how to thank them.

After that the evening sped by in a blur. She didn't remember what they ate, what selections she read from her book, though she'd chosen them carefully in advance, marking only those she'd written herself. She had no idea how many books she signed afterward, but the bookseller looked happy and Kendall's fingers ached halfway through from clutching the Sharpie. Her jaw throbbed from smiling and talking.

The only truly uncomfortable moment came when the children questioned why Kendall was staying at a hotel rather than at home. But Calvin left the explaining to her, and Melissa and Jeffrey seemed willing to believe that she'd opted for the hotel because of the next morning's stock signings and the early-afternoon flight her publisher had booked her on.

She was fairly certain Dana drove her back to the hotel, although she might have floated there on a cloud. Or in the pumpkin-turned-carriage that Cinderella had once used.

She fell asleep staring up at the hotel room ceiling, her arms wrapped around her body, too tired and too pleased to pinch herself. It had been the most exciting night of her life.

Kendall was still pinching herself three days later in Jacksonville, as they prepared to leave Florida for major cities in

Texas, followed by Louisiana, Mississippi, Alabama, northern Georgia, North and South Carolina, Virginia, Tennessee, and Kentucky.

Before each signing Kendall felt that flutter of nerves, that last-minute fear that the store would be empty and the only people who would stop at her table would be looking for directions to the bathroom. But at each store the crowds grew larger and so did the requests for media interviews.

At first Kendall had been uncomfortable on the early-morning and noon talk shows around which the book signings were scheduled. Unable to shake her sense of disloyalty to Tanya, Faye, and Mallory for taking the credit for their work, she evaded questions about her writing process and regimen. But by the time she reached Houston she'd learned how to sidestep these issues. After her sixth interview, she began to develop pithy sound bites that earned her even more exposure. She was tired but still thrilled. The bruises on her arms began to fade and the guilt began to lessen. Her belief in herself and her work grew.

"This is a very unusual reaction for fiction from a relatively unknown author," Dana said, noting the standing-room-only crowd at an independent bookstore in Louisville on their final morning together. Dana would be flying back to Atlanta; Kendall would fly on to Chicago for a signing later that afternoon and tomorrow's *Kristen Calder Show* taping.

"Fiction's such a subjective thing and very hard to promote," Dana said. "But all of these women can relate to the friendship that's central to the story. It's a real celebration of 'sisterhood.' I know that was the hot button that clinched the *Kristen Calder* appearance. I can't tell you how sorry I am to be missing it."

"I wish you'd come with me." Kendall couldn't believe how attached she'd become to Dana. She'd served as confidante and security blanket. She'd known when to keep Kendall company and when to give her space. And she knew all the best restaurants in every town they'd been in.

"I've got to get back. I've got an author to meet tomorrow. And you'll have your friends there," Dana said, referring to Mallory and Tanya's plan to fly in early the next morning so that they and Faye could be at the taping.

The very thought of *The Kristen Calder Show* made Kendall's stomach churn. Keeping the local reporters and interviewers at arm's length had been easy, but Kristen Calder was another story. She had the staff and resources to delve into anything she chose.

Enough, she chided herself. The talk show host had no reason to hunt for anything, no motive to suspect Kendall had anything to hide. Kendall was not a James Frey who had written fiction and marketed it as the truth. She just had three ghostwriting friends who'd insisted on helping her. It was a victimless crime. No one, including the public, was being hurt.

Still the knowledge that she was being less than honest left her uncomfortable and unable to completely enjoy her success. Her insides wobbled like Jell-O when she hugged Dana goodbye at the Delta ticket counter and headed to the gate for the flight to Chicago.

• • •

That morning Lacy Samuels woke in Cash Simpson's bed for the first time. Intellectually she was somewhat surprised that she'd finally ended up there, but her body had no qualms. It was doing its own little happy dance over all the attention it had received.

Her body's gratitude notwithstanding, Lacy knew that Cash was not her "Mr. Right." He was too old for her, too sophisticated, and possibly too sexually talented. But she'd decided somewhere between the second and third orgasms he'd given her that there was no reason on earth he couldn't be her "Mr. Right Now."

He moved closer, trapping the heat from their last bout of lovemaking between them. His warm breath brushed her ear. "Come here." He turned her in his arms and drew her up against him, burying her face in the breadth of his chest. His erection teased against her inner thigh. "I've got something for you."

"Why thank you, kind sir." She smiled as their lips met and felt a quickening inside as he rolled her back into the mattress and fit himself on top of her. Afterward she lay with her head in the crook of his shoulder, completely sated. Her body's dance slowed, allowing her brain to kick in—funny how they seemed unable to work in tandem.

Lacy swung her legs over the side of the bed and sat up, eager now to get moving. "I need to go home and pack."

"That's right," he said as he rolled out of the other side of the bed. "You don't want to keep Kristen Calder waiting."

He looked tousled and unbelievably attractive as he stepped into his discarded jeans. His eyes could only be called "bedroomy." Lacy sighed. If it ended today, it would have been worth it.

Cash shrugged into a T-shirt while Lacy pulled on last night's skirt and top. She still couldn't believe Hannah had arranged for her to go with Cindy and her boss to Chicago.

Outside Cash hailed her a cab and put her in it, then leaned in the open window to give the cabbie Lacy's address and a wad of bills. "Call me when you get back," he said, kissing her good-bye.

Lacy smiled and waved as the cab pulled away. But she was already thinking about what she'd take with her. And whether she'd have time to pick up her favorite blouse from the dry cleaner.

• • •

Now Lacy sat at her desk, her overnight bag packed and ready on the floor of her cubicle, reliving the night with Cash and anticipating the trip to Chicago.

Jane was in, but since the sales meeting when she'd realized Lacy was under Hannah Sutcliff's protection, she'd begun communicating primarily via e-mail and intercom, keeping personal contact to a minimum. This suited Lacy just fine.

Not so fine was how thoroughly Jane had cut Lacy out of

the loop on *Sticks and Stones*. Despite her role in getting Kendall Aims's book noticed, Lacy saw nothing of what came next: not the revision letter, not the copyedits, not the galleys, not the favorable reviews. Nothing. In fact, Lacy had had to beg Cindy Miller for an ARC, an advanced reading copy, which had been raced through production so they could be sent out for review.

Lacy had read it in one long night and been forced to admit that Jane's editing had taken a great book and made it even greater. She simply couldn't understand how such a gifted editor could be so scornful of writers. Not to mention such a failure as a human being.

The intercom on her desk squawked and Lacy jumped.

"I want you in here!" Jane's voice reverberated through the cubicle and beyond, wiping out the Cash Simpson sexual highlight reel that had been playing in Lacy's head. She rose reluctantly and picked up a yellow pad.

"Now!"

Reminding herself that she was no longer completely defenseless and that if Jane could have fired her she would have done so by now, Lacy speed-walked to her boss's office.

The door was open. Before Lacy was all the way in, Jane began to speak.

"I just got a call from Brenda Tinsley," Jane said, an odd smile on her lips. "*Sticks and Stones* has hit the *New York Times* list." The smile turned taunting. "Just as I knew it would."

"Oh, my God!" Lacy yelped with excitement as the news sank in. She wanted to hug someone—anyone—as long as that someone wasn't Jane Jensen. Who had apparently decided to pretend she'd expected this all along.

Lacy pushed aside her irritation at Jane's ridiculous claim and held tight to her excitement. Hitting the *Times* list was a pinnacle achieved by a very small percentage of authors, and it was a status symbol that once attained, never went away. No matter what happened after this, Kendall Aims's name would forever be followed by the words, "*New York Times* Bestseller."

"I'm going to call and let *my* author and her agent know,"

Jane said, making sure Lacy felt the jab. Lacy couldn't fathom how the woman could claim credit for the success of an author she'd tried so hard to bury. Nonetheless Lacy felt as if she'd won a gold medal. She could hardly imagine how Kendall would feel.

But Jane seemed more interested in Lacy than Kendall.

"Hannah may be protecting you at the moment," Jane said. "But no matter how many TV tapings they send you to or how many times you sleep with Cash Simpson, you'll never last. You're too big a Pollyanna to survive in publishing."

Lacy's blood began to simmer in her veins. She wanted to rip the smirk off her boss's face, wanted to tell Jane exactly how many times she'd slept with Cash Simpson and describe in detail each and every one of the resulting orgasms.

"Is that right?" Lacy met her boss's malicious gaze head on. She didn't flinch or shrink back. The truth was that Jane was the one who'd screwed up. Where did she get off belittling and threatening?

"So you don't think the fact that I recognized something special in a book you couldn't be bothered to read fits into this conversation somewhere?" Lacy asked. "Or that so many of your . . . colleagues . . . couldn't wait to show you up might be a sign that you should look for a new field to go into?"

Jane smiled. Or maybe it was more of a gloat. "I'm not going anywhere. I just finished editing a *New York Times* Bestseller." She paused to let the taunt sink in. "Though I sincerely doubt she'll ever hit the list again. Kendall Aims happened to write the right book at the right time. *Sticks and Stones* doesn't even read like her work. Maybe someone should look into how such a mediocre talent suddenly developed such an amazing command of differing points of view!"

Lacy's blood came to a full boil. Jane Jensen was like a cancer that grew by spreading itself over everyone and everything. Lacy was tired of being afraid of her, tired of listening to her negativity, tired of taking her abuse. Every positive thing that had happened since Lacy had started at Scarsdale had happened in spite of Jane, not because of her.

Lacy stepped forward so that she crowded Jane's space. Lacy was taller and bigger and, as far as she was concerned, she had right on her side. "You're a gifted editor—I saw what you did for Kendall's manuscript—but I'll never understand your hostility and your disdain for the people around you."

Lacy was on fire with righteous indignation; she wasn't sure she could stop the words spilling out of her mouth; she wasn't even sure she wanted to.

"Bottom line," Lacy bit out, "I'd rather be a Pollyanna than someone too . . . too . . ." She caught herself at the last minute and swallowed back the ugly words she'd been about to hurl. ". . . too cynical to do her job!"

And with that Lacy turned on her heel and marched out of Jane Jensen's office without being dismissed. At her desk, she worked out her aggression rewriting the rejection letters. Instead of rejecting the prisoners' manuscripts, she heaped praise on their work and told them to contact her personally to discuss possible publication. She signed each letter with a flourish, making sure the name Jane Jensen was legible on each one and adding Jane's direct phone line. Then she walked them down to the mail room personally so she could be sure they went out.

36

The only reason for being a professional
writer is that you just can't help it.
—LEO ROSTEN

Kendall and Faye had left Chicago O'Hare International Airport and were speeding north on I-294 toward Faye's home in Highland Park when Jane Jensen reached Kendall on her cell phone to tell her that she was now a *New York Times* Bestseller.

Once she'd determined that it was not a prank call, Kendall started to cry.

"What is it?" Faye asked, clearly shocked by Kendall's tears. "Are you OK? Did something happen to the twins?"

Kendall shook her head, but she couldn't stop crying. The enormity of what had happened hit her like a physical blow, sucking the air from her lungs and clogging her throat with emotion.

"You're starting to freak me out!" Faye's gaze was locked on Kendall rather than the highway. Even in her emotional stupor, Kendall realized this was not good, but she was struck dumb by the impossibility of what had happened.

"Are you feeling sick? Should I drive you to an emergency room?"

Kendall shook her head again as a great swell of happiness arose within her. Then she was laughing and crying. Her sobs were loud and choking things, but the joy was trying to break through, too.

The dream she had dreamed for years and finally given up on had actually come true. She, Kendall Aims, had a book on the *New York Times* Bestseller List.

"What's happened?" Faye demanded as they exited and began to work their way eastward. Street signs flew by, but Kendall didn't even try to read them. "If you don't tell me right now, I'm going to stop right here in the middle of Deerfield Road until you do." She pulled to a stop at a red light as if making good on her threat. "I'm not kidding, Kendall. What's going on? You have to tell me right this minute."

Kendall sobbed a final sob then swiped at the hot tears littering her cheeks. Her lips twisted into what she thought was a smile. "*Sticks and Stones* is number ten on the *New York Times* list." Kendall could hear the amazement in her own voice. "It's going to be announced tomorrow as part of my introduction on *The Kristen Calder Show*."

The light turned green but Faye was still looking at Kendall. Her foot didn't move from the brake.

"Are you sure?" Faye asked.

Horns blared behind them. A guy in a semi leaned out of the truck's cab to yell at them personally.

Kendall nodded her head numbly. "That was Jane Jensen. She called to tell me."

The two of them sat and stared at each other while horns blared and irate drivers raced around them. "I feel like aliens just landed and offered to take me to their leader," Kendall said, her tears still flowing. She sniffed and swiped. "I'm afraid to look," she said. "Has hell frozen over?"

A policeman appeared and pounded on Kendall's window demanding to know why they were just sitting there. "Sorry, officer." She smiled and blubbered. "We just had some . . . shocking news. We forgot where we were."

Without so much as a blinker, Faye made a hard right onto a side road and pulled to a stop at the first opportunity. They sat in the silence of the front seat, locked in their own little bubbles of wonder. "We made the list," Faye said.

Kendall's tears stopped and the fog of amazement began

to dissipate. She was on the list, but she hadn't gotten there alone. She looked into Faye's eyes and both of them registered the truth at the same time: All four of them had written the book together. Only Kendall's name would appear on the *New York Times* list.

"We have to call Tanya and Mallory right now." Faye pulled out her cell phone. "I'll dial you first so we can conference."

Kendall duly answered her phone and then waited while Faye found and then connected the others. Her excitement was now tempered by worry over the others' possible reactions. Even though they'd discussed the possibility of this happening because of Kristen Calder, not being able to claim authorship of a *New York Times* Bestseller couldn't feel good.

Kendall listened quietly as Faye gave them the news.

Tanya shrieked just as she had when she heard the Kristen Calder news, and Kendall thought how surreal it was to be sitting in a car in the northern suburbs of Chicago listening to Tanya shriek in a St. Petersburg Laundromat. Mallory was noticeably silent.

"Dang it!" Tanya said. "Hold on. I've got a customer who's having trouble with her spin cycle." The phone clattered as she set it down.

Kendall looked at Faye. Faye stared back. They were still sitting on the side of the road while traffic passed by them.

"I can't believe we've been put on hold for a laundry emergency," Mallory said. "But then that seems to be so . . . us."

Tanya came back on the line. "Lordy," she said. "Some people should not be allowed to reproduce!" And then, "This is so incredibly . . . incredible!"

"I don't see that we need to get all worked up," Mallory said. "We knew when *Sticks and Stones* became a Kristen Calder pick that this could happen. We all agreed we were willing to take the risk."

Mallory's comment was yet another reminder that everything positive that had come of their collaboration was countered by a negative. The more books sold the more money they would make. And the more visible Kendall and *Sticks and Stones* would become.

"I just want to remind everyone to be careful tomorrow," Faye said as they prepared to hang up. "The whole *New York Times* thing opens up *Sticks and Stones* to a whole new level of scrutiny. The last thing we want to do is give Kristen's people the slightest reason to be suspicious."

As they hung up, Kendall slumped in her seat. She felt as vulnerable and insubstantial as a leaf pried loose from its branch and hurled into the unknown. Somewhere she needed to find the enthusiasm and strength for this afternoon's signing and *The Kristen Calder Show* taping tomorrow. Even with her "peeps" in the audience and the Scarsdale PR people on hand, Kendall would be the one in the hot seat. Faye was right: For people with so much to hide, they were venturing into a fearfully public arena.

She stared resolutely out the window, trying not to panic as Faye pulled back onto Deerfield then headed north again. She'd simply have to play things just right tomorrow. The publishing gods had put her on the list. Now she'd have to hope they didn't intend to desert her.

• • •

At home Faye directed Kendall to a downstairs guest room and then leafed through mail in the kitchen while her friend freshened up.

Steve was out on the West Coast for a speaking engagement, so Faye had made a lunch reservation at Rosebud, where they could celebrate the news then walk around the corner to Borders for Kendall's book signing.

They ordered glasses of chardonnay and sipped them as they dipped pieces of crusty Italian bread into a shared plate of seasoned olive oil. They had a second glass of wine with their chopped salads—just enough to calm their nerves without impairing their senses—and by the time they arrived at the bookstore, tomorrow's taping had once again taken on the luster of an adventure rather than a visit into the fire pits of hell.

"Hello, Mrs. Truett." Judy Winslet, the customer relations

manager, greeted them as they entered the store. "I'm so glad you steered Ms. Aims to our store. There's a lot of excitement about *Sticks and Stones*."

"It's great, isn't it?" Faye said. "We just found out *Sticks and Stones* made the *New York Times* list." She smiled at Kendall. She'd been a bit jealous when she'd first heard the news. Happy for Kendall, but disappointed, too. This was the second appearance on the list that Faye had been unable to claim.

There was a nice-sized crowd for the signing, lots of readers and even more aspiring writers who seemed to have adopted Kendall as their poster child of possibility. Faye stood and chatted with other Highland Park residents and the customer relations manager while Kendall signed and schmoozed, something Faye noticed she'd gotten quite good at.

When the crowd had thinned, Kendall signed remaining copies while Judy affixed autographed-copy stickers onto their covers. "I'll put these on the end cap," the manager said, referring to the outward-facing shelf Scarsdale had paid to have *Sticks and Stones* placed on. "And I'll put a few extra on the new release table, too."

"Great, thank you," Kendall said. Faye could see her friend sagging from exhaustion and decided to fix a simple dinner for them at home. They could both use a good night's sleep before the *Kristen Calder* taping in the morning.

The manager walked them to the front door. Through the glass window they could see a group of women walking in a tight circle outside. They carried placards raised above their heads.

"What's going on?" Kendall asked.

The young woman sighed. "This group has been threatening to picket for a week now. They're a great big pain in the . . ." The woman looked at Faye and stopped short. "Oh, I'm sorry, Mrs. Truett. I forgot they were from your husband's church."

Judy turned to Kendall. "They're picketing because they heard Shannon LeSade was planning to come here on tour."

"LeSade, the erotica author?" Kendall asked, interested.

Faye's hands stilled.

"Yes," Judy said. "She's so reclusive I don't think the whole tour thing is much more than a rumor. But they're picketing anyway. They want us to take her books off the shelves and burn them." She frowned. "Our manager told them they could do whatever they liked with LeSade's books, but they'd have to buy them first." She smiled at her boss's one-upsmanship.

"That woman in the front is their ringleader," Judy continued, clearly warming to her topic. "She's been very unpleasant."

Faye had already recognized the woman in charge. She closed her eyes and prayed for strength.

"Do you know them, Mrs. Truett?" Judy asked.

"I'm afraid so," Faye replied, wishing she could deny it. "The woman in front is my daughter."

Judy's eyes grew wide. It was clear she wasn't sure what to say. Faye wished they could sneak out the back and pretend they'd never seen the protesters, but it was too late for that now.

"Neither her father nor I believe in book banning." Faye felt the need to clarify that this was not a family position. "But Sara's a grown woman and she's very strong willed."

"Oh, Faye!" Kendall said.

"Yes." Faye couldn't meet her friend's eye. "I expect we'd better go." Faye put her shoulder to the door and braced for combat. She nodded good-bye to Judy.

"Come on, Kendall. I'll introduce you to Sara. And then I suspect we're going to have to stop on the way home after all, because I'm probably going to need another drink."

As it turned out, she needed two. One to forget about the shouting match her daughter drew her into. The second to forget the *Chicago Tribune* photographer who documented it and then wanted to double-check the spelling of their names to make sure he'd gotten them right.

37

The photo appeared on the front page of the morning newspaper and Kendall hoped it wasn't an omen of things to come. When she slid into the backseat of the limo that Kristen Calder's production company had sent to pick her up, there was a complimentary copy of the paper waiting for her. Kendall folded it facedown and stuffed it under her seat. Did this mean that Kristen's people had already seen it? She was not going to be the one to ask.

Faye had left earlier to pick up Mallory and Tanya at O'Hare. The three of them planned to come directly to the studios, where tickets for the taping had been left under Tanya's name. They'd all insisted they wanted to be there for Kendall and had joked about wearing disguises. This gave Kendall yet another thing to worry about—as if she needed one.

The bad feeling in the pit of her stomach grew with each mile. The local station interviews she'd done during her tour had given her a certain comfort level with the whole television experience. But comparing a local talk show to the nationally syndicated *Kristen Calder Show* was like comparing a glass of tap water to the Pacific Ocean. She was deathly afraid she was going to drown.

The limo's leather interior smelled new and expensive and

the Plexiglas that separated Kendall from the driver gave her quiet within which to think. But she couldn't shake her growing unease.

She was a fraudulent *New York Times* Bestseller. She'd achieved her dream under false pretenses; she'd gotten there on the backs and coattails of her friends. What if Kristen took one look at her and sensed her guilt? What if she didn't? Kendall felt swamped by fear and self-doubt. Not exactly the sort of aura one wanted to project on national television.

Before she was ready, the limo arrived at the studio. She practiced deep breathing while the driver walked around to open her door. At the building entrance, Kendall drew another great gulp of air into her lungs then slowly exhaled, taking a moment to examine the show's marquee, which sported a life-sized photograph of the thirtysomething Kristen Calder. Kendall studied the blonde's camera-thrilling cheekbones and burnished good looks, all of which had been toned down several notches to a nonthreatening level.

When Kendall entered the lobby, a threesome dressed in New York black awaited her as she went through security and showed ID. Lacy Samuels separated from the group and moved toward Kendall. The assistant was more attractive than Kendall had imagined and much more conservatively dressed than Kendall had painted her in *Sticks and Stones*. She wore black trousers with a short black vest over a black-and-white pin-striped shirt and boots that added to her long lean look.

The assistant smiled. "I left the nose ring at home."

Before Kendall could apologize, Lacy threw her arms around Kendall, further dispelling the air of New York sophistication. "I am so excited for you!" She smiled full out, not even trying to contain her enthusiasm. "The audience is packed with book clubs. Cindy and I get to pass out copies to everyone in the audience. And Hannah back at Scarsdale just called to say that we're already in a fifth printing." She threw her arms around Kendall again and squeezed with all her might.

Kendall squeezed back. "I don't know how you did it, but I appreciate you going to bat for me." She disentangled herself gently. "I never could have imagined ending up here."

Lacy introduced Naomi Fondren and Cindy Miller and then Kristen's people began to appear. There were a lot of them, all of them smiling and efficient, most of them also dressed in black.

One perky blonde took the Scarsdale people back to the waiting area, which they referred to as the green room. Another female staffer, who identified herself as a segment producer, escorted Kendall to makeup. While the makeup person worked on Kendall's face, the producer prepped Kendall for what was to come.

"Kristen's tied up right now"—she looked away for a moment, her eyes sliding away from Kendall's—"something's come up—so you'll meet her onstage. We've got people who've had surgery to look like celebrities first, then Kristen will introduce *Sticks and Stones* and then you'll come out for your interview. After that there'll be a commercial break and then she'll open up to questions from the audience. We have a lot of book club members here today and a lot of them have already read your book. Don, our stage manager, will escort you out."

The young woman talked pretty much nonstop as they left makeup and wound their way through a warren of dressing rooms and offices, but she had a disturbing habit of looking away whenever she mentioned Kristen. Something in the woman's manner felt off, but Kendall had no experience with television of this magnitude and chided herself for glomming onto yet another worry.

People raced by, but underneath the apparent chaos Kendall sensed slick orchestration. Sights and sounds swirled around her, but Kendall was unable to absorb or catalogue them. The producer took note of Kendall's reaction. "It's a bit overwhelming," she acknowledged. "But you don't need to worry. We'll get you out there and Kristen will take care of the rest," she promised. "She cares a great deal about the book club. She's made a point of choosing less weighty books than some of the other book clubs, but she's still very aware of putting her name and reputation behind an author."

Kendall swallowed uncomfortably and this time the producer made clear eye contact. "She watched Oprah, who is her absolute idol and role model, get burned by the James Frey incident and she's very sensitive about any kind of misrepresentation."

Kendall nodded dully. Millions of people were going to see her on this show. Millions more would buy her book because of it—assuming she didn't freeze completely or blither like an idiot.

She thought longingly of the backseat of the limo and wished she was in it already heading safely back to Faye's. She had a sense of impending doom, but chalked it up to her guilty conscience.

In the green room, which wasn't actually green, Kendall took a bottle of water from a table full of food and drink and sat down next to the Scarsdale contingent. Lacy and her friend Cindy were practically bouncing off the walls with excitement. Naomi Fondren smiled nonstop. Despite her professional manner, Kendall had the sense the PR woman was mentally pinching herself—something with which Kendall could identify.

Then the monitors in the green room were filled with images of Chicago from the show's opening montage. There was a shot of the cheering audience and then another camera followed Kristen as she entered the studio and walked between the audience sections to take her place on center stage.

Kendall concentrated on drawing air into her lungs, each steady "in" followed by a not-so-steady "out." The first segment of the show featured a parade of everyday people who'd gone under the knife to resemble their favorite celebrities. There was a Gwyneth Paltrow, a Tom Cruise with his Katie Holmes, even a Paris Hilton. They talked and laughed about being mistaken for the real celebrities; several had signed autographs and another worked as a stand-in and body double for the star she now resembled.

Kendall found herself wondering what would move people to alter themselves so drastically and whether they ever regretted their decisions. It was hard enough to get rid of a tattoo; what did one do when one tired of having Angelina Jolie's lips or Kyra Sedgwick's nose?

And then the young producer came back to get her. Trying not to hyperventilate, Kendall followed her to the studio doors through which she would make her entrance. As promised, the young woman handed her over to Don, the stage manager, who had a gentle air about him.

Next to Don a TV monitor showed Kristen Calder in center stage. A projected picture of *Sticks and Stones'* cover rose giant sized behind her.

"You OK?" Don asked.

Kendall nodded numbly as she heard Kristen give a brief but accurate recap of her book. And then Kendall's stomach dropped down around her knees as Kristen Calder called out Kendall's name.

"OK then. Here we go." Don led her through the door into the studio.

Kristen said Kendall's name again and with a gentle push from Don, Kendall began to walk toward the stage where Kristen stood. She got a glimpse of herself, white faced and nervous, in a monitor as she passed. After that she kept her gaze fixed on Kristen.

The applause was loud and although the studio was heavily air conditioned, she could feel the heat from the lighting grid that hung above, raining light down on stage and audience alike. A large studio camera followed her progress toward the stage, its giant box of a lens moving with her as she walked. Out of the corner of her eye she saw two other cameras pointed toward the audience, panning for reactions. Faye, Mallory, and Tanya sat somewhere in the crowd. Kendall was very careful not to look for them. She kept her gaze fixed on Kristen Calder.

Onstage Kristen smiled her trademark smile, but there

was a question in her clear blue eyes, as if she were somehow reserving judgment.

"Kendall Aims is not an overnight success," Kristen informed her audience. "Kendall Aims was in the trenches of publishing for years. She wrote eight books that did OK, but not quite well enough. The editor who first championed her left to have a baby and never came back. The new editor assigned to Kendall didn't like her. And things began to go downhill."

Kendall drew a deep breath as unobtrusively as she could. She knew a camera was pointed at her face to record her reactions. She tried to figure out what kind of facial expression would go over best, but it took everything she had to avoid imitating a deer in the headlights. She tried for humbly interested, but had no idea if she was pulling it off.

A movement to her left drew Kendall's eye and she spotted Tanya, Mallory, and Faye seated four or five rows up. Faye was wearing beige and had kept her makeup to a minimum; she fit right in with the audience members around her. Mallory was not so easy to disguise, but Kendall could tell she'd tried. Her dark brown hair had been pulled back into a French braid and her pantsuit, though undoubtedly designer, was black and simply cut, her jewelry understated. Tanya's big hair and overly made-up face would never blend in, but while some present might know her name, they were unlikely to recognize her face.

"But Kendall Aims took the disasters that befell her and built a book around them," Kristen intoned. "And that book is now on the New York Times Bestseller List, which is, of course, a very big deal. Sticks and Stones is first and foremost a story about friendship, and that's what we're going to talk about in just a minute."

They stopped for what would be a commercial break and Kristen considered her carefully. "You all right?"

Kendall nodded then managed a somewhat wobbly, "I think so."

"Good," the host said, though the warmth of her words didn't seem to be making it to her eyes. "We're going to be seated for the rest of the interview. When we come back from the break, I have a few things I'd like to clarify."

Kendall drew another breath and tried to smile benignly at the audience as she followed Kristen to the sofa and chair at the other end of the set. Through sheer willpower, she kept her gaze from straying to Tanya, Faye, and Mallory. She was glad they were there but worried about it at the same time. She made a conscious effort to relax, but hundreds of pairs of eyes were trained on her and something in the way Kristen had said, "I have a few things I'd like to clarify," had sounded more aggressive than Kendall had expected.

A young woman whose headset was plugged into the center camera raised her hand above her head and began to count down on her fingers. When only one finger remained, she pointed it at Kristen, who welcomed the audience back.

The interview began innocently enough. How, Kristen asked, did Kendall feel about her success after so much struggle? Was she surprised by how well *Sticks and Stones* was doing? What tips would she offer aspiring writers who hoped to one day be published?

Kendall found her voice and answered as clearly and succinctly as she could. None of the questions seemed meant to trip her up. Kristen seemed genuinely interested in hearing about the writing process. When she asked what it felt like to make the *New York Times* list, Kendall did her best to explain it, jettisoning her guilt about having had help with the book and focusing on her very real amazement and excitement.

When she stole a peek at the audience, Kendall could tell they were interested in her insights into the publishing world. Kendall stopped worrying and began to enjoy herself. She even managed to squeeze in a small joke about chaining her refrigerator shut when the words weren't flowing, and she got a laugh.

As she spoke, she became aware of the strangest things:

how straight and white Kristen's teeth were. The way she seemed focused on Kendall but also managed to play to the audience. Kristen Calder might be co-opting Oprah Winfrey's city and format, but the manner in which she drove the interview forward was her own.

Then something in the air changed subtly. Kristen's attention on her sharpened. All three cameras slid closer. A red light glowed on the camera on her far left, which she had been told would get her close-ups.

It was then that the tone of Kristen's questions began to change. "Readers are always curious how much of an author's characters are based on real people," Kristen said. Kendall's close-up camera rolled even closer. "The character of Kennedy Andrews is awfully close to your real life, Kendall. My staff has confirmed that the problems your character Kennedy experiences with her publisher are almost identical to the ones you ran into at Scarsdale. Like you, Kennedy Andrews was up for a Wordsmiths Incorporated Zelda Award she didn't win. Like you, Kennedy Andrews has three very close writer friends she's been critiquing with for a decade."

Kristen paused then and Kendall realized that the talk show host was heading somewhere completely intentional. "Like you," Kristen said carefully, "Kennedy Andrews discovers her husband has a girlfriend and wants a divorce."

The blasted red camera light was still on and Kendall could just imagine what her face must look like right now as all the horror and confusion she was feeling displayed itself across it.

Her mind raced at the surprise of the attack. Kristen Calder and her staff had spent time comparing her life to her character's. Kendall blinked rapidly, trying to regain her composure. Kristen Calder knew about her impending divorce. How could Kristen know when she hadn't even told her children yet? Oh, God, she couldn't let Melissa and Jeffrey find out this way. . . .

"All of this started me wondering how much more of your book might be based on reality. What about the writer friends who help Kennedy write the book? I wondered. Could *they* be based on real people? I asked my staff to check it out."

Kendall's mouth opened and closed but no words came out. No doubt she looked like a dying fish, aground on a beach gasping for water to run through its gills.

The audience had fallen unnaturally quiet, everyone straining to hear what Kristen would say next.

"We happened on this photo in this morning's *Chicago Tribune*," Kristen said. The newspaper photo of Kendall and Faye confronting Faye's daughter, Sara, replaced the cover of her book up on the rear screen. "Isn't that Faye Truett, inspirational author and wife of televangelist Steve Truett? And wasn't this photo taken yesterday afternoon after your book signing when Mrs. Truett confronted her daughter, who was picketing against the store for carrying erotica?"

Kendall's gaze swung to the blowup of the photo in which Faye and her daughter, Sara, had squared off. Kendall stood by Faye's side as silently stunned then as she was now.

She wasn't sure what Kristen wanted from her. Would admitting that Faye was a friend be an admission of something more? Given the picture, how could she possibly deny it?

"Faye Truett's a friend of mine. I'm staying at her house and as you can see she came to my book signing with me yesterday. I'm not sure how any of this applies?"

Now the gigantic photo from yesterday's picket line was replaced by an equally gigantic shot of Kendall, Mallory, Faye, and Tanya taken during the WINC conference just before the Zelda Awards. They were all dressed in evening clothes, all smiling. All of them still believing that Kendall was going to win for *Dare to Dream*.

"Do your friends mind you using their lives as fodder for your book?" Kristen asked.

"Fodder?" Kristen's whole line of questioning left her reeling. She'd been afraid all along that someone would realize she hadn't written the book alone, but it had never occurred to her that anyone would accuse her of using her friends' lives.

She didn't understand where Kristen was going with this, but wherever she was headed, Kendall didn't want to go there.

"I'll admit I skimmed a little closer to my own life than I probably should have," Kendall stammered. "But writers use their own lives and the lives of people they know as jumping-off points all the time. That doesn't make them . . . fodder."

Kristen cocked her head and raised a perfectly arched eyebrow. She reached out a hand and someone handed two books to her. One of them was *Sticks and Stones.* Kendall didn't recognize the other.

"And what about 'borrowing' their words?" Kristen asked, turning to address the camera head on. "I believe they call that plagiarism."

She continued to stare directly into the camera. "As my staff was looking into what seemed like potentially damaging revelations that Kendall Aims had made about her writer friends, one of our researchers noticed that portions of *Sticks and Stones* felt awfully similar to one of those author's works. In fact, there is an entire scene—a love scene—in *Sticks and Stones* that is virtually word for word out of this book."

Kristen held up the second book. It was *In Plain Sight* by Mallory St. James.

Behind them the photo of the four of them was replaced by another visual—a split screen with her cover and Mallory's cover side by side. The next was a divided screen with a page from each book. Kendall's gut clenched as she started to read; the scenes were virtually identical.

Kendall was very glad they were sitting. Her legs had turned to rubber and her hands had begun to tremble. She thought back to her dead faint when she'd discovered Calvin's infidelity and craved that oblivion.

Kendall stole a glance at Faye, Mallory, and Tanya and saw the same stricken looks she felt covering her own face. Then they hunched down in their seats as if attempting to disappear.

Kristen continued to speak to the camera. "We're going to

take a small break now," she said smoothly. "But don't go away. When we get back we're going to give Kendall Aims a chance to *explain* herself." She folded her arms across her chest and allowed herself a small, dubious smile. "If she can."

*My line of work makes you aware of the fragility of
life. You can get up in the morning, eat your
cornflakes, blow-dry your hair, go to work,
and end up dead.*
—KATHY REICHS, CRIME WRITER

Kristen Calder stood and moved away from Kendall to confer with an assistant. Kendall tried deep breathing and positive thinking, but she didn't hold much hope that they'd actually calm her down. She was desperate to huddle with her "peeps" but she was afraid to call attention to them.

There was a noise as the studio doors burst open. Naomi Fondren, her hair flying, raced in followed by Cindy and Lacy. Don was trying to hold them back, but the gentle man was no match for the three New Yorkers. Shooting a look at Kendall that said she'd deal with her later, Naomi approached the star.

She held out her hand, but Kristen ignored it.

"I'm Naomi Fondren, head of PR for Scarsdale Publishing," Naomi said. "I'm not sure what's going on here. But I'm sure there's some sort of misunderstanding."

Kristen's face registered her irritation. "I think we passed the possibility of a 'misunderstanding' some time ago. When the commercial break is over, I'm going to give *your* author a chance to explain herself to *my* audience. I guess there could be some miraculous justification for the way she's exposed and plagiarized her friends. I can hardly wait to hear it."

To her credit, the PR woman didn't try to argue. She simply pulled herself up to her full height then turned and walked off the stage looking neither left nor right, stopping at the studio doors where she slipped back between Lacy and Cindy.

If Kendall could have worked up the nerve to leave the stage, she wouldn't have stopped there. She would have just kept going. Even if it meant walking back to Atlanta.

The floor person's hand went up and the countdown began. Kristen took her seat and on cue, she recapped the situation, holding up the two books, Mallory's and Kendall's, in her hands as she addressed the camera. Then she turned to Kendall. "So, Ms. Aims," she said. "Inquiring minds would like to know how this could have happened."

Kendall felt her breakfast rise in her stomach and wondered what would happen if instead of answering she simply bent and threw up on Kristen's feet. She wished she could say, "Why don't we ask Mallory?" or "Maybe we should double-check with Faye and Tanya." But she'd promised them anonymity. That promise, at least, she intended to keep.

The studio was tomblike in its silence as the audience awaited her response. Every eye as well as all three cameras were glued to Kendall's face. She was as surprised as Kristen to find out that Mallory had been plagiarized and she would have given a lot to find out how that could have happened.

But the truth was that, without the truth, Kendall had no defense. She was going to have to admit to plagiarism and co-opting her friend's secrets and be prepared to live with the consequences. What she couldn't live with was Melissa and Jeffrey hearing about their parents' impending divorce on television. She and Calvin would have to reach them before this show aired in the afternoon.

Kendall's chin went up a notch. The time had come. "As you could probably tell from the photo, Mallory St. James is also a very close friend of mine." Kendall paused. "I certainly never intended to 'steal' her life and I never would have knowingly 'used' her words."

Kendall's gaze dropped to the floor and her voice trailed

off. There was no way to defend the indefensible. "I don't really know how to explain this because . . ."

The studio remained silent as Kendall searched for a possible explanation. No one stirred. There wasn't a single cough.

"Because she didn't plagiarize me!" Mallory's voice rang out in the studio as she stood at her seat. "I did!"

Kendall's gaze flew to Mallory, who was now crossing her arms across her chest and staring at Kristen and Kendall. The lights made her dark hair shimmer. The black suit was severely tailored and probably cost more than the whole rest of the row's clothes combined. She looked irritated and unhappy.

Mallory was, in fact, royally pissed off. She'd spent the last ten minutes commanding herself to stay silent, not to get involved, not to make this worse than it already was, but she didn't seem to be listening.

Her instincts for self-preservation were finely honed; Mallory never would have survived her life without them. But she couldn't bear to watch the talk show host accusing Kendall of something Kendall hadn't done.

So what was she supposed to say now? She could feel Faye and Tanya tightening into even smaller balls beside her, a reminder that she had to be careful not to incriminate anyone but herself.

She shot Kendall a bracing smile then took the handheld microphone an assistant rushed over to her. The audience waited expectantly. A camera moved in for a close-up. Even before she opened her mouth, Mallory knew she was about to make a mistake of mammoth proportions. But she could not let Kendall take the blame for her mistakes.

"Kendall Aims is one of my best friends," Mallory said. "And although her publisher hasn't appreciated her, she's a very talented writer in her own right. She'd never steal anything from me. In fact, when I offered to help with her book because she was so overwhelmed by everything that had gone wrong in her life, she refused. At first."

There were murmurs from the audience. Tanya turned to

look up at her. Kristen's face bore an expression that was equal parts surprise and satisfaction.

Mallory closed her eyes, opened them. She'd written the truth and look where it had gotten them. After all these years of lying, what had possessed her?

It was too late to sit down, but maybe she could soft-pedal the truth a little. Not exactly take it back, but burnish it and twist it in some way that . . .

She cut her gaze to Kendall's tortured expression and knew that dissembling was out of the question. But could she tell the truth she'd hidden so carefully all these years? Mallory tried to force it back, but like the levees in New Orleans, her long-held barriers had been compromised.

"Kendall didn't 'steal' my real life. She couldn't have if she'd wanted to." Mallory paused and looked away from Kendall, unable to look her in the eye. "Because she never knew it."

"My real name is Marissa Templeton," she proclaimed in a tone a new member of AA might use. "And I wrote all of Miranda Jameson's scenes in *Sticks and Stones*."

Kristen and her audience gasped aloud. And so did her friends. Mallory hadn't even thought of her real name in more than a decade; she couldn't believe she had just claimed it on national television. But once breached, her defenses began to crumble. She knew what was coming next and was powerless to stop it.

"In fact, I gave the character Miranda my whole sordid past: parents who committed suicide. Years spent barely getting by. The creation of a whole new identity. A talent for storytelling, and a fear of losing control of her life again, which ultimately saved her."

The studio was completely silent. Even Kristen's mouth hung slightly open in surprise. Whatever she'd been expecting, it apparently wasn't a confession from Mallory St. James.

"But Kendall didn't know I was writing the truth. Nobody did. Because I never shared it with anyone." Mallory swallowed, appalled at the words spilling out of her mouth. "Not even my husband."

Mallory stole a glance at Kendall. Her friend was looking at her as if she didn't know her, which, Mallory realized, was the case.

"So you're claiming you plagiarized yourself?" Kristen seemed to be feeling her way now, trying to regroup, apparently not yet certain whether Mallory's confession was a good thing or a bad thing.

Mallory knew without a doubt that it was a bad thing, but she'd come too far to stop now. "Well I'm hoping that's not legally possible," Mallory said. "I mean I think I could be accused of redundancy and recycling, but the words were mine, both times. I don't see how Kendall or I could be prosecuted for that."

"Are you claiming you accidentally wrote the same scene seven years apart?" This clearly fascinated Kristen.

"Evidently." Mallory kept waiting for the relief that was supposed to come with confession, but she felt neither calm nor peaceful. This studio full of shocked people didn't look like they were about to offer absolution.

"The thing is, I wrote sixteen books in ten years," Mallory said, trying to explain. "Each of them was intentionally similar so that I could 'build a brand' as an author. I was, um, having trouble keeping up the pace when Kendall got into trouble." Confession was one thing; she was not going to use the term *writer's block* on national television. "And I guess that love scene survived intact in my brain, just hanging there waiting to get back out."

She saw the play of emotions cross Kendall's face and blanched when she saw the pity. Tanya had swiveled in her seat and was looking at Mallory as if she'd never seen her before. She mouthed the word "Marissa" and shook her head.

Next to Mallory, Faye was no longer in as tight a ball, but she wasn't exactly leaping into the fray.

Whoever said that the truth would set you free, Mallory

thought, was full of shit. She felt tired and angry and most definitely appalled, but free? Mallory started to sit down, wishing she'd never opened her mouth. But Kristen didn't seem to be through with her.

"So you're *Sticks and Stones*'s Miranda," the talk show host said. "What about the character Faith? She doesn't really feel like pure invention, either."

Faye flinched beside her.

Mallory was afraid to break eye contact with the talk show host, even though she could feel Faye and Tanya tensing on both sides of her. Out of the corner of her eye, Mallory could see Kendall, her face as white as the sofa on which she sat.

"But even knowing what we do now, it's hard to believe Kendall Aims would have the nerve to take such liberties with her friend Faye Truett's life," Kristen said, even though her tone indicated that was exactly what she believed.

"Pastor Steve's wife has a huge reputation as an inspirational author," Kristen said. "She helped build her husband's ministry, and she's an acknowledged philanthropist. Why, she created Rainbow House almost single-handedly." Kristen paused as if waiting for an answer to materialize. "Why would she allow Kendall Aims to create a character that resembles her but who writes 'racy' romances. And why in the world would Kendall Aims drag Faye Truett into publicly defending erotica? I just don't get it."

The talk show host was clearly fishing now. Mallory wasn't sure if she was upset at having backed a book and author that were not what they were supposed to be or if she had finally begun to recognize what kinds of ratings these revelations were likely to generate.

The photo of yesterday's confrontation reappeared behind Kristen and Kendall. The caption beneath it read, "Faye Truett Squares Off with Daughter, Defends Erotica and Author Shannon LeSade."

Kristen turned to Kendall, who appeared dazed but, to her credit, still conscious. "Did you write the character of Faith

Lovett?" Kristen asked, before swinging her gaze to Mallory. "Or did you?"

There was a long silence as Mallory and Kendall exchanged glances, silently trying to read the other's mind. Mallory had a brief vision of them both claiming responsibility at the same instant—like characters on a television sitcom.

"Which one of you created and wrote Faith Lovett?" Kristen asked. "I think at this point we have a right to know."

Mallory could hardly believe it. She'd bared her soul in front of a studio full of people. Her confession would be seen by millions, including a husband to whom she'd never even revealed her real name. And now Kristen wanted her to "out" Faye?

Kristen Calder might be a determined woman bent on giving Oprah Winfrey a run for her money. But she didn't know who she was dealing with.

39

*Your manuscript is both good and original, but the
part that is good is not original, and the part
that is original is not good.*
—SAMUEL JOHNSON (ATTRIBUTED)

Faye knew as surely as she knew her own name that Mallory
was getting ready to lie to protect her, in the same way that
she had told the truth to protect Kendall.

For a split second Faye considered letting her do it. Mallory had already admitted to a secret past that she'd never
seen fit to share with them and to working on a book without
permission from her publisher. How much worse would it be
for her to admit to writing one more character?

Mallory was so big her publisher was unlikely to drop her.
Big authors got slaps on the wrist or some sort of monetary
penalty. Even big authors who'd plagiarized and stolen ideas
from others were still being published and promoted. Chris,
of course, was another story. But admitting to writing Faith
would hardly make Mallory's husband's sense of betrayal any
larger.

Faye, on the other hand, stood to lose everything: her inspirational career, her reputation. Possibly her daughter and her
husband. And in the process Clearview Church of God and
Rainbow House would be, if not destroyed, then seriously damaged. She couldn't think of a single good thing that would
come of speaking out.

"Which one of you wrote Faith Lovett?" Kristen asked

again. "I feel like I'm on a scavenger hunt now," the talk show star said, having clearly realized the ratings potential of the unexpected show that had unfolded. "We've come this far, let's go on ahead and set the record straight." She leveled a gaze at Naomi Fondren. "Something Scarsdale Publishing should have done months ago."

Faye unfurled from her protective ball. Ignoring the hand Mallory laid on her shoulder to hold her down, Faye stood and straightened.

The camera zoomed out to include her. Seeing herself in a nearby monitor, Faye reached a hand up to smooth her hair and straighten her glasses. A close-up of her face appeared on the monitor and Faye was amazed to see that none of her inner turmoil seemed to show.

As she prepared to speak, Faye sensed that her life would forever be divided into the "before she confessed on *The Kristen Calder Show*" and "after she'd confessed on *The Kristen Calder Show*." But as frightened as she was of what she was about to unleash, she couldn't let her friends take the blame for what she had done.

"I did," Faye said. "I wrote the character Faith Lovett."

Once again Kristen looked surprised. The audience gasped as one then fell silent so, Faye assumed, as not to miss a single word.

"Why would you do that?" Kristen asked.

"Because my friend needed me." It was the truth as far as it went, Faye thought. But why had she taken the risk she had? She could have written Faith as an entirely different sort of character and risked much less.

"And why the sex scenes?" Kristen mused. "Why defend Shannon LeSade?"

This, of course, was the crux of the matter. Why had she allowed herself to stray so close to the truth? Why had she revealed things in a book that she'd been unable to admit to her friends and family?

She cut a look to Mallory. They couldn't have appeared more different. They'd lived different lives, written different things. But they'd both hidden behind their work and their public personas. And they'd both written things for Kendall that had the potential to expose them.

Surely this was no coincidence.

Faye stilled for a moment. She closed her eyes in an attempt to tune out Kristen and her audience along with the harsh lights and the red glare of the camera's light. Could God have chosen this frightening and potentially devastating way to force her to tell the truth? Could this have been His plan for her? She waited, but there was no definitive answer. No bolt of lightning. No burning bush. No voice from above.

But when she opened her eyes it was with a certainty that whatever had brought her to this place and time, there was only one answer she could give.

"The sex scenes came naturally to me," Faye said. She paused, actually unable to believe what she was about to say. "Because I *am* Shannon LeSade."

The audience erupted. Mallory turned to her in shock. Kendall gasped on stage. Tanya jumped out of her seat and turned to face her. For a few long moments pandemonium filled the studio. The cameras moved about, capturing reactions all over the studio.

Finally Kristen took charge and called for order. "I'm as close to speechless as I've ever come," Kristen said. "Can you tell us why?"

Faye thought about when it had begun, so long ago before there was anything to jeopardize. When it was a simple matter of survival. "I started writing erotica almost twenty years ago. It was just one of the jobs I took on to help pay for our children's college and to help my husband build his ministry, though he didn't know it."

Whispered murmurings filled the studio. These people only knew who she was now, or rather thought they did. "I didn't start out as a minister's wife, and personally, I don't see anything irreligious or unethical about sexual relations. I happen to think the physical manifestation of love is one of the greatest gifts God gave us."

There were more murmurs, many of them disapproving, but it was much too late to take anything back.

"But surely at some point it became unnecessary," Kristen said. "You must have realized that if anyone ever found out there would be negative consequences."

Faye looked at her friends' shocked faces. She regretted not sharing her true self with them, almost as much as she regretted not being able to tell the truth to her family. But she also felt a wonderfully lightening sense of relief. "It's those consequences that have kept me quiet for so long. But erotica has never been bigger. I've funded so many good works with the money from LeSade's work that I couldn't bring myself to cut off the income."

But if she were honest, there was more to it than that. "And I'm really good at it. For some reason I don't completely understand, I'm really good at erotica."

Kristen looked completely nonplussed. So did Faye's friends and most of the audience. She couldn't let herself think about what would happen when Sara and Steve and the Clearview congregation heard the news.

Right now, in this calm before the storm, she knew she'd done the right thing. Just as she knew there'd be plenty of time to regret it later.

· · ·

Tanya stared at Faye, trying to absorb what her friend was saying. Faye Truett, inspirational author and wife of Clearview Church's Pastor Steve, was the notorious Shannon LeSade? She simply couldn't process it.

Beside Faye, Mallory also still stood. Mallory's real name was Marissa and pretty much everything she'd written in *Sticks and Stones* was the truth. Tanya could hardly believe that, either.

Compared to them, Tanya figured she'd committed the fewest offenses; her only "sin" was secretly writing for another publisher when she wasn't legally allowed to. It wouldn't be that big an admission, but she had so much to lose. She'd worked so hard to write three short contemporaries each year.

Without her Masque money added to what she earned at the diner and the Laundromat, she'd never have enough to leave Trudy's mobile home and look after her daughters.

Without her contract, she'd no longer be a professional writer.

Tanya caught Mallory's eye and Mallory gave a subtle shake of her head. Kristen seemed more than satisfied with the morning's revelations. The truth had come out; Mallory and Faye had done their best to protect Kendall. Tanya's speaking out now would accomplish little except to annihilate her career. She turned and made eye contact with Kendall, who seemed to read her intent and also shook her head.

"Wow," Kristen said. "If there are no more confessions, I think we all need to take our seats and consider where we go from here."

Everyone around Tanya sat down. There was a swell of excited murmurings. An assistant moved toward Tanya's row and motioned for her to take her seat. She wanted to, really she did. But how could she face her friends, or herself, if she didn't admit to her part in the deception? She remained standing. "I, um, have something to say," Tanya said.

Kristen Calder cocked her head and raised an eyebrow. "This is turning into a movie of the week," she said, as she motioned for a camera to pick up Tanya. "Let me guess," Kristen said. "You're either Lucy, the plucky Scarsdale assistant, or Tina, the struggling single mother."

"Yes," Tanya said, biting back her fear. "I'm, um, Tina. I mean, I'm Tanya Mason and I wrote Tina."

"And do you really write for Masque?"

"Yes," Tanya answered. "Well, at least I did. I doubt that'll still be true once they see this show."

"And you're the one who doesn't know a good man when she sees him," Kristen observed. "Is your mother's real name Rhonda?"

"No, it's, um, Trudy," Tanya said, feeling stupid.

"Anything else you'd like to add?" Kristen Calder asked.

"No, I, um . . . I don't think so," Tanya said, feeling like a schoolgirl stammering in front of the principal. "I, um, just want to say that we did what we did out of love and friendship for Kendall. She needed our help and, well, she's always been there for us."

Tanya sat before her knees could buckle. She could already imagine Trudy's rage when she realized that Tanya had put her life in a book and then told Kristen Calder's viewing audience that it was her. Not to mention how smug Brett was going to be. Wouldn't his mother and her book club just get a hoot out of this?

"Wow!" Kristen said again. "Maybe I need to consider moving to the classics in the future; those authors might have lied and plagiarized or had help from their friends, but at least they took their indiscretions to their graves with them."

There was some laughter.

"We've seen authors write fiction and try to pass it off as the truth. But I think this is the first time I've seen an author— make that four authors—write the truth and try to pass it off as fiction." The inquisitional tone with which Kristen had begun the interview had faded to a sort of mocking irony. "You'd think four fiction writers could have come up with something besides such a thinly disguised version of their real lives. It boggles the mind."

Tanya winced at her dismissive tone, but Kristen was right. They had all bared their souls and for what? So that they could be humiliated on national television? To lose publishers and fans? And what about Kendall and Faye and Mallory, whose families would be freaking out from the secrets that had been spilled here?

Tanya felt sucker punched. She'd known she'd taken a risk when she offered to work on *Sticks and Stones*, but she'd never imagined things turning out so badly. Kristen's next words didn't help any.

"Stop tape for a minute," Kristen said, looking directly into her camera. She moved away from Kendall, leaving her sitting alone on stage. The house lights came up.

Kristen paced the opposite end of the stage, apparently

trying to figure out her next move. Then she looked into the camera again, presumably addressing the director and others in the control room. "This is what we're going to do."

The studio audience fell silent as they waited to hear Kristen's plan.

"Let's re-do the open and drop the celebrity look-alike surgery segment so that we can add more background and go with this in its entirety. And I think we should get a statement from each of their publishers—especially *Scarsdale*—that I can read on air at the end of the show just before the close." Kristen shot a "take that" look at Naomi Fondren then addressed the studio audience.

"You'll have to admit this has been an interesting hour," Kristen said. "And it's going to make great television. But I do want to apologize to all of you. I recommended this book in good faith. It's a great read. And it is an even greater story of friendship—very misguided friendship—than I originally realized." Kristen's tone was bemused. "But I don't know that I'd call it fiction. And I'm kind of appalled at the way these four hid the true authorship of this book, not to mention the legal agreements they ignored to do so."

And then without further comment Kristen waved good-bye to the audience and left the stage with her posse surrounding her.

40

When in doubt, blow something up.
—J. MICHAEL STRACZYNSKI

The studio emptied, the audience studying the four of them as they filed out in the same way a driver might slow to look at an especially awful car crash. The production staff went about putting the set to rights, moving and parking cameras, turning off stage lights, coiling cables.

Kendall felt as if she'd been caught up in the crest of a tsunami, tossed about for an eternity, flung to the ground, and then stomped on. Repeatedly. She expected she should be relieved to be alive, but she was too dazed to feel relief. Her career, which had already been in ruins, was now completely demolished. The women she considered her closest friends had stood up for her, but in the process she'd discovered that she barely knew them at all. Even worse, if she didn't move quickly, her children were going to find out about her and Calvin via national television. She knew she had to do . . . something, but she couldn't imagine what.

Mallory, Faye, and Tanya appeared equally dazed. They sat in the nearly empty studio staring at everything but each other. No one spoke.

As in a dream Kendall watched Naomi Fondren approach. She came to a stop in front of Kendall, her assistant and Lacy Samuels on either side. She addressed her comments to Kendall, but her words were meant for all of them.

"I have never witnessed such a complete fuckup in my

entire life," she said. "How we managed to put out a book cowritten with three noncontracted authors I can't even begin to imagine. Nor can I believe that I have to call New York and try to explain this . . . disaster . . . to them."

Kendall stared blankly at her. The enormity of what had happened hung over them like a shroud, dark and oppressive.

The publicist drew a breath, clearly trying to steady herself, but anger shimmered off her like a beacon. "This whole . . . debacle . . . is completely indefensible. But if I were you, I'd put my heads together and try to come up with some sort of statement. You're going to need it."

Kendall's brain noted the variety of descriptive nouns—fuckup, disaster, debacle—and wondered idly how many Naomi Fondren could come up with. She hadn't used *tragedy*. Or *catastrophe*. Or the good old-fashioned *calamity*.

"And a lawyer might not be a bad idea, either." Naomi spun on her heel then walked quickly away, her assistant behind her. Lacy remained, her gaze fixed on Kendall, her disillusionment and disappointment written on her face. "I really believed in you," she said to Kendall. "I fought for you." She swallowed and Kendall realized she was struggling to hold back her tears. "And I hate that Jane Jensen will use this to prove she was right about you."

Without waiting for a reply, Lacy turned and left. Even before they were out of the studio, all three Scarsdale employees had their cell phones pressed to their ears. Within minutes the tom-toms of the New York publishing world would be spreading the word.

A few hours from now, Kristen Calder would tell everyone else.

• • •

Kendall spent much of the drive back to Faye's house alternately staring unseeing out the windshield and trying to get through to Melissa and Jeffrey, though she hadn't yet figured out what she would say if she reached them.

There was almost no conversation between the four of

them; and although there were a lot of surreptitious glances, they were very careful not to get caught looking at each other as they tried to come to terms with how little they'd known about each other and how the only thing they now shared were collapsing careers.

It was a beautiful spring day and sunlight reflected off the glass-fronted skyscrapers and warmed their slabs of marble and granite and limestone, but the atmosphere in Faye's car on the way back to her house was frigid. Passed in silence and hurt feelings, the drive to the north shore suburb felt interminable.

In Faye's kitchen they fixed sandwiches that no one ate. Kendall continued calling the kids, frantic to reach them before the show aired in Georgia. It was possible they wouldn't actually see the show right when it aired, but Melissa was a huge Kristen fan and an enthusiastic TiVoer and had promised Kendall that she'd record her appearance. And even if Melissa and Jeffrey didn't watch today's show they were bound to hear from friends who had. With each tick of the clock, Kendall's panic grew. She could feel Faye's escalating, too.

Unable to sit still, Faye busied herself putting the cold cuts away and tidying the kitchen. She'd considered calling Sara and Steve and the boys to warn them, but yet again had been unable to bring herself to place the calls. Sara was unlikely to answer, given last night's altercation in front of Borders. And Steve, who was still out in California? She hadn't been able to tell him the truth when it was still possible to keep things quiet; how could she tell him now?

When there was nothing left to wipe or arrange, she joined the others at the kitchen table. She wanted desperately to talk this out with Mallory and Tanya and Kendall, but her secret keeping had taken its toll there, too.

Faye stole a glance at Mallory, make that Marissa Templeton, and could tell that they, like her, were still reeling from the morning's appalling revelations. By this afternoon those revelations would be airing on television sets across the country.

"We looked like complete morons," Tanya said. "And lying morons to boot. She was loaded for bear from the moment Kendall stepped out on the stage."

"Yeah," Kendall said. "And she's a good shot." She glanced down at her watch again. "And in a little while, everyone in the universe, including my children, will know that I'm a pathetic washed-up writer whose husband dumped her and who had to ask her friends to help her write her book." She shook her head as if still unable to believe it. "Did you see the expression on my face when she accused me of plagiarism?" Her voice broke and she wrapped her arms across her chest. "How could you let me go out there knowing all those secrets could be used against us?" She stood and began to pace, her arms held tightly against her body. "And how could I have considered you my best friends and not known that one of you wasn't even who you said you were and the other was the notorious Shannon LeSade?"

Kendall stopped in front of them. "The audience must have been laughing themselves silly when we kept talking about what close friends we were!"

"We were good enough friends to put you on the *New York Times* list!" Mallory retorted, clearly stung. "You think that just because Faye and I kept some aspects of our lives to ourselves that we weren't really friends?"

"A few aspects?" Tanya snorted. "Everything we knew about you was fiction. It's just too bad *Sticks and Stones* wasn't! I can't believe I'm the one who suggested this stupid collaboration." It was her turn to stand now. "I trusted and respected you all. I thought we were there for each other. My career is going to end as soon as Darby or somebody else at Masque hears about our *Kristen Calder* appearance. And you never even trusted me enough to tell me who you really were."

"This is not helping anything!" Faye couldn't stand how they were turning on each other, but she, too, felt betrayed and out of control. "Our secrets were not intended as a personal insult to you!"

"You know, my mother's been a huge disappointment my

whole life," Tanya said. "But at least she never pretended to be something she wasn't."

"Tell me that you're not holding your mother up as a model of behavior!" Mallory jumped up from her seat and distanced herself from the rest of them. "Not after all the stories and complaints we've heard all these years." She shrugged, but the movement was anything but nonchalant. "Maybe she didn't have to pretend because she had you there to pick up her pieces. I did what I had to do and I don't appreciate being attacked for it. You have no idea what it took to rebuild my life or the pressures I've been under."

"Well of course we don't," Kendall said, jumping into the fray. "Because you never bothered to tell us!"

"Yeah," Tanya added, "If you've been this secretive with Chris, I don't wonder that he left you!"

Mallory gasped in outrage. "Did you actually just say that? You, who can't even open yourself up to that poor cook because you're afraid of needing anyone?"

"Well I let myself need you all and look where it got me!" Tanya bit out.

There was a shocked silence as all of them realized that they'd gone too far. But after all the emotion of the day and all that they feared was to come, no one seemed able to retract or apologize. The foundation of their friendship had been severely compromised. The wrecking ball of their attacks on one another reduced it to rubble.

Tanya's cab to the airport arrived. "I'll pay you back for the ticket and the flight-change fee," she said to Mallory as she gathered her things. "You won't be out another penny on my account!"

Nobody tried to stop her.

"I can't spend the night now," Kendall said. "I'm going to catch a ride with Tanya. I'll call Calvin on the way to O'Hare and ask him to meet me at the airport in Atlanta so that we can drive up to Athens and talk to Melissa and Jeffrey. I just can't worry about anything else until we've explained things in person to them."

Mallory, too, felt a need to get back to New York. "I've got to sit down with Patricia first thing tomorrow and Zoe's already left three messages on my voice mail."

At Faye's door there were none of the usual hugs or talk of how soon they could get together. Everyone seemed aware that too much had been said, but instead of taking anything back, they each wrapped themselves up in their hurt and anger and turned their backs on the others.

Faye followed them out to the driveway knowing she shouldn't let them leave like this, but she was unable to summon the conviction needed to plead or implore. Not one of them had shown the slightest interest in what the revelation that she was Shannon LeSade would do to her; they had only voiced concern for how it impacted them.

All of them were about to face the consequences of what they had done together, but for the first time in a decade, they would be facing those consequences alone.

The taxi driver put their bags in the trunk. Mallory grasped the handle of the passenger door while Tanya and Kendall moved around to the back. "It seems pretty clear we won't be issuing a joint statement," Mallory said. "But everyone had best give some thought to one of their own."

Faye stood in the driveway and watched the taxi pull away. She felt as bruised and bloodied as if she had fought and lost a major battle. She didn't know where she'd find the courage for the war to come.

· · ·

From LaGuardia, Lacy, Cindy, and a still-fuming Naomi Fondren took a limo directly to Scarsdale's headquarters on West 36th. There the publicity head told Cindy she could go. Lacy followed Naomi onto the elevator and down the empty fourth-floor hallways to the conference room.

Although it was almost 8:00 P.M., most of the seats at the conference table were already occupied. The publisher, Harold Kemp, sat at one end. Brenda Tinsley sat at the other. Jane Jensen and Hannah Sutcliff were already seated and ignoring each other. Naomi took a seat next to Jane and Lacy ended up next to Hannah. When she'd settled into her seat, Lacy looked up and saw Jane Jensen smiling menacingly at her. Her skin prickled.

"Now that those of you who were on the spot have arrived," the publisher said, "perhaps you can explain how in the hell this happened."

Relieved that the question was directed at Naomi Fondren, Lacy shrank back and tried to become one with her chair. If she could have, she would have disappeared completely.

Naomi didn't shrink back or apologize, but began to explain. "Apparently a Kristen Calder staffer noticed the similarities between the Kennedy Andrews character in *Sticks and Stones* and the author, which made her look more closely at all the characters in the book. Then another staffer, who's a big Mallory St. James fan, noticed the similarities between a scene in *Sticks and Stones* and one in an earlier St. James novel.

"Although we had no warning of it, Kristen was primed and ready for a witch hunt. She just didn't realize how many witches there were until all four of them stood up and started trying to protect each other."

"It was a complete and utter train wreck!" Brenda Tinsley said. "One awful revelation after the next." She shuddered. "We've already had calls from Masque, Partridge and Portman, and Psalm Song, Faye Truett's inspirational publisher. People are freaking out all over New York City."

"I hope you're not suggesting we take comfort in the fact that we're not the only New York publishing house with egg on its face," Kemp said in the deep voice that with the power he yielded had earned him the nickname "God."

"We've got a lot more to worry about than wiping up egg," Brenda said. "There are bound to be lawsuits and ultimately we're going to have to figure out what to do about *Sticks and Stones*, which is still climbing the *New York Times* list."

"Well, I want to know how this happened," Kemp said. "How could we not have known that the book was not written by our author?"

"Jane?" Brenda Tinsley's tone was not the one she normally

used with her former college roommate. Out of the corner of her eye, Lacy noticed that the Hand of God's hands were shaking.

Jane Jensen actually looked surprised at the associate publisher's tone. She automatically began to bristle, but managed to regain control. "Even before the book was complete I wanted it buried. I had informed the author that we would not be going back to contract. I'd assigned it a recycled cover. The print run would have been minimal."

She managed to keep her tone civil, but Lacy saw the affront in her eyes. Jane Jensen wasn't used to being questioned. Or having to control herself. She shot Lacy a venomous look and then continued. "*Sticks and Stones* would never have been put out in the way that it was if I hadn't been ambushed at the sales meeting by Lacy Samuels." She pointed an accusing finger at Lacy. "She fell in love with the book and contrary to my wishes, she marshaled a whole group of supporters, including Hannah and Cash Simpson, with whom Lacy has been sleeping."

The publisher turned to consider Lacy, but whether he was trying to determine why Cash Simpson might find her attractive or was simply confused as to why this person would have stirred an insurrection at a sales meeting, Lacy didn't know.

"What is Miss Samuels's position here?" Harold Kemp asked.

"She's my editorial assistant!" Jane snapped, her outrage making her forget who she was snapping at.

"So you're blaming this on your *assistant*?" The publisher's tone was incredulous.

"Yes!" Jane snapped again, and Lacy could see how close she was to losing her grip.

"And why would your assistant feel compelled to take action on a book you were editing?" Hannah asked quietly.

"Because she's a troublemaker!" Jane Jensen spat her answer at Hannah, her fury building by the second.

"Had you read the book at the time your assistant started rallying in-house support for it?" Hannah continued to speak

calmly and quietly, in stark contrast to Jane's increasingly agitated manner.

"Well . . . of course!" Jane lied. She looked at Hannah as
if she'd like to jump up and smack the woman down—a look
Lacy knew well.

"So you read the book and didn't notice that it wasn't
written in the same voice as Kendall Aims's earlier books?"

Lacy realized now that even if Jane had read the book at
this early stage she wouldn't have known, because she'd never
bothered to read the author's earlier titles.

"And then somehow you let your assistant get other reads,
have a new cover designed, and present it at the sales meeting?" Hannah's tone remained smooth and calm. Jane was too
angry to mount a credible defense. Perhaps she was using all
her mental powers trying to keep herself from beating Hannah
Sutcliff to a pulp.

"I didn't realize what she was doing. I . . ." Jane clamped
her mouth shut, apparently just now realizing the depth of
the hole she'd just dug for herself.

"Who was assigned to edit this book?" Brenda Tinsley's
voice was cold and hard.

Lacy saw Jane struggle with her answer. Despite her rage,
she seemed to realize the trap that had been set. If she admitted she hadn't even read it until after Lacy had pulled off her
sales meeting coup, she would have to admit that she'd planned
to pass off important editorial work to an inexperienced assistant. If she claimed she'd read and edited the book, then she'd
have to accept responsibility for completely missing the fact
that the book was written by four authors and not just the one
she had under contract.

"I was Kendall Aims's editor," Jane said, her tone stiff
with anger.

"And did you actually edit *Sticks and Stones*?" Brenda asked.

"Yes, I did. But I wasn't . . ." Jane was shaking from her
efforts to hold back her anger. Her eyes took on a glazed,
unfocused look that Lacy knew precipitated an explosion.

"Were you the editor or weren't you?" Harold Kemp asked.

"I knew Kendall Aims was a mediocre talent and I had already planned to drop her. I didn't want *Sticks and Stones* in hardcover. I didn't . . ." Jane Jensen's voice rose with each statement. She looked like a teakettle coming to a boil.

"Did you edit it or not?" Harold Kemp demanded.

"Yes!" Jane shouted at the publisher. "But you aren't listening to me!" She'd lost it completely. "I knew that author was a problem. There was no way she should have been allowed to . . ." She was shrieking now. The 360 of the head on the shoulders was coming next.

But she didn't get that far. Because this time she wasn't venting her spleen all over a powerless assistant. She'd picked the wrong audience for her pyrotechnics.

"That's enough," Harold Kemp said. "You're fired."

"What did you say?" Jane Jensen was still shouting. She turned to Brenda Tinsley. "Are you going to let him do that to me?" Jane yelled.

Brenda's mouth compressed into an angry white line. "Yes," she said coldly. "Of course I am."

"You can't do this!" Jane Jensen jumped to her feet and shoved back her chair. "Not after sixteen years of working my ass off for you! You'll be sorry. You'll—"

"Brenda," Harold Kemp said. "Please call security and have them escort Miss Jensen from the building. We'll discuss what to do with the book later."

And just like that Scarsdale's publisher-in-chief performed a much-needed exorcism. Or in *Wizard of Oz* terms, he dropped a house directly upon Scarsdale's Wicked Witch and removed her ruby slippers.

Lacy watched him turn and leave the room. Brenda Tinsley picked up the phone and called downstairs. Moments later two burly guards appeared and escorted Jane Jensen out of the building.

Lacy breathed a shuddering sigh of relief as the door closed behind them. Brenda, Hannah, Naomi, and Lacy stared at each other for several long moments, but nobody seemed to be able to think of a fitting comment. They left their seats and began to file out of the office.

Lacy would have preferred a celebration. Maybe some skywriting. Or a chorus of Munchkins singing "Ding Dong! The Witch Is Dead." She wanted to hear Jane Jensen's editorial career pronounced "Really most sincerely dead." And she wanted to see her feet shrivel up and disappear beneath the killer house.

Lacy's relief was fleeting. She knew that although tonight's curtain had fallen, the drama was far from over.

41

*Critics have been described as people
who go into the street after battle
and shoot the wounded.*
—ELINOR LIPMAN

Kendall's plane landed at Hartsfield-Jackson Atlanta International Airport just before 7:00 P.M. By 7:30 she'd retrieved her bag and met Calvin outside of baggage claim. She was too tired and too numb to feel much of anything other than the hard knot of anxiety in the pit of her stomach that had been with her since she awoke this morning in Chicago.

With her bag stowed in the trunk of his BMW, Calvin merged out of the airport and headed north on Highway 85. The drive to Athens, which was northeast of Atlanta, would take about an hour and a half.

Kendall watched the familiar landmarks whiz by in silence as her brain continued in its attempts to process the horrific details of her day: Kristen Calder's surprise attack, the even more surprising revelations that followed. The meltdown of her friendship with Mallory and Faye and Tanya.

Dominating all of this was the coming conversation with her children during which she'd have to explain things that she still didn't understand herself.

Kendall closed her eyes and searched for calm. "Did you reach the kids?" she asked. "I was never able to get through."

"Yeah," Calvin replied. "And they're royally pissed at both of us. At me for, and I'm quoting Melissa on this, 'being an asshole and only thinking with my dick.' And at you for not telling them what an asshole I am. Melissa had a four P.M. class but apparently everyone in her dorm watched Kristen Calder today and couldn't wait to give her a blow by blow."

Kendall groaned. "I just can't believe any of this. I feel like I've been trapped in a nightmare since WINC in New York, and no matter how hard I try, I can't seem to wake up."

"I know what you mean," Cal said.

Kendall turned in her seat to look at him, something she had not intentionally done for a long time. His dress shirt appeared rumpled and his tie had a food stain on it. She realized, with some surprise, that he needed a haircut.

"What do you mean, you know what I mean?" she asked.

He shrugged, but without his usual cockiness. "Just that things haven't exactly turned out the way I expected."

Anger burned away some of Kendall's numbness. "Gee," she said. "Let me get out my violin." She saw his face flush and hoped it was from shame. "But don't you dare try to tell me that your abandonment of your family has been as hard on you as it has on me. Or will be on your children. Don't you dare!"

He took his gaze off the highway to look at her. The rhythmic spill of streetlights lit the hollows of his cheeks. "I did the wrong thing. I know that," he said. "I just . . . well . . . Melissa wasn't all wrong. I wasn't using my head."

Kendall closed her eyes again, not wanting to hear what part of his anatomy had held sway. He'd had to choose between his dick and his head. When had his heart been taken out of the running?

"And now you are?" she asked. "Using your head?"

"Laura, the whole . . . thing . . . was a huge mistake," Calvin said quietly. "I wish I'd never gotten involved with her." He swallowed. "I *shouldn't* have ever gotten involved with her."

The flare of westbound headlights flickered on his face. Light and dark. Truth and consequences.

She sensed what was coming before he said it; it was just one more surreal part of a science fiction kind of day.

"I'm sorry, Kendall. Really sorry. I want to put things back the way they were." He paused, apparently waiting for some sort of reaction from her. When she didn't respond, he forged on, laying out his plan, though she suspected he was making it up as he went.

"We could start fresh tonight," he said, talking himself into it even as he tried to convince her. "When we get there I'll apologize and ask their forgiveness. Oh," he added hastily, "and yours, too. And then we could try to start over again."

She realized that he'd only apologized to her as an afterthought because he assumed she'd need little convincing. He undoubtedly assumed she'd been dragging through her dreary life praying that he'd come back.

"What's happened to Laura?" Kendall asked. "How does she feel about this . . . fresh start you're proposing?" She was almost too weary to dredge up a sufficient amount of sarcasm. *Almost.*

"It doesn't matter what she thinks." He shrugged and she could picture him dismissing her to Laura in the same way nine months ago. "It's over." His tone suggested this was a minor point, hardly pertinent to the conversation. "I want you to come home where you belong. You know that's what the kids will want, too."

Kendall turned away from him. She'd taken so many emotional blows today that this one almost didn't register. He thought he could just say, "I'm sorry, I made a mistake," as if he'd brought home the wrong brand of toothpaste. "Let's forget it ever happened" and she would be so relieved that she'd take him back. With some horror, she realized that even a few months ago she would have leaped at the offer.

Despite all the years they'd spent together, he didn't know her at all. And couldn't be bothered to.

Kendall closed her eyes as the pain of the last nine months washed over her. The demise of her career followed by the disintegration of her marriage had sent her hurtling over the edge of her known life and into a pit of despair and self-doubt so deep and so wide that she hadn't thought she'd ever claw her way out of it.

But she had.

Kendall's eyes flicked open as the truth resonated within her. She'd leaned too heavily on her friends and developed a somewhat unhealthy power tool dependency in the process, but she had completed the climb.

She was still weary and bruised, but she was alive. She had survived. And so much stronger than she'd ever realized.

Calvin waited expectantly for her answer; his assumptions filled the car.

Kendall hesitated, wanting to be sure that her response wasn't simply a knee-jerk reaction to those assumptions or a misguided attempt to strike back.

But no, there was no mistake. She was horribly afraid of damaging her relationship with her children, and she wasn't sure how she was going to exist without Mallory and Faye and Tanya, but she'd already learned to live without Calvin. She was more herself without Calvin than she'd ever been with him.

And when she thought the word "home," she no longer pictured their house in the suburbs. The word conjured the soul-deep silence of her mountaintop house. With the occasional whine of her electric saw floating on the wind.

She shook her head. "If there's anything I've learned from everything that's happened, it's that no good can come from pretending." She met his gaze and saw surprise register in his.

"We're done, Calvin," she said. "But we'll always be Melissa and Jeffrey's parents. We need to try to make things right with them."

But in Athens, where they spent a terse forty-five minutes with their children, Kendall discovered that the twins were not inclined to pretend to understand. Or begin to forgive.

Instead Melissa and Jeffrey made it clear that they considered the withholding of the truth as heinous as their father's infidelity and abandonment. The fact that they'd discovered all of this on *The Kristen Calder Show* was the most heinous thing of all.

"I can't even talk to you right now," Melissa said angrily. "All I keep seeing is our personal family business coming out of Kristen Calder's mouth!" Angry tears had rushed down her cheeks.

Jeffrey had been less vocal but no less hurt. "Everyone on this campus knew you were getting a divorce before we did! How do you think that makes us feel?"

And that had been the end of the conversation.

Drained, Kendall slept in the car most of the way back to Atlanta. At her old house, where she'd left her car before the book tour, she climbed into Melissa's bed and willed herself to sleep. In the morning she'd drive back to the mountain house where she could lick her wounds. She could only pray that her children's hurt would fade and that they would ultimately be ready to listen.

• • •

Mallory let herself into the brownstone late that night and although she put on pajamas and got into bed, she didn't waste time or energy even trying to fall sleep.

Their takedown on *The Kristen Calder Show* was a top story on all of the network news programs and the lead on *Entertainment Tonight*. Leno and Letterman both poked fun at her self-plagiarism and her secret past. Conan O'Brien did his entire monologue on what might drive a pastor's wife to write erotica. Another late-night show ended with a "How many authors does it take to write a novel?" joke that gleefully bashed all of their genres.

In the morning she used makeup and dark glasses to try to hide the ravages of the last twenty-four hours, but the first thing her agent said to her when they were seated at the restaurant was, "You look like you didn't sleep a wink. But who can blame you?" Patricia Gilmore had always been one to speak her mind. In the past Mallory had thought it a positive quality.

"So where do things stand?" Mallory asked, her stomach clenching. "How bad is it?"

"It's bad," Patricia replied. "Partridge and Portman wants to sue Scarsdale for a percentage of profits as I'm sure Masque will. Psalm Song, Faye Truett's inspirational publisher, will want the book taken off the shelves as soon as possible. It's going to be a huge legal pileup.

"And the bloggers and review sites are having a field day with you, Mallory. There's a lot of negative sentiment out there. Some of the big box retailers are already talking about cutting their orders."

"Why do you think I kept my past quiet all these years?" Mallory said. "People don't want to know the real you. And when they do, they want to pick the real you apart. What they really want is the fantasy. They want—"

"Mallory," Patricia said. "They're not turned off by your past. I actually think people are inclined to sympathize with all you went through and root for you all the more. Just like they did for your *Sticks and Stones* character, Miranda." She paused to let her words sink in, although Mallory didn't want to hear them, let alone acknowledge them.

"Readers want to feel like they know their favorite authors," Patricia continued. "They've believed your PR all these years. They're hurt and angry that you didn't think enough of them to share the truth."

The words thudded against Mallory's brain, trying to gain admittance.

"I understand how they feel," Patricia said. "I've been representing you for a decade and I didn't even know you."

Mallory felt the weight of her agent's disapproval. Patricia's words were disturbingly similar to Kendall's and Faye's and Tanya's. She imagined Chris learning about her real identity and her sordid past from the media or through someone else. A casual, "Wow, I don't know how your wife kept her past secret all those years!" Or even an admiring, "Incredible that she accomplished what she did given her past!" would have been devastating blows to her husband.

Chris had been up front about needing more of her time and attention and had moved out over her inability to give it. How would he feel when he was confronted with how little of her real self she'd given him? She couldn't bear to think about it.

"Look, Pat," Mallory said. "You've done a great job for me. But you've also made a ton of money doing it. What I choose to share with people is my own business."

"Not really." Patricia gave her an enigmatic look. "Not anymore."

The waiter came to take their orders. Patricia asked for scrambled eggs and toast. Mallory stuck with coffee. The way her stomach was roiling, she was afraid to put anything in it.

"So do you want to know what you need to do about this?" Patricia asked.

"Not really," Mallory said. The only things she wanted to do were go home, crawl into bed, and pull the covers over her head. She'd love to talk everything out with Kendall and Faye and Tanya, except they weren't speaking to each other. The loss of their friendship was a gaping hole deep inside. She could feel its yawning emptiness right next to the one that had ripped open when Chris left.

Mallory set the coffee cup back in its saucer with a rattle of china against china. She'd lost everyone important to her by the time she was eighteen and somehow she'd recovered. But she was considerably older now and not so optimistic. She'd learned how to write upbeat, satisfying endings, but she had no idea how to live one.

"I can understand why you're upset," Patricia said. "And I suppose you'd be entitled to wallow in self-pity for a day or two." Patricia's sympathetic tone forced Mallory's head up. She clasped her hands together in her lap to keep them from trembling.

"But I heard from publicity at Partridge and Portman," her agent continued smoothly. "They want you to start blogging about this. Bare your soul to your fan base. Take them into your confidence. They're putting together a list of sites and a tentative schedule of 'appearances.'"

Mallory was already shaking her head. Every instinct she had shouted for her to retreat and regroup. "They're not serious."

Patricia gave her a long, level look as the waiter delivered her breakfast and refilled Mallory's coffee. "You don't want your readers angry with you, Mallory. You're already looking at a certain amount of slippage. No writer is too big to take a serious fall."

"God forbid my sales should drop off." The words were bitter on Mallory's tongue. "Next thing Partridge and Portman will be throwing me under the bus like Scarsdale did Kendall."

Patricia dug into her food when it arrived, but Mallory could barely digest her coffee. She felt like she'd already lost everyone who mattered. Now they wanted her to run after her readers and beg them not to desert her, too?

"Well," Patricia said, after a sip of orange juice and a bite of whole wheat toast, "things could definitely be worse. You could be Faye Truett right now. Or Faye Truett's publisher." She cocked her head knowingly. "Or Faye Truett's husband, the charismatic Pastor Steve."

. . .

Faye hadn't spoken to Steve since *The Kristen Calder Show* yesterday. He'd called from California more times than she wanted to count, but she hadn't picked up for fear of being forced to discuss the disaster on the phone. If ever anything required a face-to-face conversation, Faye knew that her "outing" as Shannon LeSade was it.

She would have liked to get out for a walk along the lake or a drive to almost anywhere, but she hadn't been able to leave the house due to the gaggle of reporters that had been camped out in her driveway since last night. When she'd tuned into the local news this morning, she'd actually seen a shot of their house with the drapes closed and speculation that she was hiding inside. She had no idea what the *Chicago Tribune* had to say, and she wasn't about to face down the paparazzi in order to find out.

The calls she *had* taken had only made her feel worse. At 10:00 A.M. her agent had informed her that her inspirational publisher, Psalm Song, had dropped her effective immediately and were considering legal action to recoup potential lost revenues.

Even Midnight Jade, who published Shannon LeSade, didn't seem at all happy about the revelation of Faye's true identity. The fact that their hottest author was a prominent pastor's wife struck them as "sexually off-putting," a phrase Faye had never heard before. They thought LeSade's readers might feel guilty and/or conflicted. They were panicked about sales.

When Sara's caller ID appeared on her phone, Faye answered eagerly only to discover that the last thing Sara was planning to offer her mother was her support.

"How could you do this to me?" was her daughter's shrill greeting. "Do you have any idea how humiliated we are?"

Faye recoiled from the venom in Sara's voice.

"I will never forgive you for this," Sara shrieked. "Never!"

"Sara, honey," Faye began. "There are things you don't understand. It's not—"

"I don't want to understand them," her daughter said. "It makes me sick to think of you writing that filth. Sick!"

"Why don't you come over so we can talk about this. Bring Rebecca with you and—"

"Do you honestly think I'd subject my daughter to any of this?" She let that hang in the ether, a condemnation and a threat. "As far as I'm concerned I don't have a mother anymore. Which means Becky doesn't have a grandmother!" Sara slammed down the phone, but not before Faye heard her begin to sob piteously.

Faye could hardly breathe from the stab of pain that pierced her chest.

After that, Faye simply left the phone off the hook. Ditto

for the computer and the television. She desperately wanted to call Mallory and Tanya and Kendall, but that door had been slammed shut.

Unsure what to do, she paced the house like a caged animal. Until early afternoon when the front door opened and shut and her husband strode into the house.

"Do you have any idea what you've done?" he asked by way of greeting. His tone was that of a parent speaking to a child. Or an adult with all his faculties speaking to one without.

"I'll tell you what you've done," he said, not waiting for an answer. "You've jeopardized everything we've built—the church . . . our ministry . . . your charities. Everything."

She could feel him attempting to restrain himself. The vein in his temple bulged and there was a tic in his cheek, but he didn't shout. "Everything we've built is at risk because you decided to write pornography!"

"It's not pornography!" Faye's response was automatic.

"Well it is to the people I'm talking about." He looked at her as if he didn't recognize her.

With a start, she realized she didn't recognize him, either. Always before when she'd looked at him Faye had seen Steve, her husband, wrapped in the accoutrements of Pastor Steve. Now she saw only the well-groomed televangelist; she wasn't even sure if her husband was still inside.

"And what about you?" Faye asked. "Aren't you interested in hearing what it is I actually write and why?"

"I might have been if you'd taken me into your confidence at any point before you announced it to the world. This . . . secret life of yours . . . this public admission . . . demonstrates a complete disregard for my church and everything I stand for." His hands fisted at his sides. His eyes were hard, as if all of their warmth had been suctioned out.

"You don't mean that," Faye whispered. "I helped you build Clearview because of what you stood for." Her own eyes narrowed, not because of her hurt and anger, which were all too real, but in a futile effort to see the real Steve.

"And now you seem to be single-handedly trying to tear it down," he said.

"That's not true." Faye backed away from her husband, no longer wanting to see what might remain behind Pastor Steve's façade.

"Isn't it?" His grimace of disappointment in her—and the ease with which he passed judgment on her—rankled.

"You didn't seem to have a problem with the benefits of living with Shannon LeSade," Faye retorted. "She helped put the kids through college, helped build your church, earned the seed money for Clearview's charitable works." She looked deep into Steve's eyes, still searching for the man she'd married.

"And our lovemaking—all that great sex?" She smiled at him, but he didn't smile back. "Did you never wonder why our sex life just kept getting better at an age when most couples' is on the wane?"

His eyes flickered for a moment, but his face didn't soften. His lips set into an even firmer, and in Faye's opinion, more judgmental, line.

"You had no problem living with Shannon LeSade—as long as you didn't have to know it." Her own jaw set as she tried to push past her disappointment in him. "You want to know why I didn't tell you?" she asked, finally understanding the true reason behind her inability to confide in him. "Because you didn't really want to hear it. Any more than you want to know anything at all about me that isn't a flattering reflection of you!"

He didn't acknowledge or dispute her accusation. "I don't have time for theories and rationalizations," he said, his tone clipped and dismissive. "Right now, the key to this whole mess is damage control. My congregation is upset. The media are having a field day. We're going to have to make some sort of joint statement."

It was then that she realized just how deeply the pastor had buried the real Steve Truett. Her husband would have wanted to understand her feelings and motivations. They would have mattered to him because they mattered to her.

Pastor Steve was all about how to fix things so as not to jeopardize his position or upset his flock. And one of the things that had to be fixed was her.

42

*Everything that doesn't kill you makes
you stronger. And later on
you can use it in some story.*
—TAPANI BAGGE

Tanya could barely get up in the mornings. Making it to the Downhome Diner on time, which used to be hardwired into her internal clock, became harder and harder. In fact everything had become too difficult for words.

Darby had called the day after Tanya got back from Chicago to tell Tanya regretfully that Masque was dropping her, which meant no anthology, no lead category titles. "I'm sorry, Tanya," she said. "I was looking forward to hiking part of the Appalachian Trail with you before the national conference in Atlanta this summer. And"—she cleared her voice because Darby had a large heart but lived in fear of letting anyone know it—"you're one of our most popular authors and one of the, um, easiest to work with." She cleared her throat again and Tanya could picture her running a hand through her spiky blond hair. "I'll miss working with you."

Tanya had hung up the phone and confronted the fact that she was now a waitress and a Laundromat attendant. Not a professional writer. She'd picked up her cell phone immediately, wanting to call Kendall. Or Mallory. Or Faye.

When she remembered they weren't talking to each other, she locked herself in the trailer bathroom and cried.

By the end of the week, Tanya's customers were watching

her warily. Tanya knew she needed to snap out of it before they fled her section altogether, but she just couldn't seem to concentrate.

"Darlin'," Jake Harrow said carefully. "I ordered steak and eggs."

"Yeah?" She'd been thinking about the media circus still surrounding Faye's unmasking and word that she'd been refusing to "repent" in front of the Clearview Congregation. Last night when Tanya had been surfing reader websites she'd seen Mallory's recent posts and the flurry of fan comments, which seemed to be evenly split between those willing to forgive Mallory for not sharing her true personal life with them and those whose sense of betrayal made them swear they'd never buy another one of Mallory/Marissa's books no matter what she called herself.

"I realize I'm no expert," Jake said, "but this looks a whole lot like corned beef hash." He paused, his expression pained. "With maple syrup poured all over it."

Tanya looked down at Jake's plate. "Aw, shit," she said. "I'm sorry, Jake. I just . . ." To her complete horror, her vision blurred with tears.

"And, um . . ." the long-haul trucker beside him smiled apologetically, although it was clearly Tanya who should be doing the apologizing. "I ordered coffee. This is *Coca-Cola*." He pushed it toward her with a grimace. "Diet Coca-Cola."

"Oh, Lord," she said. "I am sorry. I . . ." Tanya reached for the plate and glass, but Belle swooped in front of her and snatched them up.

"Tanya," Belle said, "why don't you go on in the back and get ahold of yourself?" Her look added, *And do it quick*. "I'll make sure Jake and Graham here get their breakfasts just the way they like them."

Belle pressed the wrong orders into Tanya's hands for disposal and began to flirt with the two regulars. "I'm sorry about the delay," Belle said. "But we're going to get you all squared away. And your breakfasts will be on me."

Tanya left Jake and Graham protesting Belle's generosity,

but it was clear they were pleased. It was rumored Belle had once given away a stick of gum some time in the seventies, but she continued to deny it.

Tanya scraped the plate into the garbage and put the plate and glass into the dirty dishpan. Then she went to sit on a stool near the open back door of the kitchen, trying to understand why she was so tired and confused now that she no longer had to sit up hunched over her laptop into the wee hours of the morning, and got a whopping seven hours of sleep every night.

Brett moseyed over and leaned against a tall metal shelf of restaurant-sized canned goods. She could just make out the words *This End Up* poking out from behind his dark hair. She'd spent the whole week either avoiding or ignoring him, but she was too far off her game today to expend that much effort.

"You look like you've been in a nuclear blast," he said.

"Me?" she asked, irritated that she'd let her guard down enough to get cornered. Or that he'd summarized her life so easily. If he offered so much as an ounce of sympathy, she'd have to work up the energy to move.

"Hell, yes, you." He folded his arms across his muscled chest. "You've been floating around here all week like you don't know who you are or what you're doing." He peered at her as if he were trying to see right inside her. "What's got into you?"

"You mean other than the fact that I made a fool of myself on national television, lost my book contract and my friends, and completely pissed off Trudy by telling the world that she's an alcoholic and a horrible mother?"

"Rhonda was not the most sympathetic character I've ever read," he admitted, once again surprising her.

"You read *Sticks and Stones*?" Tanya met Brett's gaze, certain that he must be joking. "When?"

"As soon as my mother called and told me I was in it."

Tanya groaned. "Go ahead. Make a joke. File a lawsuit. Tell me I had no right to co-opt your life and call it fiction." He had a hell of a lot of nerve smiling comfortably when her whole world had crumbled like an ancient pile of dog shit.

"It's kind of hard to object to being described as 'ruggedly handsome' and a great father. I mean I did blush a little when you described my sexual abilities in bed but . . ." He shrugged. "I guess that's the price of fame."

"God, you're full of yourself," she said, irritated and, as always when it came to Brett, intrigued. "And I guess it's my fault."

He laughed at that, his smile lighting up his whole handsome face. She wished to hell he wasn't so good looking.

"That's too bad about your contract and all," he said. "I thought this was your best writing ever. But I bet it won't take you any time at all to find another publisher. You just have to write something else." He shrugged as if there was no reason in the world why she shouldn't do this.

"My name is blacker than mud right now in the publishing industry. Masque's dropped me and I'm going to have to work more hours or pick up a third job to replace that money. I wouldn't have time to write if I wanted to."

She didn't add that the idea of writing without her friends behind her just made her heart hurt. She imagined she might be able to find a way to do it. But did she want to?

"You know, if it's just a matter of some money to tide you over while you write," Brett said, "I could . . ."

Tanya's head shot up. "No. No, thank you," she said. "I'll get this worked out. I don't need to be leaning on anyone."

He looked at her strangely. "You are the prickliest woman I have ever known. Taking a little help when you need it doesn't make you a bad person. Or a weak one. When people care about you, they want to help if they can. And I can."

"Well that's very nice of you, Brett," Tanya said. "I appreciate the offer. But I am not interested in depending on anyone for anything."

"We all have to depend on someone for something," he said.

"I don't," she said. "I won't." She looked him in the eye. She would have liked to be the sort of person who could accept his offer and believe things would turn out well. But she knew better.

"That's how disasters happen," she said. "People lull you into this false sense of security. They act like they want to take care of you; that they're always going to be there for you. And then they never are.

"My mother gave birth to me and that was the last time she willingly lifted a finger for me. I made the same mistake with Kyle, my ex. 'Oh, don't worry so much, Tanya, baby. You don't have to work so hard. I'll always be here for you and the girls!'

"Ha! One whiff of motor oil and he was off to the next race. Every once in a while he remembers he has two children and sends me fifty bucks. Think I should have listened to him?"

She was on such a tear now she couldn't have stopped if he'd had an answer, but he didn't.

"And then I meet Mallory, well, except that's apparently not her real name. And Faye. Of course, she's not who she said she was, either. And Kendall, who is what she appeared to be, but whose life I got way too wrapped up in.

"They saved me. They believed in me as a writer and a person. They were my best friends. My mentors." She smiled sadly, certain she must look every bit as stupid and pathetic as she felt.

"They were my 'peeps.'" She started crying full out then, which really, really sucked. "And now when everything's fallen apart, where the hell are they?

"I just lost my best friends," Tanya said, not liking the whine in her voice one bit. "And they never even thought enough of me to tell me who they were. Why would I ever let myself in for that again?"

She felt like an idiot crying in the back of the Downhome's kitchen. He thought it was so simple. He thought he could say, "Here I am" and she'd just faint dead away into his arms in appreciation.

"Because we're good together," he said. "And because I'm not your mother or your ex-husband or your writer friends. I've never run away from a damned thing in my life. And when I say I'm somewhere, I'm there."

She shook her head, dashing the back of her arm against her eyes to swipe away the tears. It would have been so wonderful to be able to believe.

"I never would have thought you'd turn out to be such a coward," Brett said. "You act all tough and hard, but you don't even have the guts to have a relationship with me!"

She wanted to argue, to yell some, to tell him he was full of it, but he was right. She was hanging on for dear life and she simply couldn't take the risk.

Tanya Mason couldn't afford to lose one more thing.

· · ·

A little over three weeks after her ill-fated appearance on *The Kristen Calder Show*, Faye Truett had had enough censure to last a lifetime. Her daughter refused to speak to her or allow her time with her granddaughter. Her husband, who seemed to have almost completely disappeared into the persona of Pastor Steve, came and went. But though they continued to live in the same house, sleep in the same bed, and sometimes even spoke to each other, they no longer communicated.

Faye, who had always prided herself on her ability to take action, couldn't figure out what action to take.

For the first time in almost thirty years, she faced no deadlines and had nothing she needed to write. Her presence at the church she'd helped found was no longer welcomed. Even at Rainbow House, the volunteers and staff's discomfort made her reluctant to spend time there.

More than anything Faye wanted to talk to Kendall and Mallory and Tanya, to talk about what had happened to them and what might happen next. But she was ashamed of all that she'd kept from them and felt lost in a morass of her own making.

She, who had always been so busy, now spent her days either pacing the confines of her home or walking in the Botanic Garden or along Lake Shore Drive. She'd never felt so alone or so unsure.

She was in the midst of one such walk that Wednesday when her cell phone rang. She'd almost stopped carrying it since almost everyone had stopped calling. When she flipped open the phone to check the caller ID and saw Sara's number, she allowed herself to hope for reconciliation. But when she answered it wasn't her daughter's disapproving voice she heard. It was her granddaughter's piping one.

"Gran Gran?" The five-year-old voice was wobbly and worried. "Where did you go? How come you never comed over to see me anymore?"

Faye stopped walking as she tried to get her breath; Becky's hurt had sucked it right out of her.

"Hi, sweetheart," Faye said. "I'm so glad to hear your voice."

"But where are you?" the little girl asked plaintively. "I been missing you." And then, "Don't you love me anymore?"

"Oh, Becky, honey. Of course I do!" Faye swallowed back her tears, ashamed that she'd let things slide so far. Even in the midst of the standoff with Sara, she should not have allowed her granddaughter to feel abandoned. "I've just been . . . busy," she said. "But I should have called to let you know."

She paused, realizing that this was the first time the five-year-old had ever called on her own. "Where are you, sweetheart? Did somebody dial the phone for you?"

"The babysitter helped me," Rebecca confided. "I showed her the 'mergency list with your number on it. But I don't think I'm supposed to tell my mommy. She's at yogurt class."

There was a pause while the child apparently thought about this. "Is it lying if you *don't* tell somebody you did something?"

This, of course, was the million-dollar question. For years Faye had wanted to believe the answer was *No.* That somehow her charitable ends justified her potentially objectionable means. That the sin of omission was smaller and more forgivable than that of an outright lie.

But that had been rationalization pure and simple, Faye thought, as she considered her response. A cowardly way of doing what she wanted to without facing the consequences.

And when she had finally told the truth, it was only because she'd felt compelled to protect Mallory and Kendall. Not out of any sense of moral necessity.

"You shouldn't keep anything from your mommy, Becky. It's OK to tell her we talked," Faye said. "And I've missed you so much. I'm going to talk to your mommy, too. And you know what else?"

Faye's mind began to move more nimbly, sorting through possible courses of action, considering and rejecting. "I'll see you at church on Sunday. I'm going to come by your Sunday school class right after services so we can visit."

"Do you promise, Gran Gran?" the little girl asked. "Will you really?"

"Absolutely positively," Faye assured her granddaughter, incredibly relieved to have made a decision. It would take a veritable army to stop her. "I can't wait to give you all the great big hugs I've been saving up for you."

Faye hung up the phone and continued her walk as she sorted out the best way to do what she'd just committed to. One thing was for certain. She was finished hiding as if she'd committed some mortal sin.

Sara and her group had been after her to denounce what they still insisted on calling pornography and apologize for embarrassing the Clearview congregation. Even Steve seemed to want her to speak out. She'd avoided church these past weeks rather than give in to the pressure, but she was more than ready now to address the congregation.

How they were going to feel about what she had to say was something else altogether.

43

How do I know what I think until I see what I say?
—E. M. FORSTER

Mallory was sick to death of posting apologies all over the Internet and blogging about her thoughts and feelings to anyone who owned a computer. She was even sicker of pacing the brownstone and fending off the quiet.

She hated not talking to Kendall, Tanya, and Faye. And she especially hated how much she missed Chris. But no matter how many times she picked up the phone and started to punch in his number, she couldn't seem to actually place a call.

At first, after her "outing" on *The Kristen Calder Show,* Mallory had been too frightened to think clearly. She'd been afraid that her readers would desert her in droves. That her publisher would drop her. That somehow admitting to her pathetic past and to a burnout so severe that she'd actually plagiarized herself would blot out everything she'd achieved and erase her from the bestseller lists as if she had never existed.

For a time it had looked as if all of her fears might be realized. Readers were angry and not shy about saying so and her sales numbers dropped sharply for the first time in a decade. Her publisher was not happy with her and there were more legal questions at this point than answers. But ultimately her nightmare of losing "everything" as she had after her parents' suicides, had proven to be just that—only a nightmare.

It was only now, when she was certain she was not going to be out on the street, that she'd discovered the facet of her nightmare that didn't fade in the light of day; she was alone. Horribly alone. And this time it wasn't because the people she loved had deserted her, but because they felt unloved and deserted *by* her.

Like the owner of a sinking boat who'd been so fixated on the teak trim and polished chrome that she overlooked the gaping hole in her vessel's hull, Mallory had spent so much time and energy striving for financial security that she'd overlooked what mattered most. Or rather the *people* who mattered most.

She'd heard that Chris was back in New York, but she hadn't heard from him. She didn't even know where he was staying.

She also knew that Faye's and Tanya's contracts had been terminated and that Scarsdale was planning to take *Sticks and Stones* off the shelves because of the legal wrangling between their publishers. Mallory would have given anything to talk with her friends, but she could still see the shock on their faces when they'd discovered she wasn't who she'd said she was. And her own shock over Faye's revelations.

When they'd needed each other most, rather than circling the wagons as they always had in the past, they'd turned on each other. How did a friendship survive that?

Mallory didn't know. In fact she was afraid she didn't know anything that mattered anymore. She'd rebuilt her life once before with hard, grueling work writing book after book, presenting herself as she wanted to be until she became it, making appearance after appearance.

But always she'd held her real self back. She'd given to her husband and her friends, but not of her *self*. Even when she'd been trying to help Kendall, she'd been frantically trying to get over a writer's block that she couldn't admit to. She'd accepted Chris's love and attention as her due and then doled out the bare minimum of herself in return. No wonder he'd given up on her.

Mallory walked into Chris's closet searching for her husband, but only bits and pieces of him remained. His absence taunted her and she missed him with a fierceness that she couldn't push aside.

It was there amid the unnecessary articles of clothing that Chris had left behind that Mallory realized there was no room for pride in the great emptiness yawning inside of her. If she loved her husband and her friends then she needed to demonstrate that love by offering her true self. Whether they accepted what she presented would be up to them.

Hurrying into the bedroom Mallory picked up the phone and placed a call to Patricia Gilmore. When she had her agent on the line, she explained that she was planning a month's vacation followed by major changes in her writing schedule. Then she instructed her to contact Zoe at Partridge and Portman as well as P&P's legal department. There had to be a way to salvage *Sticks and Stones* so that all of its authors could benefit from it. She charged her agent with finding a way to make this happen then placed another call to Lacy Samuels to try to get a sense of how things were playing out at Scarsdale.

Relieved to be taking action, Mallory dialed her travel agent next, explaining what she had in mind and asking that the tickets be messengered to her later that afternoon. And then before she could lose her nerve, she called Chris's secretary and scheduled a lunch appointment with her husband for the following day.

It was said that an opera wasn't over until the fat lady sang. For Mallory a love story wasn't over until the hero and heroine professed their love and agreed to live "happily ever after."

. . .

Lacy Samuels sat in Jane Jensen's empty office wondering if she should call a shaman or a priest to rid the space of any evil remnants of the editor's personality that might remain.

She'd been sent to clean out and box up the detritus of Jane's sixteen years at Scarsdale so that the space could be made ready for Hannah Sutcliff, who had laid claim to it as well as Jane's biggest authors.

With an empty box on a chair next to her, Lacy began to sort through Jane Jensen's things, realizing as she did so that she was looking for an explanation for her former boss's hostility and disdain.

She handled things as little as possible, partly because they'd been Jane's and partly because she couldn't shake the irrational fear that Jane was somehow going to storm into the office, see what Lacy was doing, and find a way to punish her for it.

Despite Hannah and Cash's assurances that this was impossible and that Jane was no doubt out interviewing for new jobs right this very minute, Lacy's fight-or-flight instinct was primed and ready to kick in.

The top of the desk yielded little in the way of clues. A chipped coffee mug stuffed with pens and pencils, an electric cup warmer, several yellow pads with Jane's aggressive scrawl across the pages, and a mostly dead plant that had bent itself in half trying to reach the light went into the box without examination.

Then Lacy pulled open the top drawer of Jane Jensen's desk.

For a time it was a simple matter of sorting: supplies like paper clips and sticky pads and red pencils stayed here, anything that looked remotely personal went into the box—though there wasn't a lot of that. There were no mementos, no personal photos, not even ones taken with the well-known authors Jane had edited. Lacy found only in-house memos and phone lists and production schedules along with crumpled wrappers and miscellany.

As she handled Jane's things, she continued to look for clues as to why a talented editor would so despise writers that she edited. Or why she had made everyone around her so miserable. Even serial killers began with a clean slate. Jane Jensen must have had her reasons.

Taking a break from the desk, Lacy turned to the shelves that held books Jane had edited over the last few years. Because she'd been an executive editor, they were mostly recent releases by Scarsdale's best-known names. Lacy handled their books reverently and felt the thrill of being a part of the publishing process. She was now an assistant editor and she could hardly wait to take the diamond of the author's work and help to polish it to an even more startling brilliance.

On a bottom shelf, Lacy found several copies of *Sticks and Stones* and she felt the elation coupled with frustration that she experienced whenever she confronted the tangled mess of claims and counterclaims now twined around the book. The book was still climbing the *New York Times* list despite, or more likely because of, Kristen Calder's "outing" of its authors. Lacy knew there was still talk of pulling it from the shelves due to the disputes over ownership. But it seemed a terrible waste to Lacy to lose such a huge moneymaker.

In her heart she believed there must be a way to satisfy the claimants without pulling the book. Mallory St. James's call made Lacy even keener to figure out a way to do it. But whenever she brought up the idea, both Cash and Hannah accused her of wishful thinking. But wasn't it wishful thinking and determination that had seen the book published in the first place? Why couldn't the same outside-the-box thinking help keep it on the shelves?

Lacy was still musing about this possibility when she came across the dog-eared manuscript crammed into the very back of a bottom desk drawer. *One Life, One Dream* was scrawled across the title page in an oversized old-fashioned font. The author's name appeared beneath it. Lacy's hands stilled as she read the name, Jana Johansen, clearly a pseudonym for "she who should not be named." The cover letter attached to the title page was dated 1983, right about the time Jane had come to Scarsdale.

Curious now, Lacy began to leaf through the manuscript pages, reading a paragraph here and there, skimming from scene to scene. She grimaced when she hit a reference to the hero's "throbbing male member." But there were also passages that betrayed Jane's attempts to be literary. Overall, Lacy thought, it wasn't bad, certainly not as bad as the submissions Jane had foisted on her. Parts of it were even good, just not good enough.

The rejection letters stacked behind the manuscript confirmed Lacy's assessment. They'd come from a who's who of New York publishing houses and every one of them concluded with the advice that the author not give up her day job; advice Jane Jensen had apparently taken to heart. And possibly never gotten over.

Was it envy that had made Jane belittle the writers she'd been hired to help? Had that envy ultimately hardened into the anger and bitterness she'd showered on those around her?

Lacy straightened the pages and bound the stack, rejection letters on top, so that Jane would know that they had been seen. Then she taped the box closed, wondering whether the anger had built into a chemical imbalance or the alleged chemical balance had stoked the envy to uncontrollable proportions.

In the end, Lacy realized, it didn't really matter which wire had blown first, and as she labeled the box with her ex-boss's address, Lacy conceded that there would never be a heart-to-heart about Jane Jensen's failed literary ambitions. Why Jane had tortured her authors and underlings was less important than the fact that she had.

It was time, Lacy thought as she carried the box out of the empty office, to stop thinking about her former boss and start thinking about how to keep *Sticks and Stones* alive. Mallory St. James's call had started her wondering whether the other three authors might also want to see some sort of agreement reached.

Maybe, Lacy mused as she carried the box onto the elevator and down to the mail room, she could help keep *Sticks and Stones* on the shelves with good old-fashioned perseverance. And a little TLC.

. . .

Steve had already left for church when Faye stepped into the shower on Sunday morning. With clumsy fingers she blew-dry her hair and applied makeup then dressed in the black pin-stripe suit she'd set out the night before.

The things she might say flitted through her head as she drove to church and parked in a reserved spot in the massive parking lot, but she just let them float through. When the time came, she didn't want to regurgitate a carefully written and memorized speech. She'd decided that whatever she said today had to come not from her mind, but from her heart.

The cameras were in place and most of the crowd in their seats when Faye entered the church. She stood just inside the massive double doors of the high-tech worship center for a moment, gathering her nerve. She had helped to build this church and had contributed in every possible way to the growth of her husband's ministry. Even though it had not been her dream, she had helped him achieve his.

She raised her chin and squared her shoulders, reminding herself what was too easily forgotten. This church had been founded to do good and to help those in need. She had done both of those things. It wasn't up to others, her daughter included, to judge her for her methods.

A hush fell as she walked up the center aisle toward their family pew. Faye felt the eyes of the congregation follow her progress. There were occasional smiles and hellos, but many of those who watched her so carefully let their gazes slide over her as if she weren't there.

As Faye approached the pew, her daughter and son-in-law became aware of the growing hush and turned in their seats. There was a flare of surprise in her daughter's eyes and she grasped hold of her husband's arm as if in need of physical support. A buzz of conversation arose but Faye ignored it. At her usual seat on the end of the front center row, she sat, keeping her eyes on the pulpit. Moments later Pastor Steve made his entrance from the side of the altar and strode vigorously up to the podium. The choir began an opening hymn. The congregation came to its feet.

For Faye the service both sped by and dragged interminably. She could feel church members studying her, eager to see if she would take a microphone toward the end of the service when members were invited to stand up and speak.

Steve's gaze flicked over her repeatedly, when he wasn't playing to one camera or another or exhorting the congregation to lift their voices to God. Both she and Sara read responsively, sang along with the choir, sat silently during the sermon, but they studiously ignored each other.

After long minutes devoted to silent meditation, Pastor Steve introduced the concluding "talking time" and asked if anyone in the congregation would care to speak.

Faye stood amid a buzz of conversation. Looking neither left nor right, Faye walked up the steps to the altar and moved behind the empty podium. She carried neither notes nor specific thoughts with her. But she did offer up several prayers to the God she knew. *Please guide my tongue so that I may be clear,* she asked silently as she stared out at the sea of faces before her. *And please know that in my own way, I love you.*

The red light on the camera aimed at her came on and, without prompting, Faye began to speak. "There are many of our members, including my family, who were upset to discover that I have been writing sensual novels under the name of Shannon LeSade." She paused as heads across the huge room bent together. "They've asked me to apologize to you because they think I've done something wrong, even shameful."

She turned her gaze to her daughter and waited for Sara to meet her eye. "But I began as LeSade to fund my children's college education and to help build this church. And I don't regret a single word I've written."

Faye allowed her eyes to scan the audience. Some faces were hard and unmoving. Others were turned away. But many watched in rapt attention, open to what she had to say. She might not change a single mind, but she was not really here to sway others. She simply needed to have her say.

"I don't believe God has a problem with novels about physical passion between men and women who love each other. And at one time, my husband wouldn't have, either. I don't know when my daughter began to judge others so harshly. It's not the way she was raised."

She paused, but did not turn to look at Steve or Sara or try to gauge their reactions. "In Deuteronomy it's written, 'Ye shall not be afraid of the face of man; for the judgment is God's.' I think there are members of our and other congregations who have tried to take over God's role as final judge," she said. "I don't believe that God has appointed us as the arbiters of others' actions. It is not up to us to tell others what they can think. Or feel. Or write. Or read."

The words came of their own accord, building in speed and intensity like they did when she wrote, when she just opened herself up and let whatever was inside her flow onto the page.

"I do apologize for not sharing this information about myself with my family and friends. I know it came as a shock and that the people closest to me felt betrayed by my silence. I regret that with all my heart."

She turned her gaze to her husband, who stood stock-still behind the other podium. Unflinchingly he met her gaze, but she couldn't read his face or his thoughts. She reminded herself that she hadn't come seeking his or anyone else's approval, but only to set things straight.

"But I will not apologize for what I've written. Or for the good we've been able to accomplish as a result."

Steve's gaze remained locked with hers, but he remained silent. There was not a sound in the massive church now, not a creak of a wooden pew, not a cough. Faye pictured the five million people viewing this live telecast sitting still and silent in their homes, weighing her words. Waiting to see what would happen next.

She looked down at Sara and saw that her head was bowed, but whether her daughter was moved or embarrassed, Faye didn't know.

So be it. She'd said what she had to say. Now she would go. She'd just walk back down the aisle and out the doors.

She'd stop off in Becky's classroom and give her all the hugs she'd promised. And then, well, then it would be time to get in touch with her friends so that she could apologize and, if God showed her the right way, make them understand. Then she thought she might call that nice young Lacy Samuels.

The church was still almost eerily silent. With a final nod to the camera Faye left the podium, swept down the steps, and began a resolute march down the aisle. She felt lighter after her "confession." Clearer headed. Resolute. But the aisle stretched out into infinity; the exit might have been twenty miles away. She judged herself to be almost halfway to the door when her husband's voice rang out in the silent church.

"My wife," he said, with conviction, "is one of the bravest women I know. And her points are well made."

Faye stopped and turned. Pastor Steve stood under a shaft of klieg light. She saw that he was staring, not into the television camera, but at her.

"It's I who owe her an apology. And my thanks," he continued in the voice that belonged to her husband. "Because she's right," he said, his gaze turning now to their daughter. "It's not our place to judge. And we're not in the business of burning books or condemning others for their choice of reading materials."

He looked to Faye once more and she felt her heart swell with tenderness and love and an awesome thankfulness to the God who had not only heard her prayers but answered them.

"She was also right when she told me that I didn't want to know the truth. But when we love someone we love all of them, even the truths that we find difficult. The things we'd rather not know."

He held his hand out toward Faye and a camera panned along with her as she came forward to join her husband at the podium for the final benediction.

She didn't know if she'd gotten through to Sara and she hadn't yet reached out to her friends, but it was a start.

Faye Truett stood in the shelter of her husband's arms as he addressed God on her and his congregation's behalf.

And then she bowed her head and cried.

44

*All good writing is swimming underwater
and holding your breath.*
—F. SCOTT FITZGERALD

"Tanya," Trudy called from the living room. "Come on out here and look at this!"

It was Sunday morning and Tanya had slept until well after ten then lay in her bed for another thirty minutes wishing she was still asleep. She'd taken to sleeping whenever she wasn't working; all those stolen minutes and hours she used to spend hunched over her laptop she now spent either asleep or trying to be.

She knew she needed to look for another job to replace her lost income. *Sticks and Stones* was still on the shelves, but she had no idea whether she'd ever see any part of that money. Masque had joined in on a massive lawsuit, but if she didn't start looking for an agent, she'd have no one but herself to make sure she was protected.

Despite all the extra sleep, Tanya had grown increasingly short-tempered. At work she and Brett nodded to each other but hadn't talked since she'd rejected his last offer of help. The Adamses' standing invitation to Sunday supper had never been rescinded and Tanya's girls kept begging to go. But it had gotten to where the mere mention of their name made Tanya long for a blanket and pillow.

When Loretta and Crystal asked why they couldn't see the Adamses anymore, Tanya just told them to leave her alone and to not ask so many questions. Because she couldn't bring herself to tell them that she was afraid to be with Brett because she liked him too much. That she didn't want to let them start imagining life in the cute little house with the great smells in the kitchen. That she was afraid if she let Brett Adams carry any part of her load she'd lie down on the ground in relief and never get up again.

"Your friend's on the TV!" Trudy yelled again.

Tanya shuffled out of the bedroom in her pajamas and slippers mumbling at Trudy and railing at the world.

Trudy had on Pastor Steve's *Prayer Hour.* "Isn't that your friend?" she asked. "The erotica writer? I usually just tune in to look at Pastor Steve. That is one fine-looking man."

Tanya lowered herself onto the couch and leaned forward to study the grainy image on the old television set. Faye certainly didn't look like she'd been moping around in her pajamas feeling sorry for herself. Her salt-and-pepper hair was neatly styled and she had on a black pin-striped suit that made her look like a CEO. Everybody in the church, including Faye's husband, seemed to be hanging on her every word.

"I expect you're sorry you ever met her and the other two. The way they left you hanging out there to dry and all."

Tanya didn't comment. She was watching Faye bow her head, and the way her husband's arm went around her shoulders as he offered a final prayer.

"It just don't pay to rely on anybody else," Trudy was saying. "It only ever leads to heartache. I taught you that from the time you were a baby. I couldn't bring myself to leave you. But I couldn't let you get too dependent on me neither, in case . . ." She hesitated. ". . . in case I caved in one day and took off."

Tanya froze. Her eyes left the bowed head of Faye Truett as she swiveled to look at her mother. Trudy took a furtive little sip of her orange juice, which undoubtedly had been spiked with a little Sunday morning vodka. There was nothing like hearing that your own mother had had to fight the urge to desert you.

Though of course she'd always known it.

"Yep," Trudy said. "I'm glad you didn't listen to me when I tried to push you into something with that Brett Adams. Things never work out the way we want them to for people like us." She nodded at the freeze-framed shot of Faye Truett and her husband. "Maybe for folks like them, but not us."

Trudy took another sip of her screwdriver. "We all have our ways of hiding out and avoiding the pain," her mother said. "Me, I've always used the bottle. It's quick and reliable. You," she said, pointing her glass at Tanya. "You use your work and your kids."

Tanya picked up the remote and clicked off the TV. She didn't care at all for the way her mother had lumped them together. Hadn't she spent her whole life trying to prove she wasn't one bit like Trudy?

Tanya wanted to go back to bed, but Trudy would not stop yammering.

"I was thinking the other day that it was my . . . struggles . . . that made you strong. It was me that taught you how to stand on your own two feet."

Although she wouldn't have thought it possible, Tanya felt even worse than she had before. And pissed off, too. Where did Trudy get off taking credit for anything remotely motherly?

"So you became a helpless alcoholic in order to make me a stronger person?"

"Well I might not exactly have planned it," Trudy admitted. "It just sort of turned out that way."

Tanya wanted to cry like Faye had done on TV, wanted to let out great big bruising sobs that might make the sick feeling inside of her disappear.

"You see, you're right to show Crystal and Loretta not to trust or depend on anyone else. They'll thank you for it one day."

"Oh, Mama." Tanya felt everything she'd been holding on to so tightly whoosh out of her. Here she'd bent over backward to be everything to her girls that her mother hadn't been to her and she'd ended up teaching them the same lesson her mother had taught her? She did not want to hear it. She did not even want to think it.

Brett had said she was afraid of him. Afraid to take a chance. Afraid to let anyone in. And he was right.

She got up from the couch, her mind racing. "So you think I'm right to give up on writing now that I've lost my contract with Masque? That I shouldn't try, say, single title? Try to sell to someone else even if I have to do it under another name?"

Tanya began to pace back and forth in front of her mother as she spewed out her questions even though she knew exactly how Trudy would answer.

"And I suppose you think I shouldn't go out with Brett, even though I like to be with him, because he might disappoint me? That I should never do anything that might not turn out the way I want it to?"

Tanya could hardly breathe as she faced the final, annihilating truth. Despite a lifetime of trying to be the opposite of Trudy, she'd turned out just like her. Only without the alcohol and lazy streak. The message she was sending her children was the same one her mother had sent her.

Not waiting for or needing Trudy's confirmation, Tanya jumped up and ran to the front door of the trailer and pulled it open. "Ya'll get ready to go over to the Adamses'," she shouted to the girls, who were playing outside. "I'm getting dressed right now!"

Tanya scooped up her cell phone and punched in Brett's number. She raced into the bedroom and started rifling through the pile of abandoned clothes while the phone rang. "It's me," she said, when he answered. "I changed my mind. The girls and I will be over if we're still invited."

"Um, sure," Brett said. "That would be great," he said. And then, "This is Tanya Mason, right? The woman who accused me of trying to lull her into a false sense of security?"

"It's real ungentlemanly of you to throw that back in my face right now," Tanya said. "I want to talk to you about that when we get there. And a few other things, too."

Twenty minutes later she was showered and dressed. She wasn't planning on inviting Trudy, but her mother had somehow gotten herself ready.

At Brett's the girls headed into Valerie's room and Trudy made her way to the waiting six-pack of Budweiser. Tanya took Brett by the T-shirt and pulled him out onto the front stoop.

All the way over in the car she'd been trying to find the words for what she wanted to say to Brett, but now that she was facing him she couldn't remember how she'd meant to start. All she knew for sure was she wasn't going to be controlled by her mother's negative thinking for one more minute. And she wasn't going to pass it on to her children for one more day.

She liked to be with Brett. He thought highly of her and said so. And he was a good father and fun to be with. And he was damned good in bed. And if it wasn't meant to be forever then so what? She'd more than proven she could take care of her girls. She didn't have to be afraid of what would happen if he left, because they would survive. She'd make sure of it. So why shouldn't she enjoy the company of someone she liked being with? After all these years of struggle, didn't she deserve some pleasure?

Brett watched her quizzically. She had the feeling he was fighting a smile, but she was too preoccupied thinking about what she wanted to say to be as annoyed as she might have been.

"So I've decided there's no reason why we shouldn't date if we want to," she said without preamble.

"OK," he said.

"Now that doesn't mean you've been elected to be in charge or anything. I'm not going to be swooning and batting my eyelashes at you or any stupid damn thing like that."

"OK," Brett said.

"And if it doesn't work out, it doesn't work out," she said adamantly. "It's not the end of the world."

"Can't argue with that," he said.

"Isn't there anything you want to say?"

"Oh," he said, pretending surprise. "You mean I get to talk, too?"

She knocked him on the shoulder as the smile he'd been holding back spread over his face.

"Raise your right hand," he said. "And repeat after me."

When she didn't move, he raised her hand for her. "I, Tanya Mason," he said.

He waited until she gave in and repeated her name.

"Do solemnly swear."

He raised an eyebrow, and she said, "I do solemnly swear."

"That Brett Adams is allowed to . . ."

He motioned her to continue and she did.

". . . do the occasional nice thing, make the occasional nice meal, and maybe even watch my kids for an hour or two now and then . . ."

She rolled her eyes, but repeated the words as instructed. ". . . without accusing him of trying to make me dependent and/or beholden."

She repeated the words, her own smile growing to match his.

"So help me God!"

When she'd repeated the final words to his satisfaction and dropped her pledge hand, he studied her for a long moment, the dimple twitching in his cheek.

"Don't you think we should go ahead and seal our vow with a kiss?" he asked, still smiling.

"I guess," she teased, wanting to do exactly that. "Unless you think pricking our fingers and signing in blood would be more effective."

Fortunately he ignored the suggestion and swept her up in his arms and kissed her soundly, just like the hero in one of her novels. Which set her to thinking about what she might like to try writing next.

And whether there might be some way to make contact with Kendall and Faye and Mallory—maybe through Lacy Samuels—without having to rehash everything that had driven them apart.

. . .

Chris was already seated at a favored table in the back of the first-floor dining room of the Spotted Pig when Mallory arrived. She felt his steady gaze assessing her as she approached and she tried to read it, but she sensed a part of him had been closed off to her. He gave nothing away. He stood as she reached the table and pulled her chair out then waited as she took her seat.

More nervous than she'd expected to be, Mallory kept her hands in her lap so that their shaking wouldn't betray her. She'd chosen the trendy Spotted Pig because it was vibrant and upbeat. Had she really believed that the lighter ambience would keep darker emotions at bay?

"I'm not sure what to call you," he said when they were both seated. "Imagine my surprise when I discovered I didn't even know my wife's real name."

Mallory nodded, saddened by the hurt in his voice, by the damage she'd done. "I know," she said, forcing herself to meet his eyes. "I'm so sorry you found out that way."

He didn't respond and Mallory fought the urge to look away. A part of her wanted to cut and run. To simply apologize and accept that she had damaged their relationship irretrievably and simply let it go. "Irreconcilable differences" sounded so much nicer than "failure to share self with spouse."

Except she couldn't bear the thought of living without him. Not now, when everything else had been stripped away and she'd finally discovered that success and financial security meant nothing if she couldn't share them with Chris.

The waiter brought a basket of bread and took their drink orders. He was friendly and the bread was warm and crusty, but Mallory found herself resenting every interruption now when all she wanted was to make Chris understand.

"I realize now," she said, "that I was drawn to writing because I was so desperate to try to control some aspect of my out-of-control life."

He'd heard the details of her past on television and in the press. There seemed little point in retelling them, but she wanted to make sure he understood her "why."

"Writers are all-powerful, you know. It's the one certain reward for all the gut-wrenching hours we spend creating a novel. A writer doesn't always get rich or famous, but she controls what her characters say and think. Who lives, who dies. Whether they achieve their hearts' desires."

She smiled at Chris. "I'm sure you can imagine how attractive that would be to someone who'd been through what I had." She looked away, searching for the right words, knowing that they were more important than any she'd ever written.

"In my mind I was already Mallory St. James when I met you. Marissa died when I was eighteen and there was nothing of her left worth knowing. She was a bundle of fear and insecurity and . . . neediness. Even a glimpse of all of that would have sent any healthy male—even a caregiving Sir Galahad like you—running for his life."

He didn't disagree, but she thought she sensed a slight thawing. "I just can't believe I married someone I didn't know at all," he said.

She waited for their salads to be placed in front of them. Chris began on his, but Mallory couldn't imagine chewing or swallowing. "But you did know the real me, Chris, the me I decided to be. You've always known her. You just didn't know the details of her life."

She didn't know if what she was saying would change anything, whether he'd be able to forgive her or even want to. She realized, as she looked into his eyes, that it was no accident that she'd chosen to write such strong female characters. It hadn't been a marketing decision or a smart business move.

She wrote what she wrote because she'd needed to believe that resourcefulness and strength of will—something with which she'd imbued all her characters—were enough to win the day. She also believed in the redemptive power of love. And at the moment, she desperately needed to believe in happy endings.

She paused and took a sip of water. The thing was, she didn't get to write the ending of their story. She could only reveal her character's feelings and motivations, throw in a final plot twist. They'd already lived their black moment. The resolution was up to Chris.

Their entrées arrived but neither of them picked up a fork or made a move to start eating. Like she did each time she confronted that first blank page of what would become a novel, Mallory made the decision to take that leap of faith.

"I love you," she said. "More than I can tell you. More than I even realized until I understood that I might lose you." She swallowed but didn't look away, horribly aware that this could be the beginning of something even better than what they'd had. Or the end of everything.

"I can't change how things have been," Mallory said. "But I can change how they will be." She looked deep into his eyes but saw no answers in them. Then she reached into her purse and pulled out an airline ticket and laid it on the table in front of him.

"I bought us tickets to Cabo San Lucas," she said. "I managed to get the casita where we spent our honeymoon. I booked it for the first three weeks of July."

Surprise registered on his face, but still he didn't speak.

"I hope you'll join me there," Mallory said. "I'd like us to spend the time together."

Still no response. Mallory continued to speak calmly, though it took all of her willpower to keep the desperation she was feeling from stealing into her voice.

"I've also told Patricia and Zoe that I'm cutting back to a book a year. So that, assuming you're willing, we can have time together. So we can have a real life." She swallowed, afraid that he was going to tell her it was too little too late. That he'd just push the ticket back across the table and tell her to have a nice life.

She saw regret and something else she was afraid to identify in his eyes. And suddenly she didn't think she could face
knowing it was over. Not here. Not now.

Mallory pushed back her seat and prepared to stand. "You
don't have to make a decision right now." She drew a deep
breath and stood, wondering if this would be it. "Your ticket
is open ended. I hope your heart still is. Because if I have to,
I'll spend those three weeks waiting for you to join me."

He stood, too, but he didn't rush around the table to stop
her. Or sweep her up into his arms. She just kept telling herself that whatever he said, she'd live with it. She was strong
enough to survive if she had to.

"I'm really sorry, Mal," Chris said, and her heart plum-
meted.

Mallory held her breath while she braced for his brush-off.
She would not cry or make a scene. She wouldn't make this
harder on either of them. It was his ending to write. And she
wouldn't be given the opportunity to edit or revise.

"I just don't have an answer," he said. "I don't know if I have
the energy to try again." He shook his head, his smile tinged
with regret.

"But you'll keep the ticket," she said. "And think about
using it."

"Yes," he said as she picked the ticket up off the table and
placed it gently in his hands. "I'll think about it. I will."

She felt his eyes follow her as she turned and walked out of
the restaurant. And as she walked down the sidewalk to where
her car was waiting, she told herself there was still hope.

Chris hadn't said no, he'd simply ended this chapter with a
cliffhanger. In Mallory's mind, that meant "to be continued."
She smiled as she played with the metaphor. With the possibility of a sequel.

The story wasn't over until somebody typed, "THE END."

. . .

More than a month after the Kristen Calder debacle, Kendall's life remained in flux. All around her in the mountains,
spring gave way to summer and Kendall took delight in the

deep pinks and whites of the flowering rhododendron and dogwood, cheek to jowl with the mountain laurel and azaleas that bloomed down the mountainsides and through the woods where she walked.

Sticks and Stones was still on the shelves despite the constant rumblings about its being pulled. One call from Sylvia Hardcastle had warned that Kendall was going to be asked to repay her advance. The next she'd been told how well the book was still selling and that there'd been an approach about movie rights. Sylvia advised her to hold tight. Each change of direction served as yet another testament to the vagaries of publishing.

Today's call caught Kendall replacing a toilet with a low-flow model and raised a subject Kendall had been too conflicted about to broach.

"Kendall," Sylvia said. "Have you done anything more about the sequel to *Sticks and Stones?*"

"Um, no," Kendall admitted, though that hardly covered her feelings about the project. She felt a pull to write, an urge to express herself that she hadn't felt since Mia, her original editor, had left to have her baby and left Kendall in Jane Jensen's hostile hands.

But she no longer trusted that urge or her ability to fulfill it. Because no matter how she wanted to whitewash it, the truth was that she hadn't hit the *New York Times* list or been noticed by Kristen Calder because of her own talent. Her only major success had come because her friends had helped her write *Sticks and Stones*.

Like an obese person who loses a hundred pounds but still sees a fat person reflected in the mirror, Kendall was deathly afraid that Jane Jensen's assessment of Kendall's talent—or lack thereof—was correct and that she'd only ceased being a mediocre midlist author because her friends had stepped in to save her. "Why?"

"I'm asking because I just found your proposal," Sylvia said. "I'd set it aside until we were forced to discuss your option book with them. And with all the hoopla we've been dealing with, I didn't read it until yesterday."

Kendall felt a shimmer of apprehension. She'd been so jazzed when she'd finished her part in *Sticks and Stones* that the proposal for its sequel, *Names Will Never Hurt Me,* had flowed out of her, the synopsis and first three chapters practically putting themselves on the page.

She didn't think she could bear to hear Sylvia tell her, even gently, that it sucked. What would she do then? Pick another room to remodel? Build a workshop to house all her power tools?

"Did you write this yourself?" Sylvia asked.

"What?" Kendall had been picturing the workshop. Found herself imagining where she'd hang her tool belt.

"Did you write the proposal for *Names Will Never Hurt Me* alone?"

Kendall sighed. "That bad, huh?" She told herself it would be OK. She'd find something else to do. Lots of people gave up writing. It was hard to stand up to the pressures of the business. She wouldn't be the first to stop writing for good. "Yep," she admitted. "It's all mine. Nobody else to blame it on but me."

"Well I'm relieved to hear that," Sylvia said, and Kendall braced for the blow. So what if she'd wanted to write since she was a child. Surely she must have some other talents. Maybe James, who had called after her *Kristen Calder* appearance and talked her into that first cup of coffee, would find her a job at Home Depot. Clayton had a Walmart, too. Did they already have a greeter?

"Because it's fabulous. With even bigger potential than *Sticks and Stones.*"

Kendall held her breath, afraid to exhale lest she erase what she thought she'd just heard. "You liked it?"

"Liked it?" Sylvia asked. "I loved it!"

Kendall clung to Sylvia's enthusiasm. Her agent was smart, straightforward, and generally positive, but she was not a flatterer.

"And if we can get this whole *Sticks and Stones* mess cleared up, it really should go to Scarsdale. Now that Jane Jensen's gone, they should have the most interest."

Kendall's heart squeezed in happiness, something that hadn't happened in much longer than she cared to remember. The details of Sylvia's plans to present it, her suggestions for who she'd submit to if Hannah Sutcliff passed on it, flew right over her head. Her agent thought the proposal she'd written was even better than *Sticks and Stones*! Right now that was Christmas and the Easter Bunny all rolled up together.

Kendall hung up in a haze of happiness that softened everything she looked at from the sparkle of sunlight off a distant mountain peak to the grace with which the branches of a nearby pine tree swayed in the breeze.

She was a writer and she had a new project under way. At the moment she didn't care where it ended up; she only cared that she would get to write it.

A burst of positive energy welled up inside her. She needed to set her life in order so that she would be free to write. Without waffling or her usual internal debate, she placed a call to both her children and this time when she got their voice mail, she calmly and succinctly read them the parental riot act. Their mother and father loved them, they simply didn't love each other. There would be no more groveling and apologizing. She was more sorry than she could ever say that they'd been hurt. But it was time to move forward.

When she hung up she felt immeasurably better, but there was still one dark cloud skulking across her horizon.

While it was imperative to know that she *could* write without the support of her "peeps," and she was embarrassingly grateful that Sylvia had confirmed that she could, that didn't mean she wanted to.

On the deck the breeze that had set the branches to swaying teased at her hair. The afternoon sun was warm and gentle on her face.

She wished her friends were here with her now to celebrate

her newfound confidence; she could never have found it without them.

So some of them had kept secrets; so everyone's good in-
tentions had gone awry and they'd all been damaged in the
process. The one thing she couldn't envision was a future that
didn't include Mallory and Faye and Tanya.

She picked up the phone, wishing she could simply call all
three of them, read them the riot act, and demand that they
all forgive each other. But they weren't her children. And they
were all facing their own demons right now.

She clutched the phone to her chest, trying to figure out
what she might do to help make things right. She couldn't sit
idly by without trying to do something.

As she listened to the stir of the leaves Kendall began to
formulate the outline of a plan. Afraid that if she waited she'd
talk herself out of it, Kendall punched in the New York number and asked to speak to Lacy Samuels. Perhaps the "plucky
young assistant," who had bucked her boss to save *Sticks and
Stones,* would consider tilting at a few more publishing wind-
mills. Or would at least know someone who could.

45

*Great is the art of beginning, but greater
is the art of ending.*
—HENRY WADSWORTH LONGFELLOW

Kendall Aims met Sylvia Hardcastle in the marbled, if not hallowed, lobby of Scarsdale Publishing on a late June afternoon, just shy of a year after she'd failed to win the Zelda at the national conference of Wordsmiths Incorporated.

As they waited for Lacy Samuels to escort them to the conference room, Kendall reflected on all that had transpired over the last twelve months. She'd bottomed out and scaled the heights, been humiliated on national television and written off a husband, but she'd also reclaimed her mountain home and regained her children. She'd lost her faith in her talent and then found it again. And according to Sylvia, an offer had been made for *Names Will Never Hurt Me*, of which she'd completed seven full chapters.

And then there was her surprising affinity for power tools and her uncontrollable urge to fix things, which she now recognized as a physical attempt to repair her broken life. Not to mention James, who was sweet and understanding and willing to let her set their pace.

In the yin and yang of loss and redemption the only things that still hung in the balance were the fate of *Sticks and Stones* and the friendships that had created it.

The clack of heels sounded on marble and Kendall looked

up to see Lacy walking toward them. She was still tall and leggy but with a new air of confidence that Kendall suspected came from working under Hannah Sutcliff instead of Jane Jensen as well as her new position as an assistant editor.

When she reached them, Lacy smiled and hugged Kendall warmly then shook Sylvia's hand.

"Everyone else is already here," Lacy said as she led them past security to the bank of elevators. "There are an awful lot of lawyers in that room. I'm not sure that's such a good thing."

Neither did Kendall, though in truth she was more nervous about seeing her coauthors than she was about exactly what kind of deal might be struck. Sylvia, however, had that gleam that stole into her eyes right before any hint of negotiation, so Kendall kept that heretical thought to herself.

Kendall spotted Mallory and Faye and Tanya the moment she entered the conference room. Each of them was flanked by an agent or an attorney or both. Even Tanya had a red-tied blue suit–wearer on one side and a woman clad in New York black on the other.

Harold Kemp, Brenda Tinsley, and Hannah Sutcliff were also there as were others Kendall assumed to be in-house counsel or accountants. She'd been told that the most combative meetings had already taken place and that today's little get-together was intended to present the suggested settlement to the four of them. Theoretically their agents could have sought their clients' approvals and gotten the pertinent paperwork signed. Yet all four of them were here.

Kendall decided to take that as a good sign.

At first their four gazes skittered over each other as if they were afraid to offend by looking too closely.

Kendall offered a tentative smile and found herself assessing and cataloguing what the last months had done to the others. Faye looked more relaxed than Kendall had ever seen her, more centered. Tanya still looked like she belonged in a country music video, but her cornflower blue eyes were sharper than ever.

Mallory sat on the opposite side of the conference table, next to Patricia Gilmore. She still held herself in a way that testified to her star power, but Kendall sensed something softer, more vulnerable, underneath.

With real alarm Kendall realized that if no one took charge they might reach an agreement and walk out better off financially, but with no need to see each other again. If she hoped to engineer a reconciliation, she was going to have to make her move soon.

She was trying to decide what to do when Harold Kemp, Scarsdale's publisher-in-chief, began his opening comments, then proceeded to bring them all up to speed on the rerelease with its new cover listing all four authors that was planned.

Kendall studied the cover and liked it, especially the way they'd interlocked all four of their names. She looked up but couldn't read the others' reactions.

The cost of production for this new version would be divided equally between all four publishing houses as would the profits, minus the authors' advances and royalties.

It sounded fairly clear cut to Kendall and she wondered again why so many people were necessary. She tuned out the rest of what was being said in order to study her friends. Or rather, the three who she hoped were still her friends.

She wanted to know if Mallory had made up with Chris; whether Tanya was still fighting off the cook and whether she'd quit all her jobs once *Sticks and Stones* started paying out. Ditto for Faye, who was rumored to be writing a time-travel erotica series set partly in biblical times.

Scarsdale's lead attorney talked next, but Kendall noticed that only the other attorneys appeared to be listening. Even the agents were busy scoping each other out. Kendall was dying to hear about Tanya's new agent and what had happened during the split with Masque.

Another attorney began to speak.

Feeling someone's gaze on her, Kendall looked up to find Mallory contemplating her. A dark eyebrow went up, then there was a roll of Mallory's green eyes. She tilted her head toward the door and Kendall felt her first real stirring of hope.

Faye noticed and nodded her head almost imperceptibly. Then Tanya joined the silent communication with a flip of her big hair.

When the attorney finished speaking and called for comment from the authors' representatives, Kendall stood and asked to address the group. Sylvia groaned quietly beside her, but Kendall was ready to make her move.

"Before we vote on the specifics, I just want to take a moment to thank Mallory, Faye, and Tanya. I'm not sure if they realize it, but they saved my life. And in the process, they made sure we all wrote a truly incredible book."

The attorneys, accountants, and agents looked slightly uncomfortable as if paying a compliment crossed some unwritten line, but Kendall only cared about her audience of three. And they were sitting up and paying attention.

"All of them paid a price for helping me and I don't think I ever thanked them properly. I wouldn't still be here—or anywhere—if it wasn't for them."

The attorneys and agents exchanged looks of alarm. A faint whiff of panic wafted into the air.

Kendall saw Mallory's smile and the batting of her eyelashes as she attempted to hold back tears. Faye ran a hand through her salt-and-pepper hair. There was a suspicious sheen behind her glasses.

Tanya stood and raised her pointy chin. "It was my pleasure," she said, as she swiped the back of her hand across her eyes. "My new agent here," she nodded to the woman seated to her left, who looked like she was about to have an apoplexy, "seems to think my future lies in Southern women's fiction. Well, hell, I guess I've got the accent for it. But I sure would like to know what you three think."

"I think we have a lot of things to discuss." Faye stood at her place now, too. "But I don't think much of it has to do with this particular deal."

"No," Mallory said. "It doesn't, does it?" She stood, completely ignoring Patricia Gilmore's gasp of horror.

Kendall looked at her "peeps" and felt a pure rush of joy as the last piece of her life's puzzle dropped into place. "All in favor of recommending that our representatives accept the split and cover credits on our behalf as offered, unless they can negotiate even better, but still equal deals, please say 'aye,'" Kendall said.

"Aye." All four of them answered as one.

Lacy Samuels, the onetime naïve but plucky editorial assistant, pumped a triumphant fist into the air.

Hannah Sutcliff, who had already made a six-figure offer on Kendall Aims's next novel, *Names Will Never Hurt Me,* which would chronicle said plucky assistant's imaginary rise up the publishing ladder, smiled serenely.

Everyone else just looked nervous, which Kendall figured was precisely what they got paid for.

"I say we adjourn to someplace where we can toast our good fortune," Mallory said.

"And find out how the hell everyone's doing," Tanya added.

"If you'll excuse us?" Faye addressed those still assembled. "We really need to leave now."

And they left just like that. Crowding into the elevator, bursting out into the lobby, throwing their arms around each other as they marched across the marbled floor and out onto the steamy New York sidewalk.

If this were the movie version that had been proposed for *Sticks and Stones,* Kendall thought, the theme music would swell up about now as the four of them shouted to and over each other as they walked, all of their energies focused on the joy of being together, oblivious to the surge of humanity forced to pass around them.

And there'd be short paragraphs typed on the top of the

screen—little capsule views of their fabulous futures—as the camera zoomed out so that the audience could see Mallory St. James's car and driver trailing sedately behind them.

Kendall Aims's sequel to *Sticks and Stones*, *Names Will Never Hurt Me*, sat on the *New York Times* Bestseller List for twenty consecutive weeks. She is also a master handyman and has built rooms onto her mountain home so that struggling writers can come and write in solitude.

Mallory St. James and her husband, Chris, divide their time between their home, the Happily Ever After, in Cabo San Lucas, their beach house in the Hamptons, and their brownstone in New York City. The author has not gone on tour since 2009 and despite her yearly bestsellers is reputed to be a confirmed homebody.

Faye Truett's time-travel bible series went into seven printings and has been translated into thirty languages. She's a guest lecturer on Pastor Steve's weekly *Prayer Hour*, and she packs lecture halls with her talks on "What Wouldn't Ruth Do?" and other sensual matriarchal parables.

Tanya Mason is a popular author of Southern women's fiction. *Publishers Weekly* has named her Fannie Flagg's heir apparent. She and her daughters live on St. Petersburg Beach, just a bridge away from the Downhome Diner, which she bought for her boyfriend Brett Adams. Her mother's shiny new double-wide resides in her backyard. They take family trips on their sixty-foot houseboat, which they have christened *Ain't Beholden*.

And then, Kendall thought, the last shot in the movie would be a real tight close-up of a woman's hands typing on a computer keyboard. Then the camera would tilt up so the audience could read the words as they appeared on the screen. Those words would be . . .

THE END